THE FLING
THAT CHANGED
EVERYTHING

BY
ALISON ROBERTS

MILLS
BOON

This is a work of fiction. Names, characters, places, locations and
incidents are purely fictional and bear no relationship to any real
life indivi...
establishn...
entirely c...

This book...
trade or o...
without th...
cover oth...
condition...
purchaser...

® and TM...
and/or its...
United K...
the Interr...

Published in Great Britain 2016
By Mills & Boon, an imprint of HarperCollins*Publishers*
1 London Bridge Street, London, SE1 9GF

© 2016 Alison Roberts

ISBN: 978-0-263-25441-9

Our policy is to use papers that are natural, renewable and recyclable
products and made from wood grown in sustainable forests.
The logging and manufacturing processes conform to the legal
environmental regulations of the country of origin.

Printed and bound in Spain
by CPI, Barcelona

Dear Reader,

Confession time…I love a bit of drama!

And what better place for it than our fabulous M'Langi islands?

I couldn't wait to get back there again, and this time I got to unleash a tropical storm that's a perfect backdrop to the powerful attraction that neither Lia nor Sam are looking for but find themselves unable to ignore.

Is it a simple story of two people unexpectedly finding their soulmates in a tropical paradise?

Of course not.

There's a reason Lia's come to Wildfire Island, and it has nothing to do with Sam. And Sam…? Well, he's got some baggage, and he doesn't realise how much it's still affecting him.

It's a bit of a wild ride. I loved writing it and I hope you enjoy it just as much.

With love,

Alison xxx

Alison Roberts is a New Zealander, currently lucky enough to live near a beautiful beach in Auckland. She is also lucky enough to write for both the Mills & Boon Romance and Medical Romance lines. A primary school teacher in a former life, she is also a qualified paramedic. She loves to travel and dance, drink champagne and spend time with her daughter and her friends.

Books by Alison Roberts

Mills & Boon Medical Romance

The Honourable Maverick
Sydney Harbour Hospital: Zoe's Baby
Falling for Her Impossible Boss
The Legendary Playboy Surgeon
St Piran's: The Wedding
Maybe This Christmas…?
NYC Angels: An Explosive Reunion
Always the Hero
From Venice with Love
200 Harley Street: The Proud Italian
A Little Christmas Magic
Always the Midwife
Daredevil, Doctor…Husband?
The Nurse Who Stole His Heart

Visit the Author Profile page at millsandboon.co.uk for more titles.

Praise for Alison Roberts

'…the author gave me wonderful enjoyable moments of conflict and truth-revealing moments of joy and sorrow… I highly recommend this book for all lovers of romance with medical drama as a backdrop and second-chance love.'

—*Contemporary Romance Reviews* on *NYC Angels: An Explosive Reunion*

CHAPTER ONE

THE SOUND OF the telephone ringing could barely be heard over the cacophony as the Roselli family gathered in their kitchen for dinner.

It wasn't a big room. If the whole family had been here, they would have had to use the huge, rustic table out in the courtyard, beneath the vine-smothered pergola, but it was raining today—the kind of tropical downpour that was familiar to people living in Northern Australia—and the vines weren't enough protection from the wet.

So, here they were, piling into the kitchen that was a long room, where Adriana Roselli presided over the benchtop and oven at one end and the scrubbed pine table that could fit ten people—if they squeezed up—filled the other end of the room. Fitting a wheelchair in made it a little more complicated, of course, and that was why the noise level was so high right now.

'*Ow…* You ran over my foot, Fiona. Watch where you're going.'

'If you didn't have your stupid ears full of your horrible music, you would have seen us coming. Move *yourself*, Guy.'

'Not until you say you're sorry. You've probably broken my toe.'

'You're the one who should apologise. Look, you've made Angel *cry*...'

'Look out, all of you. If I drop this lasagne, you'll all be sorry. *Mamma mia*...' Adriana held a vast steaming tray over her head as her youngest son elbowed his way past her. 'Why don't my children ever grow up and act their ages? What have I ever done to deserve this? Lia, why isn't the bread on the table?'

'I'm coming... Oh, is that the *phone*?'

It took a moment for the effect of her words to sink in. Adriana almost dropped the lasagne onto the centre of her table and then covered her mouth with her hands, her gaze—like that of everyone else in the room, apart from Angel—swivelling towards Nico.

Was this the call they'd all been waiting for today?

'I'll get it.'

'No, I will.'

'It'll be for Nico. Let *him* get it.'

But Nico was looking like a possum caught in headlights—too scared to move.

'I'll get it.' Lia shoved the long basket piled with fragrant homemade bread at her brother Guy, but he had his eyes shut, his head nodding to whatever mesmerising beat he was still listening to, and she was too late, anyway. Her younger sister, Elena, had reached the phone first.

'Lia? It's for you.'

'What?' Lia shook her head. Who would be calling her on her day off? Her life consisted of her work and her family and that was it. One glance around the room would have been more than enough to remind her of why there was no room for anything else. And she wouldn't want it any other way, either. This was her home and her heart all wrapped up in one delicious-smelling, messy, noisy parcel. She loved every person here so much it could be a physical ache.

'Tell them to call back, then. I'm busy.'

She put the bread on the table beside one of the salads, smiling at her father, who was already in his place at the head of the table, silently waiting for chaos to morph into a more civilised mealtime. She glanced at the place settings Elena had been put in charge of. Where was the special, modified cutlery that Angel needed if she was going to feed herself?

'It's Bruce,' Elena shouted. 'And he says it's important.'

Bruce? Her boss at the ambulance station? More than her boss, in fact. He'd been the one to push her into her specialised training that had given her the qualifications to gain her dream job on the helicopter crew. He was her mentor and a good friend. If Bruce said something was important, it was.

Were they calling in extra crew for some major disaster?

'Coming…' The noise level around her was rising again but Lia was barely aware of the small spat as her mother pulled the ear buds away from Guy. Or that Fiona was berating Elena for forgetting the special cutlery. She couldn't miss that Nico was staring into space and clearly needed some reassurance or that her father's silence was deeper than his customary patience, but paying attention to those things would have to wait.

'Bruce?' Lia pushed her long, unruly curls out of the way and pressed the phone to her ear so that she could hear properly. 'Hi. What's up?'

The noise level was still too high to hear properly so Lia slipped out of the kitchen and into the hallway.

'Say that again. You want me to do *what*…?'

* * *

The silence was one of the things Sam Taylor loved best about Wildfire Island. Especially at this time of day, when the sun was almost gone and the scent of tropical flowers grew so much stronger.

He drew in a deep breath, shutting his eyes for a moment. And then he opened them and looked out from the vantage point he had chosen to the ocean surrounding this island, which had been his home ever since he'd begun working at the hospital here several years ago.

He'd taken the highest road on the island as he'd walked from the hospital and now he was on ground that was above the gold mine that had been the catalyst for so many people besides the islanders being able to call this place home. To one side he caught a glimpse of the village and the rocky promontory with the little church on top. He couldn't see over the cliff tops to Sunset Beach on the other side, but this wasn't an evening to chill out, watching the fiery show on the cliffs that had given the island its European name, anyway. Dense clouds were scudding sideways, intermittently hiding the sun, and it wouldn't be long before they joined forces and unleashed the kind of tropical downpour that was a regular feature of the cyclone season.

Maybe it was that atmospheric tension that had pushed him into taking this strenuous walk after a busy day that had left him feeling physically jaded. They were short-staffed at the moment and having Jack, the helicopter pilot, take one of his nurses on a mission had made things a lot more stressful. It was a good thing that the plane was due in tomorrow, bringing in some new FIFO—fly in, fly out—personnel. And this time there would be a paramedic as well as a nurse so he would not only have extra hands in the hospital, they wouldn't get borrowed just when they were needed in Theatre or something.

He let his breath out in a long sigh and felt more of the tension ebb. He could always find peace in this view. Excitement, even, as he looked out at the darkening shapes that were the outlying islands. The biggest one, Atangi, had been settled for the longest time and had the infrastructure of shops and schools. He could see the misty outline of islands that he knew well due to the clinics they ran on places like French Island. He could see the tiny humps of the uninhabited ones, too, and one of them was now his own.

How lucky was it that so many tradesmen had come to the islands to work on the upgrade of the laboratory and conference facilities that was now a feature of Wildfire Island? He'd been able to quietly offer some of them more work, building his dream house and the jetty for his yacht on a bush-covered island paradise that he had yet to name.

In the not-too-distant future, he wouldn't be walking home to the accommodation provided for both the permanent and FIFO staff that kept the hospital and clinics running in this remote area. He'd take a boat and go home to picture-perfect solitude and the sheer beauty of nature. Not his yacht, of course. As much as he loved sailing, he'd have to be able to travel fast to get back here in an emergency, so he was looking at getting a new speedboat. An inflatable, probably.

For some reason, though, the prospect of that beauty and solitude wasn't generating the excitement it usually did.

For the first time, it was actually casting a shadow of doubt on if he was doing the right thing.

Was it the remnants of a hectic day that made him think it wouldn't be a good idea to have even a small strip of ocean between himself and the hospital? What if he hadn't been there to deal with that anaphylaxis from a bee sting that had seen a young mother terrified that she was about to lose her child? Or if they hadn't been able to perform that emergency appendectomy before the infected organ burst and could have caused a life-threatening sepsis?

Or was it the storm brewing? The wind picking up and those bad-tempered-looking clouds just waiting for an excuse to spark an outburst?

No. It felt deeper than anything as external as work or the weather. The shadow was more like an empty space in his soul. The alone space.

But he'd come here to this remote part of the Pacific Ocean to escape in the first place, and being alone was the ultimate escape, wasn't it?

Turning away from the view, Sam automatically looked around, forgetting for a moment that he hadn't brought Bugsy with him this time. The dog was a part of the hospital family here, and his care was shared amongst others, including him, when his owner was back on the mainland. One of the nurses had him today so Sam hadn't had the pleasure of taking him out for his daily walk.

That's what it was, he decided. That's why he had this sudden, inexplicable sense of loneliness.

Maybe it was time he got a canine companion of his own. A Portuguese water dog, perhaps, who would love boats and fishing expeditions and swimming at the tiny, perfect beach that had been why he'd fallen in love with the island he now owned.

That way he'd have the best job in the world in a place

where he could live happily ever after, and he'd have company to share it with. Company that would expect no more of him than his love.

What more could anybody want?

There was only one chair empty at the table as Lia went back into the kitchen. Plates were being passed, laden with the delicious layers of meat and cheese and pasta that had given Adriana Roselli's lasagne its well-deserved reputation of being the best.

'What did Bruce want?' Elena reached for a thick, warm slice of bread and added it to her plate. 'Was he asking you out for a date?'

'Bruce is old enough to be my father,' Lia said sternly. 'And I'm old enough to know how ridiculous that would be.'

'Oh, give it a rest,' Elena snapped. 'Mike's only thirty-nine.'

'And you're only twenty-six. Thirteen years, Lena. Count them. It's almost a generation.'

'At least I've *got* a boyfriend. You're turning into an old maid, Lia.'

'That's enough,' Adriana ordered. 'Sit down, Lia. Eat. You're far too skinny these days. I can see your bones from here.'

Lia ignored the comments from both her mother and her sister. She slid into the seat beside Angel's wheelchair.

'Look at the way you're holding your spoon, darling. Good girl… Don't forget to blow on it. That lasagne looks hot.' She leaned sideways to demonstrate but Angel giggled and tipped her spoon and the food fell off to land on her lap.

'Thanks for that, Lia.' But Angel's mother, her sister

Fiona, was smiling as she wiped up the small accident. 'Let's try that again, shall we, Angel?'

'So what *did* Bruce want?' Nico was picking at his food and clearly hoping for a distraction from his own thoughts.

'He offered me a job for two weeks. On a helicopter crew on an island about two hundred miles northwest of Cairns. It's called Wildfire.'

'An island?' Adriana shook her head. '*Pff*...what for? A holiday?'

'There's a hospital there, Mamma. It looks after a big population of people over a huge area. Bruce said it would be great experience for me. I'd have to do things I'd probably never get the chance to do here. And, if I liked it, I could go onto a regular roster to fly in for two-week stints.'

'You can't go,' Elena declared. 'Nico's going to be going into hospital for his surgery any day now and you know what Mamma's like around hospitals. You're the only one who can explain things properly and stop her crying. And even if you're here for the operation, what about the chemo? It'll be horrendous.'

'No, it won't.' Lia sent her sister a warning glance before turning to smile at her brother. 'You're going to fly through this, Nico. I know it's scary but testicular cancer has a really high cure rate and you're going to be one of those success stories. It'll be okay.'

'Promise?' Nico, like the rest of the family, looked to Lia as his medical expert.

Lia's smile was one of genuine reassurance. 'Promise.' Even if the treatment didn't go as well as hoped, she would make it okay. Somehow.

'Do you want to go?' Fiona's query was sceptical.

'It would be exciting,' Lia admitted. 'Even the name of the island is cool. Wildfire...'

'They have fires?' Adriana shook her head. 'You don't want to go somewhere that has fires.'

'Wildfire Island? Wasn't that in the news not long ago?' Guy put down his fork to fish his phone out of his pocket. 'I'm sure I heard something about a mine exploding or something.'

'Well, that's that.' The spoon clanked against the crockery dish as if Adriana's statement was final. 'I'm not having you going off into exploding mines.'

'No, it didn't explode.' Guy sounded disappointed. 'Just collapsed. People got hurt and there was a big rescue mission but it's okay now. And why would Lia be going down a mine, anyway?'

'I wouldn't,' Lia said reassuringly. 'And what makes it really attractive is what they pay. I'd earn three times what I usually do in a fortnight. Imagine how far that would get us in buying those new walking aids for Angel.'

'No...' Adriana handed a laden plate to Lia. 'It still sounds dangerous. Flying helicopters around islands miles from anywhere? What if you crash?'

'It's no different from what I do here. Apparently the head pilot is someone Bruce knows and he's top of his game. It's my job, Mamma—you know that. And I love it.'

'It's not natural,' Adriana sighed. 'You're thirty-two, Lia. You should be married and having *bambinos* by now. Look at your sister. She was a *mamma* already by your age.'

'Mmm.' Lia and Fiona shared a rueful glance that took in how well that had worked out. Angel had been born prematurely and the lack of oxygen during a difficult birth had been responsible for her cerebral palsy. Her father had walked out of their lives as soon as he'd learned of her disability.

'The money's amazing.' Guy spoke with his mouth full. 'I'd do it if I were you. Hey…you could get the roof fixed and I wouldn't have to trip over that bucket in my bedroom every time it rains.'

Her father had been silent throughout the discussion, his gaze on his plate, but he looked up as Guy spoke and Lia could see the shame in his eyes.

It's not your fault, she told him silently, her heart breaking. *And you'll get another job before the redundancy money runs out.*

The words she spoke aloud were very different. A daughter asking her father's advice.

'What do you reckon, Dad? Should I go?'

He returned her smile and the warmth in his eyes told her that her reassurance had been received and appreciated.

'If you want to do it, *cara*, you should.'

Lia nodded slowly. 'I think I do.'

'*Mamma mia.*' Adriana crossed herself as she closed her eyes. 'When would you leave?'

'Um…tomorrow. It seems like the person who was going to go has had an accident at the last minute, which is why Bruce was asked to find someone else. He's happy to give me leave.'

The reality of the offer was sinking in around the table and everyone was staring at Lia with a mix of admiration and trepidation.

'I said I'd call him back as soon as I'd discussed it with the family. Nico? You get to have the final vote. If you want me to be here for your surgery, I'll say no.'

'Go,' Nico said. 'I'll have more than enough family fussing over me. I'm only going to be in hospital for a couple of days. You can send me some cool pictures and I can boast about my fabulous sister who's off doing brave stuff and saving the world.'

Lia grinned. 'You're on. Right…' She scooped in a hurried mouthful of her dinner. 'I'd better go and ring Bruce back and start packing. I'll have to be at the airport at five-thirty in the morning.'

'I'll drive you.'

Her father smiled as he spoke but her mother burst into tears. For a moment Lia considered changing her mind but then she glanced at Angel and remembered what that extra money could mean.

Swallowing hard, she pushed back her chair and went to make the phone call.

'Whoa…' Jack Richards, Wildfire Island's head helicopter pilot, pushed his sunglasses down his nose to peer over the top of them. 'You seeing what I'm seeing, Sam?'

Two young people had climbed out of the small plane and were heading across the tarmac to where they were waiting in the shade. The man had to be the paramedic, Sam decided, so no wonder Jack had elbowed him in the ribs. The new FIFO nurse was a stunner, all right. Tall and lean, she had a mane of curly dark hair that the wind was playing havoc with and legs that seemed to go on forever beneath the short shorts she was wearing. Huge sunglasses were hiding half her face but even from this distance you could see a generous mouth that was clearly designed for laughing.

Or kissing, perhaps…?

Maybe it was just as well she'd be safely confined to

the hospital during working hours and not floating around remote islands with a good-looking young helicopter pilot. Romantic liaisons with FIFO staff happened—of course they did—and Jack was not shy about enjoying the opportunities, but for Sam it was a no-no. He'd always kept any such casual hook-ups to the times when he was on a break a long way away from here. This was his home and, as such, it was too important to mess with by indulging in something that he'd seen lead to long-lasting negative fallouts in others.

He didn't need the clipboard he was holding to remind him that this was work time. Supplies were being unloaded from the small plane that was their regular link with the mainland of Australia and, amongst them would be the important medical packs containing drugs and all the other items Sam had ordered. They'd run low on dressings and suture packs after an unusually high number of minor trauma incidents in the past couple of weeks.

'Let's check that everything we ordered has come in,' he said to Jack. 'We don't want to hold up the pilot in this weather.'

The wind had picked up even as they walked towards the plane.

'G'day, mate.' Sam extended a hand towards the male newcomer. 'I'm Sam Taylor—one of the permanent doctors at the hospital here.'

'Good to meet you. I'm Matt.'

'Welcome to Wildfire Island. Is this your first FIFO experience?'

'Sure is.' Matt's smile was rueful. 'Might be the last, too, after that flight.'

'Oh, come on, Matt.' The girl was now restraining

her hair with both hands to keep it from covering her face. 'It was fun.'

Her grin suggested that a bumpy ride had been a bonus and Sam couldn't help grinning back. A young woman who was gutsy as well as gorgeous? What man wouldn't appreciate that combination of attributes?

'I'm Lia Roselli.' She had to let go of her hair with one hand as she extended it to shake Sam's. The wind snatched the tumble of dark curls and plastered it across her face and she was laughing as she scraped it free.

The sound was as attractive as the rest of her. No wonder Jack was grinning like an idiot. It was only then that he realised that his own mouth was still widely stretched. It was an effort, in fact, to pull his lips back into line.

'I've got a hair tie somewhere.' Lia delved into the soft leather shoulder bag she was carrying. 'Sorry, I should have tried to arrive looking a bit more professional, shouldn't have I?'

'You weren't to know there's a cyclone brewing.' Jack turned to her after shaking Matt's hand. 'I'm Jack Richards.'

'Oh…you're my pilot.' The search for the hair tie was abandoned as Lia took his hand. 'Awesome. I'm looking forward to working with you.'

'You're the *paramedic*?'

Sam didn't mean to sound so astonished. He deserved the look he got from both the newcomers. Even Jack's eyebrows shot up. In just a few words he'd managed to make it sound like he not only had a prejudice against male nurses but that he didn't think females were up to the kind of dangerous work that helicopter paramedicine could throw at them. He didn't think either of those things. If he was really honest, the tone had probably come from disappointment more than surprise, and what was that about? Even the nurses tucked safely away in the hospital were not immune to Jack's charm, so what chance did Lia have?

Good grief… Was that oddly unsettling flash something other than disappointment? Jealousy, even?

'Sam didn't get the memo.' Jack was trying to rescue him. 'And, I have to admit, it's the first time we've had a female paramedic as a FIFO.'

'First time for a male nurse, too?' Matt was smiling. 'Good thing we've come, then, isn't it, Lia? Time the glass ceilings were broken around here.'

They all laughed, which broke the awkwardness. The distraction of having to check the delivered supplies off against the order form took a few more minutes and by the time the FIFOs' luggage was brought out from the back of the compartment, Sam was ready to make amends for his faux pas.

'It is a good thing,' he told Matt as the new nurse retrieved his backpack. 'We're trying to encourage more islanders to train as nurses and you'll be a role model that might open a few eyes. How would you feel about dropping into the high school over on Atangi and giving a bit of a career talk?'

'I'm up for anything,' Matt said. 'I love my job and I'd be only too happy to encourage the lads.'

'Hey… I love my job, too.' Lia was beaming at Sam. 'Maybe I could come and inspire the girls?'

Jack was grinning again. 'You up for anything, too, huh?'

The flirting was unmistakable. The flick of the long braid Lia now had her hair confined to was also an obvious message. And she could deal with more than the weather.

'Anything professional.' Her tone was a warning. Romance had been the last thing on her mind when she'd decided to take this job. It was the last thing on her mind any time these days, thanks to the time and emotional energy her family required. And even if she had been interested in meeting someone, it wouldn't be Jack. She'd met his type too many times before. Dated them. Been dumped and hurt when they moved on—as they always did if it looked like the girl was getting serious.

Had she been too abrupt? Lia softened her tone. 'I'm up for the new experience and if I like it I'll come back next time. Sounds like the guy I'm replacing got a nasty leg fracture and won't be back for a while.'

'I told him paragliding was a dodgy hobby.' Jack reached out as if he was going to offer to carry Lia's pack but then changed his mind and adjusted his sunglasses instead.

Sam hid a smile. So Lia *could* look after herself.

'Not that he wasn't good at it.' Jack seemed to be scanning the clouds now. 'Just got unlucky, I guess.'

'Lucky for me...' Lia hoisted her backpack as if it weighed nothing. 'Especially the timing. Who knew they paid so much more for coming here in the cyclone season?'

Sam's inner smile vanished without a trace. The disconcerted look on Lia's face made him realise that something of what he was feeling must be showing but he didn't care. He had better reason than most *not* to care about someone to whom money was all-important, hadn't he? He turned away.

'Let's go,' he told Matt. 'I'll show you your accommodation and then give you a tour of the hospital.'

What had just happened there?

Lia had her backpack settled onto her shoulders and she was ready to go. Didn't she have accommodation to see? Wouldn't a tour of at least the emergency department of the hospital be appropriate for someone who could be delivering seriously unwell people to a place that might be short on staff experienced in dealing with resuscitation?

Maybe it had something to do with that very unsubtle attempt at flirting that had come from Jack. Of course she'd knocked him back. She was about to spend two weeks working with the man and the only relationship she wanted was a professional one, hopefully based on mutual respect and trust.

And what about that reaction to Matt being the nurse?

Lia's high spirits dimmed a little. Was it expected to be part of the deal? Did FIFOs get paid so well because it was assumed they would provide a bonus service to men working in isolated places?

They probably did when they were working with Sam Taylor—if he was single, that was, which seemed unlikely. How many men who were that good-looking were still unattached in their midthirties, as he looked to be?

Mind you, there *was* something unusual about him. Something that didn't quite fit the picture she might have expected. Something that made him look almost as if he was here by mistake.

Not like Jack, who had the rugged good looks of a pirate and a cheekiness that suggested he liked to live on the edge, which made wanting to live in an isolated place like this quite plausible. But Sam? He looked like he was playing a role—that was it. With his sun-streaked, floppy dark blond hair and blue-grey eyes, he could easily be a film star cast as a doctor in a tropical paradise.

Intriguing.

She wasn't interested in meeting someone, she reminded herself.

But if she was, there would have been no contest between Sam and Jack, so it was probably just as well Sam hadn't shown even a glimmer of interest in her. Quite the opposite, in fact, judging by the way he'd turned his back and walked away.

'Looks like we've been abandoned.' Jack shrugged. 'Want to have a look at the helicopter before I give you the grand tour of everything else?'

'Sure.' Lia turned her head, her smile polite. 'It's a BK117, isn't it? Fully specced?'

'We've got everything your paramedic heart could desire. Even a portable ventilator and ultrasound.'

'Awesome. The only other thing I need is a pilot with exceptional skill.'

'At your service.' Jack tugged at his fringe. 'I might push the boundaries but I'm not about to risk killing myself or any of my crew.' He returned her smile. 'And, judging from your CV they sent through, you're going to be one of the best I've worked with. And…um…sorry about, you know… I'm not usually a jerk. This job is my life. Maybe I got a bit overexcited about meeting someone who has the same passion.'

He wouldn't be trying it on again, either. This time her smile was genuine. 'We're going to get along just fine, Jack.' She couldn't help turning her head to where a golf cart was sending up a cloud of dust as it carried Sam and

Matt away from the airstrip. The question of how well she might be going to get on with the medical staff here was an entirely different matter.

'Are we…um…going to have a look around the hospital some time, too?'

'It's our base.' Jack nodded. 'We hang out in the staffroom on our downtime so that we're within coo-ee of the radio. You'll probably get roped in to help with some of the medical stuff, I expect. We always seem to be a bit short-staffed.'

So she'd be seeing Sam again. Probably quite a lot of him.

Not that it should matter. If anything, it should be something that could be seen as a potential conflict, given the odd vibe he'd put out.

So why were her spirits lifting again?

Because she couldn't resist a challenge? It was intriguing, that was all. She wouldn't mind finding out how he'd ended up here and why he'd stayed.

And she'd definitely like to rub his nose in that attitude to how capable a female paramedic could be.

Yep. That would be a bonus.

And Lia was very good at rising to any challenge to prove herself.

She followed Jack towards the helicopter, which was well anchored to cope with the rising wind gusts. Not that they were likely to be flying anytime soon in these conditions, but the sooner the better, as far as she was concerned.

She could feel her fingers curling into fists.

Bring it on…

CHAPTER TWO

'WHAT'S WITH THE white coat, Sam?'

'It's my doctor coat.' The grin on his favourite nurse's face was irritating. 'You get to wear a uniform every day, Ana. What's wrong with me looking a bit more professional? Besides, I never realised how useful all these pockets were. Look—I can fit my diary and phone and even my stethoscope in here...' Sam pulled some sterile gloves from the wall dispenser and shoved those in another pocket. 'I'm ready for anything.'

'You look more like you're about to front an advertisement for washing powder or something. You know...' She dropped her voice. 'Laboratory tests have proved Wonder Wash to be a thousand percent more effective than other leading brands.'

Sam snorted. 'You've changed, Ana. You used to show a bit more respect.'

The grin widened. 'Maybe it's because I'm a happily married woman now.'

He had to smile back. 'You are. And it's great. I'm really happy for you, even if you didn't invite me to the wedding.'

'Like you would have dropped everything and come all the way to London for a few days. It was hard enough persuading my mother to be there. And you'll get your wedding fix soon enough.'

'True. Is it next week that Caroline and Keanu are tying the knot?'

'The week after. Oh…who's this coming in with Jack?'

Sam turned his head. Sure enough, there were two people entering the wide walkway that linked the three wings of Wildfire hospital around its lush tropical garden. Something in the garden had clearly attracted Lia's attention and they had paused as she'd pointed. Maybe she'd spotted an exotic bird near the pond in the garden's centre. Sam found himself checking that the lapels on his white coat were sitting flat. Not that he was about to tell Ana but there was a reason he'd wanted to look particularly professional today.

'That's the new FIFO paramedic. She came in yesterday with the new nurse. Have you met Matt yet?'

'Of course. He's giving Rangi his bath.' Her lips twitched. 'It may take a while. There's a lot to wash.'

'We've got to try and get his weight down. The diabetes and skin sores are only going to be the start of his health issues.'

'Mmm. I have to say it's going to be a treat to have a male nurse on board for a while. Matt didn't even need the winch to get Rangi out of bed.' But Ana's interest was elsewhere for the moment. 'Has our new paramedic got a name?'

'Lia…something. Sounded Italian.'

'She looks Italian. And…*gorgeous*…'

It was Sam's turn to make a sound of feigned interest but he had to turn his head again. Jack and Lia were much closer now and it was no wonder Ana was impressed.

The short shorts and wild hair he remembered from

the airstrip yesterday were gone. Lia was wearing long, dark cargo pants and the black T-shirt with the red emblem of Wildfire's rescue service. Her hair sat smoothly against her head with a complicated braid arrangement that went from her forehead on both sides to merge into a thick rope at the back.

She looked…professional.

'Hey, Ana. This is Lia, my new crewmate. Lia, this is Anahera Kopu, one of our permanent nurses.'

'It's Wilson now, Jack. I got married, remember?' Ana held out her hand to shake Lia's. 'You've got to show me how to do my hair like that. It's amazing.'

'It's dead easy. And…um…congratulations? I'm guessing your wedding was recent?'

'A couple of months ago. I just got back from London. And a honeymoon in Paris.'

'Wow… Two places I'd love to visit.'

'You haven't been yet?'

'Travelling's never been in my budget.' But Lia was smiling. 'That's why it's so exciting to be *here*.'

Because it was a new country or because it was adding to the reserves in her budget? The knot of tension in Sam's gut was as unfamiliar as the starched fabric of the coat sleeves on his bare arms. He started rolling the sleeves up a bit.

'We've got an outpatient clinic to get started, Ana.' He nodded at Lia. 'Has Jack got you settled in all right? Happy with your accommodation?'

'It's fantastic. I love it. I woke up this morning and looked out at the view of the sea and all those islands and couldn't believe how beautiful it all is.'

It wasn't just her eyes that shone with pleasure—her

whole face seemed to light up. It was impossible not to smile back.

'Looks better on a nice day.' He turned to Jack. 'Are you up with the forecast? How's that cyclone tracking?'

'Bit too close for comfort, this one. We could be in for a rough few days.'

'I'd better check the stocks in Emergency,' Ana said. 'We always get a rush on dressings and sutures and things in a cyclone. It's amazing the debris that people can get hit with.'

'Hettie might be able to do that when it's quiet later. She's on the afternoon shift, isn't she?'

Ana nodded. 'I'll see how many people we've got in the waiting room for the clinic, then.'

'I'd love to have a look around your emergency department,' Lia said. 'If that's okay?'

In the tiny silence that followed her query Sam realised that the question had been directed at him. If he was honest, though, he'd known that already. He could feel Lia's gaze on his skin.

'Sure.' He met her gaze long enough to be polite. 'Jack knows his way around. Feel free to explore the whole—' The sound of his telephone ringing stopped his invitation. He delved into his pocket to extract the phone from the tangle of his stethoscope and that was irritating enough to make him loop the stethoscope around his neck with one hand as he answered the call with the other.

He'd been expecting this. 'Yes, it's all sorted, Pita.' He stepped away from the others and lowered his voice. 'I'm tied up in a clinic this morning but I'll leave it beside the radio in the staffroom. White envelope with your name on it.'

He heard a burst of laughter behind him but he kept

moving as he ended his call. He had work to do and he knew the waiting room would be filling up fast. He didn't have time for any social chitchat. His visit to the staffroom would not even include stopping to make a coffee.

Not that being busy was enough to explain the odd tension he was aware of. Maybe that had more to do with the fact that he could still feel Lia watching him as he walked away.

Déjà vu.

Lia watched Sam walking away. Maybe she would have to get used to feeling like she wasn't overly welcome here.

She certainly needed to get over letting it get to her. She pasted a smile on her face as she turned back to Jack and Ana, but they were looking at each other.

'What's with the white coat? Has Sam been down in the lab already this morning or something?'

Ana shook her head. 'Not that I know of.' She grinned at Jack. 'He said that he just wanted to look professional.'

Lia caught her bottom lip with her teeth to stop her saying anything. Like confessing that she had started the day in exactly the same way. The French braiding of her hair hadn't been nearly as easy as she'd implied to Ana. It had taken ages and it had been Sam she'd been thinking of as she'd stared into the mirror and tried to perfect her professional look.

Had he done the same thing with that pristine-looking coat?

And if so…why?

To impress *her*?

He was still within sight on the walkway. In fact, he'd stopped in his tracks and was staring at something out-

side in the garden. Lia had been entranced by the flock
of rainbow-coloured parrots she'd seen earlier and had
had to point them out to Jack, but he'd been far less interested because it was something he saw every day so
they would be unlikely to have attracted Sam's attention, either.

'Ana?' Sam's call was calm but they could all sense
the urgency. 'Grab the resus trolley, will you? I can see
someone lying on the path.'

He disappeared behind the greenery of the lush shrubs
hedging the walkway and Lia's reaction was automatic.
As Ana raced down the walkway to vanish through a
door, Lia ran in the opposite direction—to follow Sam.
She could hear the rattle of trolley wheels behind her as
she pushed through the hedge to where Sam was now
crouched over a sprawled figure.

'Is he breathing?'

'Can't tell. Help me roll him over.'

He was a large man and it needed them both to roll
him onto his back. Lia immediately tilted his head to
make sure his airway was open and then she put her
cheek close to his face and laid a hand on his diaphragm
to feel for any air movement.

'He's not breathing.'

Sam had his fingers on the man's neck. 'There's no
pulse.'

Ana had had to go further down the walkway to find
a gap to get the trolley through, and Jack was helping
her, but there was no time to wait until they were there
with the life pack and the bag mask. Lia already had her
hands positioned in the centre of the man's chest and she
began compressions without waiting for any instruction
from Sam.

'I wonder how much downtime there's been already.'

'Not much, I hope. I think it was the sound of him falling that made me look over the hedge. He broke a few branches on the way down.'

She could feel Sam watching her as he spoke. Assessing her performance. Fair enough. This was a big man and it took a lot of strength to be able to make sure she was pushing hard enough to create an output from his heart. She could feel a sweat breaking out but she kept her arms straight and kept pushing. Hard and fast. At least a hundred compressions a minute, she reminded herself. And a third of the chest for their depth.

Ana threw a bag mask to Sam as she stopped the trolley. He caught it easily and in one swift movement had the mask over the man's nose and mouth. He hooked his fingers under the chin to help press hard enough to create a good seal and then flicked a glance at Lia, who paused her compressions to allow him to squeeze the bag and deliver a couple of assisted breaths. The chest rose and fell twice and she started compressions again as soon as she saw the chest falling for the second time. Her arms were aching with the effort now but she knew she couldn't slow down, even as Ana was cutting the man's T-shirt to pull it clear and sticking the defibrillator pads on the side just below his heart and beneath the collarbone on the other side.

She began counting aloud to let Sam know when it was time to deliver another breath. Jack had attached the oxygen bottle to the mask.

'Twenty-eight…twenty-nine…thirty…' She held her hands clear as another two breaths were delivered.

The static on the defibrillator screen was settling and

they could all see that their patient was in the potentially fatal rhythm of ventricular fibrillation.

'Come and take over the airway,' Sam instructed Ana. 'I'll get an IV in after the first shock.'

Lia could hear the tone of the life pack charging.

'Stand clear,' Sam ordered. 'Shocking now...'

The rhythm didn't change.

'Do you need a break, Lia?' Sam was pulling IV supplies from the trolley.

'No. I'll let you know when I do.'

'You're doing a good job. I'll take over after the next shock.'

The praise was enough to banish the ache in her arms and to ignore the sting of perspiration getting into her eyes.

Clearly hampered by his white coat, Sam stripped it off and shoved it onto the bottom of the trolley. Then he moved swiftly enough to have an IV line inserted and the first dose of drugs on board before the end of the two minutes of CPR that meant another shock was due to be delivered.

'Who is he, do you know?' Jack asked.

'He's Rangi's brother, Keoni,' Ana said. 'And I think he had an outpatient appointment this morning. Sam wants to test the whole family for diabetes.'

'Stand clear,' Sam ordered again.

Lia sat back on her heels this time, ready to move out of the way so that Sam could take over the compressions.

But this time the spike of the shock being delivered on the life-pack screen gave way to a blip of a normal beat. And then another and another.

'He's gagging,' Ana said a moment later. 'I'll take the airway out.'

'We'll need a bed,' Sam said. 'And a few extra hands to move him.'

'I'll get Matt,' Ana said, scrambling to her feet. 'And anyone else I can find. Or do you need me here, Sam?'

Sam caught Lia's gaze. 'No…you go, Ana. We're fine.'

The eye contact was only there for a moment but Lia felt like she'd passed some sort of test.

And she'd got good marks.

It was always a bonus to cheat death like this and have a successful resuscitation from a cardiac arrest but this felt even sweeter than usual. And the good marks went both ways. This success had been a team effort and Sam had shown himself to be a calm and competent leader.

'We'll get him into our intensive care unit,' Sam said. 'You may as well join us, Lia, and start your tour of the hospital with the pointy end.'

'I'll help you move him,' Jack said. 'And then maybe I should let them know that the outpatient clinic will be starting a bit late.'

'Give Keanu a call. He can come in early and get things started.' Sam was adjusting the wheel on the IV tubing to change the rate of fluids being delivered from the bag of saline he was holding up. His smile was wry. 'It looks like it's going to be another one of "those" days, all right…'

There was a gleam in his eye that suggested that those sorts of days were actually the ones he liked best and Lia found herself smiling back at him. She loved the adrenaline rush of dealing with emergencies, too. And the challenge of multi-tasking when it looked like there might be too much to handle but you knew the buzz of being able to cope was well worth the stress levels.

To be honest, smiling at Sam Taylor was no hardship. He looked so much better now that he'd discarded the formal white coat. His short-sleeved, open-necked shirt exposed tanned skin and he must have pushed his sun-streaked, floppy hair back from his forehead a few times during that intense scenario to have made it look so spiky and slightly disreputable.

And even with the wry twist to that smile, it was irresistible. What would he look like if he was really amused and those crinkles at the corners of his eyes deepened? What would his laugh sound like?

Lia suspected it would be a very contagious sound. Had her early impressions been unjustified? Maybe Sam was actually quite a nice guy. He was certainly a very good doctor and that was more than enough to chase away any doubts that she might not enjoy working here.

Extra sets of hands were arriving from all corners of the hospital and Sam had more than enough to do, coordinating the helpers to lift Keoni onto the bed and arrange the equipment carefully so it didn't get disconnected. He put the life pack on the bed between their patient's legs so he could keep an eye on the rhythm on the screen. The bed didn't have an IV pole attached so someone had to carry the bag of fluid high enough to keep it running. It was logical to give that task to Jack, who was the tallest person there apart from himself.

Their patient was beginning to take breaths unaided but not at a fast enough rate so he needed someone who could move alongside the bed, holding the mask in place to deliver oxygen and to assist his breathing when needed by compressing the bag attached to the mask. At any other time Sam would have asked Ana to do that because she was the most experienced nurse when it came to any protocols to do with resuscitation or post-resuscitation care. But Lia had been doing that since Ana had gone to look for extra help and she'd proved herself to be more than competent. It would be rude to push her aside and he'd invited her to come to his intensive care unit anyway.

Besides…despite how focused he was on transferring a patient who was still critical and could potentially arrest again at any moment, there was a part of his mind that was aware of appreciating Lia being there.

It wasn't due solely to the competence she'd displayed in handling an emergency situation and it certainly wasn't because of some masculine instinct that simply enjoyed having an attractive female nearby. Maybe it was his better nature asserting itself and being prepared to give her a chance to prove his first impression wrong.

Or maybe it had something to do with that smile…

'If I was at home, I'd be transporting to a facility that had a cath lab,' Lia said as they manoeuvred the bed into the walkway. 'Do you have the capacity to do angiography here?'

'No,' Ana told her. 'We've got a lot of things that remote hospitals might dream of having, like a CT scanner, but a cath lab would be taking things a bit too far.'

'So how do you treat your cardiac patients?'

'We'll take a twelve-lead ECG,' Sam responded. 'And a chest X-ray. We can check cardiac enzymes and we'll administer thrombolysis if it's indicated.'

The sound of a wolf-whistle made him blink but he ignored it.

'As soon as we've got him stable enough, we'll arrange a fixed-wing evacuation to a hospital on the mainland that can do angiography and angioplasty. Cardiac surgery, if that's what's needed.'

The wolf-whistle sounded again. Frowning, he looked up from the rhythm he was watching on the screen to see Lia reaching into the pocket of her cargo pants to pull out a mobile phone.

What the heck? Okay, she was still holding the patient's mask in place with one hand but how inappropriate could you get? Had she even been listening to the response to her query?

She was actually texting as she stepped back to let the hospital staff position the bed and hook up the equipment they now had available. Any impression he'd had of Lia's competence and professionalism was beginning to fade and maybe that was why he gave her the challenge of interpreting the ECG trace as soon as he'd put the chest leads on and printed it off.

He stepped close enough to hold the sheet of graph paper in front of her. 'So what do you think?'

Lia jumped and her gaze jerked up from her phone but she still had it clutched in her hand as she turned her attention to the trace.

Her scanning was as rapid as his had been.

'Hyperacute T waves, and there's significant ST elevation in leads V3 to V5. Looks like a sizeable anterior infarction with lateral extension.'

He wanted to test her. 'What about the bundle branch block?'

'There is a left bundle branch block but the ST elevation is greater than you'd expect and we've got Q waves here…and here…'

He hadn't noticed how delicate her fingers were before. Long and slim, with practical, unpainted nails and no rings. Her touch on the paper was light enough not to move it but he could feel the pressure transfer itself to his own fingertips.

'And there's some reciprocal changes in the inferior leads,' Lia added. 'It's pretty conclusive.'

He should have been impressed. He might have even told her that except for the interruption of that damned wolf-whistle again.

Her cheeks went pink. 'Oops, sorry. I meant to put that on silent.'

Sam glared at her. 'Maybe you could save your personal messaging for out of work hours.'

'I've got the bloods done.' Ana had a handful of test tubes. 'Some will have to go down to the lab but do you want me to do the benchtop cardiac biomarkers?'

'I'll do it.' Sam turned away from Lia. 'Set up the tenecteplase infusion, will you? And draw up some atropine. I'm not happy with his rate. It's sinus but it's too slow.'

A glance from the corner of his eye as he transferred some blood to the tiny, specialised tube that would slot into the sophisticated device he was now holding in his hand showed Sam that Lia was busy texting again. Maybe she already knew that they could measure things like troponin and creatinine kinase and myoglobin, which were all markers of whether someone was having a heart attack and how large it was, but surely she should be interested to know that she would have one of these units available in the helicopter she was about to start working in?

They hadn't been cheap but, like a fair few other items here, they were important enough for Sam to have quietly provided them from his personal funds.

Not something he would want Lia—or others, for that

matter—to know. Maybe it was better that she wasn't showing any interest or asking awkward questions.

And at least she put her damned phone away when Jack's pager sounded an alert.

'Looks like we've got a call. Come on, Lia. I'll show you how the radio system works.'

'Holy heck…' The straps of her harness tightened to hold Lia in the front seat of the helicopter as it fought the wind. 'How far have we got to go?'

'Only another five minutes.' Jack's voice was reassuringly calm inside her helmet but the sidelong glance he gave her was more concerned. 'These *are* pretty marginal flying conditions. You okay?'

'Are you kidding?' Lia laughed aloud as they slewed sideways and rocked again. 'I *love* it.'

The look she got now was impressed. 'I've had a few guys in that seat who'd have white knuckles by now.'

'How will we get to patients if it gets any worse than this? Do you think the cyclone's going to be a direct hit?'

'It's looking more likely. We might well have a day or two when we can't get airborne. If that's the case, we use boats for the closer islands. How do you go in rough seas?'

Lia grinned. 'I quite like them, too.'

Jack shook his head, silent for a moment as he focused on controlling his helicopter. The main island of Atangi was within sight now and Lia could see that it was far more populated than Wildfire. Somewhere in that cluster of buildings was the medical centre they were heading for after getting a call from the nurse who was working there.

'I used to ride horses way back,' Lia said. 'What I loved most was a good cross-country course. Boats and aircraft in a bit of rough stuff is like competing in cross-country when you never know where the next jump is or how big it's going to be.'

'You still ride?'

'No. It's not exactly an affordable hobby. Besides…' Lia let out a whoop as they were buffeted by some particularly big turbulence. 'I get all the excitement I need these days from my job.'

'Yeah…' Jack was clearly in complete agreement. 'Let's get this baby on the ground and hope that our patient doesn't get airsick on the way back. If she does, it's your job to clean up.'

'Don't think so, mate.' Lia was still grinning. 'It's *your* helicopter.'

CHAPTER THREE

THE MEDICAL CLINIC on Atangi was staffed by an older local nurse, Marnie, who met them at the door after Jack had landed the helicopter on the football field across the road. He shut the chopper down and came with her in case he needed to go back for a stretcher.

'Try not to scare her,' Marnie warned. 'I had a hard job persuading her to come in at all and she might try and do a runner. Not that she'll get very far, mind you…'

'What's her name?' Lia asked. 'And what's the story?'

'Her name's Sefina. She lives out past the edge of the village and keeps to herself, of course…'

Of course? A warning bell rang for Lia. She wanted to ask why it was expected that this Sefina would keep to herself but the nurse was still speaking quietly.

'I went out there on my way home for lunch because she missed her appointment for Joni's fifteen-month vaccinations last week and I wanted to remind her how important it was that she brings him in.'

'Joni?'

'Her kid. Anyway, when she finally answered the door, it was obvious something bad had happened. She said she had a fall on the rocks at the beach yesterday but…'

Lia touched her arm to slow their progress towards the consulting room. She needed to ask this time.

'But what?'

'Everyone knows what her husband, Louis, can be like after a few drinks,' Jack muttered. 'Is that what you're thinking, Marnie?'

The older woman shrugged and looked away. 'It's none of my business,' she said. 'I only went there because of Joni…'

Lia raised her eyebrows at Jack. What on earth was going on here? This was a village and surely everybody knew everybody else's business—and looked out for them?

'It's a long story,' Jack said quietly. 'I'll fill you in later.'

Sitting in the middle of the consulting-room floor was a small boy with coffee-coloured skin and a mop of wild curls. At the sight of strangers entering the room, his face crumpled and he let out a wail of fear and made a beeline for his mother's legs for something to cling to.

The boy's mother couldn't help, however, because she was currently vomiting into the handbasin at one side of the room.

Lia went swiftly to her side.

'Sefina? I'm Lia. I've come to help you.'

Her patient looked up as she turned the tap on and Lia was shocked by the injury to her face. One eye was so swollen it was closed and there was a cut above it that needed suturing. And even on Sefina's dark skin the bruising around the cut was obvious. She was also shocked at how young she was. Barely more than a teenager, by the look of it, and she was a mother already.

'I'm fine. I didn't want to come in here… Marnie shouldn't have called you.'

'I know.' Lia kept her smile as reassuring as her tone. 'But we're here now so let me give you a check-up? I'm new in this job so I have to make sure everything's done properly. You're my first patient, even.'

She wanted to let Sefina know that she didn't know anything about whatever it was that was keeping this young woman isolated from her community and that she was offering treatment without any kind of judgement. She wasn't going to be fobbed off, however. She'd seen more than a tinge of blood in that basin before the tap had been turned on and that was a red flag for injuries that could be internal.

'Marnie shouldn't have called you. I'm fine.'

The repetition of something that had just been said rang another warning bell for Lia. The head injury was clearly enough to have caused concussion or possibly a more serious brain injury.

'Do you know what day it is today, Sefina?'

'Marnie shouldn't have called you.' Sefina had turned away from the basin. 'Joni… Come on…we're going home…'

She started to bend over to pick up her son, who was still clinging to her legs, but then she clutched her abdomen and doubled over with a cry of pain.

Supporting her weight, Lia had to let her slide to the floor when it became obvious she couldn't get as far as the bed. Whatever this girl's injuries were, they needed more investigation than it was likely to be possible to do in this small clinic.

'Jack?' Lia knew he was waiting right outside the door and, sure enough, he appeared instantly.

'We're going to need the stretcher,' she told him. 'I don't think Sefina's going to be walking anywhere just now.'

It was impossible to start examining Sefina with Joni now trying to scramble into her arms. Lia lifted the toddler and turned to find Marnie watching, her arms folded over her ample chest.

'Can you look after Joni, please, Marnie? I need to examine Sefina.'

'*No-o-o...*' Sefina struggled to sit up but fell back with a cry of pain.

The hesitation and then grudging compliance from the nurse was enough to anger Lia. Whatever the village had against this young girl, it was not acceptable to be taking it out on an innocent child. By the time Jack returned, Lia was tight-lipped. She met him in the waiting room.

'We have to get Sefina back to the hospital. Her abdomen's rigid and I suspect she's bleeding from a ruptured spleen. On top of that she's got a head injury and there's no way of telling how serious it is. She needs a CT scan to rule out a brain bleed.'

Jack was nodding. 'Let's go, then.'

'There's another thing,' Lia snapped. 'I'm not leaving her baby here. I think there's a high chance these injuries weren't accidental. There's no way I'm letting that little boy go back to his father and I'm getting the feeling that no one else around here wants to take care of him.'

'Louis isn't his father,' Jack told her.

Lia blinked. Was that what the problem was? Had Sefina cheated on her husband and everyone knew that? Did her low-life husband think it gave him an excuse to beat her up to within an inch of her life?

'All the more reason to take Joni with us, then.'

'It'll be a rough flight.'

'So we'll strap him in. Or I'll hold him. There's not much I can do for Sefina en route, anyway. I'll give her some pain relief and get some fluids up and then what we need to do is get her to hospital as soon as possible. Hopefully before this weather gets any worse.'

Sam, Hettie and Anahera were waiting in the emergency department of Wildfire Island's hospital, having been alerted to the incoming trauma patient via radio.

Jack and Manu, the hospital porter, were wheeling the stretcher. Lia had her arms full with a very frightened-looking small child. Sam had heard of the child, of course. Everybody in this community had. But he'd never seen him. Or his mother, for that matter. Good grief, she looked *so* young…

'Let's get her onto the bed.' Sam positioned himself at the head. 'On the count of three. One, two…three…'

Sefina was transferred smoothly from the stretcher to the bed. Lia moved closer to Sam but still had to raise her voice over the crying of the child she was holding.

'This is Sefina Dason,' Lia said. 'She's sustained head and abdominal trauma. GCS is down at fourteen. Repetitive speech and vomiting. Her abdo's rigid and her blood pressure is low at one hundred over forty. Up from ninety over forty after a litre of saline. She's in sinus rhythm and tachycardic at one-three-five, and has a resp rate of thirty. Her oxygen saturation was ninety-five per cent. It's come up to ninety-eight on oxygen. She's had ten milligrams of morphine. Provisional diagnosis is a ruptured spleen and concussion.'

Anahera was changing the oxygen tubing from the

portable cylinder to the overhead port. Hettie was wrapping a blood-pressure cuff around Sefina's arm.

'Mechanism of injury?' Sam queried.

'Apparently a fall onto rocks.'

Sam raised an eyebrow at her tone as he stepped closer to Lia to take the patient report form she was holding. Glancing down at her notes, he saw the question mark in front of the words 'non-accidental injury'.

It was a serious accusation to make. He met Lia's gaze and she stared back. He could see anger in her eyes. She started to say something quietly but he couldn't hear over the noise the child was making.

'Is he injured, too?'

'Not that I'm aware of.'

'So why did you bring him? Surely there was a family member or friend who could have cared for him?'

Hettie was reaching up to hook the bag of IV fluids onto the pole at the head of the bed. She turned and her gaze was clearly caught by the sight of the scared toddler. Sam could see the way her face creased into lines of sympathy as her heart went out to the child.

'I'll take him,' she said, 'while you finish your handover.' She scooped Joni into her arms and walked away. 'He might be hungry. I'll go and see if Vailea's got something in the kitchen. Like ice cream, maybe.' She was cuddling the baby close to her body. 'Do you like ice cream, sweetheart?'

Sefina didn't seem to have noticed that her child was being taken from the room. She was drowsy from the morphine. Or maybe the head injury.

'Get another set of vitals, please, Ana. And check that her GCS hasn't dropped. I'll do an ultrasound on her belly.'

As he turned to find the equipment he needed he found himself the subject of an icy glare from Lia. She stepped away from the bed with a head tilt that summoned Sam to mirror her movements.

'Take a look at your patient,' she said, her voice quiet but fierce. 'You'll find welts on her abdomen that look like marks from the sole of a boot. Would you have left a child in the care of someone who could do that?'

'Of course not.' The tension in the air between them was enough that a small thing could ignite it, but this time it had nothing to do with Lia's looks or personality. They were both on the same side here. Sam could feel anger forming an unpleasant knot in his gut but, weirdly, there was something good to be found, as well. It felt good to have Lia on his side. As if, together, they made up a force to be reckoned with.

'Have the police been informed?'

'Not yet. I don't know what your protocols are and, anyway, the priority was to get Sefina here.'

With a nod, Sam turned back to his patient. Lia was right—they needed to work fast. As soon as he was happy that Sefina was stable, they would get a CT scan done if it was indicated and go from there, as far as her treatment went. Right now, it looked as if emergency surgery could well be part of that treatment. The full story, and any repercussions from it, would have to wait.

They were one staff member down, with Hettie having taken Joni away. 'Can you stay?' Sam asked Lia. 'We might need a hand.'

She glanced at Jack, who was manoeuvring the stretcher away. 'You may as well,' he said. 'I'm going to go back and make sure the helicopter's locked down. We won't be flying anywhere else for a while. We were lucky to get back here.' He gave Sam a wry smile. 'It was a wild ride,' he added. 'And I've never seen anyone cope as well as Lia did.'

Sam had been in a few rough helicopter rides himself. He knew how difficult it could be to try and manage a patient in those conditions. He also knew that it could be downright scary. No wonder there was such a note of admiration in Jack's voice. It shouldn't be irritating.

Maybe it was just another coal on the fire of the anger that sprang from a man hurting a woman, if that really was what had happened to Sefina. He needed to protect his patient. And maybe he wanted to protect Lia, too, from the kind of casual relationships he knew the pilot enjoyed. He'd had more than one woman in the past crying on his shoulder because they'd believed they could be the one who changed Jack's mind about being a bachelor.

The thought of Lia crying on his shoulder was strangely appealing for a moment. But it was also ridiculous and he shook it off as he began his examination of their patient. Lia could look after herself. In fact, she could probably cope with anything, and if she did hook up with Jack, it would be more likely to be their pilot who'd be crying on Sam's shoulder. The thought brought a faint curl to the corners of his mouth but they vanished as he focused on his patient.

'Let's get another line in and some more fluids up. Type and crossmatch in case we need a blood transfusion. Sefina? Open your eyes, love. Do you know where you are?'

Sefina moaned but did open her eyes. Sam could see the moment she was awake enough to be frightened again and it was heartbreaking to see how very scared she was.

'It's okay,' he told her. 'You're in the hospital, love. We're going to take care of you. You're safe now...'

Sefina rolled her head to one side and then the other. 'Joni... Where's Joni?' She was trying to sit up now. One of the electrodes that was monitoring her heart rhythm popped off her arm and an alarm began to sound.

Lia caught the dangling wire and snapped the electrode back onto the sticky dot. She had her face close to Sefina's and she caught the girl's hand in her own and held it.

'He's fine, Sefina. We're taking care of him, too.'

'Where am I?'

'You're in the hospital. I'm Lia, remember? I came to see you at the clinic. We brought you in here because you're hurt and now you're safe. And Joni's safe.'

Her voice was calm and even Sam was starting to feel the tension ebb. And that *smile*... 'I promise...'

Tears were rolling down Sefina's cheeks but she nodded slowly.

'It *hurts*,' she whispered. 'My tummy hurts...'

'I know. We're going to find out why and then we'll fix it, okay?'

Sam's glance, he hoped, thanked Lia for making this easier before he made eye contact with Sefina. The girl was still clutching Lia's hand but a lot of that fear had gone.

'I'm Sam,' he told her gently. 'One of the doctors here. Is it okay if I have a look at your tummy now?'

It was Lia the girl looked towards for reassurance before she nodded again. It was Lia's hand she had to hold whenever it was possible during the barrage of tests they employed to find out exactly how serious Sefina's injuries were.

It was more than an hour later when they could review all the results.

'There's no bleeding in her head. That's a bonus.'

'Definite concussion, though. She's still vomiting and she's very drowsy.' Anahera glanced over her shoulder to where Sefina was sleeping, now receiving a transfusion to counteract the amount of blood she was losing internally. 'I still need to suture that head laceration. Unless you want to do it?'

'Let's do it in Theatre.' Sam looked at Lia. 'Your provisional diagnosis was spot-on. She's still bleeding from the rupture to her spleen. We'll have to take it out.'

'You can do that here?'

'We can't do anything else. There's no way we can evacuate her in this weather. We weren't even able to send off our man who had the arrest this morning. We'll be keeping him here for a few days, by the look of things. Anyway, it was lucky that you and Jack could get her here so fast. A boat trip could have made things a whole lot worse.'

'Anything I can do to help?'

'Maybe go and see what's happening with the little boy. I'll need Hettie in Theatre. Do you know where the kitchens are?'

'I'll find them.'

As she went through the doorway, Sam saw her slip her hand into her pocket and take out her phone. Had it been vibrating silently even as Lia had been assisting them with this emergency?

And he'd felt the need to protect her from Jack? Irritation bubbled out.

'Hurry up,' he called after her. 'It would be better if you could attend to your love-life later.'

* * *

Love-life?

As if…

A nurse pointed Lia in the direction of the kitchens and she sped along the walkway. The windows had been shuttered against the wind and they rattled and shook with a disturbing ferocity. There was no rain yet but it wasn't far away.

She found Hettie in the kitchen, spooning ice cream into Joni's mouth. She got to her feet instantly when Lia passed on the message that she was needed in Theatre and she bent to kiss the toddler as she gave a swift farewell to the older woman working at the bench.

Lia smiled at her. 'Hi… I'm Lia.'

'I know.' The woman's smile was friendly. 'I'm Vailea. I'm in charge of the kitchens here. Can I get you a cup of tea or something?'

'That would be great—if you've got time.'

'I've got plenty of help, as you can see.' A wave of her hand took in the small group of island girls in their white aprons and caps. 'Moana? Take Joni through to the ward, will you? Ask one of the nurses to find a nappy and help you change him. And ask if they've got a spare cot. I think he might need a sleep.'

The tea was strong and sweet, just the way Lia liked it. She also liked it that Vailea came to sit at the big table with her to have her own drink.

'Sefina's going to be in hospital for a few days at least. Do you know what will happen with Joni? Will they keep him in here with her?'

'Probably. I'll have a word with my daughter later when they're not so busy. You've met Anahera?'

'Yes…is she your daughter?'

Vailea nodded. 'And she has a daughter, as well. Hana. A bit older than Joni but we're well used to looking after little ones. I might end up taking him home with me for a few days. Poor wee mite...'

Lia sipped her tea thoughtfully. Her curiosity about her first patient here on the islands was strong enough to make her push the boundaries of patient confidentiality. Vailea obviously knew enough to make her feel sorry for Joni.

She bit her lip but then raised her gaze. 'Jack said that Sefina's husband isn't Joni's father...'

Vailea's glance was sharp. Was it telling her that this was none of her business? Except it was, kind of...

'I got the feeling that she might need help. That...um... other people might need to be called in.'

Valiea clicked her tongue. 'Did that no-good Louis do this to her?' She shook her head sadly. 'It was never going to work...'

'What wasn't?'

'The arrangement.'

Lia stayed silent but her face must have advertised her confusion.

Vailea sighed. 'Joni is the son of Ian Lockhart. The family that owns Wildfire and started the gold mine way back. They're mostly good people. Max Lockhart is the one who got this hospital set up to provide for all the islanders. And his daughter, Caroline, is one of our best nurses. But Ian...well, a lot of families have a black sheep, don't they?'

Lia nodded. It sounded like this Lockhart family was the equivalent of royalty on these islands and that kind of power could be used to devastating effect by someone who lacked scruples.

'Everybody knows the story so I don't see why you shouldn't,' Vailea continued. 'It didn't surprise anyone that Ian got Sefina pregnant. What did surprise us was that he brought her back here from Fiji after her family threw her out. Not that he intended to ever marry her himself, of course. No…he hired Louis to do that because everybody knows how lazy he is and that he'd do anything for money.'

'He paid Louis to marry her?'

'Not only that. He kept paying him. Every month. Except…'

Lia's eyebrows were about as high as they could go.

'The money ran out a while back. Ian's disappeared. Nobody knows where he is. The mine got run-down and we ended up with a collapse that killed people. There's no money even for things like spraying for mosquitoes and we've lost people to encephalitis because of it.' She shook her head. 'Everybody hates Ian so nobody wants anything to do with that poor little boy. Or his mother. And Louis…well, he's like the black sheep of the village, I guess.' Vailea was scowling now. 'But if he's done something to hurt her, something will have to be done.'

Lia nodded. 'I've told Sam. I imagine he'll call the police when they've finished the surgery. Maybe he's done it already. You do have police here, don't you?'

'Of course we do.'

Oh, dear…had she caused offence? 'Sorry… I don't know enough yet. I mean, if you have police, you need to have courts and jails and things, too, don't you?'

'There's a jail on Atangi. But if a case is serious enough it does get sent to the mainland.' Vailea reached for Lia's empty tea cup but she was smiling as she stood up. 'You'll learn about us fast enough. And I hope you'll come back. It sounds like you did a very good job today.'

Wow. Word travelled fast around these parts but it was the kind of bush telegraph Lia would have expected in a small community. What had been shocking was to learn about a darker side, where a young mother and her baby could be shut off from any support.

'I'd better get on with the dinners,' Vailea said. 'And check up on what's happening with Joni.'

'And I'd better…' Lia hesitated. What was she expected to do if the weather was too bad to fly? Did she need to wait in the staffroom near the radio in case a call came in and she needed to respond by boat? 'I'd better find Jack.'

'He'll probably be in the staffroom, if he's back from the airfield. That's where he usually hangs out.'

The shutters were still rattling as Lia made her way back along the walkway but it wasn't disturbing anymore—it was exhilarating.

Lia loved a good storm. Something wild and unpredictable and exciting. And it had been a good day today. Her first case and she'd managed it well under difficult conditions. And Sefina would be okay. They could lock her beast of a husband up in the jail and keep her safe and surely, after this, things would change.

Maybe her family back in Fiji would have a change of heart after this appalling evidence of how awful her life was here and they would take her home.

At least Joni would be well cared for over the next few days. Vailea, Anahera and especially Hettie would see to that.

Even better, she'd received word that Nico's surgery

had gone well and she could let go of the guilt of not being there for him today.

Yes. It had been a very good start to her working time here. The only thing that might make the day even better was to get out into that wind for a bit. Preferably on a beach so that she would get the sting of salt water on her cheeks. And she could let the wind whip her hair and buffet her body and make her feel so alive she would have to throw her arms wide and spin around and laugh out loud with the joy of it all.

If Jack said it was okay, that was exactly what Lia intended to do.

CHAPTER FOUR

WAS SHE COMPLETELY CRAZY?

There she was, standing on the beach with big waves crashing over the coral reef and then rolling towards her in a sea of foam, probably getting soaked by the spray being picked up by the fierce wind gusts. The trees bordering the beach were bent over as if in pain and, even from this distance, Sam could hear the crack of branches about to be torn free.

And she was standing in the middle of it.

No. Not standing. She had her arms wide out to each side, like a child pretending to be an aeroplane, and she was spinning in a slow circle. Her face was tipped up and her eyes were closed and…yes…she had to be laughing, even though he couldn't hear the sound over the roar of the wind.

And then a particularly strong gust of wind knocked her off balance and Lia went sprawling onto the sand. She was struggling to get back to her feet by the time Sam reached her and she seemed happy enough to accept the offer of his hand to haul her back up.

'Isn't this amazing?' she shouted. 'I love it.'

'You're nuts,' Sam told her. 'You do realise there are

coconut palms amongst those trees and if one fell on your head it would be lights out. Probably forever.'

'I'm nowhere near the trees.'

'Branches can go a long way. And you've still got to get back up the track to get home.'

Her cheeks were bright pink from the chill of the wind mixed with sea spray. Her hair had been pulled loose from that tight arrangement of braids she'd started the day with and she looked like she hadn't been near a hairbrush in days. But her eyes were glowing with joy and that smile was wide enough to fence him in.

'You love it, too. Admit it. It's why you came down to the beach.'

'I came down to get you, you idiot. I couldn't believe it when Jack told me you'd decided to go out in this.'

But Sam was grinning now, too. She was wild, this woman. A naughty child in a grown-up's body. The sea spray had soaked her shirt and the wind had it plastered against her body. Oh, yeah…it was a very grown-up body, all right…

'He said he reckoned I could look after myself. And that he'd call me on my phone if I was needed.'

They were still having to shout to be heard over the wind. 'You think you'd even hear it?'

'It's on vibrate. I'd feel it.' Lia put her hand over the breast pocket of her shirt and Sam could see the rectangular outline of the mobile phone. How come he hadn't noticed that before when he was so aware of the way her shirt was sticking to her skin?

Because he'd been blinded by the sheer attractiveness of this woman, that's why. Something he didn't do.

The reminder of her unprofessional attention to her

phone all day was enough of a slap to bring him back to his senses.

He shook his head. 'Should have known you'd have it close. You wouldn't want to miss another text from the boyfriend.'

'What?' The smile had gone from Lia's face. The glow of exhilaration from being out in the elements had faded from her eyes, as well. 'What makes you so sure I've got a boyfriend? And when, exactly, did it become any of your business?'

'When it started interfering with how you do your job.' It was quite satisfying having to shout over the wind now. And it was good to get rid of that niggle of irritation he'd had all day. 'Every time I've seen you today, you've been fiddling with your phone.'

'And you assume that I'd let my personal life stop me doing my job properly?' Lia turned and took a step away from him. But then she turned back, almost stumbling as a wind gust caught her. 'Okay… I admit I was on the phone too much. My younger brother had surgery this morning for testicular cancer and I needed to know that he'd come through it.'

Were they tears on Lia's cheeks or was it the sea spray she was wiping away?

'I should have been there for him. I felt bad that I'd let him persuade me it was okay to come because of…of…'

The money.

That reminder should have been enough to clear his head completely of the insane attraction he was feeling towards this woman.

But there was a tiny voice in his head saying something along the lines that at least she was prepared to work for the money and not get someone else's by pretending to love them enough to score a marriage.

And she had been working. And doing a damn good job, too. If it hadn't been for her they might not have got Sefina into hospital in time.

And she was crying. She was upset because she hadn't been there for her brother and that told him something about her loyalty to the people she loved.

And maybe fate was giving things a bit of a shove. The way the wind was shoving Lia so hard she had to take a big step towards him, which knocked her off balance enough to end up bumping into him.

What was a man to do other than put his arms around her?

'I'm sorry,' he shouted. 'You should have told me. About your brother.'

'I'm sorry, too. I knew I shouldn't have been taking texts at work.'

'It didn't stop you doing your job. You were great today, Lia.'

She looked up at him, her gaze intent. 'Is Sefina okay? How did the surgery go?'

'She's fine. We took her spleen out and stopped the bleeding. She'll need a few days to get over that and the concussion but she'll be fine.'

'Has she changed her story about how it happened?'

'No. But I've had a word with our police chief, Ky. He's onto it. It's okay. I'll make sure she's safe.'

Lia was nodding. Was she actually aware that he still had his arms around her?

'And I'm sure you're brother's going to be fine, too. The survival rate for testicular cancer is great.'

She kept nodding. 'I know…'

She was still looking up at him and a new smile broke through the lines of concern for others. A relieved smile. One that underlined her apology to him and accepted his apology to her, along with the praise about her work.

It was the smile that was his undoing. On top of those huge, dark eyes that were still locked on his face. Or maybe it was the feel of her body within his arms.

Whatever…

Sam was about to do something he never did. Break a rule that was set in steel. The pull was just too strong but at least he hesitated. Made it obvious enough that Lia could stop it happening if she wanted to.

She must be more than capable of ducking a kiss that wasn't welcome…

Maybe it was because of the relief of knowing that Nico had come through his surgery and it had gone so well. She could let go of the anxiety that had been making her so tense, along with the guilt that would have haunted her forever if things hadn't gone well today.

Or maybe it was because Lia was standing in the beginnings of what was going to be a dramatic storm and the thrill of the potential danger was singing in her veins.

And maybe—if she was going to be really honest—it was because she was in the arms of a man she was already attracted to, more than she could remember ever having been attracted to any man before.

It didn't matter whether it was any or all of those reasons because Lia wasn't about to stop and analyse what was happening.

Sam Taylor was about to kiss her and she'd never wanted to *be* kissed this much.

She could feel his arms tighten around her, holding

her steady in the gusts of a wind that was more than capable of knocking her off her feet again. Could taste the salt of the sea spray on his lips. Could feel the beat of his heart through clothing that was so glued to her skin now, she felt almost naked.

For a heartbeat, that was all it was. A nice kiss.

And then something changed. Something huge got unleashed and it felt bigger than the crash of the angry sea beside them and the howl of wind all around.

If this was lust, it was unlike anything Lia had ever experienced.

The warmth of this kiss was sending tendrils of fire into every cell of her body and Lia was quite sure she would never feel cold again. The silken touch of his tongue melted her bones and made her groan with the sheer ecstasy of the sensation. The sound was lost in Sam's mouth but maybe he felt it because he pulled back.

'Not here,' he said.

Her first reaction was almost fear. He was going to stop kissing her? Stop touching her? The disappointment—or maybe frustration—would be overwhelming.

'Where?'

Had she spoken the word aloud or simply let it be written all over her face?

'Come with me.'

He held her hand but it wasn't enough as the wind pushed and then pulled at her body as she tried to step over some driftwood, so he wrapped his arm around her waist and held her against his own body. A particularly big wave began its curl and descent into foam and the shower of spray was dense enough to sting their eyes and soak them both to the skin.

But they were both laughing. Fighting the elements

together and loving the excitement of it. Anticipation of a very different kind of excitement was part of it, as well, and Lia could feel it sizzling and spreading from every point where Sam's body was in contact with her own.

And then they were away from the spray and protected a little from the wind as they left the beach and began climbing back up the path that Lia had used to come down to the beach from the hospital. Sam's hand gripping hers was enough to keep her steady now but he was moving fast up the track through the trees and she could hear the snap of branches and the thud of large objects hitting the ground nearby. Lia was too out of breath to say anything because she would still have to shout to be heard and…she wouldn't have known what to say, anyway.

Where was Sam taking her?

Back to the safety of the hospital? That was probably sensible, given that the sky had darkened so much it felt like night was about to fall hours too early and the first, fat drops of rain were beginning to fall. But there would be other people around at the hospital and that would be a guarantee that nothing more would happen between them. Or was he taking her to her own accommodation? That wasn't exactly private, either, with only thin walls between her room and that of other staff members, so it would end up being exactly the same dead end.

She didn't want that.

Even with the time she now had to consider whether this was a good idea or not, Lia felt no different than how she had the moment Sam had interrupted that passionate kiss.

She wanted this.

She wanted *him*…

'My house,' Sam finally shouted. 'On the end. Here…'

It was a small structure, not unlike the cluster of build-ings closer to the hospital that housed both permanent and FIFO staff, but it was on its own and screened by shrubbery that was currently shedding big, glossy leaves and flowers as an offering to the rising wind. Sam had to let go of her hand to pull the door open against the force of it and then he let it shut with a bang the moment Lia had stumbled inside.

They were both out of breath and for a long, long mo-ment they both stood there panting, their gazes locked on each other.

This was the moment. Either or both of them could admit that this might not be a good idea. That it might cause problems with them having to work together for the next couple of weeks. That they barely knew each other and they were both old enough to know that reck-less physical encounters like this were something they should have grown out of long ago.

But whatever extraordinary thing had been unleashed between them was getting bigger. Gaining a momentum that Lia knew she didn't have the faintest chance of re-sisting. And she saw the moment that Sam realised the same thing. Heard the sound that was both an admis-sion of defeat and an expression of a desire that echoed her own.

And then she was in his arms again and his lips were on hers and nothing else mattered. Her back was pressed against the door and she could feel her sodden clothing being peeled from her body. Her skin had to be cold be-cause the touch of Sam's hands was far too hot to be nat-ural and she had never felt anything like the softness of the bed she found herself on moments later.

* * *

Sex had never been like this before.

Ever…

Everything about Lia was extraordinary. Those long, lean limbs and gorgeous, firm breasts. That wild mane of dark hair that had somehow come loose from those braids so that he could wind it around his hands to hold her head in exactly the right position to capture those sweet lips.

The most extraordinary thing had to be the way she responded to every touch or sound he made, however. Instead of a normal focus on a satisfying climax for both parties, Sam found himself trying to slow things down and make it last as long as humanly possible. But this chemistry, or whatever it was, was too powerful to be tamed. With the background of the rain now hammering on the tin roof of his quarters and wooden shutters beating a tattoo in the fierce wind, it seemed as if the passion between them was a part of the elemental forces outside. It also seemed like it was over too soon.

Way too soon.

But that was okay. As they lay there closely entwined he wasn't sure where his body ended and Lia's began. Sam knew, beyond a shadow of a doubt, that this wouldn't be the only time. They had a whole two weeks to play with, and if Lia had enjoyed this encounter as much as her response suggested that she had, she would undoubtedly be just as keen as he was to make the most of every day of that two weeks. Or every night, at least.

His lips curled into a slow and very satisfied smile as he drew his head back far enough to see Lia's face.

'Wow…'

There were no words available but it didn't seem to matter because Lia was smiling, too.

'Couldn't have put it better myself.'

Her words were almost inaudible due to the sudden increase in the tropical downpour hitting the roof and her eyes widened.

'The worst of it will probably be over before too long. By tomorrow morning, maybe, with a bit of luck.'

'How will anyone get to the hospital if they need help?'

'They won't. Not unless they can get up from the village here on Wildfire. You and Jack won't be flying anywhere and I don't think any boats would manage the sea the way it'll be for a while. We'll all have to sit tight until it starts dying down. And then I expect we could be in for a busy time. It might take days to check the outlying islands.'

The faint sound of splintering glass could be heard, along with the crack of a shutter being torn free. Sam felt the sudden tension in Lia's body.

'You're safe,' he told her. 'I'll keep you safe.'

Good grief…where had that come from? Not just the words, which had seemed kind of corny the moment they had left his lips, but the sudden conviction that honouring those words was the most important thing in the world to him.

This wasn't part of the plan.

But, then, none of this had been part of any plan, had it?

The tension was contagious. Sam rolled away from Lia. 'I'd better check what that was. And maybe we should get back to the hospital and see if everything's okay.'

That's probably where he should have stayed. What had he been thinking? It was understandable that he'd gone after Lia when he'd heard that she'd been stupid enough to go to the beach as the cyclone hit, but to be hiding away in his quarters having *sex* at a time like this?

Nobody would expect behaviour like this from him. He couldn't quite believe it himself, now that the post-coital glow was wearing off. Never mind that he'd been due a break after a hectic day that had included emergency surgery. He had patients who might need him—like Sefina. He had colleagues who needed to be sure they could depend on him at all times, and especially in the potential disaster that a cyclone could bring. It might be just beginning but he'd been AWOL and that was unacceptable.

As unacceptable as hooking up with a temporary staff member?

His feet hit the floor. 'I'll find you some dry clothes.'

'How far is it from here to the hospital?'

'About two minutes, if we run.'

'I wouldn't bother about the dry clothes, then. I'd be just as wet by the time we get there.'

Knowing that Lia was planning to come with him somehow made things better. More professional, in a weird way. They couldn't change what had just happened between them, but they could put it aside and go back to how they'd been before. Two people who could work together as a team, focusing on others rather than themselves. And having those others around to dilute this disturbing attraction between them would make that so much easier.

Sam already knew how good Lia was at her job. Those skills could well be very necessary around here in the next couple of days.

'So it was worth it, then?'

'Sorry?' Lia knew she must look like a drowned rat,

standing there in her sodden clothes with her hair loose and dripping down her back. No wonder everybody in the unexpectedly crowded staffroom was staring at her, but why was Jack grinning as if he knew exactly what she'd been up to?

She didn't dare turn her head to look at Sam.

'Going down to the beach to see what a cyclone looks like. It was worth getting so wet for?'

'Oh…' Maybe everybody thought that the only story here was that Sam had gone down to the beach and brought her straight back here to safety. Lia's smile was probably wider than it needed to be. 'Yes… It was…it was…amazing…'

'It was stupid, that's what it was.' Sam's voice was a growl behind her. 'I'm going to find some dry scrubs in a minute. Fill me in, Jack.' He gestured towards the radio on the desk at which the pilot was sitting. 'Any news of how things are shaping up?'

Anahera was using sign language to offer Lia a hot drink as Sam was talking to Jack. Lia smiled but shook her head. Then she smiled at Hettie, who was sitting beside Anahera, holding a sleepy-looking toddler in her lap. Seeing Joni made her want to ask about his mother's condition but she didn't want to interrupt Jack.

'The northern end of Atangi seems to be getting the worst of it so far. Mobile phone coverage is out but we've got radio contact for the moment—at least with Atangi. Ky's using the school hall on Atangi as a refuge centre and a lot of families are gathering there. No word on any of the outer islands.'

'Any boats still out?'

'Hope not. Anybody with any sense would have stopped fishing a long time ago. I did see a couple of boats heading back to port when we were flying back in from Atangi earlier. Want me to check on *your* baby?'

His *baby*? Lia had to turn her head this time—a swift, startled movement. More like a horrified one, in fact. Sam had a baby? Had she just had the most amazing sex in her life with a man who had a child, and presumably a girlfriend if not a wife, tucked away somewhere?

Jack saw her expression and laughed. 'I'm talking about his yacht. *Surf Song*. The love of his life. She's moored down at the harbour here.'

Sam's face was giving nothing away. He certainly wasn't about to meet Lia's gaze.

'If she's not secure enough now, it's too late to worry about it. So…no reports of any injuries, then?'

'Not yet.'

Sam's glance swept the room and rested on Hettie. 'Is somebody watching Sefina?'

'Keanu's in there now and then I'm going to take Joni in for a quick visit. She's doing well. In a bit of pain, of course, but she's oriented well enough to use her infusion pump.'

'And Keoni—our cardiac patient?' A frown line appeared on Sam's face as he started a mental run-through of inpatients in the hospital. 'Never mind, I'll go and check myself. I just need some dry clothes.' Finally, he looked directly at Lia. 'I'll get you a pair of scrubs, too, shall I? What size are you?'

There was nothing in the look or his body language that would have given any hint that he might have a very good idea of the size of her body. And its shape and… dear Lord—she could feel a sharp twinge of renewed desire as the thought entered her head—even how it tasted.

It should be a relief that, thanks to Sam's poker face,

nobody would guess how well they now knew each other but, oddly, it felt like a putdown. As if that amazing connection they'd found didn't mean anything at all. That it was already forgotten.

'I can do that.' Anahera pushed her chair back. 'Come with me, Lia. I'll get you a towel for your hair, too. You look like you went swimming. Aren't you cold?'

'A bit.' But the goose-bumps she could now see on her arms didn't really have anything to do with her body temperature, did they? They'd been a physical response to the dismissal Sam had just dealt out.

It had been easy to pick up that Jack would have been up for a quick fling with a visitor to this island. Had she somehow missed the signals that Sam was just as likely to make the most of an unexpected opportunity, as well?

'There's a few sizes of overalls in the change room,' Jack said. 'And some waterproof undergear. You might want to be ready in case you get a callout.'

The radio on the desk behind Jack crackled as if it had been waiting for the right moment. Jack pulled the headphones perched on his head down over his ears and leaned forward to press the button on the microphone.

'Wildfire Rescue Base receiving. Go ahead…'

Voices outside the staffroom made it difficult to hear what was being relayed through the crackling on the radio and Lia found herself edging towards the wall as more people came in. A small girl ran towards Anahera.

'Mumma… It's *windy*…'

Vailea was right behind the child. She was wearing a light rainproof poncho and pushed the hood back from her head.

'Some of the villagers were too frightened to stay at home. I've brought them up here and put them in the waiting room in Outpatients. One of the lads hurt his arm when they were trying to secure the boats earlier. He might need looking at.'

'I'll do that.' Hettie got to her feet. 'Could you keep Joni with Hana?'

'No…' The small girl shook her head. 'I want to stay with Mumma.'

'You can't, sweetheart.' Anahera kissed her daughter's head. 'Mummy's got to work because people need looking after. You be a good girl and stay with Nana.'

'But—'

'I have to go. Look, Lia's all wet. I've got to go and find her some new clothes.'

'I'm wet, too…'

'Not very. You've got your raincoat on.' Anahera stepped back as Hettie passed Joni into Vailea's arms. 'You might want to take a stack of towels into the waiting room. I expect everybody will be fairly wet.'

Vailea was staring at Lia. 'You're completely soaked,' she said. 'What on earth have you been doing?'

But Lia was watching Jack. By the look on his face, he'd heard something serious on the radio transmission that he was about to discuss with Sam. By focusing on the two men, she could filter out the sound of the women around her.

'The trees coming down caused a landslide. Rocks and mud. There's a whole family trapped in one of the houses, by the sound of it. And others that have been injured. They need help.'

'I'll go.' Sam's face was grim. 'We've got to get some medical cover on Atangi anyway. We haven't got anyone at the clinic other than Marnie and even a few minor injuries will be more than she can cope with.'

Lia stepped past Vailea. 'I'll come, too. Show me where to get a kit together.'

'I brought the packs down from the chopper when I knew we wouldn't be flying anywhere. They're in the change room where the overalls are.'

Sam was shaking his head. 'It's dangerous,' he said. 'The only way we can get there is by boat and I can't let anyone else risk that trip.'

Lia met his gaze. 'You're going.'

'I know what I'm doing. And it's my boat.' There was more than the acknowledgment of a grim situation showing on his face now. This was a man who wouldn't hesitate to put himself in danger for others.

The sort of man that people could rely on. Someone honourable and trustworthy.

Someone that deserved respect and Sam had just won a huge amount of hers.

'He does know what he's doing.' Jack nodded. 'Sam's got sea water for blood. I'd go with him. You may not need to use your boat, though, mate. Ky's rounding up some manpower. I'll call him back and see if they can launch the coastguard vessel and come to get you. It's a lot more powerful than your runabout and it'll fit more people. I could come with you.'

'You're needed here. I want someone who knows what they're doing with the radio and can coordinate any rescue missions needed. Give me one of the handheld sets.'

'And me.' Lia held out her hand. She knew she was scowling at Sam with a 'don't try and stop me' expression. 'This is my job,' she told him. 'You might not have read my CV but I've had training in urban search and rescue. I'm not going to sit around here when I know that there's a family trapped in a collapsed building. There are probably *children* in there...'

'It'll be rough,' Sam warned. But there was something that looked like admiration in his gaze. 'Are you sure you want to come?'

There was something more than admiration in the way he was looking at her.

Something like the feeling she was getting, perhaps? That they might both be very good at the jobs they did but together...they were capable of something even better. Something extraordinary even—like beating the danger of a huge storm and saving lives?

Maybe it wasn't appropriate to smile but Lia couldn't help it. And Sam might not be smiling back but she could swear there was a gleam in his eyes that suggested he was smiling inside.

His slow nod, however, was completely serious.

'Let's go.'

CHAPTER FIVE

IT WAS ONE thing to expect a bit of excitement in taking on a new adventure but, in her wildest dreams, Lia could not have conjured up this scenario.

At sea—as night fell—in the teeth of a tropical cyclone. Wearing a set of bright orange overalls beneath her life jacket and hanging on to her seat with both hands to stop herself becoming airborne as the boat surged and dropped over the massive swells beyond the coral reefs.

A uniformed islander was at the wheel of the powerful motor boat and Sam was standing beside him. Somehow, they were both keeping their footing as they navigated the angry stretch of ocean between Wildfire Island and the much bigger settlement of Atangi. In calm weather the journey probably only took about fifteen minutes but this seemed to be taking forever and, despite hanging on and bracing herself, Lia was over the pummelling.

Sam turned and mouthed something at her that looked like, 'You okay?'

She loosened the grip of one hand long enough to give him a thumbs-up sign. He nodded and turned back, pointing forward at something as he tilted his head towards the man beside him, shouting something that Lia couldn't catch. Hopefully, he was pointing towards their destination. Landing and getting off the boat wasn't going to be easy but Lia was impatient to get there and get on with the rescue mission.

She had all the medical gear she might need in the heavy pack Jack had provided and Sam had another one he would be carrying on his back. Looking around this well-equipped rescue vessel, Lia took note of coiled ropes, blankets and tools and the Stokes basket rescue stretcher that could be loaded up with the extra supplies. Would there be other people available to help carry it or were the able-bodied men of the villages already at the scene of the landslide, desperately trying to dig out the people who had been buried or trapped?

Thankfully, the sea was a little calmer once they were within the reef protecting Atangi. The driving rain made visibility poor but this side of the island was not taking the full force of the wind and there were people waiting to help secure and offload the boat. There was still enough of a swell to make the task challenging. Lia passed the medical packs to Sam, who threw them up onto the jetty where they were caught by a big man wearing a police officer's uniform.

'Shall we take the Stokes basket? And some ropes and things?'

'Good thinking. Ky?' Sam waved the police officer closer. 'Have we got some manpower to help carry some more supplies?'

'Sure thing. We'll load whatever looks useful into the jeep. I'll have to drive you to the other side. It'll take too long to walk.'

Sam timed the roll of the boat and leapt up onto the jetty when they had offloaded what they wanted. Then he crouched and held out his hand to Lia.

'Wait until the boat's coming up. Then grab my hand. You'll have to be ready to jump.'

His grip on her hand was tight and the upward tug firm enough to make the leap onto the solid wood of the jetty easy. The pull was almost too firm, in fact, because it pulled Lia right against his body and he had to steady them both by catching her shoulders to stop her forward momentum.

For just the tiniest moment, when their faces were so close together, Sam's gaze met hers and Lia was aware of a surge of…something. Energy maybe. This wasn't sexual but it was just as exciting. They were about to start a task with unknown dimensions and danger involved. And they were doing it together. The shared glance was like a pact had been made. They would be doing whatever needed to be done but they would also be watching each other's back.

Taking care of each other.

There was no time for any significant moments after that. Having piled into the jeep along with all their gear, they were bouncing along a rough road that led out from the main township, going off-road in places to avoid fallen trees. The windscreen wipers were failing to cope with the deluge of water pouring down and the vehicle was rocking in the wind. More than once Ky had to stop the vehicle when they came across people who were fighting their way along the edge of the road.

He would roll down the window and yell, 'Anybody hurt? I've got the doc on board.'

If the answer was no, the islanders were advised to take care and make their way to the school hall. As they got further away from the township, the advice was to get to the nearest dwelling and stay inside, away from any flying debris.

If the answer was yes, Sam and Lia would assess and apply minimal first aid. A dressing to keep a laceration clean until it could be sutured later. A splint on a broken arm. These people were walking wounded and they could wait. Where they were headed there were likely to be injuries serious enough to need urgent medical intervention for people to survive.

The landslide was bigger than any of them had expected. There was no way to take the jeep off the track and drive around it. Huge old trees high up the side of the mountain must have been torn out by their roots, dislodging massive rocks that had kicked off a crescendo of destruction. Several metres high, the tangle of rock, mud, tree trunks and vines would have to be scaled on foot.

And Ky had messages coming through thick and fast on his radio. Roofs were lifting from houses in the township, with sheets of tin coming loose to threaten anybody still outside. The scene in the school hall was chaotic and the chain of command was not clear enough with Ky missing. Relaying instructions wasn't enough and the tone of the broadcasts was getting steadily more urgent.

'I'll have to go back,' Ky told Sam and Lia as he stopped with the headlights of the jeep shining on the mountain of landslide debris. 'I know you'll need help but, as far as we know, there's only a few people affected here. I'm responsible for the whole Atangi community right now.'

'Go,' Sam said. 'We'll find out exactly what we're dealing with and let you know. Can you send the jeep back when we need transport?'

'I'm going to have to call in any available vehicles to

get people to safety. I'll find something to send out here as soon as possible.'

Lia used her shoulder to get her door open against the wind. 'I'll get the packs out. What will we do with the stretcher?'

'We'll leave it here for now.' Sam had his door open too. 'The important thing is to find out what's going on. I'm just hoping the building isn't under this lot or we might find there's nothing we *can* do.'

Ky left the engine running as he helped them offload the gear. About to climb back into the driver's seat, he looked up, shielding his eyes from the rain.

'Hey…' he shouted.

Lia and Sam, hoisting their backpacks into position, turned to look up, as well. A man was clambering over the pile, wearing nothing but shorts and a shredded T-shirt. His feet were bare.

'Come,' he yelled, catching hold of a protruding tree branch as his feet slipped in the mud. 'Quick. My wife… my children… I need help…'

Lia was already moving. 'It's climbable,' she said over her shoulder to Sam. 'He's done it in bare feet and we've got boots.' She flicked on the headlamp attached to her helmet. 'Stay there,' she called up to the islander. 'We're coming. What's your name?'

'Afi.'

'I'm Lia. And this is Sam. Okay, Afi—take us where we need to go.'

Talk about courage.

Sam was behind Lia as she tackled the climb and he was having a hard job keeping up with her pace. Even with the heavy pack on her back, she was hauling herself up with a speed and grace that were astonishing. It wasn't a stupid headlong rush, though. She was testing branches and rocks as she followed their guide to see if they could still take her weight and choosing an alternative if they couldn't. At one point she hesitated briefly before grasping a thick vine.

'Are there snakes here?'

'Not here. We've got a nasty little adder on Wildfire but it sticks to the marshes around the lagoon.'

Her hand curled around the dark coil that could have been the tail of a snake and she was off again. It didn't take long to get to the top and then she stopped still for longer this time, staring down at whatever she could see in front of her—assessing the scene for dangers and whatever task lay ahead. Sam was by her side seconds later.

'Holy heck…'

The landslide had caught one side of the house, pushing it off any foundations it might have had and twisting it sideways. The tin roof was buckled, half of it buried under rocks with sheets bent and ripped, lethally sharp edges protruding. The wooden framework of the house had collapsed and lay like an oversized child's puzzle of pick-up sticks—flat and tangled. Was there even any space for people to have survived?

'I could hear the baby crying,' Afi said, as he led them down the other side of the obstruction. 'But I can't find her…'

'Were you inside—when it happened?'

'I was in the bedroom trying to fix the shutters. The others were in the back.'

'How many others?'

'My wife, Hika. Our children. Two older ones and the baby.'

And he'd only heard the baby crying? Sam swallowed hard.

'Are there other houses around? Other people who might be hurt?'

'I...I haven't looked.' A sound like a sob broke from the distressed man. 'I... It's my family in there... I had to call for help...'

'We know.' Lia had taken hold of Afi's hands. 'And we're going to do everything we can to help. Are *you* okay? You haven't hurt yourself or been cut by the tin or anything?'

He shook his head. 'I'm not important. I'm fine.'

'You *are* important. Afi, we need you to do something for us.'

'I'll do it.' Afi nodded. 'I want to help. Just tell me...'

'We need to know if there are any other people in trouble. You know where the houses are. You can find out for us. We'll stay here and help your family.'

It was the logical way to try and assess the wider area but it was a big ask to expect Afi to move away from where he knew his own family was trapped. Lia was asking for his trust. Had she won it by gentle persuasion rather than issuing a direct order? By the confidence in her reassurance that she and Sam were able to help his loved ones?

She was still holding Afi's hands and eye contact and, to Sam's amazement, he nodded slowly. Then he turned and began to walk away from his destroyed home into the driving rain and wind.

'Be careful,' Lia called after him. 'Keep yourself safe and come back to us as soon as you can.'

He looked back—not at the house but at Lia. A long look, as if he was using her to gather his own strength. And then he was gone, any glimpse of him curtained by the rain and then trees.

Afi had given Lia his trust and he was prepared to do what she had asked of him no matter how hard it was. Sam's heart twisted with something that felt curiously like pride. He barely knew Lia but he knew that that trust had not been misplaced.

The agreement to begin what could be a heartbreaking search was no more than a shared glance between Sam and Lia. They picked their way carefully around the edge of the house. Loose sheets of iron screeched like wounded animals as they bent and scraped in the wind. A piece of wood—maybe a fragment of a shutter—flew past, hitting Sam's helmet, and he had to peer through the water flowing over his visor. He also had to raise his voice to shout as loudly as he could.

'Can anyone hear me? Where are you?'

'Hello?' Lia was yelling, too. 'Can you hear me? *Hika?*'

It was on the far side of the house that they found an opening into the tangle of wood. A triangle of space with the roof forming one side and a broken beam holding up the rest. Lia dropped to a crouch and Sam was able to peer over her shoulder, adding the light from his helmet to hers.

The gap was a tunnel into what had been a room. And right at the end they could see a small child curled up into a ball.

They could also hear a baby crying.

Sam had to step back as Lia started slipping her arms from the straps of the pack.

'I'm going in.'

'No. Not yet. We don't know if it's safe. This could collapse on top of you. We need to find something to shore it up.'

'There's no time. And we haven't got the manpower or equipment to follow those kinds of protocols.' Free of her pack, Lia lay flat on her stomach and slid farther into the gap. 'Are you awake, sweetheart?' she called. 'Can you look at me?'

The child's face appeared from the ball of small person but one look at the bright light shining in was enough to make it disappear again. If, by some miracle, this little one was unhurt, they were too terrified to co-operate.

'*Kia orana*,' Sam called gently, using the island language. 'What's your name, little one?'

The small face remained hidden.

'What did you say?' Lia asked. 'Do the children here not speak English?'

'Everybody's more or less bilingual. Some prefer to use their own language.'

'So how do I say "hello"?'

'*Kia orana*. But you'll be understood. Don't worry about having to translate things.'

'Okay.' Lia nodded. And then started wriggling forward.

'Come out,' Sam ordered. 'I'll go in.'

'I'm smaller,' Lia said. 'Let me get this one out and see if there's any access farther in.'

There was nothing Sam could do to stop her and she was right. She had more chance of getting into a small space than he did.

And there were children here. He wouldn't have let

anyone stop him if he knew there was a chance of saving them.

Lia was his kind of person.

There was more room to move as Lia got farther beneath the debris. She could see into other pockets of space and the hope that they would find more members of this family alive got stronger. Nobody else was immediately visible so the rules of triaging a multi-casualty scene couldn't be applied. If they had been, she would have had to simply check the first victim she found and then move on to assess the others so that she could then decide on who had the highest priority for treatment. In this case, she was going to have to do the best she could with each step, rather than consider the big picture.

Sam had been right. She was breaking rules and not putting her own—and other rescuers'—safety first but this pile of building wreckage was likely to be highly unstable. Who knew how long they might have to get anyone out who was still alive?

She reached the child and pulled off her gloves so that she could feel the temperature of the skin, which was re-assuringly warm. She could see the small chest rising and falling so there was no breathing difficulty so then she ran her hands swiftly over the little body, doing a rapid check for any obvious injuries or bleeding.

'Hey,' she said. 'It's okay, sweetheart. I'm here to look after you. Do you know where Mummy is?'

'Mumma…' The child's head came up and she burst into tears. Small arms moved to wrap themselves around Lia's neck and cling hard. '*Mumma…*'

Lia heard another sound from somewhere to one side. Another child crying, or was it a groan from an adult?

She needed to move fast and she couldn't do that with a terrified child in her arms. She wriggled backwards, one hand pressed to a frizzy mop of hair to try and protect the child from any falling debris.

Sam was waiting to take the child.

'I've heard something else,' Lia told him. 'I'm going back in. I think this one's okay. Nothing obvious, anyway.'

She got past where the child had been lying and peered past the fallen beams. She could see a table with broken legs and an overturned couch and…and, yes…the bare foot and lower leg of an adult person who was lying in the space where the back of the couch had caught on the tilted table.

'*Hika…* Can you hear me?'

The response was a groan. And then a voice that she had to strain to hear.

'Help me… Help my babies…'

'I'm coming. Hold on…'

But how could she get as far as the couch? A tilted beam was blocking her way. There was enough space to kneel in front of it but there was no way she could lift the heavy piece of wood out of the way. And if she moved it, would something else collapse?

She needed help.

She needed Sam.

'I'm here.'

Good grief…had she been talking aloud to herself? And why had Sam taken the risk of squeezing himself into that narrow entrance to the debris?

'Where's the little girl?'

'Afi's back. He's brought his neighbours, as well. They're all okay. They want to help.'

'I can see Hika. And I think the baby's with her. I can't get through here. Maybe there's another way in from the other side?'

'Let me try moving that beam. If I can lift it, it looks like that pile is solid enough to support it.'

'If you can just lift it a bit, I could get through.'

Sam was moving closer. His arm was around Lia as he edged sideways to get his shoulder under the beam. His face was only a few inches from hers.

'But then you might get stuck on the other side,' he said.

The concern in his face wrapped itself tightly around Lia's heart. A tiny part of her brain told her that it was simply professional concern but she could feel his arm still around her and her face was close enough to his for the memory of what it was like to kiss him to surface. The mix of thinking about someone genuinely caring and kissing her at the same time made the squeezing sensation in her chest so big it was too hard to take a breath.

A vicious gust of wind lifted the section of roof above the tunnel of debris and it came down again with a sickening crunch and a cloud of dust. The whole, unstable structure around them seemed to shift and then settle.

There was more than concern in Sam's face now. If she gave him the smallest opportunity, he would order her out of this space to keep her safe. And maybe she would go. Imagine what her family would think if they knew she was putting herself in danger like this? What it would be like for them if she didn't make it out herself?

But if she abandoned this rescue mission, she was quite sure that Sam would not follow her example. He would stay in here himself and do whatever he could.

And that concern went both ways.

'You've got manpower outside,' Lia said. '*If* I get stuck, you can see what you can move and create another access. It sounds like Hika's injured and it might be impossible to get the Stokes basket in this way. The sooner we do this, the sooner we can all get out.'

For a moment longer, with the wind howling above them and the wreckage creaking ominously around them, Sam held her gaze.

And then one side of his mouth curled upwards into a crooked smile.

'You're quite something, aren't you?'

Lia smiled back at him. 'So are you,' she said. 'Now, get on with it. Show me how strong you are.'

He was strong enough to lift the beam. Not far enough to secure it on a higher level but far enough for Lia to crawl underneath. And there was much more space on the other side. She could actually stand up if she kept her back hunched. She climbed over broken pieces of furniture, her boots crunching on shattered crockery, to get around the table to the gap behind the couch.

A tiny baby was in Hika's arms. A boy who looked about five years old was crouched by his mother's head, holding one of her hands.

'I'm Lia,' she said. 'I've come to get you out.'

'Take my babies first,' Hika said. 'Please... Where's Ema?'

'Your little girl? She's fine. She's outside and being looked after.' Lia was scanning what she could see of the boy and trying to check the baby at the same time. Hika was conscious and talking to her, which was great. It meant that she was breathing well enough for the moment. Even a sideways glance showed Lia that the leg she had spotted earlier was lying at a sickeningly unnatural angle but the priority had to be to get the children to safety.

'What's your name?' she asked the boy.

His face crumpled and he clung closer to his mother.

'He's Rua,' Hika said. And then she groaned again. 'Oh…. It hurts…'

Rua cried more loudly and the baby joined in.

Sam's call could barely be heard over the noise. 'What's happening?'

Lia took the baby from Hika's arms. 'Come with me, Rua. Sam's waiting to help you get outside.'

'*No-o…*'

'You do as you're told,' Hika growled. With a sob, she prised her son's arms away from her body and pushed him towards Lia. 'Take him…' And then her breath caught in a gasp of pain. Her eyes fluttered shut and her head dropped back.

'Hika?'

She was still breathing but the lack of response told Lia that her level of consciousness had dropped alarmingly. She couldn't do anything with a baby in her arms. Securing the infant against her body, she caught the boy's arm with her free hand and pulled him along beside her.

He resisted enough to make the short journey around the table a struggle. Persuading him to go through the small gap under the beam was even harder. Sam reached through to catch hold of him.

'Your daddy's waiting for you outside,' he told him. 'And your little sister. What's her name?'

'Ema,' Lia supplied.

Rua shook his head. 'I want to stay with Mumma,' he wailed.

'Lia's going to stay with Mumma,' Sam said. 'And

she's going to take care of her. You have to come with me, buddy.' He pulled the little boy through the gap and lifted him so that he was on his other side and couldn't get back.

Lia crouched to pass the baby through the gap to Sam. 'This one looks like she's only a few weeks old.'

Sam took the tiny bundle. He ripped the top fastenings of his overalls open and tucked the baby against his body. Then he did up the fastenings so that only the top of the baby's head was visible. For a second, he laid his hand over the fuzz of soft baby hair and then he looked up at Lia.

'I'll get them out,' he said. 'And get the men moving things, but I'll be back as soon as I can. How's Hika?'

'Obvious leg fracture,' Lia told him. 'And her GCS has just dropped. Bring the pack back in with you if you can.'

Moving back to her patient, Lia found herself caught by that unexpected gesture of Sam cradling the baby's head in his hand. Such a gentle, reassuring touch that had probably been so automatic he hadn't realised he was doing it, but it was something she would never forget. A tiny moment in a terrifying ordeal but it gave her something so heartwarming it made her forget her own fear.

And then she was back beside Hika and able to examine her properly, and there was no time to allow herself to think of anything but keeping her patient alive and getting her out to safety.

By the time Sam got back to the other side of the beam with the kit, Lia could hear the sound of shouting from nearby, outside the house.

'The children all seem fine,' he told her. 'Barely a scratch on them.'

'Hika's got an open, mid-shaft femoral fracture,' Lia reported back. 'Limb baselines aren't good. She's got no sensation in her foot and it's cold. And she's lost a lot of blood. I need fluids and pain relief. And a traction splint.'

'I've sent someone back to get the Stokes basket. There's a lot of people out there now. They've come from all over the village. I've been in radio contact with Ky. He's sending out a vehicle to get them into the township. And a chainsaw in case that can help us get better access in here.' The pack was too big to squeeze through the gap so he was opening it as he spoke and passing things through to Lia. A roll of IV gear. Bags of saline and giving sets. The drug roll.

'I need to get in to help you. I'll get someone else to come and lift this beam so I can get underneath.'

Lia shook her head. 'It's too risky. If the roof shifts any further we'll need more than a chainsaw to get us out. I can do everything I need to do medically in here. Hika's going to need surgery when we get her back to the hospital.' She tried to summon a grin for Sam. 'You can take over then, okay?'

He shook his head. 'Bossy, aren't you?'

'You have to be when you grow up with eight siblings.'

'Eight...' Sam's eyes widened. 'I can see I'm not going to win this argument. Closest I've come to a family is looking after a borrowed dog.'

Not entirely true.

Getting back out of the tunnel took long enough for an old pain to resurface. The amazement of knowing that he was going to become a father and would have more of a family than he'd known since he'd lost both his parents when he'd been barely more than a teenager.

The agony of being told that the baby wasn't his. And

that his wife was leaving him to make a new life with the real father of her baby.

And, yes, she would be taking half his fortune with her to ensure that her new life would be the one she'd wanted all along…

It felt appropriate somehow to emerge into a wild storm and get lashed by the wind and rain. His whole life had felt this chaotic back then. So unbearable he'd run away. Taken time out to sail his beloved yacht around the world. Washed up, quite by chance, onto these islands and discovered a new purpose to his life.

And here he was, in a position to help a member of this island community that he'd grown to love so deeply. With a small crowd of islanders looking to him right now, in this storm, to provide the leadership they needed. Enough strong men that they could probably lift a roof if that was what it was going to take to get Hika and Lia out of there safely.

And, dammit, he was going to make that happen. He wasn't about to let Lia's amazing courage end in tragedy. Imagine having to face up to her whole family and tell them he'd been responsible for the world losing such an extraordinary young woman?

It took hours. Long hours of hard physical labour under appalling conditions. They had to be so careful trying to shift building materials when, at any moment, the wind could catch something with lethally sharp edges or protruding nails that could injure or even kill someone. Every so often, Sam would stop the men working completely so he could crawl back through the tunnel and check that Lia was still safe. That Hika was still alive.

'Her blood pressure has come up a little. I'm running

another litre of saline. I've got the traction splint on so I'm hoping that will help control the bleeding.'

'You're doing a great job. Are *you* okay?'

'I'm fine. I'd love to get out of here, though…'

'We're getting closer. I'll be with you before you know it.'

'I'm counting on that, Sam.'

She had to keep counting for a while longer but a space was finally cleared and the framework of the roof safe enough on one corner for a group of men to position themselves to lift it. Sam was ready, with Afi by his side and the rigid basket stretcher held between them. The men would have to hold the roof up long enough to get in, get Hika into the stretcher and for them all to get out again. Whether or not they could do it was dependent, in large part, on luck. On a window of time where there was a space between those vicious wind gusts that would make it impossible to control what was left of the iron-clad roof.

Maybe it was luck. Or maybe the ferocity of this storm was finally beginning to ebb a little as the second day of the cyclone dawned. It didn't matter. Hika was safely secured in the stretcher and there were any number of willing hands to carry her over the landslide to where Ky's jeep was waiting to transfer her. An ancient truck with a flat back had other villagers piling on to be taken to the safety of the school hall.

'Did you check the children again?' Lia looked through the back window of the jeep to where Afi was riding in the cab of the truck, his baby in his arms and his two small children glued to his sides.

'Yes. But I'll get whoever's in the clinic here to keep an eye on them.'

'Can't we take them with us? Hika's going to need her family.'

'There might be other patients who need to come over on the boat.'

'But if there's room?'

There was a plea in Lia's eyes and Sam remembered the hard time he'd given her for using her phone so much on her first day here. Her brother had been undergoing surgery and she'd needed to know what was happening.

She knew more than he did about family. How important it was for them to be together in frightening times.

And she had risked her life for this family. She deserved a medal. She certainly deserved to have a request respected.

Besides, Sam wanted to do this for her. He wanted to see her smile.

'Sure. If there's room, we'll take them all. We'll keep the family together.'

The bump in the road made their drowsy patient groan and Lia's attention was instantly drawn away from Sam.

But she *was* smiling and Sam could feel the glow of it right down to his toes.

CHAPTER SIX

WILDFIRE HOSPITAL—and every member of its staff—were pushed to their limits and beyond that day.

Sam was in Theatre repairing Hika's leg, with another doctor, Keanu, and Hettie and Anahera to assist, so they missed the drama when one wing of the hospital became damaged enough by the wind and rain to mean that patients had to be evacuated to new rooms. Taking Hika to their recovery/intensive care area was the first sign that their working conditions were already stretched. There wasn't enough space for another bed amongst the monitoring equipment.

'We need to keep Keoni in here for continuous cardiac monitoring. Sefina can be moved, though. She's stable.'

'We've lost a lot of beds,' Caroline told them. 'The windows blew in on the north wing. Nobody's had time to clean up the glass and there's a lot of water damage. The power's out on that side, too. Jack's checking the generators but we need to be prepared for some more outages.'

'Can we use some of the consulting rooms in Outpatients?'

'The waiting rooms are overflowing. We've had more injuries come over from Atangi. It's crazy in there. If it wasn't for that new paramedic, we would have no chance of coping.'

'I'll head there now.'

'I'll come with you,' Hettie said. 'I need to find out where Joni is. Sefina's been asking about him.'

Happy to leave Hika in capable hands, Sam headed for the outpatient area. It wasn't just that it was obviously where extra medical help was needed, he wanted to see Lia again. To tell her that Hika's surgery had gone well.

Maybe to also tell her that it was okay for her to take a break and get some sleep. They had enough people to cope now unless someone else needed emergency surgery. Lia had to be exhausted after the dramatic rescue mission during the night and yet she'd carried on working while he had been tied up in Theatre.

He was exhausted himself.

Not that he was about to go home to rest. There were too many people here, waiting patiently to be seen and treated. It quickly became apparent that it wouldn't be easy to find time to talk to Lia and update her on how her rescued patient was faring. It wasn't only the waiting rooms that were overflowing. Every treatment area was being used. There were lacerations that needed stitching, fractures that needed to be X-rayed and plastered. Bumps and bruises to be assessed and frightened children that needed careful checking to make sure nothing serious was missed.

An hour passed and then another as Sam moved from one patient to the next, weaving his way through the crowded rooms, having to stop and reassure people as he moved past them to the ones who needed attention first. And every time he was on the move, he noticed Lia.

At one point she was crouched in front of a child,

splinting a wrist that would probably join the queue for an X-ray. He saw her smiling. Reaching up to stroke a small cheek in a reassuring gesture.

The next time she had her stethoscope against the chest of an old man, a frown on her face as she focused on what she needed to hear instead of the background noise of the crowded room. The smile had been there again, though, before he'd looked away and she'd got one in return from her patient.

Who wouldn't smile back at Lia?

She was carrying a baby when he finally got close enough to speak to her.

'Is that Hika's baby?'

'Yes. She needs a clean nappy. And some food. I'm trying to find Vailea to see if she can help.'

Lia was wearing scrubs now. Baggy pants that completely disguised those long, lean legs. A shapeless top that left her arms bare. Maybe it was the sight of that smooth olive skin that reminded Sam's body of what it knew about this woman. What it felt like to be in very close contact with that skin. It was a moment of intensity that was completely inappropriate right then so he focused on the baby.

'Has she been properly assessed?'

'Only by me. Do you want to see her yourself?'

'Are you happy with her?'

'Yes. I think Hika had her in her arms the whole time. She was well protected.'

This might be only the second day they had worked together but it had been a trial by fire and Sam was more than confident that Lia's assessment would have been as good as his own. 'If you're happy, I'm happy.'

'I've checked all the children. Ema had a few grazes that needed cleaning but that was all. How's Hika?'

'Doing well. The fracture's set and I've started her on IV antibiotics. We've got her blood pressure back up. She's out of danger.'

'Oh…that's fantastic.' Lia's face lit up with satisfaction. 'And what about the blood vessel and nerve damage? I was worried about how bad that was.'

'Her limb baselines were looking good. We'll have to wait until she's properly awake to check sensation and movement and it'll be a while before she's walking again, but I'm confident she'll make a full recovery.'

Lia's smile widened. 'We did good, didn't we?'

Sam smiled back, amused by the childish grammar. 'We did.'

The baby in Lia's arms whimpered and she moved on with her mission of care. Sam stood still for a moment, watching her.

He'd saved lives before. Been out on rescue missions that could have ended in disaster but hadn't. He'd performed surgeries that would prevent a serious injury from becoming a permanent disability more times than he could have counted.

Why did this case feel so special?

Because he'd been working with Lia?

Because he was increasingly blown away by how amazing she was? She was not only highly skilled in the assessment and treatment of patients, she had the ability to connect with them on a personal level. She cared about them.

She had not only demonstrated an impressive level of courage, she was now showing that she had stamina to match.

Lia Roselli was one of a kind—that was for sure. Thank goodness she hadn't been injured herself last night. As Sam took yet another patient from the waiting room for treatment, he remembered how it had felt when he'd known he was allowing her to stay in danger in that house. When the roof had shifted in the wind and reminded them both of just how dangerous the situation was.

Her safety had seemed more important than anything else. Like it had when he'd been holding her in his arms in his bed and they'd heard the sound of breaking glass and he'd promised that he would keep her safe.

He'd shocked himself then. The danger signs of falling for someone had been flashing brightly enough to make him back away so fast he hadn't even taken the time to analyse and label the emotion.

Was it even harder now? Now that he knew how brave and tough she was? And what a kind heart she had?

No. Okay, he'd broken his rule about hooking up with an attractive newcomer. And yes, he was more than impressed with her personality as well as her body, but anything more than that was simply the aftermath of having shared an adrenaline-fuelled experience. And exhaustion.

This was a fling—that was all. One that would probably be more memorable than any holiday hook-ups he'd ever had before, but that was all it was. All it ever could be.

He just wasn't thinking straight, and that was hardly surprising. A few hours' sleep would fix that and that would happen.

Eventually.

He was unstoppable, wasn't he?

Lia's legs were beginning to feel like jelly and the

occasional wave of dizziness told her that if she didn't catch some sleep soon, she wouldn't be safe to be working with patients.

But Sam wasn't even slowing down and he'd been on his feet just as long as she'd been. He'd had the additional stress of the long surgery on Hika, as well, and now he was not only taking on the management of the cases that were beyond her own scope of practice, he was going back into the waiting room again and again, as the numbers of people waiting gradually lessened.

She had spotted him almost every time she'd gone to find a new patient, or taken someone to the X-ray department or through to the area where Hettie was being kept busy, applying plaster casts to the surprising number of Colles' fractures where both children and elderly had fallen onto an outstretched hand.

She'd seen how long it took for Sam to move through the groups of islanders because of the number of people who wanted to be the ones he chose to treat. He was given the respect of a true leader—royalty, almost—and yet he was clearly part of the community. He was approachable enough that everyone knew they would get the reassurance they needed.

He was their doctor and they trusted him. More than that, he'd been here long enough to have earned more than simply respect and trust. More than once Lia saw him offer a touch of reassurance to an adult or pick up a child who happily wrapped their arms around his neck. And she'd seen the expression on the faces of the mothers and the people who had been given words of encouragement or the squeeze of a hand. It was impossible not to get the impression that Sam was loved by these people.

Had she really thought that he didn't fit here? That it looked like he was playing a role in a movie? There could be no doubt that he belonged here. That he was one of these people, despite standing out as looking so very different with his much paler skin and the sun-bleached blondness of his hair.

What had brought him here? Lia wondered. And why had he stayed long enough to become such an integral part of this isolated community?

Maybe it was the level of utter weariness she was trying to push through as she kept going that made it difficult to shut out thoughts that were even less appropriate than noticing Sam's status as a doctor here. Dislocated thoughts that were more snatches of emotion than conscious recall of sequences of events. They didn't interfere with the job she was doing, but they slipped into the back of her mind every time she noticed him.

Like the memory of that first kiss—down on the beach, when the storm had first broken. That moment when something amazing had made it so much more than any kiss she had ever experienced.

That firm grip of his hand around hers as he'd led her up the track to his house.

Making love...

As Lia went back into the waiting room yet again, she stopped for a moment. There were fewer people here now and it didn't look as if any of them were seriously injured. There were no bloodstained, makeshift bandages on limbs. Nobody holding an arm as if they were scared to allow it any movement. No crying children being carried in the arms of a parent. There was no sign of Sam, for once, either.

She really did feel dizzy now. How long had it been since she'd eaten something? Or had a drink of water even?

'Are you okay?'

No wonder she hadn't spotted Sam. He'd been behind her.

'A bit woozy. I'm thinking I might need to find something to eat.'

'Come with me. I've been told that Vailea's left a mountain of sandwiches in the staffroom for us.'

'But…' Wearily, Lia turned her head to scan the waiting room.

'The urgent cases have all been seen. Keanu and Ana have had a break and they're going to take over. We've been ordered to stand down for a few hours. You won't need to come back on duty until tomorrow morning, unless things get crazy again.'

It was a relief to follow Sam. To sit down for a little while and eat the most delicious egg salad sandwiches Lia had ever tasted and to wash them down with more than one cup of wonderfully strong, sweet tea.

'Are you going to go home to sleep?'

'I'll have to. There isn't a spare bed anywhere here.'

'Is it my imagination or has the wind died down?'

Sam smiled. 'The worst is over. People are starting to go home. They want to check on their properties and neighbours. We may get a few more patients from the outer islands but it sounds like Atangi got the worst of the storm and I think we've dealt with almost all of it. And nobody's died, as far as we know. Thanks to you,' he added. 'Hika was the most seriously injured and if you hadn't been with her, she might not have made it. She lost a lot of blood from that fracture.'

Lia could feel her eyes drifting shut. Not even Sam's praise could make her smile this time.

'Come on. I'll walk you home. I have to go past your quarters to get to mine.'

The wind was definitely less ferocious as they walked out of the hospital grounds. It was easy to walk unaided, which meant there was no need for Sam to offer a hand.

There was no need for him to stop when they reached Lia's hut, either, but he did. He rubbed his forehead as though he was too tired to remember something he had intended to say and then he looked up and met her gaze.

She could see how exhausted he was. She could also see something that looked like confusion. As though he had something he wanted to ask but, at the same time, he was talking himself out of asking.

Was he thinking about asking her to go back to his quarters?

To sleep with him?

That would be all they were capable of doing but Lia would have said yes in a heartbeat.

She wanted to be with him. Just to sleep. Together. To be close.

And that was the moment she knew she was lost. She was falling in love with this man. Maybe it had already happened and she hadn't noticed. It might have been the way he'd looked at her when he'd known he was putting her in danger by leaving her under the wreckage of Hika's house.

Or it might have been the way she'd felt after she'd seen him tuck that tiny baby against his chest and cradle its head in his hand.

The realisation was enough of a shock to make Lia catch her breath. Had it shown in her face? Was that why

Sam broke the eye contact and actually stepped back to put more space between them?

'Sleep well, Lia. I'll see you back at the hospital tomorrow morning.'

She couldn't find any words. And if she opened her mouth, who knew what words might escape? Something crazy like, 'I love you'?

She'd known him for how long? Just a couple of days. Long days, certainly, under conditions that made you get to know someone very quickly, but still…

It was ridiculous.

Much safer to nod and turn away herself.

To use the last of her energy to reconnect with her real life. She'd been able to send a single text message to her family early in the day to tell them she was safe and not to worry about any news they might hear about the weather conditions around these islands, but there had been more than a dozen messages in return and she had to check them all in case there was something she needed to know about Nico's recovery or test results. Or that something had happened to Angel. Her beloved niece had had far more than her share of physical problems and unexpected hospital admissions in her short life so far.

But all was well back home and the messages were all about her family's concern for her wellbeing. They all missed her and wanted her safely back home, and the love that came through was enough to bring a lump to Lia's throat and more than a few tears that she was too tired to even wipe away. She sent the same message to everybody. She was safe. The worst of the cyclone was over. She'd be home before long and she couldn't wait to see them all.

It was true. No matter how exciting her time here was

already proving to be, or how she might think she felt about Sam Taylor, she had her real life to go back to and she wouldn't trade that for anything.

The shower felt wonderful when she finally gave her battered-feeling body the luxury of standing beneath the rain of hot water, but it didn't wash away the feeling that her life might have just changed forever.

The softness of her bed was equally appreciated but, even as sleep rushed up to claim her, Lia couldn't shake the impression that something had gone wrong here.

Finding someone had been the last thing on her mind when she'd come to Wildfire. She wasn't looking. She wasn't interested. At this particular time in her life she couldn't afford—or didn't want—the complications that came with falling in love.

But there it was. She'd been ambushed. Hadn't had enough warning to put up any defences and now it was too late.

Or maybe not. She was too tired to think straight. Maybe things would look different when she woke up.

Things did look different.

Clearer.

It wasn't just that the rain had stopped and the cloud cover had thinned enough to make the daylight feel normal. Or that the hospital was far less crowded and it felt like things were well under control.

The moment Lia walked into the staffroom and saw Sam, it felt like she had taken off a pair of emotional sunglasses that had been clouding her vision.

He looked…gorgeous.

Well, actually, he looked a bit rugged. His hair was tousled and spiky. There were deep lines around his eyes and he obviously hadn't shaved in quite some time because she knew how rough it would feel if she stroked her fingers along the line of his jaw.

And that was when she knew that the difference sleep had made was to make things worse. Because all she wanted to do was exactly that—to stroke his jaw and touch those lines of weariness. To make sure he'd had something to eat and then tuck him up into a soft bed and let him sleep.

The urge to look after him was as strong as it would have been if she was looking at Nico. Or Angel. Or any of the people who were the most important in her life.

And mixed into that desire to care for him was an underlying desire of a very different kind. Something that her family could never give her.

Something that had been missing from her life for a very long time.

On top of that, there was a sinking feeling that this was a personal disaster. She belonged in a very different world from Sam and in a matter of days she would be returning to that world and leaving him behind, and she knew that was going to hurt.

How weird that you could know so much in the space of a glance and that nobody else would even notice.

Sam hadn't even looked up from the mug of coffee he was holding in his hand. Jack was sitting at the radio desk, headphones on, fiddling with a waveband control, and Hettie was watching something turning inside the microwave oven. No. Her eyes were closed. Maybe she had fallen asleep on her feet.

'Hi.' Lia pulled out a chair to sit down at the table. 'I'm getting the feeling I'm the only one who's been sleeping.'

She risked only a brief glance at Sam as he looked up. 'How many hours did you get?'

'A few. We had a woman in labour brought over from Atangi and she was in trouble with a footling presentation. Ended up needing a Caesarean.'

'I'm going home right now,' Hettie said. 'As soon as I've heated this wheat bag for one of my patients. I think I'm going to sleep until tomorrow.'

'I'm good,' Jack said. 'I've been sleeping on and off in here between radio calls.'

'Have there been many?'

'Not since last night. I got a bit of one a while back, though, and it got cut off. I'm trying some other bands in case it's someone who's not using our frequency.' He turned the dial again, tilting his head to one side as he listened.

Hettie left the room and Lia could feel Sam looking at her but she kept her gaze on Jack. She didn't want him to guess what was going on in her head right now. Or her heart, for that matter. Especially her heart. He couldn't possibly feel the same way. Becoming aware of just the possibility of being in love with him must have sent out a vibe that had made him step away from her.

She was a visitor in his life. Like many others must had been. The last thing he'd want would be a complication that made it a nuisance. Something too heavy to be fun.

And even if she was only going to be here for a short time, she didn't want to throw away the chance to be alone with him again. To be close.

Or maybe that was the most sensible thing she could do. The closer she allowed herself to get, the harder it was going to be to walk away.

Her head started spinning and she closed her eyes, only to open them smartly as she heard the sharp crackle of the radio transmission Jack had picked up.

'Mayday…Mayday… This is the yacht *Eclipse*. Mayday…Mayday… Is anyone receiving?'

Jack pressed the transmission button on the microphone. 'Wildfire Rescue Base receiving you loud and clear. What is your location? Over…'

Adrenaline coursed through Lia and her gaze flew to meet Sam's. Any impression of exhaustion had vanished. He might still look totally dishevelled but he was as focused as Lia was.

Ready for anything.

They both were.

Minutes later, Jack was still sitting at the desk as the transmission ended, flanked by Sam and Lia on either side as he pointed at a spot on a map.

'He's here. If he's drifting, he's going to end on this reef.'

'He can't do anything but drift. He's lost his mast and he's broken his arm so badly he can't get his engine started.' Sam was frowning. 'The wind might have dropped but the swells will still be massive. He hasn't got a chance.'

'Send out the coastguard launch?' Jack was watching a computer screen now, as he brought up a comprehensive weather forecast.

'It might take too long. And the pilot's been stood down for a break, hasn't he? He's been up all night.'

'Wind's fine for flying. Might be a bit choppy but it's safe enough.'

'That would make it a winch job.' Lia took a deep breath. 'I'm up for it but we'd have to have a third crew member to operate the winch. Is anybody available that's qualified?'

There was a moment's silence.

Jack turned his head to glance up at Sam, who nodded his head slowly.

'Yes. I am.'

CHAPTER SEVEN

SAM WAS ON top of this.

If he'd been in any real danger of falling for Lia, he wouldn't be the least bit happy about sitting in the back of this helicopter with her, knowing that she was about to risk her life again for the sake of saving someone else's.

This was her job and she knew what she was doing.

Sam knew what he was doing, too. He could operate a winch as well as anybody and he'd done sea rescues like this before, both as the winch operator and the medic who was being lowered on board a vessel to bring a patient up. He knew the dangers. How you had to avoid the winch line getting caught on any of the masts or wires above deck level. That the moment of contact that would come with getting on board had to be meticulously timed with the swell of the sea so the deck didn't rush up and break your legs.

He could do that for Lia. He could keep her safe so that she could do her job. They'd get her on board and she could do whatever had to be done to treat this lone sailor who'd been caught in the storm and get him safely harnessed and attached to her own body. Then they'd pull them both up and be back at the hospital within the hour. The yacht would have to be sacrificed but that was one of the risks of the sailing game. Boats could be replaced. Lives couldn't.

So he was happy about doing this job and that meant that he had Lia safely tucked into the category of a colleague, and that was more of a relief than he cared to admit. It didn't mean he didn't care about her. Of course it didn't. He cared just as much as he had when she'd been in danger under that house but he also knew how capable she was. How much she cared about her family and how important it was for her to get home in one piece. She knew what she was doing and she wouldn't be taking any stupid risks.

Jack had been right about how rough some of these air pockets still were. And he'd been right about the size of the swells they could see beneath them. A good ten metres, he estimated, and the tops were breaking in rolls of foam that made it hard to spot their target.

'There it is. Three o'clock.'

'Roger… Copy that.' The helicopter tipped as Jack began circling. 'Turning downwind.'

Lia was checking her harness and moving so that she would be ready for permission to move onto the skid of the helicopter when the door was opened.

'Secure aft.' Sam focused on the job at hand. 'Checking winch power.'

The helicopter rocked but Jack seemed happy enough with his control. 'Speed back. Clear door.'

'Door back and locked,' Sam responded. 'Bringing hook inboard.'

He handed the hook to Lia who attached it to her harness, checking the pit pin was secure and nodding at Sam to show she was happy.

'Moving Lia to door. Clear skids.'

'Clear skids.' Jack was happy for Lia to move out and stand on the skids.

'Clear to boom out,' Sam said a few seconds later.

'Clear,' Jack responded.

Lia grinned at Sam in the moment before she stepped off the skid.

'Don't drop me, okay?'

He grinned back. 'No worries.'

She was spinning a bit as he lowered her but she put her arms out to slow the movement and her voice was calm in his headphones.

'Ten metres…eight… Hold for a bit. There's a big swell coming. Let's aim for the top of the next one.'

Jack was doing a brilliant job keeping the helicopter hovering as steadily as the conditions allowed. He was looking down at Lia. If anything went wrong, his responsibility was to keep his aircraft and those on board safe. There was a button on the dashboard that could fire an explosion that would cut the winch cable if it got tangled on anything and prevent them being brought down. Sam had access to the other explosive device. He'd never had to even think about using it, though, and he didn't expect to this time.

How it happened was hard to say. Maybe the yacht tipped unexpectedly as it reached the top of the swell. Perhaps it was the air pocket that jolted the helicopter. Or maybe it was a gust of wind that made the broken end of the mast swing on the wires that were still attached.

Whatever it was, it happened in a split second.

The cry from Lia was wordless but it was all too obvious the winch cable had caught.

'Cut the cable,' Jack yelled, as he wrestled with the controls of the helicopter.

And Sam had to do it. A moment's hesitation and it could all be over for all of them. The helicopter would drop like a stone, probably right on top of the yacht. At least this way Lia had a chance. She was within a few feet of the deck and she wouldn't land in the ocean.

Sam pressed the button before he could give himself any time to think any further. The helicopter swooped upwards but he was looking down, leaning out of the open door.

He saw Lia fall with a sickening thump. Saw her roll across the deck and for a heart-stopping moment he thought she would simply slide off and into the sea, but something stopped her.

'Lia?' Jack was on the radio. 'Talk to us. Are you okay?'

They could see her lying there. Then they saw someone emerge from below the deck. The yachtsman they had been coming to rescue was moving slowly, his arms crossed as he tried to protect the broken limb that was making it impossible for him to control his vessel. He reached Lia and knelt down beside her. Then he looked up at the helicopter and seemed to be nodding his head.

Did that mean she was alive? Conscious?

'Lia...' Sam shouldn't have to shout. His voice should be coming through loud and clear on the inbuilt headphones in Lia's helmet. Her voice should be just as clear through her microphone but there was no sound to be heard other than an ominous buzzing.

'Radio might be out,' Jack said grimly. 'She could have hit her helmet hard on landing and damaged it.'

'She's not moving.'

'There's nothing we can do.' Jack was turning them away. 'We'll have to send a boat out. There's still time before they get too close to the reef.'

'Wait… I want to see if she's moving.'

But Jack kept going and that was the right thing to do. They had to get the coastguard to launch and get out here as fast as possible. Whether Lia was conscious or not made no difference.

Except that it felt like Sam's heart was being ripped out with every passing second that was taking them farther away.

Just colleagues?

Hardly.

A bit of a fling?

Just as much of a lie.

Right now, Lia's life felt more important than his own. Sam had never felt like this about anybody in his entire life.

Because he'd never been so absolutely in love with someone before?

'Take me to Atangi,' he told Jack. 'If anyone's taking the launch out, it's going to be me.'

Lia wasn't injured.

The bump had been hard enough for it to take a short time to figure that out, though, and she'd instinctively stayed motionless until she could identify and assess any parts of her body that might be hurting in case it was important not to move. If she'd broken her neck, for example.

She'd certainly hit her head hard enough to break her radio. She could hear the men above her, albeit through a heavy crackling, and she responded to Jack to tell him she thought she was okay but her transmission obviously hadn't got back to them.

And then she'd heard Sam shout her name and she

recognised the note of desperation in the call because that was exactly what she would feel like if she thought something terrible had happened to *him*.

Did that mean that the feelings she had for Sam were not as one-sided as she'd assumed?

The thought was almost as stunning as the blow to her body had been. She tried to move. All she needed to do was to get to her feet and give them a wave but nothing was co-operating fast enough and now she had a man kneeling beside her and demanding her attention, asking if she was all right.

Lia wiggled her feet inside her boots and clenched and unclenched her fists. That felt normal. She took a deep breath without difficulty and let it out, noting with relief the absence of any pain. That fall could have easily broken a rib or two, which would have made it very difficult to move around on a rocking boat.

The crackling and buzzing in her helmet grew louder and she could only catch a word here and there as Jack and Sam talked to each other. She heard mention of a boat and something about the time before they would hit the reef, but she couldn't tell if it had been a hopeful statement or a prediction of doom.

Fear kicked in and gave her the strength to move properly. The man beside her was cradling what looked like a badly broken arm. If anyone was going to be able to start an engine and then steer this yacht and keep it out of danger for as long as it took to get a sea rescue under way, it would have to be her.

Her legs were working. And her arms. Lia pulled them into action and got to her knees and then her feet. She had to cling to the solid object that had stopped that horrible slide across the deck for a second or two until a wave of dizziness passed, but then she took another deep breath and looked up—just in time to see the dot that was the helicopter disappearing into the distance.

Sam...

It felt like an anguished shout inside her head but it came out as no more than a whisper.

Would she even see him again, let alone feel his arms around her?

She had to do whatever it took to make that happen. Lia turned to the stranger beside her.

'I'm Lia,' she told him. 'Show me how to get this boat under control and then we'll do something about that arm of yours.'

The pilot of the islands' coastguard vessel had been dragged from his much-needed sleep. He made sure the boat got launched swiftly but, adding up the flight time getting to the harbour and finally heading out to sea, nearly an hour had passed since they'd abandoned the yacht and its occupants. They were in such trouble, and who knew whether they were still afloat or if the worst had happened and they'd smashed against that reef?

The pilot was as determined as Sam to get to where they needed to be in the shortest possible time. The double engines of the powerful boat were roaring at full tilt. They cut through the rise of the swells, becoming airborne as often as not before landing with a bang and crescendo of engine noise to tackle the next swell.

Jack had come with them. They might need all the hands they could get to transfer people from one vessel to another in conditions like this, and he wasn't about to let anyone else take up the space for crew.

'You're not leaving me behind,' he'd said. 'That's Lia

out there and I'm responsible for the safety of my chopper crew.'

And that was it, in a nutshell. Lia was out there and they had no idea if she was even alive. Would they have sent out a boat and push the limits of its capability like this if they'd been going to an unknown victim alone on his yacht?

Yes. But it wouldn't have felt quite this urgent.

As if what they were going to find had the potential to change Sam's life forever.

They got to where they needed to be a lot sooner than any of them had expected.

'They're under power,' the pilot shouted. 'Well away from the reef now.'

How on earth had they managed that?

'I thought the guy on board was too badly injured to start his engines,' Sam said.

'Guess he had some help.' Jack was grinning. 'Strangely, I'm not surprised. Lia's a force to be reckoned with.'

It was more than relief that was trying to overwhelm Sam. He didn't want to allow hope to take over, only to be crushed, but—if that *was* the case, how proud would he be of Lia?

The pilot was on his radio, changing frequencies.

'M'Langi Coastguard to *Eclipse*. Do you read? Over…'

On his third attempt a response came through.

'*Eclipse* receiving. Hey… Thanks for coming. We're glad to see you guys. Over…'

It was a female voice.

Lia's voice.

Sam grabbed the microphone from the pilot.

'*Lia*…are you okay?'

The sound of laughter came through the speakers. 'I'm fine. No thanks to you, mate. You *dropped* me.'

'I'll make it up to you,' Sam promised. He needed to ask about the condition of the yachtsman and they had to find out about the condition the boat was in and whether they needed to evacuate both Lia and the man they'd initially set out to rescue, but the words caught in his throat.

Lia was making a *joke* of this? He wanted to shake her. No. He wanted to take her into his arms and hold on so tightly she could never get away and get herself into danger again.

'I broke the radio…' Lia sounded more serious now. 'Tell Jack I'm sorry.'

'I'm here.' Jack had taken the microphone from Sam. 'No worries. They're still making radios. Fill us in, Lia. What's happening? Are you really okay? How's your patient?'

The questions that Sam should have been asking instead of promising that he would make up for dropping her. Instead of being so stunned by an emotional reaction to hearing her making light of how bad the situation had been that he still had a lump the size of Africa blocking any ability to speak.

'I'm really okay. Got a bit of a bump but no more than a bruise or two. My patient is Felix Brabant. He's French, forty-three years old. He was heading for New Caledonia but got blown off course by the storm. He has a dislocated shoulder, a dislocation fracture of his elbow and a compound radial fracture. I've splinted everything as best I can and given him pain relief. He's pretty drowsy now but his GCS was good enough to talk me through getting the engines going.'

It was the pilot who took over the radio now.

'Are you able to follow us back to port? There's a tricky gap through the reef to navigate. Over...'

'I'm no sailor but I can follow directions. And I should warn you that I have no experience of navigating reefs.' Lia sounded less sure of herself. 'Over...'

'Stand by, Lia. We'll sort this out. Over...'

The men looked at each other. Transferring anyone between boats in these conditions would be difficult. Getting someone who was badly injured and now medicated to the point of being unable to help himself was going to make it even more dangerous.

'Put me on board,' Sam said. 'I need to check that the engine's powerful enough. If it's not, we'll have to transfer them and ditch the boat. If it is, I can bring the yacht in. We'll head for Wildfire and get them straight up to the hospital. You can take Jack back to Atangi to collect the chopper.'

The pilot pressed the transmission button on the microphone. 'Lia? We're going to get right alongside and Sam's going to come on board to take you in. Come up on deck. We'll need you to catch a rope. Over...'

'On my way. Over and out.'

It took more than one attempt and all the pilot's skill to get the buffered edges of the coastguard launch touching the yacht and keeping it there for more than a split second. The jump between boats was a hair-raising moment but in the end Sam didn't actually need the rope that Lia had been about to tether to the yacht because he jumped at the same instant the launch bumped against the yacht and he jumped as if he had wings on his feet.

He landed with a lurch that sent him barrelling into

Lia. She tried to break his momentum by putting her arms out but they both hit the deck.

And there they were. On a slippery deck in a fading storm, wrapped in each other's arms, and they were grinning at each other.

They could hear the roar of the launch moving away but they didn't stop grinning. Or look up. Sam couldn't tear his gaze away from Lia's eyes.

He had never felt like this in his life.

His words came out without him even thinking about what he was saying. The feeling was so huge, it had to escape.

'I love you,' he growled. 'Don't you ever give me a fright like this again.'

Lia's eyes widened. Her mouth opened and then closed. Her eyes crinkled as if she was trying not to cry and her lips wobbled as she tried to smile.

'I love you, too.'

Could there ever have been a less appropriate moment to exchange such life-changing declarations? They were still in trouble. They had to get this damaged vessel back to a safe port and they had a patient below deck that needed their help.

They had only been lying on the deck like that for a matter of seconds but it was time to move. Whatever had just happened would have to be put on hold. Sam struggled to his feet and held out his hands to help Lia up. Was this just a heat-of-the-moment thing? A reaction to the relief of him finding that Lia was uninjured and Lia now having someone to help her back to safety?

Maybe when this was over things would change and they might both be embarrassed by what had been said.

But Lia was gripping his hands and, as she regained her footing, her gaze was holding Sam's and he knew...

He knew that nothing would change.

This was as real as it got.

CHAPTER EIGHT

PICKING UP THE pieces always took so much longer than the event that had caused them.

And coping with that process could seem harder at times. The adrenaline rush of trying to survive was long gone and the relief of succeeding was also wearing off. Now was the time to count the cost. To survey the damage and put plans into action that would help people rebuild their lives and eventually reinstate the normality everybody longed for. Now, two days after the worst of the storm had passed over them, there was time to collate all the information they had and assign priorities.

Sam, on behalf of the medical team, and Ky, as the chief of police and civil defence on the main island of Atangi, had met in the hospital staffroom to do exactly that.

Cyclones were nothing new around here and Sam had done this before. He knew how hard these days of picking up the pieces could be and the strain of it all was evident on Ky's face but, for him personally, it was very different this time.

There was the same kind of destruction to be found in these islands he loved, of course—houses with roofs torn off, trees uprooted, boats that hadn't been as lucky as his own and had been bashed against rocks and destroyed. There was too much work to do and not enough manpower to do it quickly. The hospital was full to bursting, thanks to the damage to one wing that had taken some bed space away, and there were people who had been seriously injured, like Hika and the French yachtsman, Felix. Sam was worried about Sefina, too, who had spiked a temperature and would need watching in case she had an infection brewing. Yes. He was worried and tired and sad for people who had lost important things.

But he was also happier than he had ever been in his life.

Because he was in love.

And Lia had said that she loved him back…

Not that they'd had the time to celebrate this miracle that had happened in the middle of the total chaos of the cyclone. There'd been the scary time of getting the crippled yacht back into port and then many, many hours spent in surgery with Felix to try and save his arm.

Yesterday Sam had barely caught sight of Lia as she and Jack had taken the helicopter to every inhabited island in the area. They had done an aerial survey to check for serious damage to dwellings and then landed to check, treat and transport anybody who needed help. Now they had a good idea of what they were dealing with over the whole spread of this chain of islands that was M'Langi, and this was what he and Ky had been discussing.

'We were so lucky that the cyclone changed direction when it did and went back out to sea. Seems like it was only the northern end of Atangi that got really clipped. That's where the real structural damage to houses is concentrated.'

'It's great to know that the outer islands are okay.'

Sam nodded. 'There's minor damage. Roofs lifted but not ripped off. Trees down and crops ruined. A few injuries but nothing that needed transporting, according to Lia. I've got the list of people she saw and treated here…'

'I saw the chopper every time I looked up yesterday. Even out at night, with the light going. Those guys must have been exhausted by the time they stopped, I reckon. I hope they both got a good sleep last night.'

He could imagine Lia asleep in her bed, with those long limbs completely relaxed. Did she tie her hair up at night or did it spread out like a soft, dark wave over her pillows? A wave of longing washed through him. He wished he'd been there with her. Holding her in his arms. But he'd been on duty in the intensive care unit, monitoring Felix and Hika, occasionally snatching a bit of sleep on one of the comfortable armchairs here in the staffroom.

Maybe tonight he could be holding Lia. And that would be after they'd made love…

Oh, man…it was a bit of an effort to shake that train of thought back to where it belonged, which was out of work hours.

'You're looking a bit tired yourself, Ky.'

The big police officer smiled. 'I might get some sleep tonight. Last night I got a call from someone who'd spotted Louis Dason. I'd put the word out that I wanted to find him. We got a team together and went hunting for a few hours but…' He shrugged, shaking his head.

'No luck?'

'Nah… He's gone to ground somewhere and it's going to be easy enough to hide for the next few days. There's a lot of houses that have been abandoned until they can get fixed. And that's where the manpower has to go for the moment. We can't waste time searching for someone who doesn't want to be found. I've got anybody with any trade skills in building and plumbing sorted into teams and we've got a list we're working through one at a time. We'll be looking after some families in the school hall for a few days longer.' He glanced up at Sam. 'How's Sefina doing?'

'The surgery went well. We'll be keeping her in a while longer, though. She's running a bit of a temperature today.'

'Has she said anything about Louis?'

'She won't talk about it. Won't change her story. Not officially, anyway. I think she might have said something to Hettie. I don't think she realises how obvious it is that those injuries couldn't have been caused by a fall.'

'We'll find him,' Ky vowed. 'And ship him off to the mainland. Hopefully they'll lock him up and throw away the key.'

'It won't happen without a statement from Sefina. I'll see if Hettie can persuade her.'

'How's the kid?'

'See for yourself.' Sam could see the doorway behind Ky, where two women were coming into the staffroom.

Hettie had Joni in her arms. Lia was right behind her, cradling a well-wrapped baby.

'This place is turning into a creche.' But Sam couldn't have been happier to see the children arriving, given who had come with them. His gaze met Lia's and was caught. Never mind working hours—there was no way he could simply make polite eye contact and look away again.

He could spend the rest of his life looking into those eyes. Feeling that connection that went straight to his soul. Revelling in the knowledge that it would be possible to find limitless strength in that connection. Ultimate comfort. And a desire the likes of which he hadn't known existed.

It was just as well nobody else seemed to have noticed.

'Need some help?' Ky stood up to ruffle Joni's curls. He tickled the small boy, who giggled. 'We've got lots of kids being looked after in the school hall. One more wouldn't make any difference.'

'No.' Hettie looked alarmed. 'We're doing just fine. Sefina needs to see him every day.' She moved away from Ky to sit on one of the armchairs in the room. 'And we love Joni, don't we?' The question was directed at the toddler, who wrapped his arms around Hettie's neck in response. She kissed his head and answered her query herself in the kind of sing-song voice that came automatically from adults who loved the child they were speaking to. 'Yes, we do...'

Lia was smiling as she sat on the other armchair, adjusting the bundle in her arms. 'Jack's up at the airstrip. He's ready to take you back to Atangi anytime, Ky.'

'I think we're about done. You happy, Sam?'

Sam was still watching Lia, who was still smiling. He smiled back as her eyes met his again. Even with a break of only a second or two, finding that connection was still there gave him a jolt of sheer joy. Would it wear off when he'd met her gaze for the millionth time? It didn't feel like it would.

'Oh, yeah... I'm happy...'

Ky looked from Sam to Lia and then back again. He cleared his throat as if dismissing something he'd seen as being none of his business.

'Do you need me to send a team over from Atangi to deal with repairs here?'

'I don't think so. We've boarded up some windows but the main problem is water damage. Things need to dry out before we can assess what we need to replace. The windows can wait. There are people out there who need help first.'

Ky nodded. He looked at Lia again. 'Who's this little one?'

'She's Hika and Afi's baby.'

'Oh…of course.' Ky's breath came out in an impressed huff. 'Man, you guys did an awesome job there the other night. You're a legend in these parts now, Lia.'

'I was just doing my job.'

Sam shook his head. 'Hardly.' He nodded at Ky. 'She's awesome, all right.'

'Oh, stop…' But Lia's cheeks had gone pink and she seemed to find it necessary to rearrange the folds of muslin around the baby's face.

'Is Afi still here? I've got his house at the top of the list for today. We've got a big team ready to see what they can do.'

'No. He took Ema and Rua back yesterday. Someone said they'd be at the school hall.'

'I'll find him, then. He'll want to be part of the team. How's Hika doing?'

'Really well,' Sam told him. 'She'll be with us for a while, though. And we'll keep the baby with her.'

'And what about the guy from that yacht?'

'Felix?' Sam frowned. 'He might well need some more specialist surgery to make sure he regains full use of his arm but there's no point in evacuating him yet. I spoke to the chief of orthopaedics in Brisbane first thing this morning. We're going to have to wait until the swelling goes down before anything else can be done and that could take a week. He's comfortable.'

'You've got enough space? We've got a flight coming in with supplies later today. Or tomorrow. They're getting the tail end of the weather over the mainland still.'

'We'll manage. There's a few people that can probably go home today, if they've got homes to go back to.'

'Hettie?' Another person appeared at the door. 'We need you. Drug round.'

'Oh…okay… I'll be there in a sec, Matt.' Hettie gave Joni another cuddle before turning her head towards Lia. 'Can he stay here with you for a bit?'

'Sure. If I get a call I'll take him to Vailea.'

Joni wriggled happily into the small space beside Lia on the armchair and somehow she managed to put an arm around the little boy without disrupting the sleeping baby in her arms.

'I'd better go, too,' Ky said. He shook Sam's hand. 'I'll be in touch later to check how things are going but I reckon we're through the worst of this. Good job.'

'And you.'

There was a long moment's silence as Sam and Lia were left alone in the staffroom together, their eye contact saying things that had been hovering, unspoken, while others had been present and they hadn't been able to sink into this new, wonderful connection they'd discovered.

Huge things.

But Sam didn't even try to say any of them out loud. Instead, he let his gaze rest on Lia and the small people she had gathered to her body.

Something weird was happening in his head. A bit of a time warp, maybe. A flash forward in time that made him realise what it could be like to see Lia with a different baby and toddler in her arms.

Their children?

Holy heck…a week ago a thought like that would have made him break out in a cold sweat. Taking him back to a place he'd sworn he'd never go again.

But this couldn't be more different.

Even his smile felt different. Tender enough to match the lump in his throat.

'Suits you,' he murmured.

Lia grinned. 'I love kids,' she said. 'The more the merrier. Big families are the best.'

The moment the words had left her mouth Lia kicked herself mentally.

She'd been lost in the warmth of the gaze she'd been basking in. The sheer delight in knowing that what had happened between them on the deck of that broken yacht was still there.

Growing, even.

They hadn't had even a few minutes alone together since then and she'd needed this confirmation as much as she needed her next breath.

But they weren't exactly alone now, were they? She had a tiny baby in her arms and a wriggly toddler on one side. And she'd just told Sam that big families were the best.

She could hear an echo of his voice in her head.

Closest I've come to a family is looking after a borrowed dog.

Did he even know what it was like to have a family? Had he been a lonely child? Was he lonely now?

Lia's heart was breaking. She wanted to add Sam to

the pile of humanity in her arms. She wanted to hold him close to her heart and never let him go.

To make him a part of *her* family.

He was already, as far as her heart was concerned.

'Hey…'

'Hey, what?' Sam didn't seem to have been hurt by her careless words. He was still smiling. A smile that was so tender she could imagine exactly what it would be like if she was sitting here holding *his* baby.

Lia didn't bother checking that no one was coming into the room who could overhear but she did keep her voice to a whisper.

'I love you.'

Sam's chair scraped as he pushed it back. Lia's heart picked up speed as he moved towards her and it skipped a beat as he bent his head.

He didn't have to say it back. The words were written all over his face. She could feel them in the way his hands touched her face. She was living them as his lips covered hers in a kiss that blew that gorgeous smile out of the water as far as tenderness went.

And then he said it anyway.

'I love you, too.'

It was Joni who broke the moment. He tugged at Lia's arm.

'Ithe cream,' he said, with an adorable lisp. 'Pleathe?'

'I'd better go and find Vailea.'

'And I'd better do my ward round.' Sam's smile was cheeky now. 'What are you doing after work?'

'I get the afternoon off, apparently. Unless there's an emergency. But the cell phone coverage is up and running again. As long as I don't go too far away, I'm as free as a bird. How 'bout you?'

'I think I can arrange a bit of time off.'

Her breath caught as she imagined what they could do with that bit of time. Private time. In Sam's bedroom, hopefully. But there was something Lia hadn't seen in his eyes before. Something serious? Wary, almost.

'There's something I'd like to show you.'

It was something important. Instinct told her that he was inviting her into a part of his life that he didn't show to many people. This was about something private.

Lia had to swallow past a sudden tightening in her throat. And breathe past the same sensation in her chest.

'I'd like to see it,' she said softly.

'It's a short boat ride away. Want me to check with Jack that it's okay for you to be that far away?'

'I can do that. I need to take some supplies up to the chopper after I've handed over these creche responsibilities.'

'Come back soon.' Sam ducked his head and kissed her again.

He lifted Joni out of the way to give Lia room to get up. And then he lifted his hand in farewell as he moved towards the door, turning his head to smile once more.

'I'll miss you.'

Lia was smiling, too, as she stood up. But her smile wobbled as she saw Sam disappear.

She was missing him already.

'Are we going out on your yacht?' Down at the harbour on Wildfire Island, the boats were still rocking on their moorings. 'That's it, isn't it? *Surf Song?*'

'It's a she.' Sam's look was stern. 'And, yes, that's her.'

Lia remembered what Jack had said. 'The love of your life…'

'She *was*…'

The stern look vanished from Sam's face to be replaced by one that was very different. One that made Lia's heart feel so full it could burst at any moment. The very next beat, probably.

This was crazy. They'd only met a week ago. Only realised that how they felt about each other was mutual a couple of days ago. This couldn't be real, could it? The kind of love that could last a lifetime?

One of her older sisters, Carla, had married young, after only knowing her husband a short time. She and Dino were still happily married with a brood of young children, but there'd been a typical Roselli family ruckus when the engagement and wedding date had been announced back then. Lia could remember the look on Carla's face as she'd made the simple statement that had silenced everybody.

When you know, you just know.

Had Carla felt like this when she'd only been with the man she loved for such a short time?

Lia could certainly believe that.

She knew… Sam was the one for her. The person she could be with—and love—forever.

Okay, there might be a few logistical issues to figure out but she wasn't even going to think about that today.

Not when that look she was basking in from Sam suggested that *he* knew, too.

That this *was* real.

It took her a moment to tune back in to what Sam was saying.

'…so we'll take my motor boat. The seas are still big enough to need a powerful motor to get through the gap in the reef. It'll be like this for days and I wouldn't risk taking *Surf Song* out.'

Holding her hand, he helped Lia onto the small boat moored alongside his yacht.

'It'll be a bit rough but I reckon I know you well enough to know that you quite like a bit of an adrenaline rush. Here, put this on...' He eased a life jacket over her head but he didn't let go of it when it was resting on her shoulders. Instead, he pulled her closer so that only the squashy orange cushions of the jacket separated their bodies. The sea rolled beneath them and he slipped his arms completely around her body to hold her steady. It felt like the most natural thing in the world to lift her own arms and wrap them around Sam's neck. To lift her face and stand on tiptoe so that she could kiss his lips.

It was Sam who broke the kiss.

'Don't start that,' he warned. 'Or we'll never get to where we're going.'

'Where *are* we going?'

'Not far.' The engine of Sam's boat started instantly, with a powerful roar. 'Hold on to your hat.'

Everything about her time here so far had been wild enough to live up to the island's name. From that first flight in on the fixed-wing aircraft to the helicopter trips with Jack. And the work had been something she'd be telling stories about for the rest of her career. Crawling beneath the wreckage of a house. Getting dropped onto a crippled yacht and being abandoned in a terrifyingly huge sea.

Maybe the wildest story of all—and the one she would be telling her grandchildren—would end up being that she'd found the love of her life in the midst of all that adventure and danger.

This short boat ride might still be wild but it wasn't dangerous. Sam knew how to handle the boat and he'd been right, they weren't going far. Straight out from the western side of Wildfire to one of the many dots that were the uninhabited islands sprinkled right through this archipelago.

This one had a deep cleft in its shoreline, with only a narrow entranceway, but then it opened out to a small but astonishingly pretty tree-lined beach. The water was almost smooth in here, thanks to the protection of the wings of this island.

A jetty had been built to one side of the beach and it was easy enough to climb out without help. Lia looked around as she reached the end of the jetty. The only sign of the cyclone here were the coconuts and driftwood littering the pure, white sand of the beach. This was clearly a safe place to be but why had Sam brought her here?

'What's the name of this island? Who lives here?'

'It doesn't have a name yet. And no one lives here. Yet.'

'But there's a jetty. And…and is that a house?' Lia shaded her eyes with her hand as the sun broke through the heavy cloud cover for a moment. 'I can see something…up there in the forest.'

'It's a work in progress,' Sam told her. 'I needed to check that everything's still okay after the storm.'

So somebody was building a house on a tiny, private patch of tropical paradise. Lia followed Sam up a track that wound its way past huge tree trunks and tangles of vines. A flock of startled parrots took wing, chiding them for the disturbance.

The house was well under way. The foundations were complete and the framework of the walls in place.

'Kind of lucky the roof wasn't on yet, I guess.' Sam was testing the framework as he walked slowly around the construction site. 'This all seems as solid as a rock. I'll get hold of Pita later and tell him he's doing a good job.'

'Pita?'

'He lives on Atangi. He was the foreman of the crew that built the conference centre on Wildfire. They were all a bit short of work when that project got finished. He's a great builder.'

'From what I've heard, there'll be more work than all the builders here can keep up with for a while.'

'True. I'll remind him that there's no rush to come back here.' Sam smiled at Lia. 'Do you like it?'

'This house? The island? What's not to like?' From this high point of the small island, Lia could see over the trees below to the cleft of the island's shape and farther, to where Wildfire Island was sitting directly in front of them.

'Look at the shape of this island. It's like folded angel's wings.'

'It is.' Sam was staring down at the wings of land. 'How 'bout that for a name? Angel Island.'

'I just named an island? How cool. You might have to run that one past Pita.'

'I'll do that.' But Sam was looking beyond the foreshore now. 'We're facing Sunset Beach. You know, the one where you were playing windmills just before the cyclone hit?'

Lia grinned at him. How could she forget that? The place they'd had their first kiss that had unlocked the passion they'd gone on to explore in Sam's bed. And,

as huge as that passion had been, it seemed less powerful than this new depth of feeling she'd found for Sam.

The love that could last a lifetime.

'You haven't seen what happens on that beach, thanks
to the weather since you got here, but it gets its name
from the way the cliffs glow like they're on fire at sunset. It's where the name of the whole island comes from.'

'It sounds gorgeous. I want to see that.'

'This will be the best place of all to see it from. There's
going to be a big deck coming out from this living area
and it'll be a front-row seat to the greatest show on earth.'

Lia turned from the view to meet Sam's gaze. The
logistical issues were rushing up at her. Would she be
here to see one of those sunsets when the sky cleared
completely? She was due to be back on the mainland in
a week's time.

She had her family there and they needed her. How
soon would she be able to get back to Sam? How often?

She couldn't say anything about it. Not yet. Not when
this was the first time they'd been alone together since
they'd declared their love for each other. This was too
new. Too precious to risk putting obstacles in its path.

And wasn't it a bit premature to be worrying about
the future when she still had so much to learn about this
man she'd fallen in love with?

'I don't even know where you're from.' The words
tumbled out unexpectedly. 'What made you come here
in the first place and if this is where you want to be forever. I love you, Sam, but I don't really know anything
about you. Is that crazy?'

'Probably.' But Sam was smiling as he pulled Lia into
his arms. 'I don't know much about you, either, but this

feels so…right. As if I've been waiting my whole life to find you.'

This time they didn't kiss. Lia kept her head nestled against Sam's shoulder, loving the feel of his arms around her.

'I don't even know if you're single,' she murmured. 'You could be married.' Her head jerked up. '*Are* you married?'

'Not anymore.'

Lia gasped. 'You *have* been married?' It felt like she'd been doused with a bucket of icy water.

Sam sighed. 'Come on, it's a bit windy up here. Let me show you the beach and I'll tell you anything you want to know.'

So Lia asked him questions as they made their way down the track and onto the white sands of the beach. She learned that he had grown up in the north of England. That he'd done his training in Birmingham and had gone on to specialise in intensive care medicine. That he'd married a nurse who'd worked in that unit because he'd thought he was in love.

Thought?

Did that mean he knew he hadn't really been in love? Because he now knew what that *really* felt like?

They'd got to the end of the beach before Lia learned why Sam had walked away from his previous life and career.

'Vicky told me she was pregnant and I was over the moon. I was going to be a father.'

They were sitting on a huge driftwood log by now and Lia was holding Sam's hand. She knew there was something awful he was about to tell her. A dreadful accident, perhaps, that had torn his wife and unborn baby from his life?

'I wasn't the father,' Sam continued. 'Turned out that the father of her baby was another doctor in the unit. My best friend.'

'Oh, my God…' Lia breathed. 'How could she have done that?' She let go of Sam's hand to touch his face. How could any woman have done something like that to Sam? How could this Vicky have not known she had been the luckiest woman in the world with what she already had?

He must have been able to see her total lack of comprehension in her eyes. And maybe the reason behind it—that she could never even contemplate doing something like that to the man she loved.

I'm not like that, her touch was telling him. *I love you. You can trust me.*

Sam caught her hand and pressed his lips to it, seemingly lost for words.

'I'm not surprised you left. Nobody could live with that being rubbed in day after day.'

'I felt like a complete idiot,' Sam admitted. 'It felt like everybody had known she'd never actually loved me. That I'd been taken for a ride.' He sighed heavily. 'I took leave. I intended to go back but I needed a break. I took *Surf Song* and sailed off. By chance, I ended up here and they were short of a doctor at the hospital. The rest, as they say, is history. It didn't happen overnight but I'd found the place in the world I most wanted to be. I love these islands. I love the people. And…and I make a real difference to their lives. It goes both ways.'

'Haven't you been lonely?'

'I was going to get a dog.' There was a gleam in Sam's

eyes that suggested he needed to lighten the atmosphere. 'But now I've found you...'

That drew another gasp from Lia. 'Cheers,' she told him. *'Not...'* But she was smiling. She knew what he was really trying to say—that he might never be lonely again because he'd found *her*...

'It's your turn,' Sam said. 'Are you married?'

'Nope. Never got close. I've been too wrapped up in my career and I never met the right person...'

The pause seemed too significant. As if she'd left off the end of that sentence.

Until now.

'Plus, I have a family the size of Africa,' Lia added quickly. 'They take all my spare time. Especially Angel.'

'Angel?'

'My niece. She's six. She was born prematurely with cerebral palsy. Her father walked out as soon as he knew she was disabled. My sister couldn't manage by herself and moved back home a while ago. I moved back, too, to help out.' She smiled at Sam. 'It's tough but I wouldn't have it any other way. She's the most adorable kid and I love her to bits.'

'What will she think when she knows there's an island named after her?'

'Do you think Pita will like the name?'

'Doesn't matter if he doesn't. It's *my* island.'

'What?'

Sam shrugged. 'It's no big deal. The local government needed to raise some funds a couple of years back and someone came up with the idea of selling one of the islands. They used the money to build the community hall by the school—the one that the people are living in now until their houses get fixed. It wasn't that expensive compared to land anywhere in England, that's for sure.'

'Really?' Lia thought of her parents and the worry in their faces when they'd been talking about how to make the mortgage payments on their house when the redundancy money ran out. Maybe they could think of moving somewhere where the land was cheaper. Here, even? The thought was ridiculous. Or was it?

'I hadn't been planning to build a house on it,' Sam continued. 'It was just a nice place to come when I wanted a bit of time to myself. But then the work on the conference centre finished and people needed jobs.'

And he'd found a way to provide them. On top of already making a huge contribution to the community he'd made his home in.

Lia's heart squeezed. She'd learned a lot about Sam today. She already knew that he'd been without a real family and had probably been a lonely child. He'd been badly hurt by the betrayal of his wife and his best friend. And he was generous towards the people he cared about.

Love could keep growing, couldn't it? Could develop layer upon layer that made it deeper and stronger.

It was Lia's turn to be lost for words. She had to turn away from the compassion in Sam's eyes before her own filled up with tears and overflowed, which could well spoil the moment. Instead, she looked at the beach. Even now, with the sea still wild out in the open, there were only baby waves lapping against the sand here.

Angel loved the water. She loved the beach but the surf around Brisbane was too big for her to ever be able to swim in the sea. Imagine if she could come here for a holiday and play in these wavelets? Move her body in water that was warm enough to stay in for as long as you wanted?

But to live here in this isolated patch of the Pacific? Away from her family?

How could she do that?

The touch of Sam's hand made her turn her head again. The touch of his lips against hers reminded her of how private this beach was. This kiss wasn't going to stop anytime soon.

And Lia didn't want it to. She wanted to make love with Sam right here, under the palm trees that bordered this gorgeous little island.

Sam's island.

How could she leave her family behind to live here?

Sinking into the kiss and letting herself get swept away by the passion, Lia only had one more coherent thought.

How could she not live here, if it meant she could be with Sam forever?

CHAPTER NINE

Maybe there were only brief glimpses of the sun between the big, fluffy clouds this morning but it had never shone so brightly.

Sam had to shade his eyes with his hand as he stepped outside his cabin to walk to work the next morning.

It could be that the sunshine and the warmth of the day seemed more astonishing than usual because it was such a contrast to the dark side of the weather that had been around them for the past few days.

Or it could be that he was seeing life through the eyes of a man in love, and everything—including the weather—was simply perfect.

Too good to be true?

What a difference a day could make. Well, a day and night, actually.

Making love to Lia in the absolute privacy of his own island had been amazing. A confirmation of everything he'd seen in her eyes when he'd told her his story and she'd been so horrified that anyone could have done what Vicky had done to him. A physical expression of the promise he'd seen—that Lia could never do something like that to the man she loved.

And he *was* that man…

Neither of them had noticed that the surroundings weren't that ideal for that kind of intimacy but it wasn't until they'd come home and showered off the sand and then started all over again in the comfort of his bed that they realised how much better it *could* be.

Lia had gone back to her own accommodation to find a clean uniform and tidy up for work so Sam was left with a bit of time on his own to contemplate the contrasts that made life so wonderful.

Cyclones and sunshine.

Loneliness and love…

While it wasn't something he would have chosen to do, it was inevitable that Sam was making contrasts between Vicky and Lia, too. He'd never talked about his past life with anyone here because it was something he had chosen to move on from and try to forget. Talking about it had made a lot of memories resurface.

Bitter, hurtful memories. How good was it that he could superimpose memories of Lia on top of them?

There'd never been that kind of connection in working together that made him feel like he had another pair of hands that he could trust as much as his own.

Sex had never been so astonishing. So much more than a physical pleasure and release.

And Vicky had never looked at him the way Lia had yesterday. As if all the love in the world had collected in her eyes and could be freely given in no more than a glance.

He'd spent months with Vicky before deciding that this was the woman he wanted to marry and spend the rest of his life with.

Was he completely crazy to be thinking that it was

really true about Lia when he'd only known her a matter of days?

No, not thinking…

Knowing.

He probably had a goofy smile on his face as he walked through the garden to gain entrance to the hospital building.

Life was good. And it would get even better soon, because the plane from the mainland was due to arrive and Lia was going to collect the new supplies they'd been waiting for since the cyclone had disrupted normal routines, and bring them down to the hospital.

Maybe things would have calmed down around here enough for him to take a quick break. To sit in the garden with Lia, perhaps, and bask in a bit more of what her eyes could tell him.

It was too soon to tell her how permanent he wanted this to be but he could dream a little, couldn't he?

He had a few more steps before he had to enter his place of work and turn his focus to his patients and he would have been happy to use that for daydreaming. The ringing of his mobile phone seemed a rude interruption until he saw who the caller was.

'Pita… I was going to call you today. I went out to the house yesterday. It's looking great. I can't see any significant damage from the weather.'

He listened for a few moments. 'Of course… I understand. You must have a lot on at the moment. There's no rush to get back to my job. I…' His jaw dropped as he had to stop speaking to listen again. *'What…?'*

Ending the call, he moved swiftly towards the staffroom. Jack was sitting beside the radio, scribbling in a logbook.

'Hey, Sam. Gorgeous day, isn't it? Those clouds will be gone in no time. We could fly anywhere.'

'Yeah…it's going to be hot.' Sam reached past Jack to shift some books and journals. 'Did you see a white envelope here? Pita came in last night to collect it and says it wasn't here.'

'Nope.' Jack glanced at his watch. 'I'd better go. I said I'd collect Lia in the golf cart and get her up to the airfield to collect the supplies. I need to do a thorough check on the chopper. She's been put through her paces the last few days, that's for sure.' He glanced back at Sam, who was still shuffling through the piles of paper and files that seemed to always collect on the radio desk. 'How long ago did you leave it there?'

'Must be at least a week. It was…' Sam frowned. He could remember putting the cash in the envelope. Pushing the envelope into his pocket. A big pocket. Oh, yeah… he'd been wearing that white coat.

'It was Lia's first day at work.'

Because he'd put that stupid coat on to try and impress her, hadn't he? Even though he'd already written her off after that comment she'd made at the airfield.

Who knew they paid so much more for coming here in the cyclone season?

He could remember the phone call from Pita and telling him where he would leave the envelope, but he couldn't actually remember putting it where he'd said he was going to put it.

Because he'd been distracted, hadn't he? That cardiac arrest in the garden. When he'd worked with Lia and had started to revise his earlier opinion of her. He'd pulled the coat off because it had been hampering his movements. He'd pulled it off, rolled it up and shoved it…

On the bottom level of the resuscitation trolley.

'Never mind,' he told Jack. 'I think I know where it is.'

The trolley hadn't been needed since then. It would be in the storage room near Theatre.

It was. And, yes…the discarded white coat was still a crumpled heap amongst boxes of gloves and bags of saline.

He shook it out and reached into the pockets. So that was where his diary had got to. He'd been hunting for that yesterday morning because he'd needed the dates for the clinics coming up on Atangi and other islands. Important clinics where they were going to be starting trials for the new encephalitis vaccine they had available specifically for these islands.

The reminder came as a jolt. First the cyclone and now Lia. Was he losing focus on what his life was really all about? Not just the career he loved but these islands and these people. *His* people now. His home.

And that reminded him of the house he was building. And that Pita needed to be paid or he wouldn't be able to do any more work on it.

He checked the other pockets. Searched the whole trolley and poked under the shelves in the storage room but there was no sign of the envelope.

Who had put the trolley back in here?

Anahera?

He went to find her.

'Sam… I was going to call you. Can you take a look at Felix? His pain level seems to be increasing and I think the capillary refill in the nails of his injured hand is getting slower.'

'Sure. I'll be there in just a minute. Hey…do you remember the day of Keoni's arrest?'

'Of course.'

'Do you remember who put the resus trolley away in the end?'

Anahera frowned. 'Hmm. It was in the corner of ICU for a while because I put the life pack back on it after we'd switched over the monitoring to the bedside gear. I don't know who put it back in storage, though.'

Lia had been standing in the corner of the ICU, hadn't she? Sending and receiving those text messages that had annoyed him so much. Maybe she would remember.

A junior nurse poked her head around the door.

'Have you seen Sefina?'

'No, why?'

'She told me she was discharging herself this morning. I told her she'd have to wait to see one of the doctors but then I got busy with other patients. And now I can't find her.'

'Maybe she's with Joni. Try the kitchens.' Anahera caught Sam's gaze. 'Can you come and see Felix now?'

'Of course.' With an effort, Sam put the concern of the missing envelope and cash out of his mind and turned his attention to more important things. It had just been misplaced in the chaos of a crisis—that was all. It would turn up.

If it wasn't for the evidence all around her of the very recent cyclone, like bushes having been stripped of their flowers and having to dodge coconuts that hadn't been cleared from the road yet, Lia was finding it increasingly hard to believe it had even happened.

Under the clear, blue sky and sunshine that was gaining warmth by the minute, she drove the little golf cart laden with supplies for the hospital and knew that anybody who saw her would probably think she was crazy—all by herself but with a huge grin on her face.

Because she was driving towards where Sam was.

How different her life felt at this moment was even more unbelievable than how bad the cyclone had been.

This was what it felt like to be in love.

No wonder Carla had declared that when you knew, you just knew. It was *so* true.

And maybe she needed to cut a bit of slack for her younger sister, Elena, who was with the much older boyfriend the entire family had deemed so unsuitable. Maybe she was in love and maybe it was real. She could just imagine her family's reaction when she was home next week and announced that she'd met the man she was going to marry.

Lia actually laughed aloud as she pictured her mother crossing herself or slamming a pot lid and muttering something along the lines of, *Mamma mia, Lia—and I thought you were the sensible one of the family...*

The laughter—and the smile—faded.

The stab of homesickness reminded her of how much she was missing her family. The crowded dinner tables and her mother's wonderful food. Cuddles from Angel. Even the teasing and incessant arguments. They always got resolved in the end because the one thing the Roselli family had in abundance was love.

How was Nico doing now that he'd started his chemo?

And Angel? She was due for an appointment with an orthopaedic specialist down in Brisbane because there'd been discussions that a surgical release of some ligaments and tendons might be necessary to help her walk when those specially designed aids had been made.

The smile reappeared. She would be able to pay for

those aids thanks to the bonus she was earning by working here.

And then it faded completely.

On one side of her was the pull of her family and the need to be with them.

But on the other was…Sam.

And these gorgeous islands. His *private* island. Who wouldn't think it was a dream come true to live in a place like this? She wouldn't be short of friends. All the people she'd met so far, like Anahera and Hettie and Caroline and Jack, had the potential to be special people in her life. And the work… Well, she'd had more excitement and used more of her skills in the last week than she would have in a month back home. A year, even. Maybe forever. How many houses got wrecked in cyclones around Brisbane? And even if it did happen, there'd be a queue of highly trained urban search and rescue team members who'd be way ahead of her to get to the action.

Would they want a permanent paramedic on the islands? It might be less expensive for them than adding the travel costs and bonuses of bringing FIFO staff in, especially in the cyclone season.

They could still do that, though. She'd need time off when she had babies…

Whoa…

Who was getting just a little ahead of herself here?

But the grin was back as Lia parked the golf cart outside Wildfire hospital and began to ferry in the cartons of supplies. She knew where some of them needed to go, too. Boxes of IV supplies went to the storeroom near the intensive care unit. New linen went to another storage area. She didn't have a key to get into the drug cupboard, though, so she carried that box to the staffroom to find someone who did.

Hettie was on a day off but Anahera would. Or Caroline. Or…Sam…

He was sitting at the radio desk, a folder open in front of him.

'Hey…'

He looked up and Lia soaked in the way his face changed. The crinkles around his eyes that advertised a smile was on the way. The softening of those eyes that she'd looked into enough that she could describe every tiny detail. Blue-grey, with a darker rim and a ring of hazel around the pupil that was an exact match for the colour of his hair.

She loved those eyes. She loved the floppy hair. She loved the way he could look at her as though the sun was coming out again after a huge storm. A cyclone, even.

'Hey, yourself.' He stood up, abandoning whatever work he was doing, to walk towards her. 'Let me take that.' He reached for the small locked box. 'It's good to see the drugs have arrived.' Taking the box from her arms, he leaned in farther to place a slow kiss on her lips. 'You should have had security riding with you, carrying this lot.'

'It's one of my splinter skills.' Lia grinned. 'I know kung-fu.'

Sam grinned back. 'That wouldn't surprise me in the least. Oh…you don't happen to have a Brisbane Hospital staff directory tucked into that amazing brain of yours, do you? I'm trying to find the number for the guy we spoke to about Felix. I'm not really happy with the amount of pain he's in. Graham somebody, but his surname has fallen out of my head. Keanu took the call and I don't want to disturb him on his day off.'

'Graham Appleby. Professor Appleby, in fact.'

Sam shook his head. 'You really *are* amazing. How on earth did you know that?'

Lia laughed. 'It's more of a coincidence than a miracle. I told you my niece has cerebral palsy. Professor Appleby is one of the members of the multidisciplinary team that manages her problems. He's the best.'

Sam pulled a pen from his pocket and wrote on his hand. 'I'll get hold of him in a minute.' Then he glanced up, an eyebrow raised. 'While I'm picking that astonishing brain of yours, do you remember the first day you worked here? That cardiac arrest?'

'You mean when I got to see what an awesome doctor you were for the first time? When you were trying to impress me by wearing that starched white coat?' Lia's smile was the product of something warm and bubbly inside. Something very tender.

'Exactly. Do you remember that I shoved the coat onto the bottom of the resus trolley?'

'No. But I remember thinking how much better you looked without it. I'd go as far as to say *hot*…'

But Sam was frowning. 'You were standing beside the trolley in ICU when we were stabilising Keoni. You didn't see an envelope drop off it, did you?'

Lia shook her head. 'What sort of envelope?'

'Small. But quite fat. I'm paying Pita for the work on the house in cash, so he can pay the other guys and suppliers more easily. There was ten thousand dollars in the envelope and it's gone missing.'

Lia's jaw dropped. 'Who has ten thousand dollars to

put in an envelope? I knew you were rich but… That's ridiculous, Sam. How could you leave it lying around? Anyone could have taken it.'

The words were so casual.

I knew you were rich…

Part of the blame had to lie with the way his memory had been working this morning, comparing Lia to Vicky. The way stuff that had been buried for so long was too close to the surface now. It was too easy to make a very unwelcome reappearance. Like that gut-wrenching final conversation with his wife. His pregnant wife who had been carrying a baby that wasn't his.

'You said you loved me.' He could still feel the tears choking his words.

'Men are so easy to fool.'

'Why did you marry me?'

'Why do you think, Sam?' The laughter had been unforgettably cruel. *'Everybody knows how rich you are…'*

He kept his voice as neutral as he could. 'What do you mean, you know I'm rich?'

Lia had already been looking shocked. Now her face seemed to freeze and her eyes filled with wariness. Maybe his tone hadn't been as neutral as he'd intended.

'You own an island, for heaven's sake. And a yacht.'

He'd tried to make light of his assets by telling her that land wasn't exorbitantly priced in the islands. Lots of people had yachts. How much did she *really* know?

His stare was clearly making Lia uncomfortable. She looked away and he saw her fingers curl and then straighten.

'And…people have said things. About the way you…

um…buy stuff for the hospital when it's needed. About… how generous you are.' She was offering him a small smile. 'It's one of the things I love about you.'

One of the things? There was an evil voice in the back of his head—a gust of bitterness left over from a hurricane of betrayal.

More likely to be the only really *important* thing.

'Money's very important to you, isn't it, Lia?'

'*What?* What's that supposed to mean?'

Good grief…he had said that out loud? Of course he had. Lia was looking bewildered. Hurt. As if he'd slapped her.

It could be guilt, the nasty little voice whispered. *You've found out the truth.*

He could hear echoes of Lia's voice now.

Lucky for me… Who knew they paid so much more for coming here in the cyclone season?

Travelling's never been in my budget. That's why it's so exciting to be here.

He'd felt that knot of tension in his gut when he'd heard that one the first time. He'd actually wondered if it was exciting because Wildfire was an exotic location or whether she was more excited about adding to the reserves in her budget.

She could send any financial woes she might have packing forever by getting hitched to someone who'd inherited a not insubstantial fortune, couldn't she?

Even half of what was left would set her up for life.

The way it had set up Vicky and the father of her baby…

His mouth seemed to have taken on a life of its own.

'You didn't make any secret of it being why you came here in the first place, did you, Lia? For the money?'

'Are you suggesting that I took *your* money? In the envelope?'

'*No*. Of course I'm not.'

He wasn't. He'd actually completely forgotten about the damned envelope as his mind was dragging him back into the past. He would never have suggested Lia was dishonest—that was unthinkable.

He'd just been sidetracked because of the subject and now they'd come full circle and he could see why she might think that that was what he'd been leading up to. Now his mind was going in crazy circles itself. How could he put this right?

'I'm sorry... I've had stuff on my mind, that's all. And I never wanted anyone to know I was wealthy.' He rubbed his forehead with the heel of his hand. 'I told you about Vicky. That was why *she* married me. The *only* reason...'

Oh, man...this was not the time to be telling Lia the whole sorry saga of his disastrous marriage. He was making things worse. He'd pretty much confessed that he'd been thinking about his ex-wife this morning, which was true but not in the way that Lia looked like she was thinking it was.

She was so pale and still she looked like she could crumple in a heap at any moment. Fragile would have been the last word he would ever have thought of to describe Lia Roselli but that's how she looked right now.

And he'd dug a huge hole for himself by saying where the cash had been. Right beside Lia. If he tried to take that back would he put his foot in things again, the way he just had?

'You don't trust me.'

The words were a statement, not a question.

'That's not true. I do trust you. I…' He wanted to say *I love you*, but the words somehow got stuck in his head. How could you say those words to someone who was looking at you as if you'd just grown two heads or something? Had become someone—or something—that you would never choose to be near.

To make things worse, Anahera appeared at the staff-room door. 'That morphine top-up doesn't seem to have brought the pain scale down for Felix. Do you want to go ahead with taking his cast off to see what's going on?'

'Yes. I'll put in a call to Brisbane first.' To the specialist whose name he now knew, thanks to Lia.

He turned to face her, as Anahera vanished as swiftly as she'd come. He opened his mouth to say that they'd talk about this later. *Soon*. That he wasn't, in any way, accusing her of anything. That he never would.

But he didn't get the chance.

'This was never real, was it, Sam?' Her voice had a hollow tone to it. As if it was a ghost of Lia speaking, not the real woman standing in front of him. 'This…' she made a movement with her hands '…whatever we thought we had.' Her eyes looked as haunted as her voice sounded. '*None* of it was real.'

She left the room as swiftly as Anahera had. As if she were on a mission that someone's life depended on.

Her own?

CHAPTER TEN

TEARS BLURRED LIA'S vision so much that the islands were no more than green smudges on a blue background.

A week ago she would have declared that she never cried. That she could cope with whatever life threw at her and she was far more familiar with mopping up other people's tears than her own. She was the strongest person in her family—everyone knew that. She was the one they all relied on for any medical advice. The one who provided the reassurance and encouragement anyone needed when they were sick or worried. The one who'd given up her independent life and moved home to help with the enormous amount of time and effort and energy it took to raise a disabled child.

But how often had she cried in the last week, for heaven's sake?

Down on the beach that time, when she'd had to tell Sam why she'd been so unprofessional and texting on her phone all day and the pent-up anxiety and guilt and relief about not being there for Nico's surgery had come bubbling out.

And when she'd been so exhausted in the wake of the worst of the cyclone and rescuing Hika from her crushed home and homesickness had kicked in.

She'd almost cried yesterday, too, when Sam had been telling her his story and she'd realised how lonely he must have been as a child and how devastated he would have been by the betrayal of the woman he'd married. Her heart had been breaking for the boy and the man she hadn't even known.

Was that what the trigger always was? The link with family and love?

But here she was, crying again. Because she was on her way to seeing her family again?

Or were these angry tears perhaps, because she'd run away from something she should have been able to cope with?

But it had all happened so fast.

How kind had Jack been when she'd arrived back at the airfield with the golf cart, having fled from Sam's horrible accusations? That she was just like his ex-wife and only interested in his money. That she had taken the envelope with a stupid amount of cash in it.

Jack had taken one look at her face and known something was horribly wrong. Because he knew about Nico, he assumed she'd been contacted because of a family emergency and Lia hadn't tried to correct the assumption. It had *felt* like a personal emergency.

The supply plane had been about to take off, its engines already running. Jack had signalled the pilot and all but pushed Lia on board the small plane.

'But I'm here to work. You need a crew.'

'I'll use Anahera if we get a call. That's what we always do if there's no paramedic available. We've coped before. We'll cope now. Go. Your family needs you. And that's where *you* need to be.'

'But…' Her protest was weaker this time. The idea of

escaping the whole island was so appealing—even more powerful than the force that had driven her so swiftly out of the staffroom—to get away from the devastating realisation that what she had thought she'd found with Sam Taylor was no more than an illusion.

Wishful thinking…

He thought she had fallen in love with him simply because he was rich?

No, it was worse than that. He thought she was *pretending* to be in love with him. Like Vicky had? That she was so obsessed with money she could have *stolen* from him…

'I'll send your stuff on the next plane,' he told her. 'Or maybe you can come back in a day or two.'

Come back?

Not likely.

Lia blinked back her tears and her vision cleared as the plane finished banking and settled onto a straight path. A track that was taking her home.

To her family. Where she belonged.

How had she ever thought she could move away from her home town to live in an isolated collection of Pacific islands?

It would never have worked.

Sam was a loner.

And she couldn't survive without the love of her family.

She needed it now, more than ever. Not that she would be confessing how stupid she'd been, thinking she'd found the person she wanted to spend the rest of her life with. It was cringe-worthy, remembering how sure she'd been.

When you know, you just know.

Her breath came out in an incredulous huff. She wouldn't be subscribing to that belief again anytime soon.

It shouldn't have happened but at least it was over. Lia blinked again and tuned in to the radio conversation the pilot was having. He noticed her glance and raised an eyebrow.

Lia nodded. 'Sounds great.'

There weren't many seats available on connecting flights that could take her from where they were going to land in Cairns back to Brisbane. She'd have a wait of a few hours but the pilot was talking to someone who'd found a gap and would hold a seat for her.

She'd be less than an hour's drive from home when she finally got to Brisbane.

And she still had a couple of hours' flying time before they got to Cairns. Plenty of time to think up a plausible reason for arriving home without her luggage. It had been a last-minute opportunity, perhaps. They didn't need her now that the crisis of the cyclone was over and available flights were few and far between. She'd had the choice of grabbing a seat and having her stuff sent later or waiting a week to come home.

She hadn't been able to wait. That was close enough to the truth, wasn't it?

Getting the cast off Felix's arm had to be done with meticulous care, given the degree of injury it was protecting, but it had to be done because the Frenchman's level of pain suggested that he might be developing compartment syndrome, and if that wasn't dealt with urgently, he could lose the use of his arm and hand permanently. Or lose his arm, even.

It took time. And then it took more time to get in

touch with Professor Appleby in Brisbane and discuss what was going on.

Finally, Sam picked up the phone again. This time it was to call Jack.

'Is that supply plane still here?'

'Long gone, I'm afraid.'

'Can we get it to turn around? I've got a patient who needs evacuation to Brisbane urgently.'

'No can do, mate. They wouldn't have enough fuel on board. Want me to activate a rescue plane from Cairns?'

'Yeah… Tell them we'll only need a pilot, though. I want to travel with this guy myself and keep an eye on him.'

'No problem. I'll do that right now.'

'Thanks.'

'And Sam, while I've got you on the phone, can you let Anahera know that I'll need her on call in case we get a chopper mission?'

'What?' It took a sharp shake of his head for Sam to shift his attention from the problem he was already dealing with. 'Where's Lia?'

'She's long gone, too.'

'*Sorry?*' Surely he hadn't heard that correctly. 'What did you say?'

'I sent her off with the supply plane. She said she had some family emergency going on.'

Sam was stunned into silence. This was totally unexpected. Unbelievable, even.

It was also totally unprofessional. She was upset about something that he'd said so she'd just run away? Lied in order to find an excuse?

Or did she really have a family emergency? The last time he'd thought of her as being unprofessional had been when she'd been doing all that texting about her brother Nico, who had cancer and was just starting his first round of chemotherapy. Had something gone wrong?

At precisely the same time as he'd inadvertently accused her of stealing his money?

That would be a bit far-fetched.

Ending his call to Jack, Sam found himself pacing the staffroom.

No. What was really far-fetched was thinking that a meaningful relationship could have magically appeared in the form of a FIFO medic. There hadn't been anything real there. Not for Lia, anyway. She'd said so—right before she'd run away.

How could he have been so stupid?

He'd broken the rule and he deserved whatever consequences came from it, but he wasn't going to waste any more time thinking about it right now. He had too much to do.

Striding from the staffroom, he went in search of Anahera. He found her outside chatting to Manu, the hospital porter, who was raking up some of the debris the cyclone had left behind in the garden.

'We need to get another cast back on Felix. There's a plane being dispatched from Cairns and I want him ready for transport and up at the airfield, waiting for it.'

'I'll get set up.'

'Get Caroline to help, too. Jack wants you on standby in case there's a chopper callout.'

'What?' Anahera's eyes widened. 'What's happened to Lia? Is she sick?'

'No. Gone. That's something else. Can you find someone to pack her things and take the bag up to the airfield?

We're going to drop that at Brisbane Hospital, as well, so she can pick it up sometime.'

'I don't understand…' Anahera was looking shocked. 'What's happened?'

'Family emergency, apparently.' Sam was turning away. He had to step around Manu, who was scooping up leaves to put in his wheelbarrow now.

'What's *that*?' Thankfully, Anahera seemed to have been distracted from asking any further questions about Lia. She moved past Sam and pushed her hand into the pile of damp leaves in the wheelbarrow. 'Look…this isn't that envelope you were looking for, is it?'

Soggy but still intact, it was indeed the envelope. Sam took it from Anahera. The ink of Pita's name had run in the rain, as if someone had been holding it and crying.

And all Sam could think about was the look on Lia's face when he'd said that horrible thing…

You didn't make any secret of it being why you came here in the first place, did you, Lia? For the money?

He'd screwed up. He'd hurt Lia and he felt sick about it.

It didn't matter that his past had programmed him to be suspicious. Lia was as different from Vicky as it was possible to be, but his brain had somehow ignored that fact and let his mouth run away with itself. Consequences were circling like vultures and would descend to pick at his flesh as soon as he didn't have something concrete to hold up as a barrier, but he did have something.

A patient who needed a great deal of care if he wasn't going to lose an unacceptable degree of his quality of life.

It was later, as the plane took off from Wildfire Island, that Sam realised there would only be a certain number of times he could take his patient's blood pressure and check the limb baselines on his injured arm. There was going to be way too much time for his thoughts to head to where they were so determined to go.

Back to Lia.

She'd made this trip herself such a short time ago. What had she been thinking as she'd taken off and circled over the islands? Had she been able to pick out his own island? It did look like an angel with her wings folded. The name would be perfect but would he be able to use it now or would it always remind him that he'd wrecked the best thing that had ever happened to him?

The lump in his throat made it hard to swallow.

Has she seen that yacht moored off Wildfire Island that looked a bit like his own? Had she thought about what she was leaving behind?

Had she thought about *him*?

She couldn't stop thinking about Sam.

Oh, for a while it had seemed easy enough. It had been a scene of typical Roselli family chaos with her surprise homecoming. Adriana had burst into tears, of course, and kept interrupting conversations to wrap Lia in her arms or pinch her cheeks. Angel wouldn't let her out of her sight. Nico wasn't feeling great but it was Lia's reassurance that the side effects of the chemo were worth it that he'd been waiting to hear. As a bonus, her father was looking happier than she'd seen him in ages. He'd been for a job interview that day, he told her. He wouldn't hear anything before tomorrow but he was hopeful. Adriana was already preparing for a family celebration and phone calls were going back and forth as she issued invitations to Lia's siblings who weren't still living in the family house.

There'd been a bit of a blip in distraction when her

mother had announced that Carla and Dino and their three children would be coming to join them for dinner tomorrow. She'd felt a pang of something like jealousy but a lot more poignant.

Carla had known she'd found 'the one'. So had Dino. And they'd gone on to find such happiness in their marriage.

But how often did a fairytale like that happen in real life?

Had she really believed it had happened to *her*?

Telling stories of her adventures made things even harder as the evening wore on.

'You were *underneath* a house blown over by the cyclone? All by yourself? *Mamma mia…*'

'I wasn't by myself. I was working with one of the doctors from the hospital. Sam.'

'Nice name.' The nudge from Fiona's elbow was meaningful. 'Was he good looking?'

'I guess…' Lia had to block the intimate detail with which Sam's face filled her mind. That unruly sun-bleached hair. Those gorgeous eyes. The texture of the skin on his jaw when he needed a shave and how different it was to that silky, soft spot on his neck. The shape of his lips when he smiled or…or when he was about to kiss her…

'Is he married?'

'Yep.' Well, that was the truth, wasn't it? He *was* married. Once.

And he'd been hurt and every cell in Lia's body had tried to send the message that she would never hurt him.

That she loved him far too much for that to ever be allowed to happen.

Her throat closed up at that point. She had to close her eyes to force the thoughts away.

'You're tired,' Adriana declared. 'And no wonder, with all that dangerous stuff you've been doing. Get to bed, *cara*.'

'You don't have to go to work tomorrow, do you?' Fiona asked.

'I don't think so. They're not expecting me back yet. I'll call Bruce in the morning and...'

And she'd have to think up a much better explanation for her early return than the one her family had been happy to accept.

'So you could come with me, then?'

Lia opened her eyes to find Fiona grinning at her. She had Angel on her lap and she cuddled her daughter. 'How good is that? Aunty Lia's going to come with us.'

'Come where?'

'Angel's hospital appointment. I need someone to come with me and help with the driving and wheel-chair and everything. Dad needs to be here in case he's called in for another interview or something. Nico said he would but he's not feeling that great and you know what Mamma's like around hospitals. Guy's driving is... well...'

Lia held up her hand before an insult sparked off an argument. 'Of course I'll come. I'd love to.'

The more she had to do during the daytime, the better. The nights were going to be the worst because there'd be no distraction from where her thoughts were so determined to go. Back to Sam.

It hadn't been real, she reminded herself.

So why did it hurt *so* much?

* * *

It was the little girl in the wheelchair that Sam noticed first.

Yeah…right. As if the very shapely bottom stretching a close-fitting pair of jeans wouldn't have caught any red-blooded male eye, as the woman beside the wheelchair crouched to pick up a toy the child had dropped.

At least he raised his line of sight a little as she stood up, now caught by the fall of dark hair that reached the waistband of the jeans.

Something big clenched inside Sam's chest.

It looked just like Lia's hair when it was loose.

The woman was the same height as Lia, too. And her body was just as stunning.

Sam's steps faltered as the penny finally dropped.

'Lia?'

She turned so fast it made her hair swing. For a heart-beat he could swear he saw joy light up her features but then the shutters came down. There was no hint of a smile on her face.

'Sam. What on earth are you doing here?'

'I brought Felix over yesterday. He had some nerve damage that was getting worse and we couldn't do any-thing about it on Wildfire. I rang Graham Appleby and he said to bring him over immediately. It was too late for me to fly back by the time he'd been assessed and then Graham invited me to stay and watch the surgery this morning. I…' His words trailed away. He'd been talking too fast, hadn't he, and it was beginning to sound like he was making excuses for being in Lia's part of the world.

As if he would never have come voluntarily.

To see her or something.

Lia didn't even seem particularly interested. Her tone was very polite. 'How is Felix now?'

'He should make a full recovery. The surgery was amazing. I suspect you were right when you said that Professor Appleby was the best around.'

'Mmm…' Lia wasn't meeting his gaze. She was staring at something else.

'Is that *my* backpack?'

'Oh…yes. Jack asked me to bring it. He reckoned it would be easier for you to collect from here than anywhere else. I was just going to ask at Reception if it would be possible for them to look after it and…and here you are…'

'Yes. I came in with my sister to go to an occupational therapy appointment Angel had.' Lia stretched out her hand to take the pack. 'Thanks.'

She looked up as she took the bag and the connection hit Sam like a solid force. She knew he was thinking of that time on the beach together when he'd decided to name his island after her niece. Just before the sex that had been so mind-blowing that neither of them had minded the discomfort of the sand and bits of driftwood beneath them.

And she was hurting. Badly. He could feel that just as clearly and it cut through him like a knife.

He'd hurt her. The very least he could do was apologise but the crowded reception area of a large hospital was hardly the place.

Lia looked as if she would rather be a million miles away and another tall, dark-haired woman was rushing towards them, looking upset.

'Oh, God… Lia… You're not going to believe this. I can't start the car. I must have left the lights on and the battery's completely dead.'

'We'll ring Dad. He can come and jump-start us.'

'That'll take hours. Angel's tired enough as it is.'

'I could give you a lift home,' Sam offered. 'I've got a rental and I've missed the only flight that would have got me home today because the surgery took longer than expected. I'll have to reschedule one for the morning.'

The woman was staring at him. And then she turned her head to stare at Lia.

Lia sighed. 'This is Sam Taylor, one of the doctors from Wildfire Island. Sam, this is my sister Fiona. Angel's mum.'

Sam shook Fiona's hand. Then he stepped around the wheelchair so he could see the little girl's face.

'Hello, chicken. You must be Angel.'

She'd dropped her toy again so Sam crouched to pick it up. From the corner of his eye he could see the nonverbal communication going on between the sisters. Clearly, he had made an impression on Fiona Roselli but Lia wasn't playing. She looked uninterested. No. Worse than that. She was looking…angry.

The toy was an oversized stuffed clownfish and Sam made it swim towards Angel's arms.

'Bloop, bloop, bloop…'

Angel's mouth stretched into a grin wide enough to rival Lia's and her laughter was loud.

'Again,' she said, her words clearly difficult to enunciate. 'Do it again…'

This time he made it swim close enough for her to catch. Then he straightened and looked directly at Lia.

'Let me take you home,' he said quietly. 'Please?'

She held his gaze for only a moment before looking away. Had she seen how important this suddenly was for him? A chance to apologise? To try and put things right?

'That would be *awesome*,' Fiona said. 'Dad can bring

one of the boys back to get the car later. Tomorrow, even.'
She elbowed her sister. 'Say yes, Lia. I really, really don't
want to be stuck here for hours, trying to keep Angel
happy. You know how cranky she can get when she's
bored. You have to say yes.'

'We wouldn't get the wheelchair into a rental car.'

'It's an SUV,' Sam said quietly. 'It wouldn't be a problem.'

Again, her gaze grazed his. Angel looked up at the
adults around her and then threw her fish toy as far as
she could.

'Again,' she demanded.

But it was Lia who stooped to pick up the toy. Her face
was as tight as her voice as she looked up again.

'Fine,' she said. 'You can take us home. But only if
you're sure it's no bother.' She was turning away already.
'I'll go and get Angel's car seat.'

Fiona's eyes widened at her sister's tone. And then she
looked at Sam and frowned. She had caught the under-
current that something was going on here. Obviously, Lia
hadn't told her family the real reason she'd left her FIFO
post early but how long would it take for them to figure
it out? Women, in particular, were so good at picking up
on that kind of thing.

Sam swallowed. Was he about to step from the frying
pan into the fire? What if the truth came out and he found
himself facing the wrath of the entire Roselli family?

It was too late to back out now. And he didn't want
to. This was a consequence and one he was more than
prepared to face up to, if it meant he had a chance to
talk to Lia.

'It's no bother,' he said. 'I'll bring the car round to
the door.'

CHAPTER ELEVEN

IT WAS THE best thing that could have happened, being this close to Sam again.

It was also the worst thing that could have happened.

Lia's heart and her head were locked in a furious argument.

How could you possibly have agreed to this? the voice in her head was shouting. *You're stuck in a car with him, sitting close enough to touch. You have to listen to the sound of his voice. See his hands on the steering wheel, and you'll be thinking of what it feels like to be touched by those hands every time you catch sight of them. You can smell him, for heaven's sake. That wonderful, slightly musky scent that isn't any aftershave—it's the smell of the man you're stupidly still in love with...*

How could you possibly not *have agreed to this?*

It wasn't exactly a voice in her heart. More a feeling. An overwhelming one that was hard to put into words.

You saw that look in his eyes. He knows he's hurt you. He wants to fix things...

Angel, bless her, had decreed that Lia was to sit in the back seat beside her. Fiona was happy enough to take the front passenger seat after helping Sam stow the wheelchair, and then she was kept busy giving him directions to get through the city traffic. For a while Lia's head was appeased somewhat. This wouldn't take too long, it decided. He would drop them off and they'd say goodbye and that would be that. It would all be over. He'd probably apologise and maybe they'd agree that they would stay in touch. Stay friends…

But then Angel fell asleep and the traffic thinned enough for Fiona to become interested in other things.

'It must be like being on holiday permanently—living on a tropical island.'

'Not really,' Sam told her. 'The setting and the climate become normal after a while. I work, just the same as I would if I lived in a place like this. We've got a huge catchment area to look after and it's really spread out. We have clinics and emergencies on lots of islands and the hospital is almost always busy. Hectic, sometimes.'

Like it had been as the danger from that cyclone had died down, Lia remembered. She'd seen him, again and again, moving through the crowd of people who'd needed his medical expertise or sometimes just his reassurance. She'd been so aware of how much a part of this place he was. How much he was respected. And loved. And it had been at the end of that hectic, exhausting day that she'd known she was falling in love with Sam. That it had already happened, in fact, and nothing was ever going to change the way she felt about this man.

'We're often short of staff,' Sam continued. 'And we have to do a lot of extra stuff, like run laboratory tests ourselves. Plus, I'm involved in research. Right now we're rolling out clinical trials for a new encephalitis vaccine, which is really exciting…'

He sounded so passionate about his job. So sincere.

But her feelings *had* changed, Lia reminded herself.

The shock of being accused of only being interested in his money. Of—almost—being accused of stealing it…

He didn't really accuse you of stealing his money, her heart whispered. *And after the disaster of his marriage, why wouldn't he have been suspicious of a woman who'd made no secret that money was important in her life?*

'Do you have physiotherapists at your hospital?' Fiona sounded excited.

'Only a visiting one. Lots of our specialist staff just come in once a fortnight or so to run clinics.' Sam turned his head to glance at Fiona. 'Why do you ask?'

'I've almost finished my training. I'm going to graduate as a physiotherapist soon, thanks to Lia.'

'Hardly.' It was the first time Lia had spoken since this car ride had begun. She had to clear her throat because it felt clogged—with tears that were trying to form? 'You did all the hard work yourself.'

'But I couldn't have even thought about going back to school unless you'd moved home to help look after Angel. You pretty much gave up your own life, apart from your job.'

The sound Lia made was supposed to be laughter. 'I have no life apart from my job. I love my job.'

'Me, too,' Fiona agreed. 'And wouldn't it be awesome to be able to go and do it in a tropical paradise? Maybe I could be a visiting physio for Wildfire hospital.'

'Maybe you could.' But Sam's voice was wary.

'I'd love living on an island. Does your wife love it?'

'Sorry?'

'Lia said you were married.'

Lia cringed. She held her breath in the long silence that followed. She stared at Angel, trying to will her to wake up and distract everybody, but the little girl was sound asleep.

'I *was* married,' Sam said finally. 'A long time ago. It…didn't work out.'

'Ohh…' It was a meaningful sound and Fiona made it worse by craning her neck to turn and glare at Lia.

Lia turned and stared out of her window. She turned back after it seemed like enough time had passed to move on, only to catch Sam's gaze in the rear-vision mirror.

The silent communication was eloquent.

Did I really deserve that? To be reminded of the worst time of my life?

Yes. There was still a flash of that anger that came from feeling so betrayed. Maybe he hadn't really accused her of theft but he'd made it sound like he was comparing her to his ex-wife. That the possibility existed that she, too, couldn't be trusted.

No. He'd shared something private with her and she hadn't respected that. But she'd been protecting herself. It was far too raw to be ready to share what had gone on between herself and Sam so she'd had to put her sister off the scent.

Now she'd made things worse and the silence in the car was very awkward. Fiona clearly knew that there was something not being said. Something huge. To her credit, she did try and change the subject.

'Isn't it great that Dad got called back for another interview? Being short-listed must be a good sign. I *so* hope he gets this job.'

'Your dad's out of work?' Sam sounded concerned.

'Has been for months.'

'That must be tough.'

'You're not wrong there,' Fiona confided. 'Our family would have sunk financially if it wasn't for Lia.'

Lia was cringing again. How much worse could this get? They were going to talk about *money*? She could hear his voice.

Money's so important to you, isn't it, Lia?

You didn't make any secret of it being why you came here in the first place, did you, Lia? For the money?

This was her fault as much as Sam's, wasn't it? She'd set herself up for the mistrust and then she'd run away without even trying to sort it out.

Was it possible that Sam was hurting as much as she was?

But he hadn't come to see her. He'd come with a patient. He'd been going to leave her backpack at the reception desk.

Fiona's voice was only a background buzz.

'Government help only goes so far, you know, especially when you've got a disabled kid in the family.'

'I can imagine.'

'That's why Lia took the job on your island. Mamma nearly had a heart attack when she heard about it but Lia really wanted the extra money, and you know why?'

'No,' Sam said very quietly. 'I don't.'

'Well, there's these new-generation callipers that are beyond anything the government will cover because they cost a bomb, but they look like exactly what Angel needs to be able to learn to walk. Oh...turn at the next left. We're almost home.'

He should have known.

Okay, so money was important to Lia but it wasn't for anything remotely selfish.

This gorgeous, incredibly smart, astonishingly courageous and passionate woman was devoting her life—and probably a large proportion of what she earned—to the people she loved.

Her family.

And *what* a family it was…

Sam was mobbed as soon as he'd parked his rented SUV in front of the sprawling old house with its wide veranda and open doors.

There were any number of people to help get Angel and all her accessories inside. To thank him for rescuing Fiona and Lia from their transport issues. The noise was overwhelming, in fact, and there were far too many names to try and remember. There were arguments going on, and not just between the young children who were running around.

'I'll take the chair.'

'Give it a rest, Nico. You're sick, remember?'

'Oh, let Guy do it. It's about time he did *something* useful around here.'

'*Fiona*. I heard that. Don't talk about your brother like that.'

'Fish. *Fish*…' Angel seemed to be well rested from her sleep in the car and was beaming at everyone.

'Dinner's ready. What's taking everybody so long?' Wiping her hands on her apron, the matriarch of this enormous family had finally pushed her way to the front of the group. 'Who are you?'

'Sam Taylor, Mrs Roselli.'

'He's a doctor, Mamma.' Fiona pulled another bag from the back of the car. Lia's backpack. 'He's the one Lia's being working with on the island.'

'What's he doing here, then?'

'He's Lia's friend, Mamma. And he was kind enough to give us a lift home.'

'It was a coincidence,' Sam put in. 'I happened to be at the hospital because I'd come over with a patient. It was…just lucky…'

He turned his head to where Lia was settling Angel back into her wheelchair. She probably didn't think it was lucky. But now she was surrounded by her family. Protected. The chances of being able to talk to her had just got a lot more remote.

'I'd better get going,' Sam said.

'*What?* Nonsense. You're staying for dinner. Come…' Lia's mother had a grip on his arm now. 'It's getting cold. Everybody come… Is this a celebration or what?'

Lia had straightened abruptly. 'We're celebrating? Dad? Did you get the job?'

'I start tomorrow.'

'Oh…' Lia flew into her father's arms. 'I'm so happy for you.'

The mob of people were moving and Sam had no choice but to go with them.

Down an overgrown path at the side of the house. Round a corner into a courtyard beneath a pergola that was smothered by a rampant grapevine that obscured many of the fairy-lights entwined with it. In the centre of the courtyard was a massive rustic-looking table that was laden with platters of food, bottles of wine and baskets of bread. At least a dozen large candles cast a warm glow over a scene that smelled as good as it looked.

'Sit,' Lia's father ordered. 'Here, at the head of the table. You are our guest. Lia…come and sit beside your friend.'

Sam was still having trouble putting names to faces.

Fiona sat on the end of one of the long benches by the table, with Angel's wheelchair pulled up beside her. The small children squeezed in beside their parents. Carla and…Dino? Nico was easy to recognise because he was quieter than everyone else here and a bit too pale, but he'd forgotten who the young man was who had ear buds dangling around his neck, and there was another girl who had the same dark hair and eyes as Lia and Fiona. She was texting on her phone and it made Sam smile because he remembered Lia doing that when it wasn't appropriate, too. A poignant smile because he'd been wrong in the assumptions he'd made. But he'd apologised on the beach later that day, and look what that had led to…

Without thinking, he turned his head to where Lia was sitting quietly beside him.

'I'm sorry,' he said softly.

'What for?' The noise around the table as everyone helped themselves to food and admonished small children meant that nobody could hear these quiet words. Lia's sidelong glance was still full of hurt. Desperate, almost. 'Meeting me or losing your money?'

'It wasn't lost. The envelope was found under the hedge. Where we'd been resuscitating Keoni on your first day, remember?'

Lia was reaching out to accept a huge dish from one of her brothers.

'You have to try this,' she said loudly. 'Mamma's lasagne is the best there is.' She ladled some of the mix of pasta, meat and cheese onto his plate. 'And, of course I remember,' she added, but her voice was disconcertingly cool. 'I'm glad it turned up.'

Sam took a salad bowl coming from the other side of the table. 'And I could never be sorry about meeting you,' he said. 'Not in a million years.' He passed the salad bowl to Lia but still kept his hands on it as she took hold of it. The tips of her fingers were touching his. 'I'm sorry I said something so stupid. That let you believe something that isn't true.'

Her eyes were huge. 'What isn't true?'

Was anybody noticing what was going on at the end of this table? The noise level suggested not but Sam couldn't let this chance slip past in any case. It might be the only one he got.

'That none of it was real,' he said softly. 'It felt real to me. It still does.'

It *was* real.

Lia could see the love in Sam's eyes. She could feel how huge it was. How solid.

She wanted to throw her arms around his neck. To forgive and forget everything about the horrible hours since she'd walked out of the staffroom at Wildfire hospital. To start again, with this new understanding of each other that would bring them so much closer and give them a foundation that had no secrets.

But that needed complete honesty.

And trust.

'But you were right,' she said, in little more than a whisper. 'Money *is* important to me.'

They were both ignoring their food. Sam's gaze still had hold of Lia's and there was a gentle curve to the corners of his mouth.

'Only because of what you need it for. Your family. I get that, Lia. I know how blessed you are.'

'Eat…' The command came from Adriana Roselli,

who was reaching for a basket of bread. 'What's wrong with my food? Here…you need bread.'

'Nothing's wrong, Mamma. It's delicious.' Lia scooped up a forkful of the lasagne. 'It's my favourite.'

'Mine, too,' Sam said. 'Now…'

He was grinning and everybody laughed. And then they started firing questions at Sam.

'How come it was Lia who went under the squashed house?' Guy asked. 'Wasn't that dangerous?'

'I didn't want her to,' Sam said. 'It *was* dangerous. But she was the one who was small enough to get through the gap and…and she wasn't going to let me stop her.'

'That's our Lia.' Nico nodded.

'Sam came as far as he could,' Lia put in. 'There was a tiny baby we needed to get out and Sam put her inside his shirt to keep her safe.'

The memory made her eyes fill and any remnants of anger she'd been trying to hold on to evaporated.

She loved this man. With all her heart and soul.

Her appetite had gone. Instead, she sat quietly, watching her family as they got to know Sam a little better. They were impressed. Ready to welcome him as more than a guest?

I know how blessed you are…

There had been a note of longing in Sam's voice. It took her back to that moment she'd been with him when she'd been holding Hika's baby and Sefina's little boy in her arms. When she'd felt the loneliness of what was missing in Sam's life and had wanted to hold him close to her heart and never let him go. When she'd known that, as far as her heart was concerned, he already was a part of her own family.

Angel's head was drooping, down at the far end of

this long table, and Lia's father pushed his plate away and stood up.

'Let me take her. I'll put her to bed.'

It took time to undo the safety harness that kept Angel in her wheelchair and Lia could sense that Sam was about to get up to help lift her.

'They can manage,' she said quietly.

'But I want to help.'

'I know. But there's nothing you need to do. We're used to it.'

'There is something I could do.' Sam caught Lia's hand. 'Let me get those new callipers for her. The ones that might help her walk.'

Lia stiffened. 'We don't need your money, Sam.' She pulled her hand free of his. Pushed herself to her feet.

Were they back to square one?

Sam stood up, as well.

And everybody else froze. For probably the first time in history the entire Roselli family was completely silent, staring at Sam and Lia, who were staring at each other.

'Our family takes care of itself,' Lia said. 'We don't need charity.'

'I know that. But…I'm part of this, Lia. You know I am…'

'*Mamma mia…*' The whisper was loud enough for all to hear. 'What's going on here?'

Sam turned to face the whole family. Lia's father was standing behind her mother, with Angel in his arms. Fiona was standing beside him, her hand covering her open mouth. Her voice was muffled.

'I *knew* it… Lia, you have some explaining to do.'

'No.' Sam cleared his throat. 'It's me who has some explaining to do. Mr and Mrs Roselli, I haven't known your daughter for very long but I've learned a lot of things about her. I've learned that she loves her family so much she'll do whatever it takes to support you all. I've learned that she's the bravest and smartest person I've ever met and, most importantly, I've learned that…' he turned from the table to look directly at Lia '… I love her. That I always will. That she's the person I want to spend the rest of my life with. The woman I intend to marry if I'm lucky enough that she wants that, too.'

Lia was drowning in his eyes. Bursting with a joy that was going to escape as tears at any moment. Her mother was already crying—she could hear it.

'I love you, too, Sam. You're already a part of my family. I can't imagine the rest of my life without you in it.'

'Awesome,' Guy said. 'Can we come and see that squashed house? And the mine that exploded?'

'Shut up, Guy,' someone hissed.

'I knew it,' Fiona said again. She was crying, too. 'Oh, I'm so happy for you, Lia. It's about time…'

Angel had woken up in her grandfather's arms. She beamed at Sam.

'Fish…' she demanded.

'No…' Adriana was mopping her face with the corner of her apron. 'No, no, no…this is all too soon. Too fast.'

Carla and Dino were grinning.

'Where have we heard that before?' Carla said.

Lia took Sam's hand in hers and turned to face her family. She smiled at Carla but her lips wobbled. Then her gaze took in her whole family.

'We have heard it before and you all know it can be true. It's true this time, too.'

'What is?' Sam sounded bewildered.

Lia turned back to him. She let go of his hand so that

she could wrap her arms around his neck. Could stand on tiptoe and kiss him in front of everybody.

'When you know, you just know,' she said softly.

'Oh…' Sam's lips touched hers so gently she could feel them moving as he spoke. 'Yes. That *is* true… *I* know…'

'So do I.'

And then there was no way either of them could say anything else as their kiss took them into a space that only they could share. They could hear the joyous sound of a family celebrating around them as they welcomed their newest member.

They could feel the love.

But this…this was all their own and it was real.

Real enough to last forever.

* * * * *

A CHILD TO
OPEN THEIR HEARTS

BY
MARION LENNOX

Published in Great Britain 2016
By Mills & Boon, an imprint of HarperCollins*Publishers*
1 London Bridge Street, London, SE1 9GF

© 2016 Marion Lennox

ISBN: 978-0-263-25441-9

Our policy is to use papers that are natural, renewable and recyclable
products and made from wood grown in sustainable forests.
The logging and manufacturing processes conform to the legal
environmental regulations of the country of origin.

Printed and bound in Spain
by CPI, Barcelona

Dear Reader,

This is the sixth romance in the Wildfire Island Docs series, and it marks the end of one of the most dramatic, exotic series I've ever been involved in. Wildfire Island is a tropical paradise. Our heroes and heroines are our ideal lovers, the most skilled, the most gorgeous and the most fun doctors, nurses and paramedics...Oh, and did I mention the most sexy?

Meredith Webber, Alison Roberts and I have loved co-creating our characters, our worlds, our romances. Each is a stand-alone love story, but together we believe they're awesome. Linked stories push our creative boundaries, and they deepen our friendship in the process.

Max and Hettie's story tugged on my heartstrings as I wrote it, and I hope you'll be as touched by it as I've been. I love how much they deserve their happy ending. Let me know if you enjoy it—write to me at marion@marionlennox.com. If you love it as much as we do...who knows? We may be recruiting more medics for Wildfire!

Meanwhile, happy reading.

Marion

My books in this series are dedicated to Andy, whose help and friendship during my writing career has been beyond measure. I've been so proud to call you my friend.

Marion Lennox has written over a hundred romance novels, and is published in over a hundred countries and thirty languages. Her international awards include the prestigious RITA® Award (twice) and the *RT Book Reviews* Career Achievement Award for 'a body of work which makes us laugh and teaches us about love'. Marion adores her family, her kayak, her dog, and lying on the beach with a book someone else has written. Heaven!

Books by Marion Lennox

Mills & Boon Medical Romance

The Surgeon's Doorstep Baby
Miracle on Kaimotu Island
Gold Coast Angels: A Doctor's Redemption
Waves of Temptation
A Secret Shared...
Meant-to-Be Family
From Christmas to Forever?
Saving Maddie's Baby

Mills & Boon Cherish

A Bride for the Maverick Millionaire
Sparks Fly with the Billionaire
Christmas at the Castle
Nine Months to Change His Life
Christmas Where They Belong

Visit the Author Profile page
at millsandboon.co.uk for more titles.

Praise for
Marion Lennox

'Marion Lennox's *Rescue at Cradle Lake* is simply magical, eliciting laughter and tears in equal measure. A keeper.'
—*RT Book Reviews*

CHAPTER ONE

THIS COULD BE a disaster instead of a homecoming. He could be marooned at sea until after his daughter's wedding.

Max wasn't worrying yet, though. Things would be chaotic on Wildfire Island after the cyclone, but the weather had eased and Sunset Beach was a favourite place for the locals to walk. If the rip wasn't so fierce he could swim ashore. He couldn't, but eventually someone would stroll to the beach, see his battered boat and send out a dinghy.

Max Lockhart, specialist surgeon, not-so-specialist sailor, headed below deck and fetched himself a beer. There were worse places to be stuck, he conceded. The *Lillyanna* was a sturdy thirty-foot yacht, and she wasn't badly enough damaged to be uncomfortable. She was now moored in the tropical waters off Wildfire Island. Schools of tiny fish glinted silver as they broke the surface of the sparkling water. The sun was warm. He had provisions for another week, and in the lee of the island the sea was relatively calm.

But he *was* stuck. The waters around the island were still a maelstrom. The cliffs that formed the headland above where he sheltered were being battered. To try and

round them to get to Wildfire Island's harbour would be
suicidal, and at some time during the worst of the cyclone
his radio had been damaged and his phone lost overboard.

So now he was forced to rest, but rest, he conceded,
had been the whole idea of sailing here. He needed to
take some time to get his head in order and ready himself to face the islanders.

He also needed space to come to terms with anger
and with grief. How to face his daughter's wedding with
joy when he was so loaded with guilt and sadness he
couldn't get past it?

But rest wouldn't cut it, he decided as he finished his
beer. What he needed was distraction.

And suddenly he had it. Suddenly he could see two
people on the island.

A woman had emerged from the undergrowth and was
walking a dog on the beach. And up on the headland…
another woman was walking towards the cliff edge.

Towards the cliff edge? What the…?

As a kid, Max and his mates had dived off this headland but they'd only dived when the water had been calm.
They'd dared each other to dive the thirty-foot drop. Then
they'd let the rip tug them out to this reef, where they'd
catch their breath for the hard swim back. It had kept
them happy for hours. It had given their parents night-
mares.

For the woman on the headland, though, the nightmare
seemed real. She was walking steadily towards the edge.

Suicide? The word slammed into his head and stayed.

He grabbed his field glasses, one of the few things not
smashed in the storm, and fought to get them focussed.
The woman was young. A crimson shawl was wrapped
around a bundle at her breast. A child?

She was walking purposefully forward, closer to the edge. After the cyclone, the water below was a mass of churning foam. Even as a kid he'd known he had to get a run up to clear the rocks below.

'No!' His yell would be drowned in the wind up there, but he yelled anyway. 'Don't...'

His yell was useless. She reached the cliff edge and walked straight over.

Hettie de Lacey, charge nurse of Wildfire Island's small hospital, rather enjoyed a good storm. It broke the humidity. It cleared the water in the island's lagoons and it made the world seem fresh and new.

This, however, had been more than a good storm. The cyclone had smashed across the island three days ago, causing multiple casualties. Even though most wounds had been minor, the hospital was full to bursting, and Hettie had been run off her feet.

This was the first time she'd managed a walk and some blessed time to herself. Sunset Beach was relatively sheltered, but she was close to the northern tip, where waves flung hard against the headland. The seas out there were huge.

In another life she might have grabbed a surfboard and headed out, she thought, allowing herself a whiff of memory, of an eighteen-year-old Hettie in love with everything to do with the sea.

Including Darryn...

Yeah, well, that was one memory to put aside. How one man could take such a naïve kid and smash her ideals... Smash her life...

'Get over it,' she told herself, and she even smiled at the idea that she should still angst over memories from all those years ago. She'd made herself a great life. She was…mostly happy.

And then her attention was caught.

There was a yacht just beyond the reef. It was a gracious old lady of a yacht, a wooden classic, anchored to the south of The Bird's Nest. The Nest was a narrow rim of rock and coral, a tiny atoll at the end of an underwater reef running out from shore.

The yacht was using the atoll for shelter.

It'd be Max Lockhart, she thought, and the nub of fear she'd been feeling for Caroline dissipated in an instant. Oh, thank heaven. She knew the owner of Wildfire Island was trying to sail here for his daughter's wedding. Max had left Cairns before the cyclone had blown up, and for the last few days Caroline Lockhart, one of Hettie's best nurses, had been frantic. Her father was somewhere out to sea. He'd lost contact three days ago and they had no way of knowing if he'd survived.

She could see him fairly clearly from where she was, but she'd never met him—his few visits to the island during her employment had always seemed to coincide with times when she'd taken leave. But this must be him. The entrance to the harbour was wild so this was probably the safest place he could be.

She went to wave, and then she hesitated. The guy on the yacht—it must be Max—was already waving. And yelling. But not at her. At someone up on the headland?

Intrigued, she headed to the water's edge and looked up. Another islander out for a walk? Max must be stuck, she thought. He'd be wanting to attract attention so someone could send a dinghy out to bring him in. He'd seen someone up on the cliffs?

And then her breath caught in horror. Where the shallows gave way to deep water and the cliffs rose steeply to the headland, the wind still swept in from the cyclone-ravaged sea.

And up on the headland... Sefina Dason.

The woman was thirty feet above her but Hettie would know her anywhere. For the last few days Sefina had been in hospital, battered, not by the cyclone but by her oaf of a husband. She'd had to bring her toddler in with her because no one would care for him, something almost unheard of in this close-knit community.

There'd been whispers...

But this wasn't the time for whispers. Sefina was high on the headland and she was walking with purpose.

She was headed for the edge of the cliff!

And then she turned, just a little, and Hettie saw a bundle, cradled to her breast in a crimson shawl. Her horror doubled, trebled, went off the scale.

Joni!

No! She was screaming, running, stumbling over the rocks as beach gave way to the edges of the reef. *No!*

She could hear the echoes of the guy on the yacht, yelling, too.

But yelling was useless.

Sefina took two steps forward and she was gone.

Max knew the water under the headland like the back of his hand. In good weather this was a calm, still pool, deep and mysterious, bottoming out to coral. It was a fabulous place for kids to hurl themselves off the cliff in a show of bravado. The rip swept in from the north, hit the pool and tugged the divers out to the rocky outcrop he was anchored behind. As kids they'd learned to ride the rip to their advantage, letting it pull them across the shallow reef to the atoll. They'd lie on the rocks and catch their breath, readying themselves for the swim across the rip back to the beach.

But that rip would be fierce today, too strong to swim against. And the water in the pool…would be a whirlpool, he thought, sucking everything down.

All this he thought almost instantly, and as he thought it he was already tearing up the anchor, operating the winch with one hand, gunning the engine with the other.

His mind seemed to be frozen, but instinct was kicking in to take over.

Where would she be hurled out?

He hit the tiller and pushed the throttle to full speed, heading out of the shelter of the atoll, steering the boat as close as he dared to the beach. He couldn't get too close. Sheltered or not, there were still breakers pounding the sand.

There was a woman running along the beach, screaming. The woman with the dog? She'd seen?

But he didn't have time to look at her. He was staring across the maelstrom of white water, waiting for something to emerge. Anything.

He was as close as he could get without wrecking the yacht. As far as he could tell, this was where the rip emerged.

He dropped anchor, knowing he'd be anchoring in sand, knowing there was a chance the boat would be dragged away, but he didn't have time to care.

There… A wisp of crimson cloth… Nothing more, but it had to be enough.

If he was right, she was being tugged to twenty feet forward of the boat.

He'd miss her…

He was ripping his clothes off, tearing. Clothes would drag him down. If he used a lifejacket he could never swim fast enough.

He had so little chance the thing was almost futile.

He saw the wisp of crimson again, and he dived.

Sefina.

Joni.

Hettie was screaming but she was screaming inside. She had no room for anything else. Where…?

She'd swum here. There was a rip, running south. Hettie could swim well. Surfing had once been her life, but to swim against the rip in these conditions…

The guy on the boat had seen. If she could grab Sefina and tow her with the rip, maybe he could help.

A mother and a toddler?

She couldn't think like that.

As a teenager she'd trained as a lifeguard, hoping for a holiday job back when she'd lived at Bondi. Her instructor's voice slammed back now. *'Look to your own safety before you look to help someone in the surf.'*

This was crazy. Past dangerous.

Oh, but Joni… He was fifteen months old and she'd cradled him to sleep for the past few nights. And Sefina… Battered Sefina, with no one to turn to.

Forget the instructors. Her clothes were tossed onto the sand. 'Stay,' she yelled at Bugsy, and she was running into the waves regardless.

The rip was so strong Max was swept south the moment he hit the water. Anything in that pool would be tugged straight out, past the reef and out to sea.

He surfaced, already being pulled.

But Max had swum like a fish as a kid, and for the past few years gym work and swimming had sometimes seemed the only thing that had kept him sane.

He couldn't swim against the rip but if he headed diagonally across he might collide with...with what he hoped to find. That slip of crimson.

He cast one long look at the pool, trying to judge where he'd last seen that flash of crimson.

He put his head down and swam.

Was she nuts? Trying to swim in this surf? But if she got past the breakers she only had the rip to contend with. She could deal with the rip, she thought. She knew enough not to panic. The guy on the boat would have seen her. If she could reach Sefina and hold on to her, she could tread water until help came.

Even if the guy hadn't seen her, she was due to go on duty at midday. The staff knew she'd gone for a walk on the beach. If she didn't return they'd come down and find Bugsy, find her clothes... Once the rip dragged her out, she could tread water and hope...

Yeah, very safe, she thought grimly as she dived through another wave. *Not*.

What would she do if she reached them? The lifeguard part of her was already playing out scenarios.

The quickest way to kill yourself is to put yourself within reach of someone who's drowning. They'll pull you down as they try to save themselves.

There was her instructor again.

Sefina wouldn't try to save herself, though. Sefina wanted to die.

Sefina...

She'd known how unhappy the girl was, but in the post-cyclone chaos all Hettie had been able to give the young woman had been swift hugs between periods of imperative medical need. She'd promised her she was safe in the hospital. She'd promised they'd sort things out when things had settled.

She hadn't realised time had been so achingly short.

Hettie surfaced from the last breaker and looked around wildly. The rip was stronger than she'd thought. Maybe she'd missed them.

And then she saw someone else in the water, swimming strongly across the rip. The guy from the boat?

There went her source of help if she got into trouble, she thought grimly. All of them in the water? This was breaking every lifesaving rule, but it was too late to back out now. She was watching the rim of the foam where the deep pool ended and the relative calm began.

There! A sliver of crimson.

She must have shouted because the swimming guy raised his head. She waved and pointed.

He raised a hand in silent acknowledgement and they both put their heads down and swam.

He could see her now, or he could see the swirl of crimson shawl she'd wrapped around her body. If he could just get closer...

The pull of the rip was hauling him backwards. By rights it should've propelled the woman's body towards him.

Was she stuck on the edge of the reef? Had the shawl snagged?

The rocks were too close to the surface for safety. He should stay well clear...

He didn't.

* * *

This was crazy. Suicidal. She couldn't swim into the foam. She daren't. As it was, the rip was pulling so hard she was starting to doubt her ability to get herself to safety.

A breaker crashed on the rocks and threw a spray of water, blocking her vision. She could see nothing.

With a sob of fear and frustration she stopped trying and let herself be carried outward.

Free from the foam she could tread water. She could look again.

She could see nothing but white. Nothing…

There! Max's hands had been groping blindly in front of him, but the touch of fabric had him grabbing.

He had her, but she was wedged in rocks. He was being washed by breaker after breaker. He couldn't see. He pulled upwards to take a tighter hold—and a child fell free into his arms.

The child must have been clinging, or tied within the shawl. The rip caught them again and they were tugged outwards.

He had a child in his arms. He had no choice but to let himself go. To ride the rip…

He was pushing the child up, rolling onto his back, trying to get the little one into the air. The water was sweeping…

'Here!'

It was a yell and suddenly someone was beside him. A woman, dark-haired, fierce.

'Give him to me. Help Sefina. Please!'

'You can't hold him.' He didn't even know if the child was alive.

Her face was suddenly inches from his, soaking curls

plastered across her eyes, green eyes flashing determination. 'I can. I know what to do. Trust me.'

And what was there in that that made him believe her?

What was there in that that made him thrust the limp little body into her arms and turn once again towards the rocks?

He had to trust her. He had to hope.

Joni was breathing. He'd been limp when he'd been thrust at her, but as she rolled and prepared to breathe for him—yes, she could do it in the water; lifesaver training had been useful—the little one gasped and choked and gasped again.

His eyes were shut, as if he'd simply closed down, ready for death. How many children drowned like this? Thirteen years as a nurse had taught Hettie that when children slipped untended into water they didn't struggle. They drowned silently.

Somehow, though, despite not fighting, Joni must have breathed enough air to survive. As she touched his mouth with her lips he gasped and opened his eyes.

'Joni.' She managed to get his name out, even though she was fighting for breath herself. 'It's okay. Let's get you to the beach.'

His huge brown eyes stared upwards wildly. Joni was fifteen months old, a chubby toddler with beautiful coffee-coloured skin and a tangle of dark curls. He was part islander, part...

Well, that was the problem, Hettie thought, her heart clenching in fear for his mother.

She couldn't do anything for Sefina, though. The sailor—Max?—had handed her Joni and she had to care for him.

Where was he now? she wondered as she trod water. Her first impressions had been of strength, determination, resolution. His face had been almost impassive.

He'd need strength and more if he was swimming back against the reef. The risks...

She couldn't think of him now. Her attention had to be on keeping Joni safe.

Keeping them both safe?

She cupped her hand around Joni's chin and started side-stroking, as hard and fast as she could, willing him to stay limp. The rip was still a problem. Getting back to the beach was impossible. The boat was too close to the breakers, but the atoll at the end of the reef might just be possible. If she could just reach the rocks...

Blessedly Joni stayed limp. *It must be shock*, she thought as she fought the current, but she was thankful for it. He lay still while she towed.

But the rip was strong. She was fighting for breath herself, kicking, using every last scrap of strength she had, but she couldn't do it. She couldn't reach the atoll. It was so near and yet so far.

If she could just keep floating, someone would help, she thought. If she rode the rip out, if she could hold on to Joni...

But if he struggled...

She had no choice. The rip was too strong to fight.

She held him as far out of the water as she could and let herself be carried out to sea.

He had her. For what it was worth, he had her, but she was dead. He could see the head injury. He could see the way her head floated limply.

She must have crashed onto the rocks, he thought.

She'd stepped straight down instead of diving outwards. Death would have been instantaneous. It had been a miracle that the child had stayed with her.

He had her free of the reef, but what to do now? He couldn't get her to the beach. There was no way he could fight the rip. It was carrying them out fast, towards the atoll. Did he have enough strength to get them both there?

By himself there'd be no problem, but holding this woman...

He couldn't.

She was dead. Let her go.

He couldn't do that, either. A part of him was still standing at his son's gravesite.

A part of him was remembering burying his wife, all those years ago.

Somewhere, someone loved this woman. To not have a chance to say goodbye... It would have killed him.

Holding on to her might kill him. He couldn't keep fighting for both of them.

Despite the strength of the rip, the water he was in was relatively calm. He was fighting to get across the current but he paused for a moment in his fight to get a bearing. To see...

And what he saw made him rethink everything. The woman he'd given the child to still held him, but they were drifting fast, so fast they'd miss the atoll. They were being pulled to the open sea.

The woman didn't seem to be panicking. She had the child in the classic lifesaver hold. She seemed to know her stuff, but she wasn't strong enough. In minutes she'd be past the atoll and she'd be gone.

A woman and a child, struggling for life.

A woman in his arms, for whom life was over.

Triage. Blessedly it slammed back. For just a moment he was a junior doctor again in an emergency room, faced with the decision of which patient to treat first.

No choice.

He gave himself a fraction of a second, a moment where he tugged the woman's body around and faced her. He memorised everything about her so he could describe her, and then, in an aching, tearing gesture that seemed to rip something deep inside, he touched her face. It was a gesture of blessing, a gesture of farewell.

It was all he could do.

He let her go.

She'd never reach it. Her legs simply weren't strong enough to kick against the current.

She was so near and yet so far. She was being pulled within thirty yards of the atoll and yet she didn't have the strength to fight.

If she was swept out… If Max didn't make it… How long before they could expect help?

The child in her arms twisted unexpectedly and she almost lost him. She fought for a stronger hold but suddenly he was fighting her.

'Joni, hush. Joni, stay still…'

But he wasn't listening, wasn't hearing. Who knew what he was thinking?

She was being swept…

And then, blessedly, she was being grabbed herself by the shoulders from behind. She was being held with the swift, sure strength of someone who'd been trained, who knew how to gain control.

Max?

'Let me take him.' It was an order, a curt command that brooked no opposition. 'Get yourself to the atoll.'

'You can't.'

'You're done,' he said, and she knew she was.

'S-Sefina?'

'She's dead. We can't do anything for her. Go. I'm right behind you.'

And Joni was taken from her arms.

Relieving her of her load should have made her lighter. Free. Instead, stupidly, she wanted to sink. She hadn't known how exhausted she was until the load had been lifted.

'Swim,' Max yelled. 'We haven't done this for nothing. Swim, damn you, now.'

She swam.

He could do this. He would do this.

Too many deaths…

It was three short weeks since he'd buried his son. The waste was all around him, and the anger.

Maybe it was Christopher who gave him strength. Who knew?

'Keep still,' he growled, as the little boy struggled. There was no time for reassurance. No time for comfort. But it seemed to work.

The little boy subsided. His body seemed to go limp but he reached up and tucked a fist against Max's throat. As if checking his pulse?

'Yeah, I'm alive,' Max muttered grimly, as he started kicking again against the rip. 'And so are you. Let's keep it that way.'

* * *

Rocks. The atoll was tiny but she'd made it. The last few yards across the rip had taken every ounce of her strength, but she'd done it.

She'd had to do it. If Max and Joni were swept out, someone had to raise the alarm.

She wasn't in any position to raise any alarm right now. It was as much as she could do to climb onto the rocks.

She knew this place. She'd swum out here in good weather. She knew the footholds but her legs didn't want to work. They'd turned to jelly, but somehow she made them push her up the few short steps to the relatively flat rock that formed the atoll's tiny plateau.

Then she sank to her knees.

She wanted—quite badly—to be sick, but she fought it down with a fierceness born of desperation. How many times in an emergency room had she felt this same appalling gut-wrench, at waste, at loss of life, at life-changing injuries? But her training had taught her not to faint, not to throw up, until after a crisis was past. Until she wasn't needed.

There was a crisis now, but what could she do? She wasn't in an emergency room. She wasn't being a pro-fessional.

She was sitting on a tiny rocky outcrop, while out there a sailor fought for a toddler's life.

Was he Max Lockhart?

More importantly, desperately more importantly, where was he? She hadn't been able to look back while she'd fought to get here, but now...

Max... Joni...

She was a strong swimmer but she hadn't been able to fight the rip.

Please... She was saying it over and over, pleading with whomever was prepared to listen. For Joni. For the unknown guy who was risking his life...

Was he Max? Father of Caroline? Owner of this entire island?

Max Lockhart, come home to claim his rightful heritage?

Max Lockhart, risking his life to save one of the islanders who scorned him?

So much pain...

If he died now, how could she explain it to Caroline? For the last three days, when the cyclone had veered savagely and unexpectedly across the path of any boat making its way here from Cairns, Hettie's fellow nurse had lost contact with her father. She'd been going crazy.

How could she tell her he'd been so near, and was now lost? With the child?

Or not. She'd been staring east, thinking that, if anything, he'd be riding the rip, but suddenly she saw him. He was south of the atoll. He must have been swept past but somehow managed to get himself out of the rip's pull. Now he was stroking the last few yards to the rocks.

He still had Joni.

She'd been out of the water now for five minutes. She had her breath back. Blessedly, she could help. She clambered down over the rocks, heading out into the shallows, reaching for Joni.

She had him. They had him.

Safe?

CHAPTER TWO

FOR A WHILE they were too exhausted to speak. They were too exhausted to do anything but lie on the rocks, Joni somehow safe between them.

The little boy was silent, passive…past shock? Maybe she was, too, and as she looked at Max collapsed beside them she thought, *That makes three.*

'S-Sefina,' she whispered.

'Neck,' he managed, and it was enough to tell her what she needed to know.

Oh, God, she should have…

Should have what? Cradled Sefina yesterday as she was cradling Joni now?

Yes, if that's what it would have taken.

If this had happened at a normal time… But it hadn't. Sefina had been admitted into hospital, bashed almost to the point of death, while the cyclone had been building. With the cyclone bearing down on them Hettie hadn't had time to do more than tend to the girl's physical needs.

Afterwards, when there'd been time to take stock and question her, Keanu, the island doctor on duty, had contacted the police. 'I want her husband brought in. With the extent of these injuries it's lucky he didn't kill her.'

It's lucky he didn't kill her…

She remembered Keanu's words and her breath caught on a sob.

Hettie de Lacey was a professional. She didn't cry. She held herself to herself. She coped with any type of trauma her job threw at her.

But she sobbed now, just once, a great heaving gulp that shook her entire body. And then somehow she pulled herself back together. Almost.

Max's arm came over her, over Joni, enfolding them both, and she needed it. She needed his touch.

'You're safe,' he told her. 'And the little one's safe.' And then he added, 'Keep it together. For now, we're all he has.'

It was a reminder. It wasn't a rebuke, though. It was just a fact. She'd been terrified, she was shocked and exhausted, and she still had to come to terms with what had happened, but the child between them had to come first.

And Max himself... He'd swum over those rocks. Over that coral...

She took a couple of deep breaths and managed to sit up. The sun was full out. The storm of the past days was almost gone. Apart from the spray blasting the headland and the massive breakers heading for shore, this could be just a normal day in paradise.

Wildfire Island. The M'Langi isles. This was surely one of the most beautiful places in the world.

The world would somehow settle.

She gathered Joni into her arms and held him tight, crooning softly into his wet curls. He was still wearing a sodden hospital-issue nappy and a T-shirt one of the nurses had found for him in the emergency supplies. It read, incongruously, 'My grandma went to London and all she brought me back was this T-shirt'.

It was totally inappropriate. Joni didn't have a grandma, or not one who'd acknowledge him.

Max had allowed himself a couple of moments of lying full length in the sun, as if he needed its warmth. Of course he did. They all did. But now he, too, pushed himself to sitting, and for the first time she saw his legs.

They'd been slashed on the coral. He had grazes running from groin to toe, as if the sea had dragged him straight across the rocks.

What cost, to try and save Sefina?

He'd saved Joni.

'I never could have got him here,' she whispered, still holding him tight. The toddler was curled into her, as if her body was his only protection from the outside world. 'I never could have saved him without you.'

'Do you know…? Do you know who he is?' Max asked.

'His name is Joni Dason. His mother's name is…was Sefina.'

'A friend?' He was watching her face. 'She was your friend?'

'I… A patient.' And then she hesitated. 'But I was present at Joni's birth. Maybe I was…Sefina's friend. Maybe I'm the only…'

And then she stopped. She couldn't go on.

'I'm Max Lockhart,' Max said, and she managed to nod, grateful to be deflected back to his business rather than having to dwell on her shock and grief.

'I guessed as much when I saw your yacht. Caroline will be so relieved. She's been out of her mind with worry.'

'My boat rolled. I lost my radio and phone three

days ago. Everything that could be damaged by water was damaged.'

'So you've been sitting out here, waiting for someone to notice you?'

'I reached the island last night. It was too risky to try for the harbour, and frankly I wasn't going to push my luck heading to one of the outer islands. So, yes, I've been here overnight but no one's noticed.'

'I noticed.'

'Thank you. You are?'

'Hettie de Lacey. Charge nurse at Wildfire.'

'I'm pleased to meet you, Hettie.' He hesitated and then went on. 'I'm very pleased to meet you. Without both of us… Well, we did the best we could.'

'You're injured. Those cuts need attention.'

'They do,' he agreed. 'I need disinfectant to avoid infection, but the alternative…'

'You never would have saved Joni without swimming over the coral,' she whispered, and once again she buried her face in the little boy's hair. 'Thank you.'

'I would have… I so wanted…'

'Yes,' she said gently. 'But she jumped too close to the rocks for either of us to do anything.'

'Depression?'

'Abuse. A bully for a husband. Despair.'

The bleakness in her voice must have been obvious. He reached out to her then, the merest hint of a touch, a trace of a strong hand brushing her cheek, and why it had the power to ground her, to feed her strength, she didn't know.

Max Lockhart was a big man, in his forties, she guessed, his deep black hair tinged with silver, his strongly boned face etched with life lines. His grey eyes were deep-set and creased at the edges, from weather, from sun, from…life? Even in his boxers, covered with abrasions, he looked…distinguished.

She knew about this man. He'd lost his wife over twenty years ago and he'd just lost his son. Caroline's twin.

'I'm sorry about Christopher,' she said gently, still holding Joni tight, as if holding him could protect him from the horrors around him.

'Caroline told you?'

'That her twin—your son—died three weeks ago? Yes. Caroline and I are fairly…close. She flew to Sydney for the funeral. We thought…we thought you might have come back with her.'

'There was too much to do. There was financial stuff to do with the island. To do with my brother. Business affairs have been on the backburner as Christopher neared the end, but once he was gone they had to be attended to. And then…'

'You thought it might be a good idea to sail out here?'

'I needed a break,' he said simply. 'Time to get myself together. No one warned me of cyclones.'

'It's the tropics,' she said simply. 'Here be dragons.'

'Don't I know it!'

'But we're glad you're back.'

That got her a hard look.

Max Lockhart had inherited the whole of Wildfire Island on the death of his father. The stories of the Lockharts were legion in this place. Max himself had hardly visited the island over the past twenty years, but his brother's presence had made up for it.

Ian Lockhart had bled the island for all it was worth. He'd finally fled three months ago, leaving debt, destruction and despair…

Ian Lockhart. The hatred he'd caused…

She hugged the child in her arms tighter, as if she could somehow keep protecting him.

How could she?

The sun was getting hotter. She was starting to get sunburnt. Sunburn on top of everything else?

She was wearing knickers and bra. But they were her best knickers and bra, though, she thought with sudden dumb gratitude that today of all days she'd decided to wear her matching lace bra and panties.

They were a lot more elegant than the boxers Max was wearing. His boxers were old, faded, and they now sported a rip that made them borderline useless.

'You needn't look,' Max said, and she flashed a look up at him and found he was smiling. And in return she managed a smile back.

Humour… It was a tool used the world over by medical staff, often in the most appalling circumstances. Where laypeople might collapse under strain, staff in emergency departments used humour to deflect despair.

Sometimes you laughed or you broke down, as simple as that, and right now she needed, quite desperately, not to break down. Max was a surgeon, she thought gratefully. Medical. Her tribe. He knew the drill.

'My knickers are more respectable than your knickers,' she said primly, and he choked.

'What? Your knickers are two inches of pink lace.'

'And they don't have a hole in them right where they shouldn't have a hole,' she threw back at him, and he glanced down at himself and swore. And did some fast adjusting.

'Dr Lockhart's rude,' she told Joni, snuggling him

some more, but the little boy was drifting towards sleep. Good, she thought. Children had their own defences.

'My yacht seems to be escaping,' Max said, and she glanced back towards the reef.

It was, indeed, escaping. The anchor hadn't gripped the sand. The yacht was now caught in the rip and heading out to sea.

'One of the fishermen will follow it,' she told him. 'The rip's easy to read. They'll figure where it goes.'

'It'd be good to get to it now.'

'What could a yacht have that a good rock doesn't provide?' she demanded, feigning astonishment. And then she looked at his legs. 'Except maybe disinfectant and dressings. And sunburn cream.'

'And maybe a good strong rum,' he added.

'Trapped on an island with a sailor and a bottle of rum? I don't think so.' She was waffling but strangely it helped. It was okay to be silly.

Silliness helped block the thought of what had to be faced. Of Sefina's body drifting out to sea...

'Tell me about yourself,' Max said, and she realised he was trying to block things out, too.

'What's to tell?' She shrugged. 'I'm Hettie. I'm charge nurse here. I'm thirty-five years old. I came to Wildfire eight years ago and I've been here ever since. I gather you've been here once or twice while I've been based here, but it must have coincided with my breaks off the island.'

'Where did you learn to swim?'

'Sydney. Bondi.'

'The way you swim... You trained as a lifesaver?'

'I joined as a Nipper, a trainee lifesaver, when I was

six.' The surf scene at Bondi had been her tribe then. 'How did you know?'

'I saw how you took Joni from me,' he reminded her. 'All the right moves.'

'You were a Nipper, too?'

'We didn't have Nippers on Wildfire. I did have an aunt, though. Aunt Dotty. She knew the kids on the island spent their spare time doing crazier and crazier dives. I've dived off this headland more times than you've had hot dinners. We reckoned we knew the risks but Dotty said if I was going to take risks I'd be trained to take risks. So, like you, aged six I was out in the bay, learning the right way to save myself and to save others.' He shrugged. 'But until today I've never had to save anyone.'

'You are a surgeon, though,' she said gently, looking to deflect the bleakness. 'I imagine you save lots and lots.'

He smiled at that and she thought, *He has such a gentle smile.* For a big man…his smile lit his face. It made him seem younger.

'Lots and lots,' he agreed. 'If I count every appendix…'

'You should.'

'Then it's lots and lots and lots. How about you?'

'Can I count every time I put antiseptic cream on a coral graze?'

'Be my guest.'

'Then it's lots and lots and lots and lots and lots.'

And he grinned. 'You win.'

'Thank you,' she managed. 'It takes a big surgeon to admit we nurses have a place.'

'I've never differentiated. Doctors, nurses, even the ladies who do the flowers in the hospital wards and take a moment to talk… Just a moment can make a difference.'

And she closed her eyes.

'Yes, it can,' she whispered. 'I wish…oh, I wish…'

He'd stuffed it. Somehow they'd lightened the mood but suddenly it was right back with them. The greyness. The moment he'd said the words he'd seen the pain.

'What?'

Her eyes stayed closed. The little boy in her arms was deeply asleep now, cradled against her, secure for the moment against the horrors that had happened around him.

'What?' he said again, and she took a deep breath and opened her eyes again.

'I didn't have a moment,' she said simply. 'That'll stay with me for the rest of my life.'

'Meaning?'

'Meaning Sefina was brought into hospital just before the cyclone. Ruptured spleen. Concussion. Multiple abrasions and lacerations. Her husband had beaten her to unconsciousness. Sefina's not from M'Langi—she came here eighteen months ago from Fiji. Pregnant. Rumour is that…Joni's father…brought her here and paid Louis to marry her. Louis's an oaf. He'd do anything for money and he's treated her terribly. She's always been isolated and ashamed, and Louis keeps her that way.'

There was a moment's silence while he took that on board, and somehow during that moment he felt the beginnings of sick dismay. Surely it couldn't be justified, but once he'd thought of it he had to ask.

'So Joni's father…' he ventured, and she tilted her chin and met his gaze square on.

'He's not an islander.'

'Who?'

'Do I need to tell you?'

And he got it. He looked down at the little boy cradled in Hettie's arms. His skin wasn't as dark as the islanders'.

His features...

His heart seemed to sag in his chest as certainty hit. 'My brother? Ian? He's his?' How had he made his voice work?

'Yes,' she said, because there was no answer to give other than the truth. 'Sefina is... Sefina *was* a Fijian islander. As far as I can gather, Ian stayed there for a while. He got her pregnant and she was kicked out of home. In what was a surprising bout of conscience for Ian, he brought her here. He paid Louis to marry her and he gave her a monthly allowance, which Louis promptly drank. But a few weeks ago the money stopped and Louis took his anger out on Sefina. The day before the cyclone things reached a crisis point. They were living out on Atangi. We flew her across to Wildfire, to hospital, but then the storm hit...and I didn't have that moment...'

'I'm sure you did your best.' It was a trite thing to say and he saw a flash of anger in response.

'She needed more.'

'She had no one else?'

'You need to understand. She was an outsider. She was pregnant by... And I'm sorry about this—but she was pregnant by a man the islanders have cause to hate. She married an oaf. Her mother-in-law wouldn't have anything to do with her, and vilified anyone who did. And the only person responsible—your brother—is now missing.'

'He's dead,' he said, and her gaze jerked to his.

'Dead?'

'That's another reason I couldn't get back here until now. Ian's been gambling—heavily. Unknown to me he racked up debts that'd make your eyes water. That's why he's bled the island dry. And that's why…well, his body was found two weeks ago, in Monaco. Who knows the whys or wherefores? The police are interested. I'm…not.'

There was a long, long silence.

She was restful, this woman, Max thought. Where others might have exclaimed, demanded details, expressed shock, disgust or horror, Hettie simply hugged the child in her arms a little tighter.

She was…beautiful, he thought suddenly.

Until now, despite the lacy knickers and bra, despite the attempt at humour, she'd seemed a colleague. A part of the trauma and the tragedy. Now, suddenly, she seemed more.

She was slight, five feet four or five. Her body was tanned and trim, and the lacy lingerie showed it off to perfection.

Her dark hair was still sodden. Her curls were forming wet spirals to frame her face.

Thirty-five, she'd said, and he might have guessed younger, apart from the life lines around her shadowed green eyes.

Life lines? Care lines? She'd cared about Sefina, he thought. She was caring about Joni.

Her body was curved around him now, protective, a lioness protective of her cub. Everything about her said, *You mess with this little one, you mess with me.*

His…nephew?

'You realise he's yours now,' she whispered at last into the stillness, and the words were like a knife, stabbing across the silence.

'What…?'

'This little boy is a Lockhart,' she said, deeply and evenly. 'The M'Langi islanders look after their own. Joni's not their own. He never has been. He was the child of two outsiders, and the fact that an oaf of an islander was paid to marry his mother doesn't make him belong. The islanders have one rule, which is inviolate. Family lines cross and intercross through the islands, but, no matter how distant, family is everything. Children can never be orphaned. The word "orphan" can't be translated into the M'Langi language.'

'What are you saying?' There was an abyss suddenly yawning before him, an abyss so huge he could hardly take it in.

She shrugged. 'It's simple,' she said softly. 'According to the M'Langi tradition, this little one isn't an orphan, Dr Lockhart. This little boy is yours.'

He had complications crowding in from all sides but suddenly they were nothing compared to this one.

Ian had had a son.

The boy didn't look like Ian, he thought. He had the beautiful skin colour of the Fijians but lighter. His dark hair wasn't as tightly curled.

He was still sleeping, his face nestled against Hettie's breast. Max could only see his profile, but suddenly...

It was a hint, a shade, a fleeting impression, but suddenly Max saw his mother in Joni.

And a hint of his own children. Caroline, twenty-six years old, due to be married next week to the man she loved.

Christopher, buried three weeks ago.

Christopher, his son.

This little boy is yours...

How could he begin to get his head around it? He couldn't. Every sense was recoiling.

He'd loathed Ian. Born of gentle parents, raised on this island with love and tenderness… There'd never been a reason why Ian should have turned out as he had, but he'd been the sort of kid who'd pulled wings off flies. He'd been expelled from three schools. He'd bummed around the world until his parents' money had dried up.

Max thought back to the time, a few years back, when Ian had come to see him in Sydney.

'I'm broke,' he'd said, honestly and humbly. 'I've spent the money Mum and Dad left me and I can't take the lifestyle I've been living anymore. I need to go back to Wildfire. Let me manage the place for you, bro. I swear I'll do a good job. We both know it's getting run-down and you don't have time to be there yourself.'

It was hope rather than trust that had made him agree, Max thought grimly. That and desperation. It had been true; the island had needed a manager. But Max had needed to be in Sydney. Christopher had been born with cerebral palsy and he'd lurched from one health crisis to another. Max had been trying to hold down a job as head of surgery at Sydney Central, feeding as much money as he could back into the island's medical services. Caroline, too… Well, his daughter had always received less attention than she'd needed or deserved.

If Ian could indeed take some of the responsibility…

Okay, he'd been naive, gullible, stupid to trust. That trust was coming home to roost now, and then some. He was having to face Ian's appalling dishonesty.

But facing this…

This little boy is yours…

His son was dead. How could he face this?

'You don't need to think about it now,' Hettie was saying gently, as if she guessed the body blow she'd dealt him. 'We'll work something out.'

'We?'

'I love Joni,' she said simply. 'I'm not going to hand him over until I'm sure you want him.'

'How can you love him?'

Her eyes suddenly turned troubled, even a little confused, as if she wasn't quite sure of what she was feeling herself. 'He has no one,' she said, tentatively now. 'His mother trusted me and depended on me. I was there at his birth.' She took a deep breath. 'Maybe...until you're ready to accept your responsibilities, I can take care of him for you.'

'My responsibility...'

'Whatever,' she said hastily. 'Until there's another alternative, I seem to be all he has. He needs someone. He has me.'

'You're not saying you'll take him on?'

'I'm not saying anything,' she whispered, and once again her lips touched the little one's hair. 'All I'm saying is that for now I'm holding him and I'm not letting go. Oh, and, Max...'

'Yes?'

'There are people on the beach,' she said. 'Waving. I think rescue is at hand. Time to get back to the real world.'

He glanced around sharply. There were, indeed, people on the beach.

'Caroline will be overjoyed,' Hettie told him. 'Your daughter. Your family.'

And there was something in the way she said it...

He knew nothing about her, he realised. Nothing at all. He was a Lockhart. The islanders, including Hettie, must know almost everything there was to know about him. But Hettie? He knew nothing about her other than she was holding…

His son?

CHAPTER THREE

THE CORAL CUTS on Max's legs were treated by his about-to-be son-in-law. Keanu, the island doctor Max's daughter was about to marry, greeted him with overwhelming relief, but was now insisting Max submit to his care.

It seemed Sam, the island's chief medical officer, had had to fly out that morning, transporting an urgent case to the mainland. 'We're always short on medical staff,' Keanu told him, 'so you're stuck with me. But I think we can get away with no stitches. Now, anaesthetic?'

'The last thing I need is a general anaesthetic,' Max growled. 'And no blocks. I've wasted enough of my time here. I don't intend to lie round, waiting for anaesthetic to wear off. Keanu, leave it. I can clean them myself.'

'So who'll explain to Caroline that you can't give her away because your legs are infected?' Keanu demanded. 'Not me. You'll let me clean them properly.'

So he had no choice. He lay back and thought about biting bullets as Keanu cleaned, disinfected and dressed his cuts.

Thankfully the cuts were on his legs and not his face, he thought. He might still manage to look okay at Caroline's wedding.

'You have no idea how relieved she'll be when she

finds you're here,' Keanu told him as he worked. 'She's been out at a clinic at Atangi but she's due back any time now. Our wedding plans are all in order and now she has her dad. We were starting to think we'd have to send Bugsy down the aisle in your place.'

'Bugsy…'

'The dog,' Keanu said briefly, inspecting a graze that almost qualified as a cut. 'This one's nasty. Hold your breath for a bit, there's a bit of muck stuck in here.'

Max held his breath. Maybe an anaesthetic wouldn't have been such a bad idea.

'Dog,' he said at last when he could concentrate on anything other than pain.

'Bugsy, the golden retriever. He's responsible for us finding you so fast. Hettie left him on the beach. Normally Bugsy would loll around, waiting for her to come out of the water, or go for a swim himself, but he must have figured something was wrong. He came haring up to the hospital, soaking wet. We were already worried about Sefina and Joni. Sefina had discharged herself but we knew she couldn't go home, so when Bugsy appeared looking desperate, running back and forth to the beginning of the path to Sunset Beach, and we couldn't find Hettie, we put two and two together and figured we needed to investigate.'

'You let Sefina discharge herself?'

'Junior nurse,' Keanu said grimly. 'But it wasn't her fault. Short of holding Sefina by force, which was impossible, there wasn't a lot she could do when Sefina decided to leave. She let us know as soon as she could, and then Bugsy arrived.' He hesitated. 'Bugsy's a shared dog, devoted to all of us. He officially belongs to one of our fly in, fly out doctors, but Maddie's on maternity leave right now so Bugsy's main caregiver is Hettie.'

'Hettie has…no one else?'

Keanu cast him a sharp look. 'Hettie has everyone on the island.'

'Is that a warning?'

There was a moment's silence, and then Keanu gave a reluctant shrug. 'I know you're not Ian,' he conceded. 'I need to keep reminding the islanders.'

'Meaning they think if I was Ian I couldn't be trusted with anything in a skirt.'

'Ian couldn't be trusted with anything at all,' Keanu said bluntly. 'But he was your brother and Hettie tells me he's dead. I'm sorry.'

'Are you? Will anyone on this island be sorry?'

'No,' Keanu admitted bluntly. 'Maybe Sefina might have mourned him, but now…' He shrugged again, and then went back to focussing on Max's knee. 'Maybe a stitch here…'

'Steri-Strips,' Max growled. 'A scar or two won't hurt.'

'You can always cover it with pantyhose,' Keanu said, and grinned. 'It's good to have you home, Max. You've done so much for the island.' And then he glanced up as the door opened a crack. 'Hettie. Come in. That is, if Dr Lockhart doesn't mind you seeing his bare legs.'

'I saw a lot more than his legs out in the water,' Hettie retorted. 'And there's nothing our Dr Lockhart has that I haven't seen a thousand times before.'

'Shall we let the lady in?' Keanu asked.

And Max thought, *What the heck?* It was true, Hettie was a professional. Right now, he was a patient, she was a nurse. There was no reason he should feel odd at the idea of her seeing him dressed in a hospital gown with bare legs.

'Sure,' he growled, and Hettie popped in, smiling. It was a professional smile, he thought, just right, nurse greeting patient. She was in nurse's uniform, blue pants and baggy blue top. Her curls were caught back in a simple ponytail.

She looked younger than she'd looked on the atoll, he thought, and then he thought… She looked lovely?

She wasn't beautiful in the classical sense, he conceded. Her nose was too snub, her cheeks were strong-boned, and her mouth was maybe too generous to be termed lovely.

She was wearing no make-up.

He still thought she looked beautiful.

'How's Joni?' Keanu asked, before Max could form the same question, and Hettie smiled, albeit sadly.

'Clean and dry and fast asleep in the kids' ward. He's the only occupant, now that any kids with minor injuries after the storm have gone home. I left Bugsy asleep beside his cot.'

'The dog?' Max stared. What sort of a hospital let dogs stay in the children's ward?

'We have monitors,' Hettie told him. 'The moment Joni stirs I'll be in there, but the first thing he'll see when he wakes will be Bugsy. Bugsy's a friend, and Joni…well, Joni needs all the friends he can get.'

'What will you do with him?' Keanu asked. Keanu was still cleaning. Hettie had moved automatically to assist, handing swabs, organising disinfectant. They were both focussed on Max's legs, which was disconcerting, to say the least.

The question hung and suddenly Max realised Keanu was talking to *him*.

What will you do with him?

'He's not mine to do anything with,' Max growled, and Keanu raised his brows.

'That's not what the islanders think.'

'They'll think he's yours,' Hettie said. 'I told you. He's your brother's child, your brother's dead, therefore he's your family. You don't want him?'

'Why would I want him?'

'Goodness knows,' Keanu said, and kept on working. It was disconcerting, to say the least, to be talking to two heads bent over his legs—plus talking about a child he'd only just learned existed. 'Family dynasty or something?' Keanu suggested. 'He is a Lockhart.'

'I have no proof he's a Lockhart.'

'You don't, do you?' Hettie was concentrating—fiercely, he thought—on his legs, and yet he could tell that her thoughts were elsewhere. On a little boy in the kids' ward. 'He could be anyone's.'

Yeah, but he looked like a Lockhart.

'Is there any sort of Child Welfare in the M'Langi group?' he asked.

'We don't need Child Welfare,' Hettie snapped, and Keanu cast her a surprised look. But then he shrugged and addressed Max.

'We don't normally need Child Welfare,' Keanu agreed. 'The islanders usually look after their own, but Joni's an exception. He's an outsider.'

'He's not an outsider. He belongs here, and if Max won't look after him, I will.' Hettie murmured the words almost to herself, but for a murmur it had power. The words were almost like a vow.

They made Keanu pause. The doctor stood back from the table and stared at Hettie, who was still looking at Max's legs fiercely.

'What the…? Het, are you suggesting you adopt him?'

'If no one else claims him, yes.'

'You can't decide that now.'

'I have decided. If his family doesn't want him, I do. I mean it. Keanu, do you want to keep cleaning or will I take over?'

Keanu stared at her for a moment longer and then silently went back to cleaning. There was a tense stillness, broken only by the sound of tiny chinks of coral hitting the kidney basin.

His legs really were a mess but, then, everything was a mess, Max thought grimly. So what was new? When hadn't life been a mess?

For just a moment, this morning, watching the sun rise, watching the fish darting in and out of the water, watching a pod of dolphins give chase, he'd given himself time out. He'd thought, What if…?

What if he finally let himself be free?

Twenty-six years ago his wife had died on this island, giving birth to twins. He and Ellie had been babies themselves, barely twenty.

He'd met Ellie at university. They'd both been arts students, surrounded by friends, high on life. They'd fallen in love and when they'd discovered a baby was on the way they'd accepted the pregnancy with all the insouciance of youth.

'Maybe it's not a mistake,' Ellie had told him. 'Maybe we're meant to be a family.' The knowledge that she'd been carrying twins had only added to their feeling of excitement.

'How do you feel about marrying on Wildfire?' he'd asked, and she'd been ecstatic.

'The Lockhart family home? Your real-life island? Max, can we?'

They could, but not until summer vacation. They'd travelled to the island as soon as exams had ended. Ellie had been thirty-two weeks pregnant, excited about her pregnancy, excited about her sheer bulk.

He remembered their welcome. His mother had been wild with joy at their homecoming. His father had been gravely pleased that his son had found someone so beautiful to wed. No one had worried that Ellie had been pregnant at the ceremony. After all, what trouble could come to this truly blessed couple?

No one had worried that twin pregnancies sometimes spelled trouble.

He remembered his brother the night before the wedding. Ian had been blind drunk, toasting him for the hundredth time. They'd lit a campfire on the beach. Ian had waved his glass towards the island and then out at the stars hanging bright and low over the ocean.

'Here's to us, bro. We've got it all.'

He'd even been stupid enough to agree. The next day, he'd married. They'd danced into the small hours.

Ellie had gone into labour that night.

There had been no medical centre on the island then. They'd faced an agonising wait for medical evacuation, while Ellie had bled and bled.

She'd died before help arrived. The twins, Caroline and Christopher, had survived, but prematurity and birth trauma meant Christopher would be burdened with cerebral palsy for the rest of his life.

Christopher. His son.

'Family dynasty or something? He is a Lockhart.'

No. Christopher was his son, he thought grimly. Not some child called Joni. How could he ever want another child?

He closed his eyes and Keanu paused again.

'If this is hurting too much, let me knock you out.'

'Just go for it.'

There was silence as Keanu started work again. Undercurrents were everywhere, Max thought, gritting his teeth against the pain.

'Het, you won't be able to just…adopt him,' Keanu said at last into the stillness. 'You'll have to go through channels. If it's really what you want then we'll support you, but you're not deciding this today. This suggestion seems right out of the blue. It's a huge decision and there are legal channels to be dealt with. You know we come under Australian legal jurisdiction. If Joni doesn't have relatives on the island…' Here he cast a quick glance at Max. 'As the island's acting medical director, I'll need to report Sefina's death and Joni's status to the mainland authorities. A kid like Joni…there'd be mainland couples lined up to adopt a toddler like him. You'll need to plead some special case to be allowed to keep him.'

'Sefina was my friend,' Hettie told him.

'Sefina was your patient.'

'I let her down.'

'We all let her down but her death is not our fault. I'm not about to let a guilty conscience force you into adoption.'

'I'm not being forced.'

'Why would you want to adopt?' Max asked, and they both paused in their work, as if they'd forgotten he was there.

Maybe they should have had this discussion without him, Max thought. After all, it had nothing to do with him. Just because it was Ian's child…

This little boy is yours.

No. He wanted nothing to do with Ian's child.

His own son was dead. His daughter was about to be married to the man of her dreams and he might even be free of another responsibility.

All his life he'd accepted the responsibility the Lockharts had carved for themselves through generations of ownership. Every spare cent he'd earned had been ploughed back into this hospital. He'd worked so hard…

But now… In the next couple of days Max would meet the man who'd funded a world's best tropical diseases research facility and tropical resort on Wildfire. Ian had conned a Middle Eastern oil billionaire—a sheikh, no less—into purchasing island land for the resort, but the sale had been built on forged signatures and falsehoods. Island land was held in a Lockhart family trust for perpetuity and Ian had had no power to sell. Amazingly, though, once he'd known the facts, the sheikh had still been prepared to invest, leasing instead of buying. He had seemingly limitless money and resources. He was giving work to the islanders, giving hope, and for the first time since that night before his wedding, twenty-six years ago, Max was feeling a taste of freedom.

Maybe he could walk away from here and never come back.

This little boy is yours. Hettie's words, Keanu's words meant nothing. They couldn't. He did not want any more responsibility.

But finally Hettie was answering his question. 'I want to adopt because I can,' she said. It was as if she'd needed time to work out her answer, but now she had it clear. 'I've spent my life looking out for no one but myself. Sitting out on the atoll this morning, holding Joni, knowing Sefina was dead, it crowded in on me. I give nothing. I love…nothing. If I can have Joni… I will love him, Keanu. I promise.'

'But it won't be up to me,' Keanu told her, giving her a searching look. 'We'll report Sefina's death to the authorities and see what happens.'

'I won't let him leave the island.'

'Het, the islanders won't accept him,' Keanu said gently. 'He's Ian's child and Ian robbed them blind.'

'He'll be my child.'

'Let's see what the authorities say.' Keanu fastened a last dressing on Max's legs. 'There you go, Dr Lockhart. All better. You're free to go.'

Free to go…

It sounded okay to him, Max thought, swinging his legs gingerly from the examination table. Hettie held his arm while he stood, and he had the sense to let her. Lying supine during medical procedures could make anyone dizzy.

And dizziness did come, just a little, but it was enough for him to be grateful for Hettie's support.

She was small and slight. She'd been through an appalling experience, too, and yet he could feel her strength. She was some woman. How many women would have backed up such a morning with heading into work; with continuing to keep going?

With offering to adopt a child?

'Are you okay?' Hettie asked, sounding worried.

She was worried about him?

'I'm fine. Just a bit wobbly.'

'Take your time,' Keanu told him. 'We'll find you a bed in the ward.'

'If you can find me some clothes I'll head up to the house.' His clothes were either in the water or on board the boat. And where was his boat?

'You need someone to keep an eye on you,' Hettie said. 'With those legs, you need care. I'm not sure where Caroline is…'

And, as if on cue, the doors to the theatre swung open. Caroline burst through the doors, looking frantic.

'Dad,' she said as she saw him. 'Oh, Dad…' And she flung herself into his arms and burst into tears.

Hettie stepped back.

'You'll be okay now,' she said softly. 'You're with your family.'

And she walked out and left him with his daughter.

Keanu was waiting as Hettie finished her interview with the local constabulary. He'd protested as she'd donned her nurse's uniform instead of civvies the moment she'd reached the hospital. Now, though, with Max settled with his daughter and Joni asleep, there seemed no reason for her to stay. The hospital on Wildfire had settled to a new norm. Without Sefina.

Hettie could hardly think of Sefina without wanting to be sick. Of all the senseless deaths…

'There's nothing more you can do, Het,' Keanu told her as the policeman left. The young doctor was starting to sound stern. 'You've had an appalling shock. For you and Max to save Joni was little short of miraculous. You need to give your body time to recover. Take Bugsy home with you and sleep.'

'How can I sleep? Keanu, we failed her.'

'The island failed her,' he said. 'The islanders hated Ian Lockhart, and Sefina was someone they could vent that anger on.'

'It wasn't her fault.'

'We all know that. Even the islanders know that. It was only her husband who was overtly cruel and he'll be prosecuted. Now you need to take care of you.'

'I'll stay with Joni.'

'Not on my watch, Het,' he said, even more firmly. 'Joni's a problem we need to solve but not now, not when you're emotionally distraught. If I let you stay with him all the time it'll tear your heart out when he leaves. I don't know where your offer of adoption came from, but it's crazy. You know it is. You haven't had time yet even to absorb the enormity of Sefina's death. So let's be professional. We're taking care of him. Go home.'

'I don't want to.'

'I'll give you something to help you sleep,' he said, as if he hadn't heard her objection, and he took her shoulders and propelled her to the nurses' station. 'But you're signing off now and that's an order.'

It was all very well, following orders, but Hettie needed to work. She was exhausted but work seemed the only way to get the events of the morning out of her head.

She couldn't—but neither could she get rid of this certainty of what she had to do.

She'd tried hard not to get emotionally involved with her patients. Why did she suddenly, fiercely, want to adopt Joni?

Why did she *need* to adopt Joni?

She walked slowly around the lagoon, in no hurry to get to her neat little villa overlooking the water. The island was lush, beautiful, washed with rain. Most of the storm damage had been cleared. A few palms had fallen but tropical rain forest regenerated fast. Soon there'd be nary a scar.

Except Sefina was dead.

Maybe it'd be easier, she thought, if there was a body to bury. To keen over?

It'd be a tiny funeral if the body was ever found. Nobody here had loved Sefina.

No one would love Joni. He was Ian Lockhart's son.

He'd be adopted off the island, she thought bleakly. Here he'd never get over the stigma of being Ian's son. He'd never be accepted.

'I could make him be accepted.' She said it out loud but even as she said it she faced its impossibility. On this island Joni was an illegitimate outsider. He always would be.

'But I want him.'

Why? She sank onto a fallen log and stared sightlessly over the lagoon. Why did she want, so fiercely, to hug Joni to her? To hold?

Her maternal instinct was long dead. Killed by Darryn...

'Oh, get over it.' She rose and stared out at a heron standing one legged at the edge of the water. She often saw this guy here. He was a lone bird.

'And that's what I am, too,' she told herself. 'Today was an aberration. Joni will find himself some lovely parents on the mainland who'll love him to bits. And I...' She took a deep breath. 'I'll take the pills Keanu gave me and go to sleep. And I'll wake up in the morning feeling not maternal at all. I'll feel back to normal.'

But she couldn't stop thinking of Joni.

And, strangely, she couldn't stop thinking of Max.

Max, swimming strongly towards her in the water as she felt herself pulled out to sea. Max, risking his life to save a woman he didn't know, almost killing himself in the process. Max, tugging a small child from a dead woman's arms.

A decent Lockhart?

She'd watched his face when he'd told her Sefina was dead. She knew it had almost killed him to release her body, to make the choice to save her son instead.

He'd be feeling sick, too. She knew it.

Would Max stay in hospital for the night? Would Keanu insist he stay, or would he let Caroline take him home to the big house, the homestead owned by the Lockharts for generations?

'So what's that got to do with you?' she demanded of herself. 'You've never had anything to do with the Lockharts.'

Which wasn't quite true. As nurse administrator she'd had conflict after conflict with Ian Lockhart. The funds for the medical administration came from the Australian government, augmented by donations from a trust Max Lockhart had set up when his wife had died. Ian, however, had swaggered onto the island a few years back and had tried to take control. For a while, because of his name, they'd let him sit on the hospital board but pretty soon they'd realised the hospital hadn't been a priority. Equipment had been purchased from the trust but had mysteriously never appeared. If she hadn't been on the ball...

She had been. There'd been an almighty row, she'd threatened to bring in lawyers and she and Ian had hardly spoken after that.

Max looked like his brother.

They were so different… Ian was a con man, out for what he could get, morally empty.

This morning Max Lockhart had risked his life trying to save a woman and her child.

Max had poured money into this island's medical services for years.

Max had mourned his dead wife and had cared for his son until the end.

'Yeah, he's a hero, and he looks great in boxers.' She ran her hand through her hair and her tight ponytail came free, letting her curls cascade to her shoulders. She hauled them back up with something akin to anger.

She was so confused.

No, she thought. What she was feeling was shock. It'd be shock making her thoughts so tumultuous.

'So go home and sleep,' she said out loud. 'You know that's the most sensible thing to do. Go home and stop thinking of Joni. And stop thinking of Max.'

She tried. The pills Keanu had given her put her to sleep but her sleep was full of dreams.

Sefina's body, drifting on the tide.

A little boy, unloved, lying alone in the hospital ward.

Max Lockhart.

Why was he superimposing himself over all the rest?

Despite Keanu's objections, Max discharged himself. 'I have my own home and my daughter's a qualified nurse. She can report in if my condition gets interesting,' he'd told Keanu. So Caroline drove him the short distance to the Lockhart homestead, but once in the jeep a silence fell between Max and his daughter.

Where to start? There'd been silence between them for twenty-six years, he thought grimly. He hadn't treated her fairly and he knew it. He'd had two children. Ninety five per cent of his attention had been taken by Christopher. Caroline had had to fit into the edges.

'Caro,' he started, dubiously, and she flashed him a look that might even have been amusement.

'You're going to say sorry again?'

'There's not a lot else to say. I shouldn't have tried sailing here. Hettie says you were terrified.'

'I was.'

'And…I shouldn't have left you alone for so long.' He had to say it. He'd had no choice, but now that Christopher was dead the ghosts had to be hauled into the open. 'I'm so pleased you and Keanu are together.' Keanu was an island kid, grown up to be a fine doctor. He was loyal, intelligent and courageous. There was no one he'd rather have for a son-in-law, but that Caroline had met him and was marrying him was in no way down to her father. He'd done so little for her.

'Dad, I understand.' They pulled up in front of the homestead. She switched off the ignition but made no move to get out. 'Yes, there were times during my childhood when I resented the time you spent with Christopher, but the older I get the more I understand. You could never have looked after two babies on your own, not with Christopher's needs. And Grandma and Aunt Dotty were wonderful. I had Keanu as a playmate and his mum as our housekeeper. I had this whole island and I had freedom. If you'd taken me to Sydney I'd have had childcare and no one apart from the snatches of time you could spare.'

'I should have spared more.'

'And taken that time from Christopher? How could you?' She put her hand on his and held. 'Dad, you know

I loved him. You know how much I wanted him to live—how much I've been hoping a miracle would save him. That last rally, I so hoped… It wasn't to be, but my comfort was that you were there, loving him for me, for us, right to the end. I guess I've accepted now that he was always on borrowed time, but it must have broken your heart, watching him fade. Yet all the while you've supported the medical needs of this island every way you know how. And I know you're blaming yourself for Ian's dishonesty but maybe you had to trust him. Ian was *your* brother, and this was his island, too.'

Redemption? Forgiveness? His daughter was handing it to him, but could he take it? His legs ached. His head hurt. The morning's tragedy hung heavily in his thoughts.

So much tragedy…

'Hey!' Caroline released her seat belt and gave him a hug and then kissed him. 'Don't look like that. Dad, it's over. The new guy investing in the resort is pouring money into the island—did you know he wants to help with the medical facilities, as well? I know there are legal things you have to sort, but they're minor. And, Dad… Christopher's dead. You did everything you could do for him, but now it's over. And I'm marrying the man of my dreams. For the first time in your life you're responsible for nobody, for nothing. You're free, Dad. It's time you shook off the guilt and enjoyed yourself.'

'And Joni?' He said it heavily, as if he couldn't help himself, and maybe he couldn't. 'Joni's a Lockhart. I can't escape that.'

Caroline took a deep breath. 'So he is,' she said gently. 'So I guess he's my cousin. If no one else will take him, maybe Keanu and I could.'

'You can't go into a marriage with someone else's child.'

'Honestly, it's not something I ever planned for,' she said diffidently. 'But if Joni is indeed my cousin… Dad, we may have no choice.'

'That's crazy. The social welfare system works well for orphaned children. Lots of families will want him.'

'Dad, you don't understand.' Caroline put her hand on his. 'You were born here. You should get it. According to the islanders, Joni's now yours.'

'How can he be mine?' He felt as if a vast leaden weight was descending onto his shoulders. 'Hettie wants him,' he said abruptly, and Caroline's eyes widened.

'Hettie?'

'She wants to adopt him.'

'That's crazy.' She shook her head in disbelief. 'She's shocked. It's been an appalling morning. She'll be devastated by Sefina's death. We're all upset but as for taking him on…'

'Yet you're saying you could take him.'

'It wouldn't work with Hettie,' Caroline said, thinking it through. 'He'd be the illegitimate son of an outsider, with the stigma of Ian as a father to add to it. He'd have no father to watch his back. If Keanu and I adopted him, the islanders would know he's our family. They love Keanu. They'd come to accept him soon enough.'

'But he's my responsibility.' There. He'd said it. The words were heavy and hard, but they were true. Whether he liked it or not, he was the closest kin. To have a situation where his daughter took on that responsibility because he wouldn't…

It made him feel ill, but what was the alternative?

Adoption off the island? It *was* an option, but no one else was seeing it.

'You're tired,' Caroline said at last into the stillness. 'Come into the house. You can have some sandwiches and those nice painkillers Keanu's given you. Then you can sleep until morning. Problems always seem smaller in the morning.'

'I need to visit the mine. I need to talk to—'

'You need to do nothing except sleep,' she said soundly. 'Bed, this instant.'

'Yes, Mum,' he said meekly, and she chuckled and hugged him, and he thought that at least he was here with his daughter.

But…why was he still thinking of Hettie?

CHAPTER FOUR

SLEEP WAS NOWHERE. At 3:00 a.m. Hettie lay staring into the dark, and ghosts she'd thought were long buried resurfaced and started swirling.

Dawn, long ago, a morning like this one. Breakers hurling in from the east, pounding the beach. The lingering remnants of a vast southerly storm.

Darryn, waking her, exuberant with excitement. He'd organised the press for a photo shoot.

'Come on, babe. The surf's perfect.'

She'd protested, still sleepy, still tired. 'Darryn, the waves are huge. You know the doctor said—'

'Honey, the doctor's just covering himself. Our kid's born to surf. Honest, he'll come out hanging ten. Let's go.'

'I don't want to.' There, she'd said it. 'I'm seven months pregnant. I'm off balance on my board. It's dangerous.'

'You're not turning into a wuss on me. Babe, I married you because you're a surfing legend. The pictures will be awesome. Come on!'

And now, sixteen years on, her hands moved instinctively to her belly.

For sixteen years she'd buried this hunger. Today one

little boy had unleashed it to the extent it was threatening to overwhelm her.

She couldn't go back to sleep. She was trying to be logical but logic was nowhere. All she could see when she closed her eyes was Max, in the water, holding his arms out for Joni. Demanding she release him to keep him safe.

She could still feel the wrench as she'd let him go. A little boy who needed her.

How could she let him go again?

This was nonsense. It was emotional fluff. She had no business to be thinking of it.

But she was more than thinking of it. She was tossing back the bedclothes, tugging on jeans and heading for the children's ward.

He was in the bedroom he'd moved into when he'd married.

When he'd been a kid Max had had a small room at the back of the house. From his window he'd been able to see all the way to the sea.

But Caroline had that bedroom now. She'd assumed he'd want to sleep in this big room. This place of ghosts.

He and Ellie had hardly had any time at all here, he thought bleakly. A break from university while they'd planned the wedding, the wedding itself, and then tragedy.

Ellie had given birth in this bed. How could a man sleep in it?

It was history. Twenty-six years of history.

He'd decided to come back now, see Caroline married, sort out the financial affairs with the sheikh who was prepared to pour money into the place and then walk away.

For the first time since the birth of the twins he'd be responsible for nobody.

Except one little boy. Fifteen months old.

A Lockhart.

Caroline had suggested she could take him on. She would, too, he thought. His daughter had a heart big enough to take on all comers. But, like him, she had her whole future ahead of her. She was marrying Keanu.

He couldn't—he wouldn't—ask them to take on Joni.

Hettie, then?

A single woman. A woman who'd instinctively said she'd care.

It'd be different in the morning, he thought. Hettie would be back to being sensible.

So… Adoption off the island…

Why did that feel so wrong?

This little boy is yours.

'I'm too much of an islander,' he said into the dark. 'But I don't believe it. The child needs parents who want him. Adoption's the only way.'

This little boy is yours.

And suddenly he was thinking of a toddler, waking in the small hours, calling from his cot. As Christopher had called for him.

Where was sleep when he needed it? Nowhere?

He lay and stared into the dark until the dark seemed to take shapes and mock him.

This little boy is yours.

Useless. He swore and threw back the sheets. He hauled on pants and a shirt and headed for the children's ward.

The children's ward was empty, apart from Joni. 'He's asleep,' the night nurse told Hettie. 'I checked on him twenty minutes ago.'

But he wasn't asleep anymore. He was lying on his

back, wide-eyed, staring upward. The ward had luminescent stars all over the ceiling but Hettie wouldn't mind betting Joni wasn't looking at the stars. He seemed almost to be looking past them. He had a corner of the sheet in his mouth and was sucking fiercely, but he wasn't making a sound.

'Louis hits us both if Joni cries,' Sefina had told her. 'Joni's good, but he can't be good forever.'

'Joni?' she said softly, and the baby's gaze flicked to her and then away again. He went on sucking fiercely.

'Hey.' It was too much. Hettie scooped him up and cradled him against her. He was stiff and unresponsive. She tugged the sheet with her so he could keep on sucking. Anything that gave him comfort was okay by her. Anything...

'How is he?'

It was a low growl. Max. He was standing in the doorway. She wasn't startled. For some reason it seemed almost inevitable that he was here.

'He should be crying,' Hettie whispered. 'But even so young he's been trained not to cry. With his stepfather... there were consequences.'

'You're kidding.' Max spoke softly, his words seeming little more than another shadow in the night. 'What kind of creep...?'

'He's nothing to do with Joni anymore.' Hettie kissed Joni on the top of his head. 'Louis didn't let Sefina name him as father on the birth certificate. She named Ian. He never adopted Joni so he has no hold. No one will hurt you, little one. You're safe with me.'

She stood and rocked while Max watched. He could retreat. There was no need for him to stay.

He stayed.

'He's not sleepy?'

'Are any of us?' Hettie asked hollowly, and Max shrugged.

'Not me.' Then he looked up at the ceiling. 'How about bringing him outside so we can see some real stars?'

She nodded without a word, and carried the little boy out through the glass doors to the courtyard and down to the lagoon beyond. The courtyard and walkway down to the lagoon were set up so healing patients could lie under the palms, still under the watchful eye of the staff on duty. Hettie sank down onto one of the loungers, still cradling Joni. Most children would be wailing, Max thought. It was the middle of the night. Joni was with strangers. Why wasn't he sobbing for his mother?

How did you train a child not to cry? The question made him feel cold.

'See the stars?' Hettie whispered to Joni. 'See how many there are? They're up there, guarding us. Every one of them is your friend. Aren't they, Max?'

'They surely are.'

'And the moon's the biggest friend of all. He watches over the whole sky and keeps us safe.'

She almost had him believing it.

He sat on the lounger beside them while Hettie crooned her words of comfort to the little boy. In truth, he wasn't quite sure what he was doing here. Keeping guard? That's what it felt like, but who needed guards when there was Old Man Moon and his minion stars?

But it felt okay. More, it almost felt as if something inside him was settling. The last few weeks had been fraught and this day had been steeped in tragedy and grief. Sitting here under the stars with this gentle woman brought a measure of peace.

Around them was strewn the detritus from the cyclone. Trees had been uprooted, stripped foliage was everywhere and clearing up had barely started, yet here the darkness hid the damage. Here was an oasis of calm. Here was peace.

Hettie rocked and rocked, and then she started a gentle singing, a silly little tune that children must know the world over.

'My nanny sang that to me,' Max said softly, as he watched Joni's body finally lose its rigidity. The little boy was slumped, exhausted, against Hettie's breast, as if he'd finally lost the fight. He had no one else to turn to. Hettie was his last resort and he may as well submit.

'My grandma sang it to me, too,' Hettie whispered back between tunes. 'Hush, little one. Sleep.'

And amazingly Joni did. His eyes fluttered as he fought against the inevitable but finally he slept.

There was a long silence, broken only by the faint lapping of the water at the edges of the lagoon. It felt okay, Max thought. It felt good.

'Did you sing it to your twins?' Hettie asked at last.

'To Christopher,' he said shortly. 'I had to leave Caroline behind.'

'On the island?'

'Yes.'

He didn't tell people his personal business, but suddenly it was out there. A long-ago tragedy.

'My wife went into labour here on the island,' he said. 'We had no medical facilities. The twins were premature and came fast. Caroline was four pounds, big enough to survive. Christopher was only three. He survived but with cerebral palsy. Ellie haemorrhaged and died the day before she could be evacuated.'

'I guess… I knew that much,' she said. 'That's why you set up the hospital.'

'I was twenty.' He said it with muted fury, remembering the waste, the realisation of a loss he could never make good. 'We were arts students, studying in Sydney, young enough to think we knew everything. We came home to the island in our summer vacation to shock everyone with our pregnancy and to marry. We never thought…'

'Kids don't.' She hugged Joni a little tighter.

'So I grew up fast,' he said. 'Christopher needed excellent medical care. I decided there and then that Wildfire was going to get the best medical facilities I could manage, but I couldn't care for twins, not with Christopher's needs. So Caroline stayed here with my mother—her grandma. She came to Sydney later when she was ready for boarding school. I went back straight away, though. I moved from studying arts to medicine. I studied and I cared for Chris. Then I worked and cared for Chris. So, yes, I sang to Chris but I never sang to Caro.'

'She doesn't resent it,' Hettie said softly, as if she guessed his bone-deep grief. 'I'm sure she understands.'

'It doesn't stop me feeling like I've failed her,' he said heavily. 'At least she has Keanu now. At least she has someone who she knows will love her.'

'I'm sure she knows you love her.'

He paused and stared at Joni and tried to get his thoughts in order. 'We should never have got pregnant,' he said at last. 'We were two kids without a sense of responsibility between us. It was an accident but we weren't being careful. Planning a baby is huge.'

'It is.'

'And yet you say you want Joni.'

'Yes.'

'Within a day of his mother dying. It's an impulse decision.'

'That doesn't make it bad. Having Christopher and Caroline...no, it wasn't planned but they were loved. Joni will be loved.'

More silence. Sitting under the stars with this woman seemed to lead to silence. There was something about her, he thought, some restful quality that seemed to make his world settle. The huge bundle of regret and grief that had been his world since Christopher's death all at once seemed to take a step back.

'Tell me about you,' he said into the night, and was it his imagination or did she stiffen?

'What about me?'

'You know about me,' he told her. 'Max Lockhart, owner of Wildfire Island, brother of criminal Ian, father of Caroline...'

'Uncle of Joni,' she added, and he winced.

'Don't. Just tell me about you. You're the head nurse here. You've been here for years. Did you come here to escape?'

'Why would I do that?'

'People do. My great-great-grandfather bought this place as an escape after a scandal with a married woman. He brought her here, waited for years for her divorce to come through and then married her with all honour. But the initial decision to buy the island was as an escape.'

'I didn't know that.'

'You have no idea how many skeletons there are in the Lockhart family closet. So show me one of yours. Why did you run here?'

'I didn't!'

And for a while he thought she wouldn't say more. It didn't actually matter if she didn't, he decided. The night was warm and still, Joni was deeply asleep and the sky was aglow with stars. There was a sense of peace that couldn't be messed with, no matter what skeletons were exposed.

'I'll tell you,' she said at last, though. 'If you'll support me caring for Joni.'

'I can't decide if you can have Joni.'

'No. Sorry. I guess… All I'm thinking is that you're Joni's uncle. You deserve to know a little about the woman who's fighting for custody, and I will need your support.'

'So you will fight for custody?'

'Yes.' She said it harshly, and Joni stirred uneasily in her arms. She hushed and crooned and Joni slipped back to sleep, and Max sat on while she decided what she wanted to tell him.

'I was a bit like you,' she said at last. 'I married young. My parents were surfers, hippies, based at Bondi Beach in Sydney but following the waves. I learned to surf when I was three but they often left me behind. My grandma was my rock. She died when I was fifteen and after that I sort of drifted. But by then, wow, I could surf. I was competitive. I won a couple of world championships and then I met Darryn.'

'Your husband.'

'We thought we were so cool,' she told him. 'Both champion surfers. Both invincible. We had this crazy, amazing wedding on the beach in Hawaii. We had the world at our feet—nothing could touch us.' She shrugged. 'Only then I fell pregnant and I was fat and clumsy and I backed off in the surf. Darryn wasn't doing too well, either, and he couldn't stand it. He hated not being in the limelight. Finally he organised a photo shoot with one of the big American surfing magazines. He said it'd be stunning publicity, me hanging ten when I was so pregnant. It'd tell the world why we weren't out front in the surf scene anymore. But on the day, the swell was huge. I should never have agreed to do it.'

'And…' He hated to ask but he had to.

She sighed. 'And something went horribly wrong. To this day I have no idea how, but I bombed and the board hit my belly. I lost my baby and I also lost the chance to have any more children.'

'Oh, Hettie…'

'So Darryn couldn't cope with my grief,' she said, as if she hadn't heard him interrupt. 'He left me as soon as he decently could. I went back to Sydney, knowing I had to make a living. I scraped through a nursing course but I hated being anywhere I could meet any old friends. I got the best qualifications I could, and then this job came up. I've been here ever since.'

'So you're hiding?'

'I'm not hiding,' she snapped, and then bit her lip as Joni stirred again. 'This is my family. I love the island, the islanders, the hospital, my colleagues. I'd never had a place to call home until I reached here. This is where I want to be.'

'And now you want a baby?'

'I didn't know I did,' she murmured, cradling Joni to her. 'I thought I'd blocked it out. Until today. Until I held him. Suddenly I realised that this was someone I could help. He's injured, Max. Not just today, though heaven knows how he'll remember the terror of today. But he's already had his tiny lifetime marred by abuse at the hands of the man who was supposed to be his father. He's been hit. Sefina told me on that last appalling day when she was admitted. He's seen his mother being hit. How old do you have to be to remember such things? All I know is that he's quiet when he should cry. I know his background. I knew Sefina, and I can bring him up to love her. I've been thinking and thinking. It may seem selfish to you, but it's not. I can give him…all the love he needs and more. If he's adopted on the mainland this part of his life will be a blank. It shouldn't be. He needs to be here.'

'And you need him.' It wasn't a question.

'Maybe I do,' she said softly. 'Maybe until today I didn't realise how much. But I will look after him. We will be a family.'

'He might not be accepted on the island.'

'Because he's Ian's? He's not Ian's. He's mine.'

Was there anything else to be said? There were questions everywhere, Max thought, but he couldn't voice them.

He should go back to bed. His legs ached and he had a power of issues to face in the morning. Ian had left a legacy of debt and deceit. He needed to start sorting the mess. The sooner he got it sorted, the sooner he could leave.

But somehow, tonight, the thought of leaving was slipping into soft focus. Ever since Ellie had died, twenty-six years ago, he'd thought he hated this island. The horror of Sefina's suicide should have made it worse.

Somehow it didn't, though. Somehow, sitting here in the peace of the night, with this woman, with this child, the grief of the past seemed to lessen.

'Has Caroline told you all her wedding plans?' Hettie asked.

And he thought, *Great, we're moving on, away from the grey of the past*. But there was another shadow.

'I guess she doesn't have to. She'll have it all arranged.'

'She hasn't run things by you?'

'She's been independent forever. She's known she can't count on her dad.'

'She's known why,' Hettie said gently. 'You can't beat yourself up over something that's not your fault.'

'You'd be amazed at what I can beat myself up over.'

'Well, that makes two of us.' She grinned. 'Glum and Glummer, that's us. It doesn't help, though. Tell you what, how about a swim tomorrow?'

'The sea…' he said, startled, and she shook her head.

'Not in the surf. I'm no longer a surfer. You needn't worry, a wave doesn't have to be very big to have me a screaming wuss and backing away.'

'You weren't a wuss today.'

'Neither were you. No choice gives us no choice. But below the resort…'

'The resort?'

'The research station. You know it? Have you seen it yet? I don't suppose you have. But you must know that Sheikh al Taraq—or Harry, as he's known, the guy who's rebuilt the research centre—has converted it into a world-class conference venue. It'll take your breath away. I know you're leasing the land to him. I know the scandal. Everyone here knows now that Ian conned him into thinking the land was his, but he seems to have accepted the facts and moved on. So as owner I reckon you need to do a tenancy inspection, and if you do, how about in your swimming gear? There's a lagoon between the resort and the sea. It's fed by rainwater from the mountains so it won't hurt your legs—but you'll know that.'

Then she glanced at Max's legs and grimaced. 'Okay, maybe not tomorrow,' she conceded. 'Maybe tomorrow's for sitting on the verandah and trying not to wince. But by Tuesday you should be up for a swim. It might even do you good. I swim most mornings so if you're up for it… Tuesday morning? Seven o'clock?'

'Hettie…'

'I know, you have a power of stuff to face,' she said, gently again. 'And so do I. Neither of us may be able to do it. But if we can… Look, it's just a thought. I'll be at the track at the back of the house at seven. If you're there, you're there. If you're not, you're not, and no hard feelings.' And then she stood, still cradling Joni. 'That's it,' she said briskly. 'Time to move on. Goodnight, Dr Lockhart.'

'Goodnight, Hettie.'

She smiled and gave a brisk little nod and turned away.

He stood and watched her as she walked back into the hospital. A woman holding his nephew. A woman claiming him as her own?

The child was a Lockhart, if not in name, certainly in everything else.

Hettie wanted Joni.

And Max… Who knew what he wanted?

Hettie disappeared and he dug his hands into his pockets and gazed back out over the lagoon.

He could settle things here and disappear, to a life, finally with no responsibilities.

That's what he'd thought he wanted. So why did watching a woman disappear into the darkened hospital suddenly make him feel…hungry?

Hettie returned Joni to his cot, then settled in a chair beside him. There was no need to stay—the night staff would be here in moments if there was a peep out of him—but somehow it seemed impossible to leave him. Whatever ties had been created in the morning's drama seemed to be strengthening by the moment. She couldn't leave him.

She might have to. She had no right to him. He was an orphan. Keanu had already told her that the mainland social services had been contacted. She'd have to fight.

'And I will,' she whispered into the night, and part of that fight seemed to start right now. She fetched a rug from the linen bank, tugged it over herself and tried to settle.

But not to sleep. Sleep was nowhere. The events of the day were too horrific.

Joni's needs were too overwhelming.

Max's presence was too…invasive.

What was that about?

She didn't know. All she did know was that every time she closed her eyes, instead of the horrors of the day, somehow superimposed was Max.

Max, sitting beside the lagoon, gazing reflectively into the night. Max, describing his past, the pain of choices he'd had no part in making.

Max, taking Joni from her just as she'd felt herself sweeping out to sea, out of control. Saving her baby.

Not her baby. Joni.

Max, trying with everything he had to save Sefina.

She shouldn't be thinking of Max. The day had been a swirl of trauma. There was so much else to be thinking of besides Max, so why did he seem beside her now? Why had sitting beside him on the edge of the lagoon seemed to settle not just the terrors of today but past terrors?

She'd asked him to go swimming with her. How stupid was that?

He wouldn't come. Even if his legs didn't hurt, why would he come?

But if he did…

Stop thinking about it, she told herself fiercely. Her life was suddenly complicated. It'd get more complicated if she was to have a hope of adopting Joni, and stupid teenage thoughts about a guy with a good body could mess things completely.

But he has more than a good body. She almost said it aloud but she was in the hospital so the monitors were on and anything she said could be heard at the nurses' station. She still had some remnants of sense.

Did she want…more than a good body?

The question was suddenly out there. Why?

Relationships terrified her. She'd stepped into marriage that one horrendous time and the scars were still with her. She'd made a vow to stay single, to stay in control, for the rest of her life.

So why was Max Lockhart messing with that control? Why did the image of him, the sound of his voice, make something inside her feel as if it was stretching to breaking point?

'It was the day,' she said, and it seemed her subconscious was taking over her sense as well as her thoughts because she did say it out loud. 'It's just the way he held Joni and the way he saved him—it's the way he saved me… We both could have drowned without him. It's made me feel vulnerable.'

But…vulnerable? Was that the word she was looking for?

She was gazing down at the sleeping Joni, aching to

lift him and hold him again. But there was suddenly a deeper ache, and it was an ache she couldn't acknowledge. She couldn't begin to define it. Max…

But she had spoken out loud, and Beth, the nurse on duty, was bustling down the corridor to see what was happening.

'Hettie? Is anything wrong?'

'No.' It was as much as Hettie could do not to snap but somehow she managed it. She was off balance and if she was to have a chance to adopt Joni then she needed to be more on balance than she'd ever been in her life. She certainly didn't need to be letting her subconscious have weird thoughts about his uncle. 'I'm just muttering to myself before I go to sleep.'

'You know, if you want to go home to bed, I can look after him,' Beth said, and Hettie nodded.

'Of course you can. And me sleeping here is ridiculous. But that's pretty much how I'm feeling right now. Ridiculous. Indulge me.'

'He's pretty good-looking, isn't he?' Beth said softly, and to her horror Hettie felt herself blush. Blush! She hadn't done such a thing since she was a kid.

'You're talking about Dr Lockhart?'

'Who else would I be talking about? Only the guy you were stranded on the reef with. Who risked his life with you. Also, the guy you've been sitting outside with for an hour.'

'An hour?'

'And five minutes. I timed you. And all the time I thought, he's gorgeous.'

'He's too old to be gorgeous.'

'Are you kidding?'

'He's Caroline's father!'

'And Caroline's twenty-six and her parents were twenty when she was born. That only makes him forty-six.'

'For heaven's sake, after all that's happened today…'

'Especially after what's happened today,' Beth said, becoming serious. 'Honest, Hettie, you do so much for everyone, and now you're talking about adopting Joni…'

'That's not being generous. It's entirely selfish.'

'Maybe, but it's left out a whole chapter of your life. It's called your Love Life. You run this hospital brilliantly, you watch all your staff have affairs, fall in love, have fun. But you—'

'Am I or am I not your boss?' Hettie demanded, and Beth chuckled.

'Yes, you are, ma'am.' And she gave a mock salute. 'But I've never heard that giving your boss a bit of well-meaning advice is insubordination. Max Lockhart's gorgeous. I say go for it.'

'Beth…'

'That's all,' Beth said, and stooped and kissed her. So much for respect, Hettie thought. Beth was an island girl, born and bred, and she knew everything about this island. She probably knew far too much about Max Lockhart. 'But, honest, Hettie, it's been an appalling day and we all know there's appalling stuff behind that mask you wear. You're going to fight for Joni? Good for you, but while you're about it, what about fighting for his uncle, as well? He might be Ian's brother but to my mind he's *bee-yoo-ti-ful*.'

CHAPTER FIVE

To HIS ANNOYANCE Max slept half the next day. He emerged from his bedroom at noon, feeling disoriented. Weird.

Caroline was in the kitchen, cooking and humming an old island folk tune. For an instant she could have been his mother. The tune was an ingrained part of his childhood, as was the smell of the meal she was cooking.

She turned as he entered, and smiled, and she was his daughter again and time had moved on, but the surge of emotion didn't move with it.

He'd been raised on this island. He loved it. He loved its people. He loved this house.

He'd been away for more than half his life, yet it still felt like home.

'Hey,' Caroline said, and smiled some more.

And he thought, *That was Ellie's smile*. But he could hardly conjure her now. Ellie. His wife.

'Welcome to the world of up,' Caroline said. 'Would you like breakfast or would you like curry? Keanu will be here in ten minutes. I've made his mum's recipe— fish curry with a magnificent red emperor caught this morning. Coconut milk and limes picked an hour ago. There's nothing like it. Oh, and Hettie rang to find out how you were. I asked her for lunch, too, but she's staying with Joni.'

'She still wants to keep him?'

Caroline looked troubled.

'Yes, but I don't see how she can. Keanu's contacted social services. A couple of welfare officers will be on the flight the day after tomorrow. They'll make an interim decision.'

'So soon?'

'If he's to be adopted, the sooner the better. His stepfather doesn't want him.' She eyed her father for a couple of moments and then ventured, 'Unless... Dad, do you want to keep him yourself?'

And there it was, front and centre, and with her words the past slammed back. Standing in the intensive care nursery in a Sydney hospital, with the two tiny scraps of humanity that were his children. He'd been twenty years old, a kid himself. Ellie was dead. The doctor had just spelled out Christopher's probable future.

'How will you care for them?' the doctor had asked, and Max hadn't been able to answer. But he'd muddled through. His parents had suggested taking Caroline home to Wildfire. Christopher had needed specialist care, though, so unless he abandoned him to foster care, Max was stuck on the mainland. His father had agreed to fund him through a medical degree, and somehow he'd cared for Christopher. After Ellie's death, though, he was determined to get a decent medical service for Wildfire, so somehow he'd found time to put pressure on politicians. He'd made noise in the right places and even sent money home to help get the Wildfire hospital up and running.

It had all just been reaction, though. He'd done what had come next. That's what he'd been doing for twenty-six years. Was this another such moment?

'Hey, Dad, don't look like that,' Caroline said softly.

'If Hettie really wants him, we'll support her. Maybe we can organise things so she can. If worst comes to worst, we've discussed it and Keanu and I will adopt him. No one's forcing Joni on you.'

'No one's forcing anyone.' He shook his head. 'And you can't adopt a child as worst-case scenario. Sorry, love. Let's think this through later. Your curry smells great.'

'It does, doesn't it?' Caroline agreed, and then Keanu arrived, filthy after clearing fallen palms from behind the hospital. There was cyclone damage to talk over, then the wedding to discuss and island affairs and arrangements to be made. The rest of the day passed in a blur and Max had to put the thought of one small boy aside.

And the thought of the woman who loved him?

Hettie had a busy day at the hospital, followed by another sleepless night, and then she was faced with something she would have rather forgotten.

Had she been nuts, suggesting this? It had been an off-the-cuff suggestion and she was hoping Max had forgotten. What had she been thinking, suggesting an early morning assignation? A swim below the research station? Why would he want to do such a thing—and with her?

She should leave a message at the Lockhart place for him to forget it. Or tell Caroline.

Ha!

'Tell your father I don't want to meet him tomorrow morning,' she'd say. She could imagine Caroline's re-action.

He would have forgotten, she decided, but if he hadn't…

Okay, if he hadn't then he had a choice. He'd be there

or he wouldn't. It wouldn't worry her either way. She loved swimming—she swam most mornings. If you blocked out the fallen trees and mass of leaf litter, the island was at its gorgeous best and she wasn't on duty today.

But did she want to go swimming with Max?

Who wouldn't? He was…

Gorgeous?

Yes, he was, she told herself, and if she was interested she'd think he was very gorgeous indeed, but she wasn't interested, at least not like that. She was well over such nonsense. She had to be.

But if he happened to be there…

Then they'd have a brisk, businesslike swim, she told herself. Joni was still in the children's ward—Keanu wasn't letting her take him home until after the welfare visit. Caroline was on duty. Bugsy was asleep under his cot. The child welfare visit the next day was looming large and she needed exercise to drive her thoughts from it.

And she reached the fork in the track and Max was sitting on a fallen palm, looking for all the world like he was waiting for her.

But he didn't look like he was heading for a swim. He was dressed almost formally, in chinos and a short-sleeved, open-neck shirt, almost a business shirt. He was wearing brogues, for heaven's sake. He was clean-shaven, smart—no, more than smart.

He was almost breathtakingly good-looking.

She was wearing a sarong and sandals. She'd let her hair cascade to her shoulders.

All of a sudden she felt practically naked. Like she should turn and run?

'I thought you might have forgotten.' He rose and smiled at her, for all the world like he'd been looking forward to this strange assignation.

'I don't…I don't forget appointments.'

'I can see that about you,' he said approvingly. 'Nice sarong.'

'I… Thank you. Neat…shirt.'

'Thank you, too.'

'And brogues?' She couldn't help the note of teasing.

'You know they found my boat?'

She did know. They'd towed it into harbour yesterday. They'd also found Sefina's body, but Hettie wasn't going there.

'I… Yes.'

'So I have my clothes—and I have an assignation other than the one with you. I hoped we might combine them.'

'Sorry?'

'With the sheikh,' he told her. 'The businessman who's funded the reopening of the research station and the resort. He's invited me for breakfast. I've never met a sheikh. I've only spoken to him on the phone. See me nervous.'

'Hence the brogues.'

'It seems disrespectful to wear sandals.'

'So you're inviting me? With sarong and sandals?'

'Women get latitude. I dare say every woman in his harem wears sarong and sandals.'

'He's not like that,' she said sharply, and he raised his brows.

'You've met him?'

'Sheikh Rahman-al-Taraq? Otherwise known as Harry? Yes, I have. You know he's an oil billionaire? He's also a brilliant paediatric surgeon but a near-fatal brush with encephalitis has left him with hand tremors that prevent him from operating. He's now intent on wiping encephalitis from the face of the planet, which is why he invested here. But you must know that already, and we all know now that your brother conned him into thinking he could buy the land here. We're just so grateful he's bigger than…'

'My shady brother?' Max sighed and fell silent.

They started walking towards the resort, easily, almost with the familiarity of longtime friends. There was still fallen timber on the track. They needed to concentrate on where they walked. A couple of times they faced logs fallen over the path. The first time it happened Max offered his hand to Hettie to help her over.

'You're the one with the cut legs,' she said, and he smiled.

'I'm the one with brogues. Indulge me.'

'I'm fine on my own.'

'Aren't we both,' he said softly, but still he held out his hand. 'Indulge me,' he said again, and there was nothing for it but to put her hand in his and let him support her as she stepped over or through the litter.

It was nothing more than a gentlemanly gesture, she told herself when it happened the second time. It was good old-fashioned courtesy, and why it had the power to make her feel…?

She didn't know how she was feeling.

As if she was almost looking forward to the next fallen log?

Weird.

Focus on practicalities, she told herself, trying hard to block out the feel of Max's hand holding hers. Trying to block out the strength of him, the way he made every nerve ending seem to tingle.

Think of Max, the man. Max, the owner of Wildfire Island, finally about to meet the sheikh who was helping to save it.

For the last couple of years things on the island had been a mess. While Max's son had been gravely ill in Sydney, Max's brother had illegally 'sold' the land and buildings to Sheikh al Taraq. By the time Max had discovered that documents had been signed in his name, the research station had been rebuilt as a state-of-the-art conference centre.

The Sheikh would have been within his rights to walk away and sue for millions. Thanks to Max's frantic phone negotiations, somehow the situation had been saved.

It seemed almost ludicrous now, though, that Max had never met him.

'I've only seen the sheikh in my work gear, though, and only as a nurse,' Hettie told him. 'Breakfast in my sarong… You do realise I'm wearing my bikini underneath.'

'Excellent.' Max's magnetic smile flashed out again. 'I'm wearing boxers.'

'Better than the last ones I saw?'

His grin broadened. 'Yes, indeed. I'm almost respectable.'

'As opposed to me.' She tried to glower, which was hard when his grin made her want to smile back. His grin seemed to be made for sharing. His grin seemed…almost dangerous. 'One slip of the tie at my breast and I'm… Well,' she managed. 'I'll sit still, that's all I'm saying.'

'So you will join us?'

'You'll be wanting to talk business. I can't imagine it's anything to do with me.'

'I can't imagine there's anything on this island you don't know about,' Max said gently. 'Support me, Hettie. I need your strength.'

'You know, I'm very sure you don't.'

'Then you don't know anything about me,' he said, and suddenly his voice was grim. 'Not many people do.'

The breakfast with the sheikh went brilliantly. They sat outside the resort's wonderful new restaurant, under the bougainvillea and frangipani, with brilliantly coloured island parrots squawking in the trees above them and occasionally daring a brave foray to try and filch a sugar lump. The sheikh—'Call me Harry'—was polite, gentle and non-accusatory.

'Every family has troubles,' he told Max, when Max tried to apologise as he'd apologised over and over, via telephone, via his lawyers. 'And now your brother is dead. I'm so sorry, but we need to move forward. You know I invested in this facility to make a difference to the worldwide scourge of mosquito-borne encephalitis. This is my passion. I have other facilities around the world but this one is important to me, and Wildfire itself seems to have found its way into my heart.' He smiled. 'You know I've married a woman who loves Wildfire as much as I do? How can I argue with my heart? So now how can we make the best of the situation, for us, for the islanders and for the researchers who I hope will use this island?'

He then launched into plans that Max found impossible not to engage in. Clinical trials for the encephalitis vaccine were well under way, but meanwhile Harry was offering Max assistance in an insect eradication programme, and in other island medical needs, as well. The two men were soon deep in conversation, and Hettie sat back and listened.

She listened with intelligence, though, Max thought. Through the hour they sat there she asked four questions, each simple but each intensely focussed. She spoke little, but when she did, it was to maximum effect.

It took him little time to realise she already had Harry's respect. She spoke and Harry deferred to her local knowledge—and to her intellect.

As she sat, demure and quiet, he found himself more and more drawn to her. She was wearing no make-up. Her curls were free to tumble to her shoulders. The tie of her sarong sat low in the curve of her breasts.

The work he and Harry were talking of was vital. All his attention should be on business, but it was as if there was some magnetic pull, tugging his gaze to that tie.

Hettie looked…almost like a girl.

Except she wasn't. There were life lines around her eyes. Her hands were worn from a career in nursing where she washed them a hundred times a day. And the way she held herself, with quiet dignity…

She was no girl. She was every bit a woman.

'But I'm holding you up.' With their business finished, the sheikh rose. 'I can see by Hettie's outfit that you're heading for the beach. For the rock pool below the resort?'

'You've taken away the barriers,' Hettie said. 'I assume it's okay?'

'The barriers were only there during construction,' the sheikh told them. And then his voice softened. 'The rock pool where Joni's mother died is a favourite place to swim, as well. I know you swim there, Hettie. I hope you can return to swim there again, but for now please use our pool. I'm so sorry. It's an appalling tragedy and I know this is none of my business, but, Max… The little boy…your nephew… How will you care for him?'

And there it was again.

This little boy is yours.

'The welfare people will be on the island tomorrow,' Max said brusquely. 'They need to assess what's best for him.'

Harry glanced at Hettie. 'My sources say you would take him.'

'I could,' Hettie said, and unconsciously tilted her chin. 'I would. If I'm permitted.'

'You know that isn't an ideal solution.'

'Why not?' Max asked, and Harry cast him a curious glance.

'This is your island. You don't know the mood of the community?'

'Max hasn't spent any time here for years,' Hettie told the sheikh, obtusely defensive on Max's behalf. 'He's been supporting his son in Sydney. He's also been doing everything he can to support the islanders.'

'This I already know.' Harry held up a hand as if in apology for what he had to say. 'But, Max, I also know how your brother has besmirched your name. Your brother was hated. The mine collapse, the death of a beloved island elder… These are only two of the many crimes put to his account.' His voice gentled. 'I've only been on this island a short while, but already I know the stigma the child will carry. And Hettie, as a single mother, you won't be able to protect him from that stigma.'

'I can.' Hettie rose abruptly. 'This isn't the time to discuss it, though. Meanwhile, if you two need to talk more, I'll leave you to it. Max, if you still want a swim, I'll see you in the pool. Otherwise I'll see you back at the hospital.'

She walked out, leaving the two men gazing after her.

But she couldn't disguise her distress. Harry's words had battered her.

'She might be able to care for him,' Max said softly into the stillness that followed, but Harry shook his head.

'The child will be seen as a Lockhart.'

'I'm a Lockhart.'

'Yes. And I understand the situation. Even though your brother was hated, this community still looks to you for leadership. If you stayed...you might afford this child some protection.'

'I'm not staying. I'm here for my daughter's wedding and then I'll leave.'

'To be free?'

'I... Yes.' What was the purpose of denying it? Besides, this man deserved honesty. 'This island killed my wife. I've been away for twenty-six years. The island has little to do with me.'

'And yet you love it.'

'I don't.' It was an angry snap but as he stared out over the sea to the cluster of islands beyond he felt that age-old tug that made a liar of him. And Harry knew.

'How can you not?' Harry shook his head. 'I know. You don't want the mantle of responsibility and yet it's yours regardless. I, too, have responsibilities I can't walk away from. This is your community, and, like it or not, the child, Joni, is your responsibility.'

'Hettie can have him.'

'That's just the problem,' Harry said gently. 'You know and I know that Hettie can't.'

* * *

When all else fails, swim. It was a mantra that had held her in good stead all her life. Maybe that was one of the reasons she loved Wildfire. The sea was tropically warm, turquoise waters washed over brilliant coral, and fresh-water pools dotted the island. Apart from the occasional storm, she could swim year round.

She needed to swim now. The pool behind the resort was a naturally formed rock pool, fed by waterfalls from the mountains above, with an outlet at the end where the water tumbled to the sea. The water was crystal clear, the rocky bottom dotted with clumps of water grasses. Brilliantly coloured fish darted from clump to clump, but here in this protected place there were no large predators. If she floated she could almost touch the fish with her fingers.

But today Hettie wasn't floating. She put her head down and swam the full length of the rock pool, up and back, up and back. She blocked out everything except the need to expend energy, to get rid of this grey hopelessness that had been with her since she'd seen Sefina walk off the cliff edge.

Or maybe before that. Maybe a long time before. Maybe Joni's helplessness was bringing out emotions she'd suppressed for years.

And with that thought came another. Did she want to adopt Joni for Joni's sake—or for hers?

And then there was the way she was feeling about Max. The way he made her feel…

Like she was a vulnerable kid again. Out of control. Scared.

Her mind was a kaleidoscope of emotions that swimming couldn't settle. She swam and she swam…

And suddenly Max was swimming with her. Suddenly he was right beside her, pacing her stroke for stroke.

He swam with ease. She was pushing herself but she was aware that his power was constrained. He could lap her if he wished.

He didn't wish. He simply chose to swim beside her.

For a moment she considered stopping, pulling back, telling him to find his own space to swim. But that'd be impolite. Besides, he owned this island. Okay, Harry was leasing this part but she wasn't too sure of landlord rights and she didn't feel up to treading water and telling Max Lockhart to take himself off.

So she kept on swimming and Max kept on pacing her. Stroke for stroke. On and on.

And finally she found herself relaxing, just a little. The tension that had been with her since Sefina's death eased. Her mind was focussing on Max instead, and strangely, thankfully, her irrational fear was fading, as well.

But it was a strange sensation, swimming in tandem with this man. He'd eased his power back so he exactly matched hers. It meant there was no sound apart from the precise, matched strokes. The morning sun was glinting on the water. The fish were darting every which way underneath them and the grasses were swaying lazily as they passed.

It was almost mesmerising. It was…beautiful.

So was the man beside her.

That was dumb. She was trying to make her thoughts practical. Prosaic. She needed to be matter-of-fact about this. She'd invited Max to swim with her this morning and that's what he was doing. Nothing more, nothing less.

So do it.

They swam length after length, diving as they reached

the rocks at the ends, tumble-turning and swimming back. Over and over. Not connecting. Simply pacing each other.

Except they were connecting in a way she didn't understand. It was disturbing. It wasn't bad. It wasn't threatening. But it was...disturbing.

She shouldn't have asked him to join her, she decided. She was a loner. Since divorcing Darryn all those years ago, she'd retired into herself. She had friends, she was sociable enough, but she held herself to herself.

Over the past few months there'd been a flurry of romances between the medics on the island, so much so that she was thinking of buying wedding gifts in job lots. But each time she'd watched one of her staff fall in love, a part of her had been flinching. *Be careful*, she'd wanted to warn them. *Fall with your head, not your heart.*

They wouldn't have listened. Hormones had held sway.

And right now hormones were having a fine time with her and she couldn't prevent it. The sensation of Max's body beside her, not touching and yet moving so his strokes matched hers, the rush of water that followed his strokes... It was almost a caress. His body was so large. So male...

And this water wasn't cold enough. She needed to go and find a cold shower—but that'd mean breaking the moment and she couldn't. Whether she willed it or not, she was held in thrall by the sensation of a man she hardly knew swimming beside her.

The sun warmed her body, glinted on the water, glistened on the large male body beside her. This was like a trance, a dream. Soon she'd wake up, but not yet, not yet.

For some reason an illusion crept into her mind and stayed. The illusion that she wasn't alone. Not just here.

Not just now. But somehow her customary solitude had been invaded in a way she...wanted?

This was crazy. Her mind was all over the place.

All she could do was keep on swimming.

He hadn't meant to lap with her. At first Max had settled onto a rock at the water's edge. He'd watched Hettie for a while—she really was a wonderful swimmer—and finally he'd stroked out to meet her.

But she hadn't seen him come, and as he'd reached her it had seemed right not to interrupt her solitude. But somehow it had also seemed right to keep swimming, to stroke beside her, and then to match his pace to hers.

Maybe it was an intrusion. If it was, though, surely she'd have raised her head and glared? She knew he was with her. At the last turn she'd fallen a stroke behind. Instead of staying behind, though, she'd raised her stroke rate until once again they'd been in rhythm.

They were swimming as one.

It was almost a kind of lovemaking.

Where had that thought come from? And how crazy was it? This wasn't a woman to make love to. This was Henrietta de Lacey, charge nurse of Wildfire Island hospital. She was practically his employee.

She was not his sort of woman.

Who was...his sort?

No one, he thought as he swam. His one foray into marriage had catapulted him into a catastrophe so great it had overtaken his life. Since then he'd had the occasional relationship but they'd mostly been with colleagues, and all had been on a strict no-future basis. There were many women in medicine who welcomed such friendships. They were career oriented, focussed on getting ahead, knowing a family would interfere with what they wanted in life.

What did he want in life?

Why was he wondering that now, as he stroked back and forth?

Because he hadn't had time to think about it until now? Because there'd never been a choice? Christopher's needs, the island's needs, his daughter…

Now suddenly the future lay ahead like a blank slate. What did he want?

Freedom? Yes!

He swam some more and Hettie swam with him, and he found himself thinking of what Hettie wanted. To take on a child who wasn't her own.

To knowingly step into responsibility.

The thought made him shudder. Freedom had hung before him for twenty-six years, unattainable, a dream he could barely imagine. To give it up…

What was Hettie thinking of?

He shouldn't want to know, he told himself. It was none of his business—as the child she wanted was none of his business.

He should stop swimming alongside her. He should…

No. There was no *should*. He was free. Harry was willing to pour money into the island's medical facilities, making his own small contribution almost unnecessary. Christopher was dead. Caroline was marrying the man of her dreams.

And one little boy? If Hettie wanted that responsibility it was up to her. He could walk away.

Except for now all he wanted was to swim.

They swam for almost an hour and in the end it was Max who called a halt. He reached the flat rock at the end of the pool, and as Hettie turned to do another lap he hauled himself out of the water.

She did another two laps alone. It felt like she'd lost something.

That was fanciful. She'd lost nothing. She'd swum in this pool often since she'd arrived on the island. Sometimes colleagues swam with her but mostly she swam alone.

She didn't mind being alone.

She wouldn't be able to do it with Joni.

Yes, she would. She could teach him to swim. The thought gave her a surge of pleasure, of hope, but it wasn't enough to dispel the weird, desolate sense of losing Max's presence beside her.

Wow, she was being dumb. She had no right to be thinking like this.

Right? That was the wrong word, she decided. She had no *desire* to be thinking like that.

Desire. There was a loaded word.

She shook it off, almost with anger. She finished another lap.

If she kept swimming, would Max go away? How ungracious was that? She slowed, reached the rocks and pulled herself out.

The rocks were slippery. Max's hand came out and caught her wrist. She was tugged up, faster than she expected, a little closer than she expected.

He was so…male. He must spend serious time in the gym, she thought tangentially. A twenty-year-old would kill for Max's body.

A twenty-year-old could never have this body. Wet, clad only in board shorts, his silver-shot black hair dripping, rivulets of water running down his bare chest, he looked…

Distinguished?

It was the wrong word but she was too close to him to think of another.

Mature. Strong.

Very, very sexy.

Whoa...

'That was some swim,' he said, and smiled at her, and that smile was almost her undoing. How could a guy's smile light up his face? More. How could it light up... something inside her she didn't know had been dark?

He'd tugged her up on the rocks to sit beside him. Mosses covered the surface. The sun was warm on her face. The moss was as soft as bedding, and this man beside her was so...

Near.

She should edge away. She couldn't. Her body wouldn't move.

'You're some swimmer,' he said, and she tried smiling herself. She wasn't sure it came off.

'You're not so bad yourself. Not many men can keep up with me.'

'I can see that about you.' One of her curls had flopped over her eye. He leaned forward and tucked it behind her ear.

'Th-thank you.'

'My pleasure.' His voice was deep and resonant, almost a caress on its own. 'So...no men in your life?'

'Is this a come-on?'

'It's not.' His smile lit his face again. 'Not that I'm not interested...'

'Don't do that,' she snapped, and his smile died.

'What?'

'You sound like your brother.'

That produced a sharp intake of breath—and instant anger. 'You'd judge me like Ian?'

She hesitated. 'No,' she said at last. 'That's not fair. But you look like him.'

'And he…came on?'

'He tried,' she said darkly. 'He regretted it. He also tried messing with a couple of my nurses. He regretted that, too.'

'That sounds scary.'

'I invoked you,' she told him, and lightened up a little, remembering a late-night conversation when she'd found Ian propositioning one of her very young ward assistants. 'Rumours were that you didn't know half the stuff Ian did, so I told him that if he messed with my staff I'd personally fly to Sydney and lay every folly I knew about him in front of you. I said it once in desperation, and to my astonishment he backed off. After that I only had to glare at him.'

'He was scared of me?' Max said incredulously.

'I believe he was afraid of you finding out what a toerag he was.'

'I wish you *had* told me.'

'You had enough to worry about,' she said gently. 'That was the island consensus. We knew how ill Christopher was. I'm glad we didn't worry you.'

'But if you had…'

'No.' And this time it was her turn to touch him. His face had grown grim. She could see the pain of remembrance, of regret, and she couldn't help herself. She reached out and traced the strong contours of his face, a feather touch, a touch of comfort and nothing more. 'Max, you've done all you can for this island. To stop Ian you would have had to leave Christopher, and that would have been unthinkable. Your first care had to be for your son.'

'As your first care will be?'

'If I'm allowed to keep Joni, yes.'

'You'll make a formidable mother.'

'Don't you believe it,' she said, suddenly feeling shaky. 'I'm tough on the outside but I'm squishy in the middle.'

'Which is the best combination for a mum.'

'You think so?'

'I know so.' His hand came up and caught hers. 'Hettie, you know it'll be hard.'

'It'll be hard but it'll be fun.' She should pull away from his touch, she thought. His hand was holding hers and it was totally inappropriate, but to pull away seemed…ungracious?

Impolite?

Unthinkable.

'It might not happen,' Max warned.

'I know that. But I will fight for it.'

'You have no one to help you.'

'I won't need help. Like you, I've learned to be independent.'

'I don't see Child Welfare seeing independence as an attribute.'

'Strength must be.' She looked down at their linked hands. Once more she thought about pulling away, but once more came the realisation that pulling away was impossible.

'I hope you're right.' He, too, was looking at their linked hands and his face twisted into a wry, self-mocking smile. 'Strength has to be fed, though.'

'So how did you stay strong? All those years?'

'I'm not sure I did,' he confessed. 'Maybe on the outside…'

'I guess that's the important part. The part we show to the world.'

'That's the part you'll show to Child Welfare when they assess you?'

'What else should I show them?'

'Maybe the softer bits,' he suggested.

'Softer?'

'The distress you feel at Sefina's death. The regret. And the way Joni makes you feel…'

'How do you know how he makes me feel?'

'I had twins, remember?' he said gently. 'I was twenty years old, I was grief-stricken, I was terrified, and I held them and knew I'd do anything in my power to protect them. It was enough to make me study medicine, to make me vow to learn everything I could for Christopher. It was even enough for me to send Caroline back to the island to live with my parents and my aunt. I loved her enough to let her go.'

There was a long silence at that.

Their hands were still linked. It *was* inappropriate, Hettie thought inconsequentially, and everything seemed inconsequential just now.

Everything except that link.

But somewhere in that conversation was something she had to pursue. A warning?

'Are you saying…maybe I should let Joni go?' she asked into the stillness, and he didn't answer for a while. His fingers started massaging hers. It was a comfort touch, maybe something he'd learned to do for Christopher, she thought, but it didn't feel like something he'd do for Christopher.

Or maybe it was just that she was a woman and he was every bit a man...

A man who was too close.

A man to whom she wouldn't mind being closer.

'I don't know,' Max said at last, heavily now, still massaging her fingers, using his thumb and middle finger to knead their length, strong, firm, sure. 'I only know you're offering something I can't. To commit... Hettie, it's for a lifetime.'

'That's what I want.'

'I've done a lifetime.' His words were suddenly angry. She flinched. He closed his eyes and shook his head. 'I'm sorry.' He released her hand, then absently lifted the other and started massaging again. She had a sudden image of Max, a surgeon, always on call, finding time every day to be at his son's bedside, gently working his magic.

For a lifetime...

'You can't regret,' she whispered, and he shook his head.

'No. Except the time I couldn't spend with Caroline.'

'Caroline understands.'

'Will Joni understand that you need to work?'

'Other women work when they're on their own.'

'So do men, as I did, but believe me it's usually not by choice. Sole parenthood is just plain hard.'

'So if they ask—Child Welfare—will you support me?'

'Why would you need my support?'

'You're his uncle. His legal guardian. Your wishes should make a difference.'

There was a long pause.

'Why do you want him?'

And what did she say to that? She hardly knew herself.

She thought of all the things she should say, the logical arguments she'd already lined up for the welfare people. How she had a secure job, a supportive community. How she already knew Joni and he seemed to trust her. How she'd been a friend of Sefina's, and how, with her, Joni would grow up knowing his background, his heritage. How she'd raise him with love and with all the skill her nursing background could give her.

But that didn't answer Max's question.

Why do you want him?

And there was no answer to that other than the truth.

'I don't know,' she confessed. 'I know I can't have children. Yes, I lost my baby and I mourned, but then I got on with life. My work satisfies me. I love caring for people. I've loved caring for Joni. And yet I've cared for many children without wanting them.'

'But you want Joni.'

'All I know is that when you handed him to me in the water, something changed,' she whispered. 'I held him to me and I wouldn't have let go, even if the rip had carried us both out. Something just…stuck. It was suddenly like he was part of me. Keanu's sent me away now. He says I shouldn't take on all the caring because it'll hurt more when…*if* I have to give him up. But it can't hurt more than it'll hurt right now. Because in that moment…' She shook her head. 'I'm sorry. It doesn't make sense.'

'But it does,' he said gently. 'At twenty years old I held my twins and that was how I felt.'

'They were yours. Their mother was your wife. It did make sense.'

'I don't think sense comes into loving.'

'No,' she said bleakly, 'it doesn't. But Keanu's right. My chances of keeping him…'

'Hettie, I will support you. I will ask that you be allowed to keep him. I can't do more than that, but I'll do my best.'

She closed her eyes. Swallows were swooping across the pool. It was so quiet she could hear their wingbeats as they fluttered back and forth, snatching insects above the water.

Joni wasn't hers yet—but this man would help her.

'Thank you,' she whispered, and he put a hand under her chin and lifted her face and waited until her eyes were open.

'You'll make a good mother,' he told her. 'You're a good person, Hettie. You deserve…'

'I don't deserve…'

'Okay, maybe "deserve" is the wrong word. But you long for a family. I'm over family. I'm free, so holding on to Joni would hold me down. But you… You'll give him all the love he needs. I know you will.'

'How can you know that?' She shouldn't ask, she thought. He'd given her the assurance she wanted. Why ask for more? But the question was out there.

'Because you're you,' he said, and she looked into his eyes and the combination was too much. The stress of the last two days, the tragedy, the shared danger. The shared worry for a small boy. The swim this morning, the sun, the gentle lapping of the water, the sound of the birds…

Whether she raised her face still more, or whether he bent to her, she could never afterwards remember. All she knew was that he was cupping her face. She was moving those last few inches.

And he was kissing her.

CHAPTER SIX

HE HADN'T MEANT to kiss her. Why should he? There was nothing between them. There could be nothing.

His life had just stopped being complicated, and he needed another complication like a hole in the head. He did not need to have an affair with the woman who wanted to adopt his nephew.

But she wasn't just the woman who wanted to adopt his nephew. She was Hettie, a woman who'd risked her life trying to help him, a woman of strength and character, a woman of past tragedy and determination born of that tragedy.

Or…she was none of those things. She was a nymph, a water creature who'd swum beside him, a desirable, beautiful woman.

She was wearing a sliver of a crimson bikini. She was wet but sun-warmed. Her curls were tumbling, still dripping, in tendrils, to her shoulders.

Her eyes were a deep green, slightly shadowed as though she hadn't slept. She had crinkly life lines at the corners of her eyes… Smile lines?

Which brought him to her mouth…

Yeah, it was her mouth where the trouble was. Her

lips were full, her mouth was slightly open and his whole consciousness centred on it.

When her face tilted to his, when he drew her to him and he touched her…

When he tasted…

It was an explosion of senses that almost blew him away.

He'd had women—of course he had—lovers as well as friends. A widower was sexy, he'd discovered early. It evoked a nice mix of availability, sympathy and, for some reason, intrigue. It was much sexier than a divorcée. More reliable, too.

Or maybe it was Christopher who evoked the reliability response. Christopher had been his out, but, then, he'd never really needed an out. He'd never let himself get close enough.

I have a disabled son…

He'd used it in his head more than he'd used it out loud. It stopped him getting close. He didn't want to get close.

He was close now. He was so close his brain was in danger of shorting out. Hettie's body was against his, wet and sun-warmed and soft and curvaceous. Her slip of a bikini was barely there. Her mouth was lush under his, and she was taking as well as giving.

This kiss was blowing his mind.

When had a kiss ever tasted like this? When had a woman ever felt like this?

She was ordinary! She was a thirty-something charge nurse, a career medic, someone employed in the hospital he helped fund. She was sensible, determined, capable.

She had no right to be making him feel…

Like this kiss had to be deepened. Like he needed to hold her tighter and tighter still, until her breasts were crushed against his chest and until it felt as if their bodies were melting into each other. Becoming one. He heard a whisper of a moan. Her hands were clutching the small of his back, tugging him as close as he wanted to tug her.

The sea grasses were soft. This place seemed deserted. They could…

'No.'

And suddenly she was pulling away.

The world somehow steadied. Or sort of steadied.

Thank heaven she had some sense, he told himself, because he seemed to have lost his.

He had still lost it. She'd pushed back from him, but her gaze was still locked to his. She was breathing too fast. She put a hand to her heart as if to try and control its beating.

Control. That was what they both needed. This was madness.

'This is crazy.' It was a whisper, words he could barely hear, but behind the whisper he suddenly heard…fear.

What was she afraid of?

And then the image of his brother flashed into his mind. *Anything in a skirt…*

'I'm not like Ian.' If she could think that…

'I know.' Her voice wobbled. 'It's just…'

She couldn't explain further but the moment was shattered. How could she be fearful? Her fear made him feel ill.

'You don't trust me and why should you?' He snagged her sarong from the rocks and tossed it to her, then watched as she tugged it round herself like a shield. She was shaking. Because he'd kissed her?

What sort of damage had his oaf of a brother done on this island?

He was a Lockhart. He couldn't escape that. His neglect had caused grief and heartache for the islanders. Was it now causing this woman to back away?

'I'm sorry.' She had herself under control now, and she even managed a weak smile. 'Whew. That was some kiss.'

'But I'm not Ian.' It was all he could think of to say.

'I know you're not.' But still her voice trembled.

'That kiss,' he said slowly into the silence, 'was not a kiss of seduction. Neither was it a kiss that said I'll kiss anything in a skirt. Or in your case—' he managed a smile himself '—anything in a bikini.'

'I know you're not like Ian. Of course I do. But it didn't mean anything,' she whispered. And then she took a deep breath, hauling herself together. 'Sorry. I'm not usually a wimp. It's just… I'm usually in control. That feeling… okay, it scared me. Max, I'm not in the market for a relationship, and I don't think you are, either.'

'I'm not.' He had to be blunt. 'I'll be leaving the island after Caroline's wedding. Harry has the research station under control. The mine's being made safe and will be running as a co-operative from now on, and Caroline and Keanu are happy to oversee things. If I need to, I'll come back, but only for fleeting visits.'

'Can I ask why?'

'My wife died here.'

'That seems a bit…excessive.'

'It does, doesn't it?' He shrugged. 'I can't help that. My father brought me up to be the lord of the island, Lord Lockhart, if you like. Dad never had a title but he acted like he did, as did my grandfather before him. I rebelled. I insisted on heading to Australia to university. Then I met Ellie and brought her here and she died.'

'Which was the end of your freedom,' she ventured, and he shrugged.

'What do you think? Dad wanted me to put Christopher in a home. He insisted the island needed me. In my conceit I thought medicine needed me more. Christopher needed me more. And I was right. My grandfather set up a trust for the islanders' medical care but it wasn't enough for a hospital. With me on the ground in Australia, and with my medical knowledge, I was able to badger the authorities into proper funding, and for years now my income has augmented the terrific service you provide. But the choice I made had costs, so much so that even stepping on the island fills me with regret. So now? I'll see Caroline married, and then I'll go back to work. I still command an exorbitant salary so I can still feed funds here. But Harry is promising to help so the load is lessening. Now, in my spare time…'

'You'll be free?'

'Yes.' He said it with vehemence. 'What's wrong with that?'

'Nothing, if it makes you happy.'

'It will.'

'Be careful what you wish for,' she said softly, and looked out over the sunlit water and smiled. Her smile wasn't for him, though. It was a smile filled with sadness, filled with the same regret he was feeling. A smile that looked back over the years and saw…nothing.

Enough. What was he doing here with this woman? She stirred things up in him he had no wish to be stirred. He needed to get back to the house.

Back to…what?

'You had Christopher,' she said gently. 'You loved him. And you have Caroline.'

'I've let her down…'

'It doesn't matter what you have or haven't done in the past,' she snapped, suddenly angry. 'It's what you do today and tomorrow that counts. I can't see running away as an option.'

'I'm not running. No one needs me.'

'Joni…'

'Has you.'

'What if I'm not allowed to adopt him?'

'Then he'll go to adoptive parents in Australia who'll love him. He'll get over this awfulness and so will you.'

'And I'll be free again,' she said in a strange voice, and he couldn't bear it. He wanted to kiss her again. He needed to kiss her.

But she was backing away even more, slipping her feet into her sandals, fastening her sarong tighter.

'I need to get back to the hospital. Joni might be awake. I don't want to leave him for too long.'

'You might have to leave him forever.'

'So why would you care?' she snapped. 'You think freedom's so great? You might even think it's a good thing for me to be alone again.'

'Hettie…'

'No. I didn't say that.' She bit her lip. 'I have a great life. I'm perfectly happy. I don't need Joni. And I don't need you, either, Max Lockhart, which is just as well, seeing you're flying in and flying out. So you can just keep your hands and your mouth to yourself while you're here.'

'You liked kissing me.'

'What if I did?' she snapped. 'I have very poor choice in men.'

And with that she turned and stalked away, leaving him to follow if he wished.

He decided…maybe he shouldn't follow.

* * *

Joni was awake when Hettie reached the hospital. She hadn't stopped for a shower or to change. For some reason she felt deeply unsettled.

She needed to ground herself.

But if she needed Joni to ground herself, then she was in trouble. She knew it but she couldn't help herself. She headed for the children's ward and Caroline was sitting beside Joni's cot. She had him out of the cot and was cuddling him, but the little boy was asleep.

'Hey,' she said as Hettie walked in. 'What's up?' Her eyes widened as she saw what Hettie was wearing. Hettie was nothing if not proper in the way she dressed for work.

'I just thought I'd drop by and see how he's doing,' Hettie said defensively.

'I'm not talking about the sarong,' Caroline said gently. 'I'm talking about your face. What's wrong?'

'Nothing.'

'Liar, liar, pants on fire. Hettie, I've only worked with you for three months so I still don't know you very well, but I do know enough to recognise trouble.'

'Your dad…' Hettie said, before she could stop herself, and Caroline's face stilled.

'What about my dad?'

'I…' Hettie shook her head. 'Sorry. Nothing. I was just talking to him…'

'In bathers and a sarong?'

'He was telling me…' She fought for a minute for composure. What if she really said what had happened? That Max had kissed her until her toes had curled, that he'd made her feel as young and vulnerable as a teenager, and she'd felt so out of control she was terrified? Um…not.

'He'll support me if I want to keep Joni,' she managed.

'But he doesn't think it will happen?'

'I think he thinks it's a whim.'

'It's not?'

'No.'

'But you're not family.' Caroline looked down at the little boy in her arms. 'He's my family. My uncle's child. My cousin.'

'Do you want him?'

'N-no,' Caroline told her. 'Is that selfish? But if no one else will…'

'He'll be adopted in Australia. It's sensible.'

'Yeah,' Caroline muttered. 'Sensible. Like Dad sending his daughter back to Wildfire while he stayed in Australia. Sensible.'

'Did he have a choice?'

'No,' Caroline conceded. 'But it did hurt, no matter how much I reassure Dad. And it'll hurt Joni. He should stay here. I'll talk to Dad. See if he can apply more pressure…'

'He's said he'll support me,' Hettie said again, and Caroline's eyes frowned.

'Is there something between…?'

'No!'

'There is! Hettie… You and Dad?'

'There's nothing!'

But Caroline's eyes had lit with excitement. 'Hettie, that'd be awesome. You and Dad and Joni…'

'Caro, cut it out. It was one kiss.'

'He kissed you? My dad kissed you?'

'That makes me feel about eighty. Stop it.'

'It shouldn't make you feel eighty. Dad's gorgeous. Oh, Hettie… You could make him stay here. He could take on work at the hospital—heaven knows, the islands could use a full-time surgeon. You could be a family. Hettie, this is amazing. We just have to get it sorted before the welfare people arrive…'

'Will you stop it?' Hettie was half angry, half laughing. 'Of all the ridiculous… One kiss doesn't make a romance.'

'No, but the way you're looking… I know a romance when I see one. Oh, it'd be so wonderful for both of you.'

'Caro, don't.' The laughter faded. She looked down at the little boy in Caroline's arms and she felt…ill.

And Caro's teasing faded. She looked up at Hettie for a long moment and then she rose and gently lowered Joni back into his cot.

'I won't,' she said softly. 'It's just…it would be so perfect. Why did he kiss you?'

'Heaven knows. He's a Lockhart?'

'That's unfair,' Caroline told her. 'As far as I know, Dad hasn't had a single serious affair since Mum died. I asked him once when I was a kid when he was getting married again. You know what he said? He said he had his family. He'd married my mother, he had Christopher and me, and we were all the family he ever needed. Only you know what? From here, with Chris gone and Mum gone and me marrying Keanu, his family's looking a bit lean. But I'd imagine he's still not even thinking about anything serious. Twenty-six years…maybe he's out of the habit.'

'That's none of my business.'

'It's not, is it?' Caroline said seriously. 'But, oh, Hettie, wouldn't it be great if it was?'

Sam, the island's medical director, arrived back later that morning, and he strode from the plane looking immensely pleased with himself. Apparently the patient he'd escorted to the mainland was on the way to full recovery. There was also a woman, Caroline told Max, a paramedic called Lia whom Sam had hoped to see in Brisbane. His grin said that he had seen her, and his love life was just fine.

His grin got even broader when he learned that Max was back. 'Great to have you here, sir,' he told him, and they celebrated by going through the hospital finances. Maybe both men wanted to be thinking of other things but it had to be done. Ian had managed to bleed funds from the hospital, but not enough to cause significant problems. Max's job was to figure out where the gaps were and plug them.

There was also the damage done by the cyclone. There'd been a power surge, and the CT scanner was damaged. A leak had also caused problems behind the kitchen stoves and one of the wards was unusable.

He needed to get back to the mainland and start working again, he thought. He couldn't ask Harry to donate for general maintenance.

Some things he was still responsible for.

'I'm sure Harry would help with this if we asked him,' Sam said as they reached the end of the bookwork. 'If he was allowed. You know he's a doctor himself, a surgeon and a good one. Encephalitis damaged the nerves in his hands so he can no longer operate but he appreciates what we're doing and supports us to the hilt.' He hesitated. 'Speaking of surgeons… I have an islander with suspected appendicitis in room three. Our only surgeon, Sarah, is currently completing her fly in, fly out roster—did you know she and Harry have just married? But at the moment she's on the mainland. Tomas seems to be settling, but if he flares in the night can I call on you?'

'Of course. You'd normally fly him out?'

'Keanu and I can cope with a simple appendix, which is what this looks like, but Tomas is in his sixties. With the CT scanner out of action I'd like to send him to the mainland. I'm all for avoiding surprises when we open things up, but the islanders hate leaving.' He hesitated. 'Max, there are many things we could use a specialist surgeon for. At the moment we have Sarah for one week a month but it's not enough and now she's married Harry. Harry loves this place but he has his own country. He has research facilities elsewhere and Sarah will travel with him.'

'You're telling me the position's vacant.'

'Interested?'

'For tonight, yes.'

'But not forever?'

'A week and then I'm gone.'

'You hate it here so much?'

Max hesitated. Did he hate the island?

No. He loved it. The island was like a siren song, calling him home.

The problem was, though, he'd never been able to see it as home. He saw it as responsibility.

When he'd been born his grandfather had still been alive. He had vague memories of walking with the old man, hand in hand, as old Henry Lockhart had started the process of handing over.

'You'll own this,' he'd said. 'You'll own every square inch, but don't you dare waste it. And don't think of it as pleasure. It's a burden, boy, a sacred trust. My grandfather bought this island and what he didn't realise was that buying it meant responsibility for every islander who makes their living from it. These are your people, Max, boy. You'll work for them for the rest of your life.'

Even then—aged, what, about six?—Max had felt the burden of responsibility. As a kid, roaming the island with the island kids who were his friends, he'd already felt it. If anything happened to his mates, his family and their families, had looked to Max. He remembered his best mate, Rami, falling from the cliffs while they'd been checking birds' nests. Rami had broken his leg. Max's father had belted Max and then sent him to Rami's family to apologise.

'You're a Lockhart,' he'd growled. 'Your responsibility is to keep people safe, not put them in danger.'

Keep people safe...

That's what he'd been juggling all his life. Keeping his children safe. Keeping the islanders safe.

If he allowed Harry to fully fund the hospital... To finally walk away...

'This is your home, isn't it?' Sam asked curiously, and Max dug his hands into his pockets and thought about it.

'I don't do...home,' he said at last. 'When I was in Sydney with Christopher I always thought I should be here. When I was here, Christopher needed me. Home has always meant...guilt.'

'Hell, Max.'

'I'd been thinking I might take a break. I thought I might take *Lillyanna* and sail round the world.' He was attempting lightness he wasn't feeling. 'Until she rolled. The night of the cyclone put me off like you wouldn't believe.'

'I can imagine it would.' Sam hesitated. 'But if you did decide to settle... We might not need your money

anymore but your presence would be a godsend. The islanders need a figurehead. Persuading them to get their
kids vaccinated. Mosquito eradication. Disease control.
So many things… They still look up to you.'

'Even after Ian?'

'Especially after Ian. They knew he was the wrong
Lockhart. And, Max…'

'Yes?' He was starting to feel…goaded.

'Hettie and Joni.'

'What about Hettie and Joni?'

'Joni's Ian's son and the islanders treat him as that. If
you stayed…he'd be your son. The difference would be
unimaginable.'

'I can't take on another family.'

'No one's asking you to take on another family,' Sam
said gently.

'But you are pressuring me.'

'I'm just telling you the truth.'

Hettie was on duty that afternoon and she was busy. All
she wanted was to be in the children's ward with Joni,
but Joni was happy, playing with Leah, the ward clerk,
and the hospital seemed suddenly to be full of acute patients who needed her skills.

Tomas Cody was one of them. Sam had examined him
and given him pain relief but Tomas wasn't settling and
was obviously afraid.

By late afternoon Hettie was thinking of calling Sam
back, just to reassure him, but before she could, Max
appeared.

He was dressed semi-formally again, and he carried a
stethoscope. He paused at Tomas's door and smiled at her.

'Good afternoon, Nurse. Good afternoon, Mr Cody.

Dr Taylor's asked me to see you, Mr Cody, in my capacity as a surgeon. Do you know who I am? Max Lockhart...'

'I know who you are,' Tomas muttered. 'Damned Lockhart who ran away...' And then he paused and seemed to regroup. 'Nope, that's wrong. You've been the one sending money, I know that. Keeping this place going. It's your brother who was the bad egg. Blasted pain's got me confused.'

'That's why I'm here,' Max said gently. 'Dr Taylor— Sam—suspects appendicitis. He could send you to the mainland tomorrow but if it is appendicitis I could whip it out here. That is, if you trust me.'

'Of course I trust you. Your mother used to say you'd made a brilliant surgeon. If you can stop this gut ache I'd be grateful.'

'It's okay to examine you?'

'Be my guest.'

So Hettie watched as Max gently questioned, gently examined, gently probed. His questions said he'd confronted this situation hundreds of times before. His very assurance as he performed the examination had Tomas relaxing. Pain could often be augmented by fear, Hettie knew, and somehow Max's very assurance was taking the fear out of it.

And at the end of the examination Max sat by Tomas's bed as if he was prepared to chat.

How many surgeons did that? Hettie thought in astonishment. In her experience surgeons arrived, did a fast examination and then left to discuss the outcome with the lower orders. Not with the patients themselves, at least not first off.

'I think it is appendicitis,' Max told him. 'You have a tender abdomen and a slight temperature, but I can't be sure without a CT scan. Sadly our CT scanner is out of order. It was damaged by a power surge during the cyclone.'

'I don't want to go to the mainland,' Tomas said, startled. 'Not for just an appendix.'

'Well, here's the thing.' Max glanced up at Hettie, a single glance that somehow encompassed her, that told Tomas that Max was part of a medical team, working for the best for him. How did he do that? Hettie wondered. She didn't know. All she knew was that this man engendered trust. It seemed to ooze from him like radio waves, encompassing all in range. 'You're older than most people who present with appendicitis. There's a slight chance you could have some kind of bowel blockage, something that might have caused your appendix to get inflamed. You don't seem very sick so I doubt if that's the case, but it might be. Without a CT scan I can't guarantee it.'

There was a long silence while Tomas took that on board. 'I guess…' He hesitated but then forged on. 'You're saying… Guys of my age… You're saying things can go wrong, huh? If it was a kid with a bad appendix, you'd just think it was their appendix, but with me… well, there's all the C-word stuff. You're saying there's a chance it's cancer?'

He'd repeated what Max had told him in terms of acceptance. How had Max done that? Hettie thought. More and more, she thought, this man had skills that were needed here.

If he could stay…

He wasn't staying, and it was just as well, she reminded herself. After that kiss…

'The chance is small,' Max said. 'But we can't exclude it.'

'So if you operated…' Once more Tomas hesitated and then he forged on. 'If there is something in there, you could fix it?'

'I could try.'

'No promises, right?'

'There never are in medicine,' Max told him, and once more Hettie was stunned by Max's skill in telling it like it was.

'So if I went to the mainland and they did one of those CT scan things and it told them there was cancer…'

How hard had that been to say? Hettie thought, but Max didn't react. It was like cancer was just like a normal word. A non-scary word. A workaday word.

'If I was in Cairns,' Tomas forged on. 'If it was cancer… Someone like you would do the operation, right?'

'That's right.'

'And you'd cope with what's in there when you found it.'

'We'd have a better idea of what we were dealing with,' Max told him. 'We might be better prepared but, yes, it'd be someone like me doing the operating.'

'So you can operate here?'

'I can,' Max said steadily. 'If you trust me. But, Tomas, remember, there's still a very good chance it's just appendicitis.'

But Tomas had relaxed, Hettie thought. The big man had straightened in the bed and was looking directly at Max, man to man. It was like saying the word 'cancer' out loud had brought the bogeyman out in the open where it could be fought, not just by Tomas but by all of them as a team.

'I trust you, Doc,' Tomas said, and Max grinned and reached for his hand to shake it.

'I'm glad to hear it. After so long off the island…'

'You're a real Lockhart,' Tomas muttered. 'Not like the other one. Now, about this gut ache…'

'I'll do something about that right now,' Max said. 'Nurse de Lacey…'

'Hettie,' Tomas growled. 'She's one of us. Our Hettie.'

And what was there in that that made Max flinch? Hettie saw the brief flash of bleakness, but then it was gone.

'Hettie,' Max corrected himself, and he smiled at her, and there it was again, that smile, and why it had the power to disconcert her so much she didn't have a clue. 'I'll write Mr Cody up for—'

'Tomas,' Tomas growled, and Max grinned.

'Only if I'm Max.'

'You're Mr Lockhart,' Tomas growled. 'Some things don't change. Some things shouldn't change. We've needed a Lockhart to be in charge here forever.'

Max's smile faded. He stood looking down at Tomas for a long, long moment and finally he nodded.

'I'll see what I can do,' he said. 'But, meanwhile, we'll give you painkillers and let you sleep. Sam's started you on antibiotics and there's still a good chance things will settle down. But if nothing's changed in the morning then we'll go in and fix things.'

'That's exactly what this island needs,' Tomas muttered. 'Finally, a Lockhart who can fix things.'

Max had dinner at the resort that night. He spent time with Harry, discussing out how to keep the islands, Wildfire and the rest of the M'Langi group, safe into the future.

Yes, Harry was prepared to put funds into the hospital. Yes, there were good men prepared to oversee the mine. Yes, the mosquito eradication and the vaccination programmes could go ahead.

Things were under control. There was no need for Max to stay after Caroline's wedding.

He walked home—no, he walked back to the homestead—late. He walked around the lagoon and then he paused. Hettie was where she'd been that first night he'd sat with her. Looking out over the lagoon.

He paused, and decided not to intrude. He could sense her need for space even from where he was.

There'd been a burial service for Sefina late that afternoon. He'd stood in the background then, too, hating to intrude.

It had been a simple island service with less than a dozen people in attendance. Hettie had stood at the graveside with a couple of the nurses from the hospital. She'd held Joni, and she'd placed a spray of frangipani on the grave. Sefina's son and Sefina's friend saying goodbye.

A part of him had ached to go and stand by them, but he had no right. It wasn't his place. His brother had done such harm...

Some of the island women watched from the background as well, as if, like him, they were ashamed.

In time these women could support Hettie, he thought, if she was allowed to keep Joni. The anger and resentment of Sefina's husband had driven them away, but maybe the fact that Joni was Ian's son could eventually be forgotten.

That had been a moment of hope amid the bleakness, but there seemed only bleakness now.

Hettie was still in her nurse's uniform. She must have just come off duty. She didn't have Joni with her. She was simply staring out over the moonlit water.

He could feel her desolation.

He'd only known her for three days. How did he feel he knew her so well?

Shared experience? They'd been through grief, but hers had been the bleaker harvest. He'd been left with two children. Despite his appalling medical problems, Christopher had brought him joy. Caroline would continue to bring him joy. Hettie had none of that.

In time Caroline and Keanu could even give him grandkids. That was a sudden blindside. Surely he was too young to be a grandfather, but the thought was… amazing. He'd have to come home for that.

Home?

This wasn't home.

Nowhere was home.

He stood on, in the shadows of the palms, and watched Hettie for a few moments more, careful not to make a move, not wanting to intrude. Was he being a stalker, just watching? The thought crossed his mind, but he pushed it away. He needed this time to watch her.

She seemed so bereft. So alone.

Sam seemed to think the authorities would come down hard on her wish to keep Joni. Maybe she was mourning that already, as she was mourning the death of her friend. But Hettie must've known more than most that she could survive grief and move on.

But did she need to?

An image flashed into his mind, a tiny nebulous thought. A thought so ridiculous…

He and Hettie and Joni. A family. They'd let Joni stay then.

A family. Was he out of his mind? This was tiredness speaking, he decided, and grief, and a bit of shock and pain thrown in for good measure.

Enough. He could justify watching her no longer. He turned and slipped away, aware as he did so of a sharp stab of loss.

Like leaving part of him behind?

No!

He was still raw from Christopher's death, he told himself. He was in no state to be thinking of anything other than the needs of himself, his daughter and the island.

So why were the needs of one nurse suddenly so important?

Why, when he went to bed, did he lie awake and think of Hettie?

Why did the faint idea of family suddenly seem possible?

How did she know he was there?

She had no idea. It was like a sixth sense, telling her there was someone among the shadows.

Maybe she should be nervous. Maybe she should be creeped out.

She wasn't. It was Max. She knew it, and she also knew he was fighting shadows that were as long as her own.

She didn't move. She didn't by as much as a blink let on that she knew he was there. There was no need, for it seemed he was doing the same as she was.

He'd be looking into the future and seeing only echoes of the past.

This was dumb. She was tired and she had to be at her best tomorrow. She had to make a good impression on the welfare people. More, she had to convince them she could be mother and father to Joni and that she could care for him better than some adoptive parents in Australia.

Could she?

It was too huge a question for her to answer.

Max would support her. The thought was comforting but strangely it wasn't enough.

She wanted more. From Max?

Why was she thinking that? She had no right.

'Enough.' She said it out loud, knowing, once again without understanding how, that Max had gone, and the night felt emptier for his going.

CHAPTER SEVEN

Tomas was no better the next morning. The drugs Max had prescribed had had to be topped up in the small hours and when Max saw him at eight, he was starting to slip into an abyss of pain.

'Enough,' Max told him. 'If it's okay with you, Tomas, we're going in. I'll operate. Sam will do the anaesthetic.'

'And Hettie will be there, too?' Tomas demanded. Hettie had come into the ward with Max and was standing at his side, waiting for orders.

'I'm not much use,' Hettie told him. 'I just get to stand around and watch the doctors do their thing.'

'Yeah,' Tomas growled. 'Like we know that's true. There's no one on this island we'd rather have than Hettie in an emergency,' he told Max. 'We're limited in doctors. The number of times she's had to step in, stitch people up, help mums with bubs, cope until a doc can get here... She ought to be a doctor, our Het. Some of us reckon she already is.'

'Hush,' Hettie told him. 'Don't give him any ideas. If you think it's fun to chop people open...'

'I reckon you could do it if you had to,' Tomas said stubbornly, and Max glanced at Hettie and saw her blush, and thought he wouldn't be the least bit surprised if Tomas was right.

'So you want Hettie there in case Sam or I fall over?' he asked, and Tomas managed a weak grin.

'That's the one. With Hettie I know nothing will go wrong.'

She's that sort of woman, Max thought. Though the weird fantasies of last night had slipped back where they belonged, into the realms of tired night dreams that could be safely ignored, it still gave him curious comfort to think that when he left the island Hettie would stay on. It was as if the island was safe in her hands.

His daughter intended to stay here. Maybe in time Hettie could even deliver her babies. She could be here for her.

As he couldn't? Because he could no longer do family?

Enough. He turned to the drug chart and started writing up pre-meds.

He had a patient to operate on. Medicine.

He needed to concentrate on practicalities, not emotion.

How many appendectomies had he performed in his working life? Max had lost count. He should be able to do this in his sleep, and yet enough had presented challenges over the years for his adrenaline levels to rise as he stepped into the theatre.

This place didn't have back-up, either. It had no highly equipped intensive care unit and no specially trained theatre staff.

It shouldn't matter. He'd already figured that Sam Taylor was extremely competent. A fly in, fly out surgeon and anaesthetist came once a month, but in the interim Sam and Keanu did most of the low-key surgery, even though they weren't specifically surgically or anaesthetically trained. Sam surely knew what he was doing now. He discussed the levels of anaesthesia with a calmness that spoke of years of practice.

And Hettie was good, too. She worked silently in the background, not ready to pick up doctors as they collapsed, as Tomas had suggested, but surely ensuring nothing would collapse on her watch.

As Tomas slipped into drugged oblivion Max checked and rechecked the monitors, and got the go-ahead from Sam—'All systems go!'

And from Hettie came a curt, 'Yeah, why are you asking me?'

He made a neat incision—and almost immediately suspected something was wrong.

The appendix was gangrenous.

'No wonder he was hurting,' he muttered, and then concentrated a bit more and the mood in Theatre became tense around him.

Hettie and Sam had assisted in enough surgical procedures to know when things weren't great. There'd been the odd comment, a joke from Sam as Max had made the incision, and now there was silence.

'Blast,' Max muttered, and the silence intensified.

He closed his eyes for a nanosecond and then stepped back from the table. Hettie moved in with swabs.

'I need to change the incision to midline,' he told Sam. 'I'm thinking caecal carcinoma. That's what it looks like.'

'Can you cope with that here?' Hettie asked. It was a dismayed whisper.

Max was looking at Sam. 'It's extensive—I'm thinking a right hemicolectomy. Couple of hours, mate. You up for it?'

'We can't close him up and send him to Cairns?' Sam asked, and Max shook his head.

'Worst case—if we have to—but the mess of the gangrenous appendix is going to knock him around anyway. There's no way I can close and leave it. To close and send him for further surgery… The outcome's shaky anyway.'

'Okay,' Sam said grimly. 'What are we waiting for?'

And as if on cue the door to Theatre swung open. Caroline stood there, in her nurse's uniform, looking… scared.

'Dad?'

'Problem?' Max was checking the equipment tray with Hettie, figuring what else they needed on hand before he did the midline. 'We'll be a while, Caro.'

'That's just it,' Caro said, and he thought, *Uh-oh, she's scared*. 'We need a doctor out here. Billy Tarla's just come off his boat. He was dropping lobster pots on the reef and the rope wound round his leg. He fell and the pot pulled him under. His mate got him out but he was five minutes underwater. They've got him breathing but he's still unconscious. The boat landed five minutes ago. They should be arriving now.' She paused and listened and they could hear a car being revved up the hill, engine screaming. 'That'll be him. Dad, Sam…'

'Where's Keanu?' Max snapped.

'On one of the outer islands. Clinic.'

'Damn.' Two doctors. Two patients. Two situations ideally calling for two doctors each.

'Close and wait?' Sam asked, and Max looked down at the incision he'd already made and swore. The appendix was a mess. The longer he took, the more likely it would be that infection would spread through Tomas's body.

'If it's important… If I have to,' Hettie ventured. 'If you give me instructions every step of the way… I've given anaesthetics before.'

And Sam's face cleared. 'She has. She's good, Max.'

'Good enough to give an anaesthetic?' he demanded.

'I know it's unusual but we've used her before. She follows instructions to the letter. I trust her.'

And he knew Hettie well enough by now not to argue. Moving on… If Sam left… If Hettie took over the anaesthetic…

'I'll still need an assistant.' He wasn't being precious. To do the complex surgery he was proposing and have to turn constantly to locate the equipment he needed was impossible.

'How about I stay?' Caroline suggested.

'Sam'll need the best help possible,' Hettie said. 'Send in Beth. She's not theatre trained but—'

'What's her training?' Max demanded, and Hettie gave a strained smile.

'Registered nurse, basic qualifications. She's only just returned from the mainland after qualifying. So no theatre experience yet but she's calm and she doesn't faint. You talk me through the anaesthesia, I'll talk Beth through what she needs to be doing.'

Outside the truck had screeched to a halt. 'Okay, Max?' Hettie said. 'Caro, Sam, go. Billy's Tomas's mate's son. If we give up on his life to save Tomas, Tomas will never forgive us. Let's give it our best shot and save them both.'

Hettie was, quite simply, incredible.

The surgery he was performing was complex, technically difficult and messy. Normally there'd be a team of at least four highly qualified medics. Beth was a scared newly qualified with just basic training. She was totally reliant on Hettie's directions. The thing was, though, that Hettie gave directions softly and succinctly, and so subtly that Max found himself snapping a request for something and it was in his hand almost before he needed it. Hettie was watching Tomas's breathing, watching the monitors, watching Max's hands, as if she had six hands and six eyes. And she wasn't even a doctor!

Occasionally she'd slip the odd query his way—or a warning as blood pressure dropped—and once she hit the intercom with her elbow. A scared kitchen lad came to the door and she requested plasma. He returned before Max needed it.

She was amazing.

He couldn't pay her any attention. If Tomas was to end up with a working bowel, Max needed to use all the skill at his disposal, and he could only be grateful that Hettie's skills seemed to match his.

Grateful? 'Astounded' was the word he wanted, he thought as he finally stepped back from the sutured and dressed wound and moved to help Hettie reverse the anaesthetic. He saw the sag of her shoulders as he took control; he knew how much stress she'd been under.

This woman must have spent her entire working life learning 'more', he thought. She must have watched and watched, and learned and learned, and he thought that for Tomas's sake, the day she'd decided to move to Wildfire had been a blessing.

'Thank you both,' he said simply, as Hettie started to help Beth clear up. 'You're two amazing women.'

'You're not so bad yourself,' Hettie murmured, but her voice shook and he thought she could hardly talk. Her concentration had been so fierce…

'We all did good,' Beth said in satisfaction, and then looked down at Tomas's drawn face. 'Will he…? Is he…?'

'He'll need chemotherapy,' he told her. 'But it's looking good. I'm pretty sure I've removed everything. He'll need to go to the mainland for scans and to see an oncologist. It's unfortunate but it's a small sacrifice when he's looking at years of life ahead of him. The appendix was a bit of a blessing. If it hadn't flared, the tumour could have grumbled and spread for a long time without us knowing. As it is, we've caught it early. Also, Sam ran blood tests yesterday and there's no sign of anaemia. Lack of anaemia in caccal carcinoma is related to a better outcome. If I was a betting man I'd say he has a few good years left.'

'Oh, thank goodness,' Beth said, and burst into tears.

No man is an island… Nowhere was that so true as on Wildfire. Tomas was Beth's uncle. Hettie had known that when she'd asked her to assist. It hadn't been fair but there hadn't seemed a choice and Beth had handled herself brilliantly. Now it was over, it was fine to burst into tears—and Max had said exactly the right thing.

He hadn't treated Beth as a junior helping out, Hettie thought. His response to her had been as one medic to another. He hadn't patronised or sympathised and Beth had taken his words and held them. They'd be repeated to Tomas's wife, his mother, his children, and the reassurance would be all the better coming from Beth.

And by adding the comment about going to the mainland for chemotherapy... By the time Tomas was fit enough to put up a fight the family would have plans in place.

It's a small sacrifice when he's looking at years of life ahead of him.

That line would be repeated across the island, and Tomas wouldn't have a leg to stand on.

Max had saved Tomas's life today, Hettie thought, and he'd save it into the future.

So why did her knees suddenly feel like jelly?

'Sit,' Max said, and her gaze jerked up to his in surprise. *What...?*

'Sit,' he said again, more gently, and suddenly his hands were on her shoulders and he was propelling her into a chair at the side of the room. It was a chair put there for just such a purpose, only she'd never used such a chair in her life. But she was sitting and Max was easing her head down between her knees with gentle, inexorable pressure.

'Watch Tomas,' he growled to Beth. 'Tell me the minute his breathing changes. The second.'

'Go back to him,' Hettie muttered. 'I can manage.'

'I know you can,' he said softly. 'You can and you can and you can. You're amazing, Henrietta de Lacey. I wonder if this whole island knows how wonderful you are.'

'She needs to be even more wonderful now,' Beth interjected. The nurse was bent two inches from Tomas's nose, watching his breathing with total attention, following Max's instructions to the letter.

'What—' Max started.

'The Child Welfare people.' Beth pointed to the clock. 'They'll be here in thirty minutes.'

'I need to check on Billy,' Hettie murmured. 'Sam and Caroline might need help.'

'I'll check on Billy,' Max said firmly. 'You go and get yourself ready to be a mother.'

Billy looked like he'd make it. He had water on his lungs. He'd need intravenous antibiotics and careful watching for a couple of days but for a potentially lethal accident the outcome looked promising.

'He was under for almost five minutes,' Sam told Max. 'He's probably knocked off a neural pathway or two, and, to be honest, he didn't have all that many pathways to begin with. Not the sharpest knife in the block is our Billy, which explains why he was tossing out lobster pots without checking where the ropes were. But he's conscious, he knows what day it is and with luck he'll walk away with no consequences. And Tomas?'

'Hopefully the same.'

'Excellent,' Sam said. 'You sure you don't want to join us permanently, Dr Lockhart?'

'No,' he snapped, possibly with more force than necessary, and Sam looked at him quizzically.

'I've hit a nerve?'

'I've had responsibility since I was twenty. I wouldn't mind some freedom.'

'Right,' Sam said slowly. He glanced at his watch. 'You going to this meeting with Child Welfare?'

'I'll go for Hettie but he's not my responsibility.' Why did he feel the need to say that so forcefully? Sam was looking at him in mild astonishment.

'He is your brother's child,' Sam reminded him. 'Ian's name is on the birth certificate. It seemed even though

Ian paid for Sefina's marriage, Sefina was still adamant that Joni was a Lockhart.'

'He was Ian's son, not mine.'

'Yes,' Sam said gently. 'But with Ian's name on his birth certificate, and you being next of kin to Ian, you're his closest relative. You get to choose.'

'I choose Hettie.'

'I meant choosing whether to keep him yourself,' Sam said. 'I've been on the phone to the mainland for a couple of hours, being grilled on the situation, and I can tell you that Hettie will need your support and more if she's to be allowed to adopt him. So why are you still here? Or does your lack of responsibility mean you're not even interested enough to attend?'

'There's no need—'

'To be blunt? Maybe there is,' Sam said. 'If you care about Hettie, you need to be there now.'

He'd always intended to be there. Joni was his last responsibility. This was the last of Ian's messes to be cleared up.

But because of the medical emergencies of the morning he was late. He walked into the meeting, he looked at Hettie's face and he knew things weren't going well.

Sam had volunteered his office for the meeting and two officials were seated behind Sam's desk. They had a chair apiece and had pulled in a folding chair for Hettie. She was sitting facing them. It had the effect of making Hettie seem younger, vulnerable, like a schoolkid in front of two headmasters.

The man and woman were both suited, formal. Hettie had changed in a rush. She was wearing a simple blue skirt and white blouse. Her hair was still tugged back as it had been in Theatre. She was wearing no make-up.

She looked scared.

'Good afternoon,' Max said, and formally introduced himself. 'I apologise for being late—we've had medical emergencies, which have also prevented Dr Taylor from being here. I believe those incidents have also meant Ms de Lacey is less prepared than she'd wish to be. However, we have saved two lives so I'm sure it was worth the inconvenience. Now, before we go any further, this seating arrangement seems inappropriate. Let's pull this desk back and get ourselves a couple more decent chairs. Ms de Lacey has had a stressful morning; we don't want to put her under more stress.'

There were harrumphs and sighs but he went ahead and reorganised the room. He'd learned early with patients that behind-the-desk consultations could push stress levels through the roof. Informality put everyone on an equal footing and Hettie needed that.

Hettie cast him a grateful glance as they all re-settled, but he saw her fingers clench as soon as the woman in the suit started talking again. It seemed they were well into the discussion.

'Dr Lockhart, please understand that we've done some intense research on Joni's situation in the last two days.' The woman addressed Max as if she'd already finished her discussion with Hettie. 'His mother is dead. His stepfather doesn't wish to have anything to do with him—indeed, he's making threats if the child stays on the island. We understand criminal charges are pending but we can't take that into consideration—our principal job is to keep Joni safe. We've made some tentative enquires to his grandparents in Fiji but it seems they'd lost contact with their daughter and want nothing to do with her child. Dr Lockhart, you're Joni's uncle but Dr Taylor says you don't wish to take on the responsibility, either.'

Then her voice softened a little. She became the compassionate counsellor, still talking only to him. Ignoring Hettie.

'Dr Taylor told us your son died three weeks ago,' she murmured. 'If that's the case, we don't blame you for stepping back now. You have no wish to replace your son. No one would.'

You have no wish to replace your son.

The words felt like a kick to his gut, and Max felt himself freeze. He'd never thought of such a concept.

He felt ill.

But to his astonishment Hettie's hand came out and touched his. She flashed him a look that said she understood; that the woman's words were ridiculous.

'No one can replace Christopher,' Hettie said, to the room in general. 'We all know that. Joni and Christopher are two different people. "Replacement" is the wrong word, and to put Joni's care into the context of Max's grief is inappropriate.'

'I didn't mean...' The woman paused, disconcerted, looking towards her colleague for help.

'What Maria means,' the man said evenly, 'is that you don't want the child, Dr Lockhart, and that's understandable. Your grief aside, you are his next of kin. We've made tentative enquiries. You've raised two children already. You seem admirably responsible so of course you could have custody if you want him. But you don't, so we need to make other arrangements. Ms de Lacey here has kindly offered—'

'There's no *kindly* about it. I *want* Joni,' Hettie said, and maybe only Max heard the faint tremble in her voice. Her hand was still touching his. Was she taking reassurance now instead of giving it?

'Very well,' the man said. 'Ms de Lacy has expressed a desire to keep him, but we fail to see it as an appropriate option.'

'Well, I do,' Max said firmly, and he found himself holding Hettie's hand. Staring down this officious pair together. 'Hettie's competent, caring and loving, and she has the backing of the entire hospital staff. She also has my backing. As Joni's uncle, do I have a right to ask that Joni stay in her care?'

'Frankly, no,' the woman said, collecting herself and moving on. 'As next of kin, if you want him yourself it's a different matter, but you have no right to delegate. Ms de Lacy, we've talked to the island doctors and to some of the island elders. It seems there's reluctance to accept the child among the islanders. As well as that, Ms de Lacey, you've never expressed a wish to adopt a child before. You knew Joni's mother only in a professional capacity. You certainly didn't know her well enough to prevent her suiciding—'

'That's unfair,' Max snapped, beginning to seriously dislike this woman. But the woman shook her head and continued.

'Ms de Lacey was occupied with her professional duties while Mrs Dason was distressed. We understand that, but we also understand that she'd still be occupied with professional duties if we allow her to try and raise Joni. She has no means of financial support apart from her career. Also, Ms de Lacey, if we allowed you to adopt Joni, he'll be staying on an island where the local community consider him an outsider. That disadvantage might be mitigated if he were to have the support of two loving parents, but our feeling is that you alone have little chance of providing sufficient support. We therefore think it's best for the child if he leaves the island and starts life in a new community with two parents. We're sorry, Ms de Lacey, but Joni will be returning to the mainland with us. Tonight.'

Silence.

Other women might have sobbed, Max thought. Other women might have reacted with anger. Hettie simply sat staring at the woman who'd made the pronouncement.

The silence lengthened. Max tried to think of something to say, and couldn't. Her hand still lay in his. He found himself gripping tighter. Was he feeding her reassurance—or taking it himself?

Or was it something other than reassurance? Guilt?

Or more. She was hurting and he couldn't bear it. And the vision of Joni was all around him, too, a little boy who was partly a Lockhart, his parents' grandchild, a toddler in his cot, keeping quiet because he'd been hit...

Hettie had had the courage to do something about it. Why didn't he?

And the thought he'd had the previous night suddenly was there, front and centre. Family...

Could he?

'Is there any way I can appeal?' Hettie asked at last in a small voice, and the woman gave her a sympathetic smile.

'My dear, you're not family. From all reports you're hardly even a friend. You have no support for the child among the islanders, and you have no family support yourself. What do you possibly have to offer Joni?'

'Love?' Hettie said in a bleak voice, in a voice that said it was already hopeless. And then she seemed to pull herself together. She tugged her hand from Max's and she made one last try.

'What if I leave the island?' she said. 'I can get a job in Cairns. That takes away one of your objections.'

What? Max thought. For the island to lose Hettie...

But it seemed that also wasn't an option. 'The islanders' antagonism is only one of many objections,' the woman said, more firmly now. 'This seems a spur-of-the-moment offer and we can't decide a child's future on such a whim. The issue is settled.'

More silence. Hettie stared down at the floor, her face blank. She looked...stoic, Max thought. She'd accept it and she'd move on.

But why should she?

What had the woman called this? A spur-of-the-moment offer? It was no such thing, Max thought. What Hettie was offering—had, in fact, given—was something as old as time itself. It was love. He'd watched Hettie when she'd realised Sefina was dead and he'd seen the grief—and the love. He'd seen her at the simple burial service for Sefina. Hettie had looked stoic then. She'd loved and she'd lost.

Hettie had offered to move to Cairns. The woman had called it a spur-of-the-moment offer. It hadn't worked.

Love...

The situation was a muddle, a chaotic tangle in his head. He was trying to get it clear, but, no matter how tangled, one thing stood out.

For whatever reason, however unlikely, Hettie loved Joni. And wasn't love the most important thing?

And as he looked at Hettie he felt something deep within his gut, something that hadn't stirred for years.

Love?

No. He didn't understand it. It was too soon, too fast, too crazy. He had to get himself together. He had to get this on a solid, unemotional footing.

He had to say the only sensible thing there was to say.

'I have a proposition,' he said into the silence.

Behind him the door swung open. Sam had promised to try and attend to back Hettie up, and here he was. He opened the door but then he paused, as if he knew how momentous were the words Max was about to say.

'I've told you,' the woman snapped, her professional smile slipping. 'You can't delegate responsibility.'

'No, but I can share,' Max said, and he thought, *What am I doing? I want no responsibility.*

But surely this wasn't taking it. This was simply handing it over in another way.

'How?' the woman snapped, and Max turned to Hettie and took her hand and smiled at her.

'Easy,' he said. 'Hettie de Lacey, will you marry me?'

Up until now this discussion had been loaded with silences. None had been as long as this one. It stretched seemingly all the way to the horizon and back, and then zoomed off into the distance again.

The woman was the first to recover. 'Is this some kind of joke?' she snapped, but Max didn't take his eyes from Hettie.

'I'd get down on one knee if I didn't have coral grazes all over both of them,' he said. 'But, Hettie, I'm serious.'

She didn't look like she thought he was serious. She looked like she thought he'd lost his mind.

'What...? Max, for heaven's sake...'

'Think about it,' he said, urgently now because he could feel the rising anger of the two officials behind him. 'Hettie, can we go outside for a moment?'

'Say what you need to say here,' the woman snapped angrily. 'We'll not condone any arrangement made purely—'

'For the good of Joni?' Max finished for her. 'Isn't this what the entire meeting is about?' Still he watched Hettie. 'Hettie, think about it. I believe I'm Joni's lawful guardian. I'm his closest kin. As Louis has refused any responsibility, any court in Australia will give me first right of custody, especially as I know what parenthood entails. I know what I'm taking on.'

'You don't intend to take it on,' the woman snapped, and finally Max turned back to her.

'In times of stress families need time to adjust,' he said. 'You know that. I've changed my mind, and that's understandable in the circumstances. The responsibility's mine, and I'll take it on as long as I have a wife to support me. If Hettie agrees to marry me, we'll take Joni for our own.'

'But...you don't even want to stay on the island,' Hettie whispered, and Max turned to her again, his gaze meeting and holding hers. His gaze was an urgent message— *Hush*, he was saying without speaking. *Don't argue. Go along with this.*

'I will need to come and go,' he agreed. 'But half the workers on these islands seem to work on a fly in, fly out basis. I will support you, Hettie, and I'll support Joni. I swear.'

'You can't...' Hettie whispered.

'Why can't I?'

'This is ridiculous,' the woman snapped, and Max shook his head, determined not to look at her again.

'It's not ridiculous. Hettie and I share a very deep friendship. She's been in my employ for many years now.' There was no need to mention it wasn't totally his employ—the hospital was part funded by the Australian Government and he hadn't actually met Hettie until this week. That was irrelevant.

'Hettie's one of the best nurses I've ever met,' he continued. 'She's competent, she's caring, she's wonderful. She also swims like a champion and when she kisses me she knocks my socks off. Hettie and I have both been married before. Up until now we've been looking at life through sensible, pragmatic glasses, but suddenly I'm thinking, Why not? Why not, Hettie, love?'

To say Hettie looked astounded was an understatement. She looked like she'd just been slapped on the face with a wet fish. It couldn't matter. There was nothing he could do to make this proposal more romantic. Or sensible.

He wanted to whisk her outside and talk through practicalities, but there was no way he'd leave these officials time to reorganise their opposition. This was a rearguard attack. They'd been left floundering—it was just a shame that Hettie had, too.

'Well, about time.' It was Sam, coming to Hettie's rescue. Coming to both their rescues. He stooped to kiss Hettie, as if the thing was already decided and she'd said yes. 'You two have been smelling of April and May forever.' He grinned across at the officials. 'The whole island's been wondering... I had a text from one of my more impudent twelve-year-old patients when I flew in yesterday morning,' he told them. 'Bobby "borrowed" his dad's phone to take a picture of the big fish he was planning to catch. Instead, he spotted our Hettie and Max at one of the most beautiful of the island's water-holes. He sent me the photo in twelve-year-old indigna-tion, and asked should Nurse Hettie be allowed to do "yucky stuff"?'

His grin broadened as he flicked open his cellphone and held it up. And there were Max and Hettie after their morning swim yesterday. Or rather there was Max—you could scarcely see Hettie but there was no denying she was under there.

It had been quite some kiss. All the emotion in the world was in that kiss.

Hettie opened her mouth to say something but nothing came out. Actually, Max was fighting for anything to say, as well. Hettie's normal tan had turned to bright crim-son. She looked like she was blushing from the toes up.

This was one kiss recorded for the world to see. It was one kiss that meant these officials just might see their relationship as real.

It was one kiss that didn't mean anything?

'So we have Joni's uncle and Joni's mother's friend,' Sam said, smiling from Hettie to Max and back again. 'Two people who risked their lives trying to save Sefina and who saved Joni. Two people who love Joni and who wish to marry.'

'But Dr Lockhart doesn't want the child,' the woman managed.

'I didn't see how I could love him,' Max told her, deciding he should stop looking at Hettie. He'd sprung this on her with no warning. It wasn't fair, but then, he hadn't planned this. He just had to go with it. 'But if Het-tie's willing to share,' he continued, 'then I think we can provide Joni with a safe and loving home. Hettie? This is much earlier than I'd like. I know it's rushed but suddenly it seems the only sensible option.'

He turned fully to her then and took her hands in his. He held them, firmly, and waited until she looked up at him. His gaze held hers. *Trust me,* he was saying in his head, but the words he said out loud were different.

'Hettie, we can be a family,' he said. 'We can make a home for Joni.'

'And no one will ever give Joni grief about his background when he's our Hettie and our Doc Lockhart's son,' Sam said triumphantly.

'Sam?' Max was still focussed on Hettie.

'Yes?' Sam was practically bouncing.

'Shut up,' Max growled. 'It's time for Hettie to speak. Hettie, do you think…? Is it too soon to ask you to marry me?'

His eyes were doing all the talking. He'd thought previously that this woman seemed to be a kindred spirit. Could she guess what he was thinking now?

She looked at him for a long time. The lady from welfare made to say something but the guy beside her put his hand on her arm as if to restrain her. All attention was on Hettie.

'We can do this,' Max said softly. 'We can work this out. Together.'

And she got it. He saw the moment when she decided to trust him. He saw the moment she decided to put Joni's fate—and hers—in his hands.

'You really want to marry me?'

'I do.' How hard was that to say? To be honest, though, it didn't seem to be adding to his responsibility. In some way it seemed to lessen it.

'Yes,' he said. 'We can give Joni a home. We can make it work.'

'Okay, then,' she said, and he blinked.

'Okay?'

'Until I get a ring, okay is all you get,' she managed. 'Okay is fine until I see the diamond to match.'

And amazingly he saw the hint of laughter, the slight twitch of her lips. She was amazing, he thought. Stunning.

'When?' the woman snapped in a last-ditch attempt to gain control, and Sam looked from Hettie to Max and back again and obviously decided a little help was needed.

'The islanders don't have mandatory waiting periods like the mainland does,' he said, grinning broadly. 'I know,' he added as the woman made an involuntary protest. 'They'll need to satisfy the Australian legal requirements, but for now… I'm sure you won't object to an island marriage. This island is, after all, part of Joni's heritage, or it will be with these two as his parents. Now, is there anything else, or is Joni's future settled?'

The officials left soon after, without Joni, making angry noises about Max's indecision costing them time and money but with no arguments left. Sam needed to head back to the wards.

'But this is the best possible outcome,' he told them, shaking Max's hand and kissing Hettie. 'Brilliant. Max, we'll make an islander of you yet.' He left, still grinning, and they were left alone in Sam's office.

What had just happened? Max was feeling like he'd been hit by a truck, but Hettie looked like she'd been hit by a bigger truck. The wet-fish analogy was no longer big enough.

'You know this won't be a real marriage.' He said it too fast, wanting to wipe the look he didn't understand from her face. Was she feeling trapped? He hadn't meant that.

'I didn't…' She took a deep breath and tried again. 'I didn't think so. You're offering…'

'A marriage in name only.' Once again he'd said it too fast. 'I don't intend to stay on the island, but neither do I…did I…intend to marry again. I've had enough of responsibility to last a lifetime.'

'You will be responsible…for Joni. If you marry me…'

'I'm already responsible for Joni.' He said it more forcibly than he'd intended, but he seemed to have little control over his emotions right now. 'What I'm doing by marrying you is assuring his future.'

'By delegating the responsibility.' Her voice sounded as if it came from a long way away.

'I'll pay,' he said. 'Of course I'll cover the cost of his upbringing. And, Hettie, I will treat Joni as my son.'

'Even though you won't be here.'

'I'll visit. He'll be a Lockhart of Wildfire.'

There was a pause. 'How will Caroline feel about that?' she asked at last.

'I think she'll be pleased. She said if worst came to worst she and Keanu would take him.'

'But worst hasn't come to the worst,' Hettie whispered. 'Because you're marrying me to stop that. Max, I don't think I want to be married.'

'But we've both been married,' he said, cautiously now because there was no need to bulldoze her. If indeed she didn't want Joni enough to take this step, things had to be reassessed. 'We married with our hearts before. This is marriage made for practical reasons, sensible reasons. It's a marriage made with our heads.'

'But you kissed me.'

And there it was, the elephant in the room. The kiss…

'In retrospect,' he said cautiously, 'maybe that was a mistake.'

And, amazingly, a glint of laughter crossed her face again. It was an echo, a trace, and it was gone as fast as it had appeared, but it left him disconcerted.

'Meaning kissing could get in the way of a marriage of convenience?' she asked.

'It could,' he said, just as cautiously, and she nodded and fell silent again, and then she turned and looked out the window.

'Why?' she asked, without looking back at him.

'Why?'

'Why are you making this offer?'

He had to get this straight. 'Because I know how much you want Joni. Because I believe you'll make Joni a wonderful mother. Because it'll give you and Joni the respect you deserve on this island.' He took a deep breath. 'And because there's no one else I want to marry.'

She didn't turn back. 'What if…what if there's someone else I'd like to marry?'

'Is there?'

'Call me stupid,' she whispered. 'But I've always thought…one day I'd like to end up with someone who loves me. Darryn never did. My parents never did.' She shrugged. 'Sorry. Pipe dream. It's not going to happen. This is a fine offer, a wonderful offer. It's more than kind.'

'I don't believe I made the offer to be kind.'

'You did,' she said gently. 'And of course I knew as soon as you said it that the sensible thing was to accept.'

'You can still back out.'

'And lose Joni? No.'

'If you meet someone else… Hettie, there's always divorce.'

'You think I don't know that?' Still she was staring out the window, as if there was something out there that took her entire concentration. 'Max, you took my breath away—back there. I was prepared to lose him.'

'I wasn't prepared to let you lose him.'

She turned then to face him. Her face had lost its colour. She looked strained to breaking point. 'It'll have to seem…real,' she whispered. 'At least while you're on the island. I mean, if we marry in name only and never go near each other it'll get back to them soon enough. The authorities. For the first year at least…'

'The Lockhart house is huge,' he told her. 'Caroline doesn't want to live there after her marriage. You could move right in. It's big enough for us…'

'To be separate?'

'Yes.' And then he added, and afterwards he wasn't sure why, 'If that's what you want.'

'Why would I want anything different? But, Max… the big house? I'm staff.'

'You won't be staff. Of course you could still nurse if you want—but you'd be my wife.' And then he paused. The word seemed to echo.

My wife.

He'd had a wife once. It had been a disaster. He'd sworn…

'Things don't need to change,' she said—fast, as if she'd read his mind. 'Max, my villa is fine. I'm happy to stay there.'

'Your villa isn't my home. You said yourself the marriage needs to be seen to be real, and if Joni's to be a Lockhart he has the right to be raised in the big house.'

'But you don't want a wife there.'

'I'll get used to it.'

'You won't have to. You'll be coming and going.'

'Yes.'

'You really won't expect…'

'You to be a wife?' He tried to smile. 'I'm pretty good at cooking for myself these days. I iron a mean shirt. I've even been known to scrub a bathroom.'

'Wow, now we really are getting into the nitty-gritty of marriage proposals.'

'I do have a housekeeper, though,' he added. 'So we don't need to take turn about.'

'This is getting more and more romantic.'

'It is, isn't it?' he agreed, and then he grinned, suddenly relaxing. This'd be okay. He'd marry Hettie. Hettie would live in the big house and care for Joni. He'd stay here for a little longer than he'd intended, but he'd go back to work in Sydney. He'd fly in, fly out, maybe once a month to check things were okay.

They could live in separate wings of the house. He could still be independent. He could still be free.

But there were a few words that niggled, that Hettie had said, that couldn't be unsaid.

But I've always thought…one day I'd like to end up with someone who loves me.

She deserved that, he thought, and suddenly he was back at the pool, with Hettie in her crimson bikini, with Hettie melting into his arms.

He wouldn't mind—

'Don't even think about it,' she snapped, and he stepped back as if she'd slapped him.

'What?'

'If you're thinking about a little nookie on the side.'

'Nookie?'

'You know what I mean.' She glowered. 'This is complicated enough. No nookie.'

'Sheesh, Het, no sex? What sort of marriage is that?'

'A marriage of convenience. It'll be like the olden days. You're a Lord Wotsit with debts up to your ears and I'm a plain little heiress with warts and a crooked nose and millions you can use to restore your castle.'

'I can't see a crooked nose. But do you have warts?' he demanded, fascinated.

'Not that I'm admitting to.'

'You can show me. I'm a doctor.'

She choked then, laughter bubbling up again unbidden. But then it faded and her lovely green eyes grew serious. 'Max, if you indeed do this…it will be the kindest—'

'It won't be the kindest. It's self-interest,' he growled.

'Marriage with no nookie is not self-interest.'

'Providing my nephew with a woman like you for his mother is self-interest. You're brave, kind, funny… Not to mention skilled.'

'My head will explode. Cut it out.' Still her gaze was serious. 'Max, can we really do this?'

'I think we can.' He reached out and took her hands. He looked down at them for a long time. They were good hands, slim, tanned from years in the island sun, worn from years of nursing. Years of caring.

'I know we can,' he said, more surely now. 'This is sensible, Hettie. We can make this work. So when? Next week? We'll get Caroline married off and then do the deed ourselves.'

'No fuss,' she said anxiously, and he could only agree. He was having trouble getting his head around…everything.

'I need to find Caroline,' he managed. 'I need to tell my daughter I have a brand-new family.'

'A family of convenience.'

'I suspect you and I both know that's the only type to have.'

CHAPTER EIGHT

FOR THE NEXT few days Max hardly saw Hettie. Lawyers arrived from the mainland to help him sort out the mess Ian had left. He and Harry spent hours planning directions the island management could take. A new fly in, fly out nurse arrived and Hettie took leave from nursing. She took Joni back to her villa.

They weren't avoiding each other on purpose—were they?

Max couldn't think about it. After so many years of neglect, all his focus had to be on seeing his daughter wed. Arrangements between him and Hettie had to take second place.

Which suited him. He needed time to get his head around what was about to happen.

Caroline and Keanu had organised a wedding rehearsal and then a dinner for their closest friends the night before their wedding. Max dropped by Hettie's villa that morning and asked her to be there, but she refused.

'It's Caroline's time,' Hettie said firmly. 'She needs her dad to herself. She's had to share him often enough.'

Max had to agree. He went to the dinner alone but Caroline cornered him afterwards.

'What's going on, Dad? Are you marrying Hettie or not?'

'Not until after your wedding. Hettie and I both agree that comes first.'

'But Hettie's my friend and your fiancée. She should be here.'

That's what he'd thought but Hettie had been adamant. 'I don't need a social life,' she'd told him. 'Especially not now. Joni needs me. We need to bond.'

Hettie had been dressed in shorts and a T-shirt. She'd let her hair loose. She'd been hugging Joni. She'd stood in the doorway of her villa and she hadn't invited him inside, and he'd thought that was just as well.

After they were married they'd move to the big house and things would change. Or would they? He'd be leaving, heading back to Sydney, doing what came next.

'Dad, talk to me,' Caroline was saying. 'You are marrying Hettie?'

'You know I am.'

'Then she has to be included in tomorrow's ceremony. I thought the hope was that the islanders start looking on Joni as yours and Hettie's. You need to be a family for that to happen.'

'You're my family.'

'Yes, but now I have Keanu, and you have Hettie and Joni. You offered this marriage, Dad. You need to go through with it.'

How to tell his daughter that one part of him would love to 'go through with it'? One part of him thought Hettie was the most beautiful woman he'd ever met.

But the other part of him wanted—needed—to head back to the mainland and soak up the freedom he'd wanted for so long.

'You'll walk me down the aisle tomorrow,' Caroline said, and he forced his attention back to the here and now.

'Of course.' He smiled at his beautiful daughter. Caroline was showing no signs of nerves. She was glowing in anticipation of spending the rest of her life with the man she loved.

Was he jealous?

'I love it that you're here,' she said softly, and suddenly she reached out and hugged him. 'I know responsibility has always kept you in Sydney but I've always known you love me. I'm so glad the *Lillyana* didn't sink. I'm so glad you're free to start again.'

To start again... What did that mean?

'But you have to start,' Caroline continued. Since when had his little girl got bossy? She was certainly bossy now. 'Dad, tomorrow you'll walk me down the aisle, you'll give my hand to Keanu and then you'll sit in the front pew. And you'll sit with Hettie and Joni. I've chosen my new family. You've chosen yours.'

'Caro—'

'It's the way it is,' she said gently. 'We're both moving on, and isn't it wonderful?'

Max went round to Hettie's as soon as the dinner finished. It was late but there was still a light on in her front room. He knocked and she opened the door a notch and peered out.

The door was on a chain. That took him aback a bit. Most islanders didn't even bother to lock their doors.

'Hettie?'

'It's you.' She sounded relieved. She closed the door and fumbled with the chain and a moment later the door swung wide.

She was wearing pyjamas. Pale blue pyjamas adorned with pink flamingos. Her hair was tousled. Her feet were bare and she looked so desirable it was all he could do not to gather her up and claim her as his wife there and then.

Boundaries would have to be worked out, he thought. Boundaries were like fine gossamer threads—he had to look close to see them and they could be broken with one misstep. But they were important.

So he forced himself to stop looking at the woman before him and looked instead at the chain.

'Do you get nervous?' And then he looked more closely. The chain was shiny new, and there was a trace of sawdust on the doorknob. Like it had only just been put on.

'Is this about you and me?' he managed lightly. 'Are you scared I'll come to claim my own?'

'What, club me and drag me by the hair back to your lair?' She said it lightly but he could hear the trace of strain behind her words. 'Nope. It seems to me that I've agreed to go willingly to the big house—if that is indeed your lair.'

'It's the closest thing to a lair I can think of. You reckon I should put down a few bearskin rugs and hook mirrors to the ceiling?'

'And pop in a dungeon complete with shackles and whips. Um…maybe not.' She was smiling but still there was that strain.

'Hettie, what are you afraid of?'

'N-nothing.'

'You don't put chains on your doors for nothing. What's going on?'

'I… Louis was here,' she said.

'Sefina's husband?'

'Yes.' She bit her lip. 'Look, I'm overreacting. He was drunk. You know he bashed Sefina before she died? There's a warrant out for his arrest but Ky's the only policeman on Wildfire and he hasn't been able to find him.'

'But he was here?'

She tilted her chin, looking all at once brave, defiant and vulnerable. 'He was drunk,' she said. 'Well, that's nothing new. But it seems things have changed for him. He's a bully. He accepted Ian's money to marry Sefina but he bad-mouthed her and he threatened everyone who even tentatively tried to befriend her. He threatened me.'

'When?' She was so small, he thought, but then he thought she wasn't small. She was defiant even now. She was five feet four of courage.

'When I reported her injuries to the police,' she said. 'When I told Louis he'd pay for what he was doing to her. He said he'd hurt me and anyone else who tried to interfere with…well, I won't tell you what he called Sefina.'

'That didn't worry you?'

'I told Ky.' She flinched and he saw her regroup. 'And now Louis's in hiding but he's running out of places to hide. He came to find me today, and he yelled at me. He says the islanders are starting to blame him for Sefina's death. They are, too. There are a lot of guilty consciences; a lot of people who looked the other way. Her death has made people see the appalling place she was in. So Louis is getting a hard time and no one's willing to support him. He says… He said, "The kid should never have survived. If you keep him the locals'll be rubbing my nose in it for the rest of my life. Don't you dare try and keep him. You and the doc… Bloody do-gooders. Get rid of the kid or I'll do it for you."'

There was silence at that, silence while Max assimilated her fear; while he looked down at the chain she'd obviously had installed in a hurry; while he looked at the defiance of that tilted chin and saw the fear behind it.

'You told Ky this, too?'

'Yes. He's trying to find him. But word is that he's all talk and he's gone back to Atangi. It was only the booze talking. I should be okay. But Ky sent a guy to put on the chain.'

'Wise but not wise enough,' Max growled. 'You'll stay in the big house tonight. Both of you. We'll pack what you need and you can come now. There's room.'

'Max, it's ten o'clock. I'm in my pyjamas.'

'And very cute they are, too. You can put on some slippers, or I'll carry you.'

She choked on that, laughter bubbling despite the seriousness of what she'd been saying. 'You couldn't.'

'Want to see me try?'

'Yeah, you might manage it if you sling me over your shoulder like a bag of potatoes, and I cling to Joni while you carry me. Not. Max, I've just got Joni to sleep. I can't move now.'

'But you would feel safer in the big house?'

'I… Yes,' she admitted. 'Bessie and Harold are there. With a housekeeper and gardener on site, Louis wouldn't dare come near.'

'And me.'

'And you,' she admitted with another attempt at a smile. 'Macho Max.'

'There's no need to be sarcastic.'

'Believe it or not, I'm not being sarcastic,' she told him. 'You are macho. I've watched you swim into danger to try and save Sefina. You did save Joni. I've also watched you perform as fine a piece of surgery it's ever been my privilege to watch, and now you're threatening to throw me over your shoulder in a fireman's hold. So, yes, macho.'

'So you will come.'

'No,' she said. She took a deep breath. 'Not because I'm being stubborn. Not because I have any sense of bravado. I know I'll have to live there when we're married. But not tonight, Max, when it's Caroline's last night in her home before she marries. Tell me the house isn't full of guests? It is, isn't it?'

'You could sleep in my room. I could sleep in the living room.'

'And have all your guests trip over you in the morning? Max, I'm not moving in until Caroline is well and truly married, until we can divide the place into sensible sleeping quarters, until we can start as we mean to go on.'

And she was right. The place was full.

He thought of Sefina. He'd seen the pictures Hettie had taken when she'd been admitted before the cyclone. She'd been thoroughly, brutally bashed.

Somewhere out there was the guy who'd done it. Somewhere out there was the guy who was threatening Hettie. Rumour said he'd gone back to Atangi. Rumour wasn't enough.

'I'll sleep here tonight, then.'

'You're kidding.' She shook her head. 'Max, you can't. Firstly, I only have one bed. Secondly, it's the night before Caro's wedding. She needs you.'

'Caroline is surrounded by bridesmaids,' he said. 'We've arranged to have breakfast together, alone. I can go home by then, after I've checked with Ky that he has someone to keep an eye on this place. I can kip on your sofa. Okay?'

'I… Okay,' she managed, and he realised that underneath it all she really was scared.

'And, Hettie, you are coming with me to the wedding tomorrow.'

'Caroline's already invited me. I thought I'd slip in…'

'You're slipping nowhere.'

'But—'

'You'll sit with Joni, in the front pew, as my future wife, as my family. You and Joni are under my protection and the sooner Louis understands that, the sooner the threat to you will fade. We're a united front, Hettie. That's what this marriage is all about.'

'Until you leave.'

'I'll keep returning. I'll keep you safe. You're my—'

'Responsibility,' she said flatly. 'I know.'

'I meant to say you're my family.'

'It's the same thing, isn't it?' she said, attempting lightness. 'I'm sorry, Max. I'll try to make your load as light as possible.'

'I didn't mean—'

'I don't want you to explain,' she said, and he heard the faint note of bitterness in her voice. 'I'm enormously grateful and I'm sure Joni will be, too. Okay, then. Let's go find you a blanket and a pillow. My sofa's not bad. Let's both of us see if we can get some sleep.'

As a surgeon on call, and as a father of a disabled son who had spent his life in and out of hospital, Max should have been used to sleeping wherever he found himself. He usually could.

Tonight he couldn't. He found himself staring up at the ceiling, listening to the bush turkeys scrabbling in the undergrowth outside the villa. It wasn't that he was nervous. In truth, he wouldn't mind if Louis appeared. He had Sergeant Ky's number on his phone. He'd spent time training in karate. He wouldn't mind a chance to face off with the guy who'd caused so much grief.

So it wasn't that that was keeping him awake. It was the fact that Hettie was sleeping right through that door.

She had Joni in with her. Soon after she'd left him to his sofa, he'd heard him stir. She'd heard Hettie rise and comfort him, crooning him back to sleep.

For years Max had cuddled Christopher to sleep. The sound of someone else doing it...

Someone else taking his responsibility?

Someone else doing the loving?

It was a strange sensation and it left him feeling unsettled. Especially as the one doing the loving was Hettie.

His wife-to-be.

Wife. The word kept echoing in his head. She wasn't his wife yet, but she would be.

She was so different from Ellie. Ellie had been young, vibrant, carefree. She'd been full of the promise of life to come.

Hettie was sensible, practical, bruised by life.

Which was why this would be a sensible, practical marriage.

She'd be taking on Joni. He wouldn't have to feel responsible.

Why did he suddenly want to feel responsible?

There was a crazy thought. It wouldn't go away, though, and at four in the morning, when Hettie padded through the lounge in her bare feet to heat a bottle, he was still wide awake.

He watched her from the shadows as she quietly heated Joni's milk, and when the bottle was ready he spoke.

'Bring him out here,' he said softly.

She jumped almost a foot. She yelped.

'Yikes,' she managed when she came down to earth. 'Don't do that. I forgot you were there.'

So much for the vague thought—hope?—that she might be lying in the dark, thinking about him.

'Sorry,' he told her. 'I just thought…maybe Joni should start seeing me as part of the furniture.'

'Because?'

'Because I will be,' he growled. 'Hettie, I will keep coming back. He should see me as…'

'His father? He's never had one.'

'I don't—'

'How about he calls you Papa?' Hettie suggested. 'That's a nice encompassing word that could be Dad or could be Papa.'

'And you'll be Nana?'

'That's the Fijian word for mother,' Hettie said softly. 'I can't replace Sefina. I have no wish to try.'

'But you could be Mama.'

'I guess…'

'At least Mama doesn't sound like Grandpa,' he growled, and she chuckled.

'That's settled, then…Papa. He's waiting.'

'Bring him out. Unless you think it'd distress him.'

'No,' she said softly, slowly, as if thinking it through. 'He's got so much to get used to but he needs to get to know his papa.'

Which explained why two minutes later Hettie was perched on the sofa, watching him feed Joni.

She'd simply walked out and handed him over. 'Papa is going to give you your bottle,' she told Joni, and she sat right down beside Max, easing the little boy onto Max's knee. They were right beside each other. Feeding their…son?

Together.

And for some unknown reason it evoked sensations so strong it almost blew him away.

He'd never done this.

Oh, he'd fed children, all right, mostly Christopher. He remembered hours, days, weeks in the nursery for premature babies, and then in a succession of hospitals. Feeding his son. Watching nurses feeding his son.

In the times when his mother had brought Caroline to the mainland, she'd leave her to him to feed so they could 'bond'—but Caroline had hardly known him. Feeding her had been fraught, tense, with Caroline making it very clear she preferred her beloved grandma.

But now… Joni didn't know him. Joni hardly knew Hettie. Yet somehow he was lying cradled in Max's arms, sucking fiercely at his bottle, casting an occasional glance at Hettie as if to make sure she was going nowhere but then looking up at Max again.

It was like he was learning Max's face.

'He's learning to know you, Papa,' Hettie whispered, and Max managed a grin.

'Don't you start using it. I can see it now. One marriage ceremony with a difference. Will you, Mama de Lacey, take you, Papa Lockhart…?'

She chuckled, a lovely low chuckle that lit the night. That even had Joni looking up in wonderment and his eyes lighting with something that might even be a smile— if he wasn't concentrating so fiercely on his bottle.

'You want me to call you Max?' Hettie asked.

'Of course.'

'You mean you want it to be personal?'

There was a question. It hung between them while Joni kept feeding, his sucking slowing as he grew sleepier. He shouldn't need a night bottle anymore, Max thought obliquely, but it was a comfort. A personal need.

Do you want it to be personal?

Was that what Hettie wanted? Support in more ways than one?

A proper marriage?

'Max, I didn't mean... With personal... I'm not asking for romance. I'm not one for hearts and flowers,' she said hurriedly.

'I didn't think you were.'

'But I'll not have a husband who calls me Mama.'

'And if anyone else on this island's seen you in your bikini and heard me call you Mama they'd think I was nuts.'

She chuckled again. 'So I'm not past it?'

'You're not past it at all,' he murmured. 'You're beautiful.'

'There's no need to get carried away.'

'I'm not carried away,' he said, and suddenly the laughter was gone from the room. 'Hettie, you are beautiful.'

'I'm thirty-five years old. I might have been beautiful a long time ago.'

'How long since you looked in the mirror? How long since you listened to your chuckle? How long since you saw your smile?'

'Max...don't.'

'I'm only speaking the truth.'

She sighed then and lifted the now sleeping Joni from Max's knee. She carried him into the bedroom. She had a nightlight on. He watched through the open door as she settled the little boy into the hospital cot she'd borrowed.

She took her time settling him, crooning a little, making sure he was deeply asleep.

Then she straightened and he thought she'd close the door on him and return to bed. Instead, she came back to the doorway and stood and looked at him. It was a direct look that seemed to bore straight through him.

'Max, don't,' she said.

'Don't what?'

'Start something you have no intention of continuing.'

'Hey, I only said—'

'That I'm beautiful. I know. At least, I don't know that I'm beautiful, and you know what? I can't afford to think it. I put beautiful away a long time ago and it's staying away. We need to keep this impersonal. If we need to refer to ourselves as Papa and Mama…'

'In your dreams…'

'Max, that's all we can be to each other.'

'We can be friends.'

'Friends don't call each other beautiful.'

'Of course they do.'

'Friends don't kiss each other…as you kissed me,' she whispered and he had no answer.

'You want to be free,' she said, still whispering. She made no move to come forward out of the doorway. It was as if she was making sure she had an escape route. 'You'll leave after the marriage ceremony.'

'I'll come back.'

'As often as you need to. I know. You take your responsibilities seriously and I honour you for that. I'm not exactly happy that Joni and I need to be your responsibility, but I'll wear that. It's…anything else that I can't wear.'

'Like?'

'Like falling in love,' she said, and her whisper was so low he could hardly hear it. 'Max, I can't do that. I can't afford to. Not with a man who doesn't want to be here.'

'I don't want you to…'

'Fall in love? Of course you don't, and I won't, at least I think I won't, unless you keep calling me beautiful. Unless you keep cradling Joni and looking up at me as if you want me to share how you're feeling. Unless you kiss me again.' And then she hesitated but finally the rider…

'Unless you care.'

'I don't think…' he said, carefully, because in truth he had no idea how to respond to this. 'I don't think I can stop caring.'

'Care as my boss, then. Care as my acquaintance. You can't care as my husband.'

'How can I not?'

'Stay separate,' she said. 'We've both been separate for many years now. We're probably good at it.'

'I'm not.'

'But you don't want to love me. You don't want me to love you.'

There was a long silence at that. A loaded silence.

Love.

He thought of the way he'd loved Ellie, fiercely, passionately, throwing all cares to the wind. What a disaster.

He thought of the pain of loving Caroline, knowing he couldn't give her what she wanted, knowing he'd had to let her go to keep her safe.

He thought of the agony of loving Christopher, of losing him little by little by little.

Did he want to love again? Could he?

It was too hard an ask, and Hettie saw it. She smiled, a tiny, rueful smile that was almost self-mocking.

'Don't, Max. Don't even think about going there. You've done an amazing thing for Joni and for me. All I'm saying is that we can't complicate things by going further. Yes, I'll call you Max. I won't call you Dr Lockhart because you'll be my husband but you'll be my husband in public only.'

'So you'll call me Dr Lockhart in private?'

'Are you kidding?' she said with sudden asperity, with the return of the Hettie with courage and humour. 'That would be just plain kinky. You know exactly what I mean, Max Lockhart. I have no need to explain further. Just cut it out with the beautiful. Now, if you don't mind, I'm going to bed.'

'But you will sit beside me at the wedding tomorrow.'

'Yes, because that's public.'

'Of course.' He didn't have a clue where to take this from here, and apparently neither did she, because she backed a few steps into her bedroom.

'Goodnight,' she managed, and closed the door behind her.

'Goodnight,' he repeated, but it was all he could do not to add a rider.

Goodnight, beautiful.

'Fall in love? Of course you don't, and I won't.'

That was what she'd said but she was wrong. She'd just uttered an out-and-out lie.

Hettie settled Joni into his cot and tried to settle herself but settling was impossible. She'd just watched a man who would be her husband feed a child who would be her son, and while she'd watched, she'd felt her world shift.

He was big and tender and kind. He'd held Joni as she knew he'd held his own son for years. She'd watched the expert way he'd held the bottle, his big hands cradling Joni, manoeuvring the bottle so Joni wasn't sucking air. She'd watched the way he'd constantly checked that all was right with the baby's world.

With her baby's world.

He was staying here to protect her.

He'd put his life on the line to try and save Sefina.

He held her heart in his hands.

And there it was, as simple and as complicated as that. It was crazy to say she'd fallen in love. It was far too soon, far too crazy, far too unthinkable.

But still…

He was lovely. He was in her living room.

He was to be her husband and if he wanted her…

It was totally, absolutely unthinkable but the sentence kept ringing in her head.

He held her heart in his hands.

CHAPTER NINE

Happy is the bride the sun shines on?

It wouldn't have made one speck of difference if it had been pouring, Max thought as he walked his daughter down the aisle. Caroline clung to his arm as if she needed his support, but he knew it wasn't true. She'd woken smiling and she hadn't stopped smiling since.

His beautiful daughter was marrying a man whose smile matched hers. Her Keanu was an islander, a doctor, a man of fierce intelligence and integrity, and Max couldn't have chosen a man he'd be more proud to call his son-in-law. Caroline didn't need his support.

No one did.

'Who giveth this woman…?'

'I do,' he said in a voice that was choked with emotion. He released his daughter's arm and stepped back to the pew reserved for him. The pew where Hettie sat, cradling Joni. At his insistence.

Hettie reached out and took his hand and he was grateful for it. The way his daughter looked… A man could dissolve into tears.

'Hold Joni,' Hettie said, and suddenly the sleeping Joni was on his knee. He had something…someone…to hold. To care for.

He didn't need him, he thought, but as the ceremony proceeded he was more than grateful for the baby's presence. And for Hettie's. She sat by him, pressed lightly against him as if there wasn't quite room in the pew, but of course there was, for this pew was reserved for the bride's family and there was only him.

The ceremony was over. Handel's Trumpet Voluntary sounded out through the little chapel, joyfully triumphant, across the headland and over the island beyond. Caroline was laughing and crying all at once. She was hugging her father and because he was holding Joni she was hugging the bemused little boy, as well. And then she took her husband's hand and somehow enveloped them all in a wedding hug—Caroline and Keanu, Max and Hettie and Joni.

'I have so much family,' she whispered through tears. 'I'm so happy. Dad, you need to go for it, as well. Love Hettie as much as I love Keanu.'

And then she was gone, in a mist of white lace, to envelop Keanu's aunts and uncles, his grandma, the staff of the hospital and anyone else who was brave enough to come into her orbit.

'You must be very proud.' The voice behind him made Max turn. It was Harry, holding the hand of a woman Max now knew as Sarah, the woman who'd acted as a fly in, fly out surgeon one week a month. Sarah enveloped Hettie in a hug. They turned to talk, and Max was left with Harry.

'Are you ready to leave?' Harry asked, smiling across at Caroline and Keanu. For all his distraction, though, Max knew this man to be an astute businessman. A billionaire with power. It behoved him to stop thinking about Caroline for a moment—and also stop thinking about the way Hettie had felt beside him in the chapel.

'You're wanting to take over responsibility?'

'In a word, yes. These islands… In a sense they've cured me,' Harry said. 'They've made me see there's life beyond my injury and it would be my privilege to give back. But you, Max, you've been injured, too, and you've been giving back for years. Forgive me but I've made some enquiries about your background. It seems you're a skilled surgeon working in the public sector but you've also honed your skills in cosmetic surgery. You're the go-to surgeon for Sydney's society darlings. Do you enjoy that?'

Did he enjoy it? After a day working in the public sector, operating as he had here, to turn to men and women who were paying to keep the years at bay… No, he hadn't enjoyed it.

'It's lucrative,' Harry said softly, watching his face. 'I, too, am a surgeon. I know the choices we make. I know the doctors who choose to work for money and those who don't. I know you, Max Lockhart, and I believe you're the latter. But my spies also tell me that every cent of your lucrative cosmetic practice has been channelled back to the Wildfire hospital. Max, we've already discussed this, but the money you contribute would be a drop in the ocean compared to my fortune. I've already said I would like to assist. It would be my very great privilege to endow the hospital in perpetuity. You no longer need to do cosmetic surgery. You can step back and let someone else take over. Will you accept?'

And with that Max felt the last great burden of responsibility lift from his shoulders. He thought of the CT scanner, blown in the power surge at the hospital, and of the usual mass of paperwork to try and get government help to repair it, or the scores of cosmetic surgical procedures he would have had to perform if government help wasn't forthcoming.

Would he accept? Here was freedom in a form he had never dreamed.

'Thank you,' he said simply. 'The whole island would be honoured to accept your help.'

And then he paused as a burst of delighted laughter sprang from the crowd. The islanders were tossing armfuls of frangipani over the bride and groom. Some had landed in Joni's hair. The toddler had lifted a handful, stared in wonder and then tossed the petals towards Caroline.

And he crowed in delight.

It was the first time Max had seen the little boy laugh, and, by the look of it, Hettie hadn't seen him laugh, either. Max watched Hettie blink away tears. He watched her hug Joni and then stoop with him, gathering more flowers to toss again. She was wearing a soft blue dress—incredibly simple, elegant, right. She had a frangipani tucked behind her ear. She looked…happy.

A happy ending.

And for a brief moment he forgot about freedom and let himself think, *What if?*

What if he stayed?

What was he thinking? Abandoning his dream? Harry was right beside him, telling him his dream was real.

For years, from the time he'd been twenty years old and he'd stood in the premature nursery as the father of twins, he'd thought of freedom. And now it was being handed to him. His financial obligations had been lifted. Caroline was safely married. Joni? He had to take responsibility there, but Hettie had shouldered that, as well. He could easily support them, from a distance.

Louis had been a threat to Hettie but the news there was reassuring, as well. Sergeant Ky had arrested him late last night, drunk, outside Wildfire's only bar. With island sympathy for Louis completely gone, the bartender had rung Ky to tell him where he was. Louis had broken the bartender's jaw, he'd smashed furniture, he'd even lunged at Ky with a knife. He was currently on his way to the mainland, facing a lengthy jail term, and the consensus was that the islanders, both on Wildfire and Atangi, were pleased to see him go.

So that left Max free. Hettie was safe. Joni was cared for. He could do whatever he wanted. He could work wherever he wanted.

He could lie on a beach in Hawaii and do nothing at all.

Suddenly Hettie was back beside him, linking her arm in his. But this was a plan they'd talked about before the ceremony. This whole family thing was a pretence, a plan to have Joni accepted by the islanders. It wasn't real.

'What are you two plotting?' she asked. Joni was still on the ground, happily sorting frangipani flowers. She smiled down at him and then smiled up at Max, a smile that took his breath away.

She was beautiful. This place was beautiful.

Freedom... He did want it—didn't he?

'Harry's making plans for the island,' he managed, and Hettie turned her smile on Harry.

'Good ones?'

'Excellent ones,' Harry told her. 'We'll make your hospital first class. I'm thinking we won't stop at repairing the cyclone damage. I'm thinking we need a new wing with the extra services we could offer. More full-time staff.' He eyed Max speculatively. 'You know, if you decide to stay, Wildfire needs a good surgeon.'

'Of course it does,' Hettie said stoutly, and her arm tightened in Max's. 'But don't you look to Dr Lockhart. Apart from a few fly in, fly out visits to check on his new family, our Max is free.'

And that should've made him feel amazing.

It did—didn't it?

Their own marriage took place three days later. It was a quiet ceremony. 'Max's son died so recently. There's no way we want a fuss,' Hettie told everyone, and their friends were disappointed but understanding. But they had enough people in attendance to make a public point.

Caroline and Keanu were there, smiling and smiling. They were leaving the next day on an extended honeymoon but they'd stayed to see Max wed.

'Because even if this is only a marriage of convenience, I think it's lovely,' Caroline told Max before the ceremony, hugging him soundly. 'And if you can make it more...'

'Neither Hettie nor I want more.'

'Really?' Caroline looked across to where Keanu was talking to Hettie and her eyes reflected her love and her happiness. 'I can't think why not. Dad, why don't you go for it?'

'You know why not.'

'I do,' she said, softening and hugging him again. 'But, honestly, Dad, freedom's not all it's cut out to be. I understand what's driving you,' she said, as he tried to frame words to explain. 'I've figured it out but I don't have to like it. Off you go and see the big wide world but know always there are people who love you. Including, I suspect, your Hettie.'

'She's not my—'

'She would be,' Caroline said softly. 'Given half a chance. She has all the love in the world to give, your Hettie. Just say the word.'

'Caro…'

'I know. Not my business. But let's get you wed and see where things go from there.'

So here they were. *Getting wed…*

They didn't use the chapel. It didn't seem right to make time-honoured vows in the chapel when their vows were being made for convenience, not for love.

Instead they stood by the lagoon, in the place where he'd sat that first night with Hettie and Joni. Hettie was wearing the same blue dress she'd worn at Caroline's wedding. Caroline had made her a wreath of frangipanis and pinned it to her hair. Her curls were tumbling softly to her shoulders. She was bare-legged, wearing simple golden sandals. She was devoid of all jewellery and as Max slipped the ring of gold on her finger he thought he'd never seen her look as lovely.

With this ring, I thee wed.

He'd made that vow before, as a carefree student, a boy who'd never imagined what responsibility that vow entailed.

Now he was making that same vow—without the responsibility?

It felt wrong.

'I will look after you,' he murmured, as she placed a matching ring on his finger and made the same vow, and she flashed him a look that might almost be anger.

'I don't need looking after,' she whispered. 'This island is my home and my family. Max, I love that you're doing this. I love your reasons, but I don't need your care. I'm not your responsibility, so if that's what you're thinking I'll take off this ring right now.'

'Really?'

'Really.'

'That would be the shortest marriage in the history of the universe.'

'I'm up for record breaking.' She was smiling, for the sake of their audience, he thought, but her voice was deadly serious. 'We're doing this for Joni. Don't you dare take me on, as well.'

'I want to take you on.'

'As my friend.' Her chin tilted. 'As your wife in name only. As someone you can leave and leave again. I'll not hold you down.'

He couldn't reply. Their tiny audience was watching, a little bemused. They were speaking in undertones, only to each other. What did brides and grooms generally say to each other in such circumstances?

'Go ahead or not?' Hettie whispered. Still her eyes were challenging.

And how could he not go ahead? Why would he not?

But he would take care of her, he thought. He just wished…

What? There was no time to decide.

The vows were made. They were man and wife. The island's celebrant beamed a blessing.

'You may now kiss the bride.'

Their friends were smiling and waiting. Caroline and Keanu, with Keanu cradling Joni. Harry and his Sarah. Sam and his Lia, just flown in from Brisbane, via Cairns. Bessie and Harold.

Couples who'd listened to the wedding vows and were remembering or looking forward to their own. He could see it in their eyes as they smiled and clapped and waited for him to kiss his bride.

As they waited for him to kiss Hettie.

And it felt...wrong? It felt dishonest, like some sort of travesty, that he'd make these vows to this woman, that he'd kiss her now and claim her as his wife and not mean it.

It was sensible. It was what they both wanted.

He needed to kiss his bride and move on.

He set his hands lightly on her shoulders and drew her to him.

He kissed his bride.

She should take this lightly. She'd deliberately pulled back during the ceremony and she'd deliberately added a prosaic reminder that this wedding was in name only.

So this kiss should be a brief, formal kiss, as this ceremony was supposed to be. And indeed for an instant that was all it was. Max's hands took her shoulders, she tilted her face to meet his and their lips brushed.

She should have pulled back fast. He should have released her. They should have turned to their audience, job done, formalities complete.

Except they didn't. They couldn't.

Because they were still kissing?

How did that happen? One moment there was a light brushing of lips against lips. The next moment the hold on her shoulders tightened. The brush of lips was repeated and then she found herself standing on tiptoe so the brush could be something more.

For it was something more. It was a whole lot more.

Max was kissing her as if he meant it, as if this was no mock wedding. He was kissing her as if he wanted her.

Want...

It was such an alien sensation that she had no way of dealing with it. She was shocked into submission—but no. Submission? This was no such thing.

She was shocked into desire.

He was kissing her and she was giving as good as she got. Why not? she thought in the tiny amount of brain she had left for processing such thoughts. It's not every day a woman gets married.

It's not every day a woman marries a man like Max.

And with that thought came another, insidious, sweet, a siren song. What if this marriage was real?

What if Max wanted her?

It was a fleeting thought in the few sensuous moments as his mouth claimed hers, as warmth flooded her body, as his hands held her to him.

As she felt herself mould against him.

As she kissed him as she'd never dreamed she could ever kiss.

And as the kiss ended, as she surfaced to laughter and applause and Max smiling down at her, his hands on her shoulders, she thought, *My world has changed.*

She was married.

It was a marriage of convenience.

Yes, it was, she told herself. Her head knew that it was true. It was only her body telling her it was a lie.

Or maybe it was more. For somehow she knew, deep down, admit it or not, it was her heart that was telling her that for richer or poorer, in sickness and in health, for as long as they both should live, this man was her husband.

Her heart was saying, Marriage of convenience or not, from his moment, with this kiss, she was truly married.

Only, of course, it *was* just a marriage of convenience. They signed the register. They received laughing congratulations from their friends. They got through a sumptuous wedding feast that Caroline had organised and then their friends dispersed and they were left alone.

With Joni.

'Let Keanu and I take him for the night,' Caroline had begged, but Hettie wouldn't hear of it.

'He's only just starting to relax with me. And with Max. He needs to stay with us.'

Plus she needed the little boy, she thought as she walked up the steps into the palatial Lockhart mansion. She looked at all the photographs of Lockhart ancestors and felt the presence of her new husband behind her and thought, *What have I done?*

Joni was practically a shield. She hugged him tight, thinking this was for him. Joni's rightful place was here. Max had wanted her to move in here three days ago but when Ky had assured her there was no further threat from Louis she'd opted to stay in her villa.

'Only until our wedding,' Max had growled, and she'd agreed, but now there was no reason not to live here.

Except she wasn't a Lockhart. This wasn't her home. It'd be more suitable if she was here as Joni's nanny, she thought, and a bubble of laughter that was half fear rose within her.

She should be the hired help. She had no place here.

And the way she felt about Max… It scared her.

'This is your room,' Max told her. He'd led her across

the grand entrance hall and along a short passage. He threw open double doors and she caught her breath in awe.

This room was amazing. This room was bliss.

For a start it was vast. It was also old. The worn, wooden floor was honey gold and faded by sun. The bed was an enormous four-poster, with soft white netting draped around it. There was a faded chintz sofa and armchairs, a small, elegant antique table, faded rugs, and wide French windows opening to the verandah and the lagoon beyond.

The room invited her in, welcomed her in a way nothing else could. A woman could sink into this room.

'Check the bathroom,' Max said, smiling, watching her face. He threw open a door and revealed an enormous tub on crocodile feet, a shower the width of the room and massive towel rails with lush, white towels. All still looking over the lagoon.

'And this is where Joni can sleep,' he told her. He opened another door and there was a perfect child's room, already decorated with pink wallpaper. With ponies and roses and tiny forget-me-nots.

'This was Caroline's. Maybe we should get rid of the pink.'

'I don't think Joni's noticing,' Hettie said. 'But we… Maybe I can do something later? Max, it's beautiful. But where do you sleep?'

'At the other end of the house. But I'm leaving next week so you'll have the whole house to yourself.'

'That's…fine,' she managed, and hugged Joni a bit tighter.

'Bessie and Harold will be here. Ky says Louis is no longer a threat.'

'You don't need to worry.' But she must have sounded strained because Max looked at her in concern.

'Hettie, I didn't resign from my job,' he told her. 'I took leave. I'm not sure what I'll be doing in the future but for now, my job at Sydney Central is waiting.'

'Of course it is.' She struggled to make her tone light. 'But you will come back?' Heck, she sounded needy. She could have slapped herself but the words were out and she couldn't get them back.

'Once a month,' he told her. 'I have it planned. If I stay at Sydney Central I'll do what most fly in, fly outers do. I'll work through a couple of weekends and then spend five or six days here once a month. That way I can catch up with Caroline and with you and Joni.'

That was the deal, she thought. This was the agreement going into their marriage. This arrangement had given the little boy to her, and more. It had given her the backing of the Lockhart name, this sumptuous place to live, and a live-in housekeeper and groundsman to help with Joni's care.

How could she possibly want more?

It was just that kiss.

Those kisses.

They were somehow imprinted on her heart. How Max could stand there and calmly talk about catching up with her once a month when he'd kissed her like that...

'What you're planning... That doesn't sound like freedom to me,' she ventured. 'Max, this has been all about me. I wanted Joni and I have him. What do you want?'

'I have everything I need.'

'I didn't say need. I said want.'

'Want doesn't come into it.'

'So all that talk of freedom...'

'Leave it.'

It was a snap and she flinched. He saw it and swore. 'Hettie, I didn't mean—'

'It doesn't matter.' She cut him off. 'I'm tired. Max, I need to settle Joni and go to bed myself.'

'Of course.' But there was a strain between them that was almost tangible. He was standing back, apart. That's what he wanted, she thought. His body language was almost spelling it out.

Why did she want to weep?

Some wedding night, she thought bleakly, with the groom backing out of her room as fast as he could go, with her holding Joni like a shield.

They were alike. Two people with ghosts, with shadows so deep they'd never move past them.

But she was overthinking things. This, after all, was a business arrangement, a great outcome for all concerned. If she could just get the kisses out of her head... If she could just look at Max and see the patriarch of the island, the hospital's benefactor, a fine surgeon, her friend...

Not the man. Not the toe-curlingly sexy male her heart told her he was. Not a man who knew how to love and who could be loved in return.

Not a man with needs he couldn't admit to.

No. That was wishful thinking and she needed sensible thinking. And action.

'I don't need anything else,' she told him, striving to sound brisk and efficient. 'I know where the kitchen is if Joni needs a bottle and everything else can wait until morning. Thank you, Max. Thank you for everything and goodnight.'

'It's me who should be thanking you,' he said heavily. 'You're the one taking on the responsibility for Joni.'

'I'm not taking on responsibility for anything,' she snapped, suddenly angry. 'I'm choosing. They're very different things and I'm sorry you can't see it. Meanwhile, I don't need gratitude.'

'Hettie—'

'Goodnight, Max,' she said, as firmly as she could manage, and she turned away fast, and if it was to hide the sudden moisture welling behind her eyes, well, how stupid was that?

A woman had to be sensible. A sensible woman said goodnight to her brand-new husband and closed the door behind him.

And where was sleep after that?

Max didn't even try to go to bed. Instead, he wandered down to the lagoon where a few short hours ago he'd made the vows to love and to honour Hettie de Lacey for the rest of his life.

They'd been mock vows.

They hadn't felt like mock vows.

It didn't matter, though, he thought as he stared out over the still water. He'd always look out for her. He'd keep her safe and he'd keep his nephew safe.

He was responsible for them—and he didn't want to be responsible.

But neither did he want to walk away.

He could stay. He could pretend those vows were real. To love and to honour... Well, the honour was real at least.

Love? He'd known her a week.

She was a convenient answer to the problem of Joni.

Could he love Joni?

As he'd loved Christopher?

A few short weeks ago he'd stood by his son's grave and he'd felt his heart break. Simple as that.

He'd done the same when Ellie had died. He'd had no idea that grief was a physical thing, a crumbling from within, a physical reaction that had left him gutted, helpless, without an anchor. Drifting as the *Lillyanna* had drifted, buffeted by whatever wind, whatever tide took her.

That's what grief did to you. That's what love did to you.

He'd longed for freedom and now he had it. If anything happened to Caroline, yes, he'd be gutted again, but she had her Keanu to look out for her. He was free.

A man without responsibilities.

Why did it feel so empty?

He was still feeling grief; of course he was. With his son so recently gone…how could he think of making new connections?

Of filling the void.

Of replacing Christopher?

Hell.

It was hell. His head was filled with a special kind of torment, a tangle of pain and confusion and emptiness.

What he wanted—what he ached for—was to walk back into the house, take Hettie into his arms and hold her. To take comfort in her body. To forget himself in the love he suspected she could give.

She'd given her heart to Joni but he was starting to know this woman. He'd kissed her and she'd kissed him back, and there was a matching need in that kiss. The difference was that her need wasn't a product of aching loss.

What was it, then?

The beginnings of love?

If it was…

If it was then he had to move away fast. It wasn't fair on Hettie to take this one step further. He'd married her because it had been the sensible thing to do. To even think about making that marriage something other than a signed contract would be to invite disaster.

To let her hold him when he couldn't give back… To ask her to love him when all he felt was fear… It was unthinkable.

He swore and a night heron startled and flew straight upward into the starlit sky.

The night stretched on but still he didn't go inside. He needed to go back to Sydney, he thought, and quickly. He needed to bury himself in his work. There was always enough medicine to fill the void. In Theatre, with lives under his hands, there was no room for the questions hammering in his head.

He could go back to swimming laps, lifting weights, running, filling the empty crevices of his life. He could finally figure where he could go from here without pain.

Except…why was the pain still with him?

It was Christopher, he told himself. Of course it was Christopher. He ached for his son.

He stood and looked out over the lagoon until the first rays of dawn tinged the sky.

He thought about Christopher. And Ellie.

It was sheer discipline that stopped him thinking about Hettie.

CHAPTER TEN

THE NEXT FEW DAYS were busy—deliberately so. He and Harry spent hours delving into the island's finances, deciding what needed to be invested and where. The knowledge that he wasn't on his own was incredible. Since his father's death he'd felt the full responsibility for the island's welfare. Now…the sensation of sharing made him feel almost light-headed.

'Harry's hiring choppers from the mainland within the next week,' he told Hettie on the night before he left. 'We've planned a full spray of all the M'Langi islands. Until now I've only been able to do Wildfire but if we can get rid of the mosquito breeding grounds… With the new vaccine available for clinical trials, with the money injected to get stocks, with the spray covering the swamp areas, encephalitis might become a thing of the past. And the ulcers… Without them, this island will be so much safer.'

He'd come back to the house—briefly. He'd done a couple of minor operations during the week and he'd told Sam he'd do a ward round that night.

'There's no need,' Sam had growled. 'Spend your last night with Hettie.'

But that was dangerous territory. He did need to be

seen to spend time with her. That was part of the plan—
to have the islanders see them as a family, to see Joni
as a Lockhart—but that could easily be done with Hettie living in the house and Max dropping in and out at
need. And sleeping—or not sleeping—there. Lying in
the dark, thinking…

Trying not to think.

'You and Harry seem to have done a wonderful job,'
Hettie was saying. She was sitting at the kitchen table.
Joni was in his highchair. She was giving him his dinner,
making the spoon into an aeroplane, making him giggle.

What was there in this scenario that made him want
to run?

He didn't need to run. He was leaving tomorrow.

'Harry's amazing. I'm leaving the island in great
hands.'

'But you still own the island,' Hettie said.

Was that a rebuke?

Maybe not. The aeroplane swooped, Joni chortled and
the moment was past.

'You will be okay,' he told her.

'I'm not worrying about me,' she said, and then she
stopped zooming the aeroplane and turned and looked
directly at him. 'I'm worrying about you.'

What was there in that that took the air from his lungs?

'Why would you worry about me?'

'Going back to the mainland alone. Max, tell me you
have good friends who'll meet you at the airport, who'll
take you out to dinner, who'll watch your face and know
you need to be taken for a drink or a walk or just have
silent company. Christopher's so recently gone. Tell me
you have friends who care.'

'My colleagues care.' They did, too, he thought. The

hospital team had been incredibly supportive through-out Chris's illness. Some of his colleagues had attended the funeral. There'd been a vast arrangement of exotic flowers delivered to his apartment. His anaesthetist and a couple of his fellow surgeons had clapped him on the shoulder and said things like, 'We're with you, mate. Anything we can do, just ask.'

But he'd been so busy... For twenty-six years he'd been busy, working two jobs and caring for Christopher. He'd had an apartment at the hospital and a full-time carer for Chris, so that any gap in his working day could be spent with him.

Gaps hadn't included making friends.

Maybe he could now. Maybe that was what this new-found freedom would give him.

Friends.

He looked down at Hettie serenely feeding Joni, and he thought...

No. Run. Get out of here before the whole nightmare starts again. The nightmare of caring.

'I'm heading back to the hospital now,' he told her. 'I'll do a ward round tomorrow, too, before I go. I expect I'll see you at breakfast.'

She didn't move. 'I expect you will.'

'What will you do while I'm away?'

She concentrated on another aeroplane. 'Pretty much what I'm doing now, I expect. My role as charge nurse will be filled while I have some family leave.' She smiled up at him then. 'Actually, you know what? I intend to do...nothing. Or not quite nothing. I intend to play with Joni, to hug him, to take him to the beach and teach him to paddle, to lie under the palm trees and read silly kids' books to him. I intend to feed him his dinner via aeroplanes. I expect to leave my hair untied, wear my sarong, wake when Joni wakes, sleep when Joni sleeps. I intend to love my son.'

There was nothing to say to that. He glanced at Joni, who was picking up a rusk and inspecting it for possible poison. It was obviously a Very Suspicious Rusk, covered with Vegemite, the lovely black goop beloved by every true Australian kid but obviously not by Joni. He eyed it from every which way, then smeared it carefully onto his nose before carefully dropping it overboard.

Bugsy had been lying unnoticed in his basket by the corner. With the speed of light the rusk was hoovered up and Bugsy was back in his basket, smirking.

Joni chortled with delight and then looked expectantly at Hettie and held out his hand.

'Rusk?' he said, and Hettie giggled and Max grinned. But inside…his heart twisted.

'I have to go,' he said, and Hettie rose and searched his face.

'Do you?'

'You know I do.'

'I guess I do,' she said evenly, and then she took a deep breath. 'Max… I have to tell you, though…'

And then she fell silent.

Don't ask, he thought. *Just go.* But she was standing in front of him, shorts, T-shirt, snub nose, her curls a bit tangled. One curl had dared to drift across her eyes and she didn't seem to notice.

He really wanted to lift it and tuck it behind her ear.

He couldn't.

He should turn and walk out the door but his feet seemed glued to the floor.

'What?' he asked, heavily, and here it came.

'You should know that there's a choice,' she whispered. 'These last few days... I know you don't want it and I don't want you to take it any further. But what I feel for you... It's not gratitude. It's not respect and it's not friendship. You know how I held Joni after his mother died and I knew I could love him? Well, like it or not, that's how I feel with you.' She gave a wry grin then, as she heard what she'd said.

'Okay, sort of different,' she conceded. 'It's something to do with you being six feet tall and so gorgeous it's not fair to expect my hormones not to react.' She caught herself, trying to make what she was saying make sense. 'Um... Max...hormones or not, I understand you need to leave. I respect that. I know your reasons. But when you come back... I'll stay at my end of the house for as long as you wish, for Joni's sake, but if you ever want me... If you ever want to take it further...'

And then she broke away. She took a step back, looking appalled.

'Whoa, I'm sorry,' she managed. 'I can't imagine why I'm laying this on you. I know it's not fair. But, Max, you know I'm fine on my own. You know I'm happy. It's just that I thought maybe if we're husband and wife I should just say it. Just so you know...the hormone thing is sort of...there.'

'I can't,' he said, because it was all he could think of to say, and she nodded as if this was a normal conversation between a married couple, maybe Mum asking Dad to take the kid to school, Dad saying he couldn't.

Dad saying he couldn't commit.

Dad saying he couldn't be a dad. Or a husband.

Or a lover.

And there was the crux of everything. He wouldn't

mind being a lover. No, that was wrong. He *wanted* to be a lover. The more time he spent with Hettie the more he wanted to pick her up and carry her to his bed. To love, to protect, to honour…

To hold her as his own.

But with that came the rest. Husband. Father. Island patriarch. All the things that had weighed on him for twenty-six years.

'Hettie, love…'

'I know I'm not your love.' She managed to say it evenly, emotion gone from her voice. She sat down again and started wiping Joni's face. 'I'm not your anything,' she added mildly. 'I shouldn't have said it but it seemed only honest and I think honesty has to be front and foremost in this…arrangement. Go back to work, Max. Go back to what you do and forget all about my dumb little confession. It means nothing. Your plane gets in at ten in the morning. I'll feed Joni between seven and eight but then we'll go and play by the lagoon. So if you can arrange not to be in the kitchen between seven and eight…'

'Why?'

'Because goodbye should be now,' she said, and she looked up at him and he saw the emotionless facade slip. He saw distress. 'Because I've just made a fool of myself and I need time to recover. You'll be back in a month and by then I'll have myself nicely under control. Joni and I will have our lives sorted. So you head off and sort your life as you want it to be—as you deserve it to be—and leave us to get on with ours.'

'Hettie—'

'Leave it, Max,' she said, and she tugged Joni from the highchair and held him close. 'I'm taking Joni for a bath so we'll say goodbye now.' And then she slipped forward and reached up and kissed him, lightly, a faint brush on the cheek. And then she stepped away fast.

'Goodbye, Max,' she whispered. 'And thank you.'

How was she to calmly bath Joni after that?

Luckily Joni pretty much bathed himself. He splashed in the big tub, crowing with delight as he ran water from a plastic mug down his tummy. He was entranced with his cleverness.

So was Hettie, but not completely. She sat on the floor next to the tub and she kept a hand on Joni's shoulders, keeping contact, keeping the reassurance that she was always there, and stupidly, foolishly, she let herself weep.

She'd just let down all her defences.

She was married and, for better or worse, she wanted her husband. She wanted to keep contact. She wanted the reassurance that he was always there.

More, she wanted him.

At midnight, twelve-year-old Indi Hika and his two mates sneaked out of their parents' houses, took Indi's dad's dinghy and tried to catch flounder in the lagoon. Two hours later, hauling the dinghy out through the marshes, Indi felt a sting on his ankle. It hurt, but twelve-year-olds didn't make a fuss in front of their mates. By the time he limped home it was hurting a lot, but he was understandably reluctant to let his parents know he'd been out on the water after midnight. He sneaked back into bed and pulled up the covers.

He didn't even look at his ankle. If he had he would have seen two distinctive fang marks. Instead, he lay silent for two hours while his foot grew more and more painful and the venom spread through his body. Finally he cried out loud. His parents investigated, to find him twisting in agony and having trouble breathing.

The family had no phone. Max was standing on the house verandah, staring into the darkness, when he saw the truck race up the hill.

His thoughts were so tangled that a medical emergency was almost a relief. He reached the hospital almost as the Hikas did, and by the time Sam arrived he had the lad intubated.

It took the two doctors' combined efforts, considerable skill and the rest of the night to keep the boy breathing. Finally, though, Indi decided to live and Max walked out of the hospital to a new day. The day he was to leave.

He glanced at his watch. He had an hour until the plane left.

Hettie and Joni would have already breakfasted. She'd have taken him to the little beach at the end of the lagoon.

His time on the island was over.

He walked back to the house to shower and collect his gear. His thoughts were still drifting, the drama of the night fresh and real. Just do what comes next, he told himself as he walked up to the airstrip with his kitbag. Any number of people would have driven him but he wanted no one. He felt curiously disengaged, as if he was moving in a vacuum.

The *Lillyana* was in harbour, waiting for repairs. Most of his gear was still on her and could stay there.

His kitbag was light. He was…free.

It was the end of an era. He'd come back, he knew, but only as a visitor. The responsibilities had all been taken care of.

He'd be welcomed as a friend.

He wasn't part of this island.

The incoming plane hadn't arrived yet and the airstrip was deserted. He sat on a cyclone-smashed palm beside the hangar and looked out over the island. From here he could see the sea and the lagoons dotting the island. He could see across to the research station with the beautiful pool where he and Hettie had swum.

She'd keep swimming there.

And suddenly her words from the night before were replaying in his head. Not the ones concerning him. Not the ones that had him closing down, the words he didn't know what to do with. What he was remembering was her talking of taking family leave to get to know her new son.

'You know what?' she'd said. 'I intend to do…nothing. Or not quite nothing. I intend to play with Joni, to hug him, to take him to the beach and teach him to paddle, to lie under the palm trees and read silly kids' books to him. I intend to feed him his dinner via aeroplanes. I expect to leave my hair untied, wear my sarong, wake when Joni wakes, sleep when Joni sleeps. I intend to love my son.'

He found himself smiling at the thought of Hettie free from her responsibilities as nurse manager, free to do what she wanted.

Free to love her son.

And all at once he was hit by a sensation so powerful he couldn't deal with it. It was like a blow to the side of the head, a blow that sent him reeling.

He wanted…what Hettie had chosen.

Of course he did, he told himself, rising and striding across to the edge of the clearing, staring across at the island and then out to the farther islands dotting the sea beyond. He wanted freedom. He'd ached for freedom. That's what Hettie now thought she had.

So…had he got it wrong?

Was freedom sitting under a palm tree, reading a kids' book to a child who wasn't his?

Was freedom dipping his toe again into the pool of loving?

Was freedom jumping right in?

The memories of the night just gone were still swirling in his head. Indi, twelve years old, agonisingly close to death. Indi's parents, clutching each other in terror, every fibre of their being centred on the life of their son. If he'd died, everything would have fallen apart.

As his life had fallen apart when Ellie had died. And then when Christopher had died.

He never wanted that pain again. If he walked away now, he'd never have it, and that was what he wanted—wasn't it?

'I intend to love my son.'

There was the rub. What if Joni were to be bitten by a snake or stand on a stonefish? Hettie would bear the trauma alone.

No, she wouldn't, he told himself savagely. She'd have every islander beside her. His own daughter and her husband would be here. Caroline and Keanu would support her. Everyone here would love her and stand by her.

It should be him.

He wanted it to be him.

He thought tangentially of Christopher. His grief for his son was still a raw and jagged wound. Surely he couldn't open his heart to that sort of loving again?

Surely he couldn't.

But as he stood in the morning sun, as he watched the silver glint of the incoming plane slowly grow bigger, he thought somehow, some way, he already had.

It wasn't a betrayal of Christopher. Or of Ellie.

He remembered Chris in one of the last few lucid moments before he'd slipped into unconsciousness. His lovely son had reached out and taken his hand.

'Dad, get a life…'

Chris had said it to him often, sometimes teasing, sometimes exasperated, a kid not able to see how seriously a man had to take the world.

Get a life.

A life could be…right here on the island.

Hettie was right here.

The choking fog that seemed to have enveloped him since Christopher's death was lifting, and with its lifting came a knowledge so deep, so fundamental that he must have been blind not to see it all along.

He was free to choose.

He could choose to love.

If she'd have him.

'Please,' he said out loud, and he left his kitbag where it lay and turned and started walking down towards the house. Towards his home.

And then he started to run.

Hettie and Joni and Bugsy had sat on the beach at the lagoon for a couple of hours. Joni was ready for a sleep but she hadn't wanted to risk running into Max by heading back to the house too soon. The plane's schedule was tight, though. It'd come in, drop off, pick up and be gone, so as soon as she saw it coming in the distance she knew it was safe to go home.

Home? To the Lockhart homestead.

She was a Lockhart. It'd take some getting used to. She was Max Lockhart's wife.

She was a wife without a husband.

She pushed the all-terrain stroller along the path to the house. The going was rough through the bushland, over leaf litter strewn from the cyclone. Joni was growing sleepier and she was in no hurry. What was the use of hurrying?

As she walked somehow she kept noticing the glint of gold on her ring finger.

She was married—and yet not.

She was married to a man who was even now boarding a plane to head back to Australia.

'Well, what did you expect?' she muttered to Bugsy, who was trailing at her side. 'He's given you Joni. What else did you want from him?'

'Nothing,' she told Bugsy.

She lied.

'Yeah, and didn't I do that well,' she demanded. 'Telling him I was available if he wanted me. Throwing myself at him. What sort of a goose must he take me for?'

Bugsy looked supremely disinterested. Joni, however, looked up sleepily from the stroller and looked a bit worried.

'It's okay, sweetheart,' she said, giving the stroller a final shove up the path into the clearing by the house. 'I'll forget to blush in a while. Life will settle down. We're fine on our own.'

But then Bugsy gave a joyful woof, as if he'd seen someone in the bushes. He lurched ahead. Hettie shoved the stroller up the last bit of rough path—and Max was in front of her. Max, looking dishevelled. Max, out of breath.

Max, looking as if he'd been running.

For a moment neither of them spoke. She couldn't,

and it seemed neither could he. Possibly because he had no breath.

'Hey,' she whispered at last. 'You'll miss…you'll miss your plane. It's landed.'

He told her where the plane could go and she blinked. 'Pardon?'

'You heard. But I hope Joni didn't.' He smiled then, a tired, rueful smile. They were standing eight feet apart, as if he wasn't ready to venture closer. 'I guess…I need to start watching my language all over again. Toddlers are parrots.'

She hesitated, still confused. 'Joni's nearly asleep. I think you're safe. But…Max, I saw the plane coming in to land. That's why we're going home. Because you won't be there.'

There was a silence at that. It stretched on, while a couple of crazy parrots turned somersaults in the palms above her head, while a blue-winged butterfly idled past her nose, while she became aware of the look of strain behind Max's eyes.

'I guess,' Max said at last, as if he'd finally regained his breath and was ready to go on. 'What I'm about to ask… Hettie, do you think, in the future—or even now—do you think you can go home because I *am* there?'

She thought about it. Thinking was hard when there was a butterfly doing circles around her head, but it seemed it needed to be done. She needed to concentrate really hard.

She waved away the butterfly. The butterfly was beautiful but Max's words were better.

But this was a time to be practical, she told herself. She needed to say it like it was.

'Max, I'm truly grateful,' she managed. Why was it

so hard to get her voice to work? 'I'm incredibly grateful for all you've done, but you've done enough. I won't
have you staying because you feel responsible for me.
For us. You need your freedom, and you deserve it. You
need to leave.'

The silence stretched on. There were sunbeams fil-
tering through the wind-battered canopy of palms. They
were making odd shadows on the path. She concentrated
on the patterns, on the shifting shadows.

Joni was drifting off to sleep in his stroller. He gave
a tiny, sleepy murmur and Hettie checked him, grateful
for the distraction. When she glanced up again Max's
face had changed a little. The tension on his face lifted.

'Hettie, I know you don't need me,' he said, and it was
as if he was talking from a long way away. This was a
voice she hadn't heard before. 'But what if I realised…'
he said slowly. 'What if I said I needed you? You take
the world on your shoulders, Hettie, love. Could you take
me on, too?'

What was he saying? She stared at him and then
looked down at the shadows again. This felt terrifying.
She felt as if she was on the edge of something so huge…

So fragile…

'Hettie, this might not make any sense to you,' he said
slowly, as if he was still putting the words together in his
head before he spoke. 'But I sat up on the runway, waiting for the plane to land, and I thought of you building
sandcastles with our son—*our son*—and I had a wash
of need so great it knocked sense into me.'

'Sense?' She was having so much trouble getting her
voice to work.

'Perspective? Heaven knows what. I only know that
at twenty I was landed with twins and financial obliga-

tions and responsibility and I coped. But you know what? Sometimes I even had fun. I loved Chris. I adored my daughter, even though I seldom saw her. But I loved it that Caroline grew to love this island, so much so that she's now married an islander. And I loved my work. Heaven help me, sometimes I even loved the weird and wonderful people who lined up to have themselves look younger. But all the while, all these years, a voice has been hammering in my head, saying, *What if you were free? What if you had none of these responsibilities?* And then suddenly…I was.'

'You deserve—'

'Who knows what I deserve?' he said frankly. 'But is what I deserve what I want?'

'I don't know what you mean.' It was barely a whisper.

'I mean I sat up there, waiting for the plane to take me to this new freedom, and I thought, Harry's taken financial responsibility from me. You've taken the care of Joni from me. Caroline and Keanu are here to take care of the island. I'm not needed. I can go and lie on a beach in Hawaii. I can do anything I want. And the plane was coming closer and I thought, I can get on that plane and go anywhere in the world. I'm needed nowhere. But then I thought, *Where do I want to be?* And suddenly the answer was so obvious it was like a punch to the side of the head. Because I knew. Hettie, I knew that you were at the lagoon, playing with our baby—*our* baby, Hettie—and I realised that this is where I want to be. More, this is where I need to be. Hettie, love, I'm not here because you need me. I'm here because I need you.'

The butterfly had landed on the leaf litter just beyond

her feet. Its wings were still fluttering, seemingly in time with the beats of her heart.

She was trying to get Max's words into some sort of order. Some sort of sense.

For some reason, it was easier to watch the butterfly.

'This is probably way too soon,' Max said ruefully. 'I know you said you could love me but maybe you need time. Maybe we both need time.'

'Do you need time?' Her voice was still strangely calm.

'No,' he said, and he said it almost fiercely. 'I need no time at all. For I know what I want and I want you. Hettie, love, suddenly I have freedom and it's the greatest gift of all. Up on the airstrip as the plane was coming in to land… It was like a clearing of the fog. I could see it and why I couldn't see it before… But I am seeing it now. Hettie, it means I have the freedom to love. If you'll have me, my love. If you'll take me on, then I have the freedom to love you.' He paused, still apart from her, still holding himself back. 'But if it's too soon… if indeed we are rushing things… Hettie, tell me to go away and I will.'

'N-no.' It was so hard to make her voice work. 'Can you really want to stay?' she managed.

'For as long as you need me.' And then he shook his head. 'No. Let's make that as long as I need you.'

'And how long could that be?' Her voice was scarcely a whisper.

'Forever?'

Maybe she hadn't heard right, she thought. Maybe this was nothing but a dream.

But he was stepping forward. He was moving the stroller with the sleeping Joni aside and he was taking her hands. He was smiling at her, tenderly, lovingly but, oh, so uncertainly.

He thought she didn't need him.

Ha!

But let him think it, she decided, a hint of the inner Hettie returning. A man who thought he wasn't needed… A man who wanted to be needed… This could be excellent. She could graciously allow him to unblock her plumbing. She could kindly permit him to push the stroller up the rough part of the track—or maybe she could even suggest if he could rebuild the track.

'Hettie?' He sounded nervous.

'Yes?'

'What are you thinking?'

'Nothing,' she said with insouciance, and suddenly Max was grinning. He could read her, her Max, and suddenly he was with her, the Max she knew and loved, the Max in charge of his world, who'd returned to take his rightful place as Lockhart of Wildfire.

Her husband.

The father to her son.

'You get to push the stroller,' she said firmly, and he looked astonished.

'What, now?'

'Certainly now. You can push faster than me and we need to go home.'

'I… Yes.' And then he added, still not completely sure, 'Back to the homestead?'

'Certainly. We have work to do.'

'Work?'

'We need to shift those bedrooms,' she said astringently. 'Get all your stuff up to my end of the house, or my stuff up to your end of the house. Depending on whose bed's biggest.'

'Het—'

'And we need to do it before Joni wakes up,' she told him. 'We could make a bed right here but I'm scared of small boys and cameras.'

He choked on joyful laughter, and then, even though speed was imperative, even though his beautiful, bossy Hettie was giving orders he fully intended to comply with, he firmly gathered her into his arms.

'Hettie de Lacey?' he managed and then he kissed her so her answer couldn't come for quite a while.

'Y-yes?' she managed when she came up for air.

'Will you marry me?'

'I thought…I thought I already did.'

'Not properly,' he told her. 'Not the way it ought to be done. I'm a Lockhart of Wildfire and I know what's due to my bride.'

'What?'

'The whole island,' he said in satisfaction, holding her against him, folding her to him so she moulded against his breast, so she felt truly as if she'd found her home. 'We need to repeat our vows in front of every islander, from Wildfire, from the whole of M'Langi if they'll come. Every single islander present, a feast that lasts for days, a celebration to say this is a new beginning. You and me, my love, with Joni and Bugsy and Harry and all our hospital friends and all the islanders… It's a joyous beginning for all of us. I want to work here, Hettie, and I hope I can be needed. I hope together we can make a difference to this place. But we'll do it side by side, my love. As husband and wife. I know you don't need me, but this new system, do you think we could share?'

'It sounds good to me,' she told him, and smiled and smiled. And then she pulled back so she could see him. So she could see all of him, this man she loved with all her heart.

'It sounds wonderful,' she told him. 'Let's start now.'

EPILOGUE

EIGHTEEN MONTHS ON marked the twenty-fifth anniversary of the opening of the Wildfire hospital. When Ellie had died Max had vowed to get a hospital on the island. It had taken a herculean effort to see it built but now every islander, plus every medic who'd ever worked in the hospital, seemed to be here to celebrate. They were also here to celebrate the new Christopher Lockhart Surgical Wing, built by Harry.

Harry had also funded tonight's *hangi*. It was held on Sunset Beach, below the hospital, and it was a feast to outdo any feast the island had seen before. All day there'd been hospital tours, tours of the new research centre, tours of the amazing new resort, even an underground tour of the now fully operating gold mine. Two years before, Wildfire had been in such financial straits that half the islanders had been unemployed and the hospital threatened with closure. Things couldn't be more different today.

'We've done well.' Harry and Max were standing apart, looking out over the crowd of islanders and medics gathered around the vast fire pit on the beach. Harry gripped Max's shoulder in a gesture of companionship, a gesture that spoke of shared troubles and a similar happy ending. 'This is better than we could ever have hoped,' Harry said in quiet satisfaction, and Max could only agree.

And he wasn't only thinking of the hospital.

Harry's Sarah was helping Hettie build a sandcastle for Joni. At three, Joni was a bossy toddler, happy and self-assured and certain that his way was the right way to get those turrets up, even when they kept falling over. Sarah and Hettie were giggling over the latest disaster, while Joni stomped down to the water's edge with his bucket to get more water.

Both men watched and both men had goofy smiles on their faces.

'We have done well,' Max said softly. 'Thanks to you.'

'Thanks to us,' Harry said firmly. 'Mine was the money. Yours was the persistence and power. Not to mention the encouragement of the two women in our lives.'

'We wouldn't have done it without them,' Max agreed. He tried to change his smile from goofy and failed. Hettie was laughing. Hettie was gorgeous. She was his wife. How could he do anything but smile?

And there was so much more to smile about than the laughter of his lovely wife, he conceded. He had a grandchild now, tiny Christie, born six weeks ago to Caroline and Keanu. Ana and Luke were here, with their daughter, Hana, and their baby, Julien. Sam and Lia were helping Joni scoop up water but Lia was having trouble bending. Eight months into pregnancy, Lia had an excuse not to bend.

And she wouldn't have to go to the mainland to have her baby. That was an amazing source of satisfaction. With the new wing on the hospital and with Harry's funding, they now had a full-time obstetrician on the island, plus an anaesthetist. Max's grandchild had been born on Wildfire with every precaution taken care of.

'And we've not had a single case of encephalitis for the season.' Harry's beam was almost as wide as Max's. 'The trials of the new vaccine seem to have been a resounding success. We can almost rest on our laurels, Dr Lockhart.'

Max grinned back. 'Do you think my Hettie will let me rest? That woman has so many projects…'

'She did tell me you like to be needed,' Harry conceded, smiling across at the doctors in charge of the new clinic out on Atangi. Josh and Maddie and their beautiful baby daughter had come to Wildfire for the celebrations. 'Has she told you her idea for a preschool?'

'No,' Max said, startled, and Harry chuckled.

'I might have known. The elementary school's good but she thinks early schooling's important, especially now we have so many more babies. She's thinking of setting one up on each of the islands and she's already hit me for funding.'

'You've done enough,' Max told him, but Harry shook his head.

'How can I ever have done enough? If I've done enough then I'm not needed. What about you, Max? Have you done enough?'

And Max thought of what he had.

He had enough surgery here to keep him busy full time. He had a wife who loved him. He had a son who came running every time he came into the house, greeting him with joy. He had his daughter and son-in-law and he had a granddaughter who was already promising to be Joni's best friend.

He had friends, he had family, he even had a dog because Hettie decreed that since Maddie had taken

Bugsy out to Atangi, there had to be another hospital mascot. Not that Roper was much of a mascot, but the great shaggy crossbred was certainly a favourite. Max needed to put in a bit of dog training. He had projects to make the M'Langi islands better and better, and Hettie kept thinking up more.

He smiled at her now and she looked up from what she was doing and smiled back, almost as if she could sense he was thinking of her. Her smile was warm, intimate, loving, and it still had the capacity to make his heart turn over.

'What are you plotting?' she called. 'You and Harry?'

'Just what comes next,' he called back, and he couldn't help it. His smile turned goofy again, just like that. 'Just how to be needed for the rest of my life.'

* * * * *

MILLS & BOON®

Helen Bianchin v Regency Collection!

40% off both collections!

Discover our Helen Bianchin v Regency Collection, a blend of sexy and regal romances. Don't miss this great offer - buy one collection to get a free book but buy both collections to receive 40% off! This fabulous 10 book collection features stories from some of our talented writers.

Visit **www.millsandboon.co.uk** to order yours!

MILLS & BOON®

THE ULTIMATE IN ROMANTIC MEDICAL DRAMA

A sneak peek at next month's titles...

In stores from 21st April 2016:

- **Tempted by Hollywood's Top Doc** – Louisa George *and* **Perfect Rivals...** – Amy Ruttan

- **English Rose in the Outback** *and* **A Family for Chloe** – Lucy Clark

- **The Doctor's Baby Secret** – Scarlet Wilson
- **Married for the Boss's Baby** – Susan Carlisle

Available at WHSmith, Tesco, Asda, Eason, Amazon and Apple

Just can't wait?
Buy our books online a month before they hit the shops!
visit www.millsandboon.co.uk

These books are also available in eBook format!